DRAGON KINGDOM
of Wrenly

CINDER'S FLAME

By Jordan Quinn
Illustrated by Ornella Greco at Glass House Graphics

LITTLE SIMON

New York   London   Toronto   Sydney   New Delhi

LITTLE SIMON

An imprint of Simon & Schuster Children's Publishing Division
1230 Avenue of the Americas, New York, New York 10020
First Little Simon edition May 2022
Copyright © 2022 by Simon & Schuster, Inc.
All rights reserved, including the right of reproduction in whole or in part in any form.
LITTLE SIMON is a registered trademark of Simon & Schuster, Inc., and associated colophon
is a trademark of Simon & Schuster, Inc. For information about special discounts for bulk purchases,
please contact Simon & Schuster Special Sales at 1-866-506-1949 or business@simonandschuster.com.
The Simon & Schuster Speakers Bureau can bring authors to your live event. For more information
or to book an event, contact the Simon & Schuster Speakers Bureau at 1-866-248-3049 or visit our
website at www.simonspeakers.com.
Designed by Kayla Wasil
Text by Matthew J. Gilbert
GLASS HOUSE GRAPHICS Creative Services
Art and cover by ORNELLA GRECO
Colors by ORNELLA GRECO and GABRIELE CRACOLICI
Lettering by GIOVANNI SPATARO/Grafimated Cartoon
Supervision by SALVATORE DI MARCO/Grafimated Cartoon
Manufactured in China 0222 SCP
2 4 6 8 10 9 7 5 3 1
Library of Congress Cataloging-in-Publication Data
Names: Quinn, Jordan, author. | Glass House Graphics, illustrator. | Quinn, Jordan. Dragon Kingdom of Wrenly ; 7. |
Title: Cinder's flame / by Jordan Quinn ; illustrated by Glass House Graphics.
Description: First Little Simon edition. | New York City : Little Simon, 2022. | Series: Dragon kingdom of Wrenly ; 7 |
Summary: Cinder has always been a little envious of Ruskin, the legendary scarlet dragon, after all it can be hard
to be friends with a legend, but when the Witch-Dragon Villinelle casts a Soul Blazer spell on Cinder, her envy
blossoms into an uncontrollable wildfire, and Ruskin must save his friend from Villinelle's curse. |
Identifiers: LCCN 2021017775 (print) | LCCN 2021017776 (ebook) | ISBN 9781665904551
(paperback) | ISBN 9781665904568 (hardcover) | ISBN 9781665904575 (ebook)
Subjects: LCSH: Dragons—Comic books, strips, etc. | Dragons—Juvenile fiction. | Magic—Comic books, strips, etc.
| Magic—Juvenile fiction. | Witches—Comic books, strips, etc. | Witches—Juvenile fiction. | Envy—Comic books,
strips, etc. | Envy—Juvenile fiction. | Graphic novels. | CYAC: Graphic novels. | Dragons—Fiction. | Fantasy—Fiction. |
LCGFT: Graphic novels. | Fantasy fiction.
Classification: LCC PZ7.7.Q55 Ci 2022 (print) | LCC PZ7.7.Q55 (ebook) | DDC 741.5/973—dc23
LC record available at https://lccn.loc.gov/ 2021017775

Contents

Chapter 1

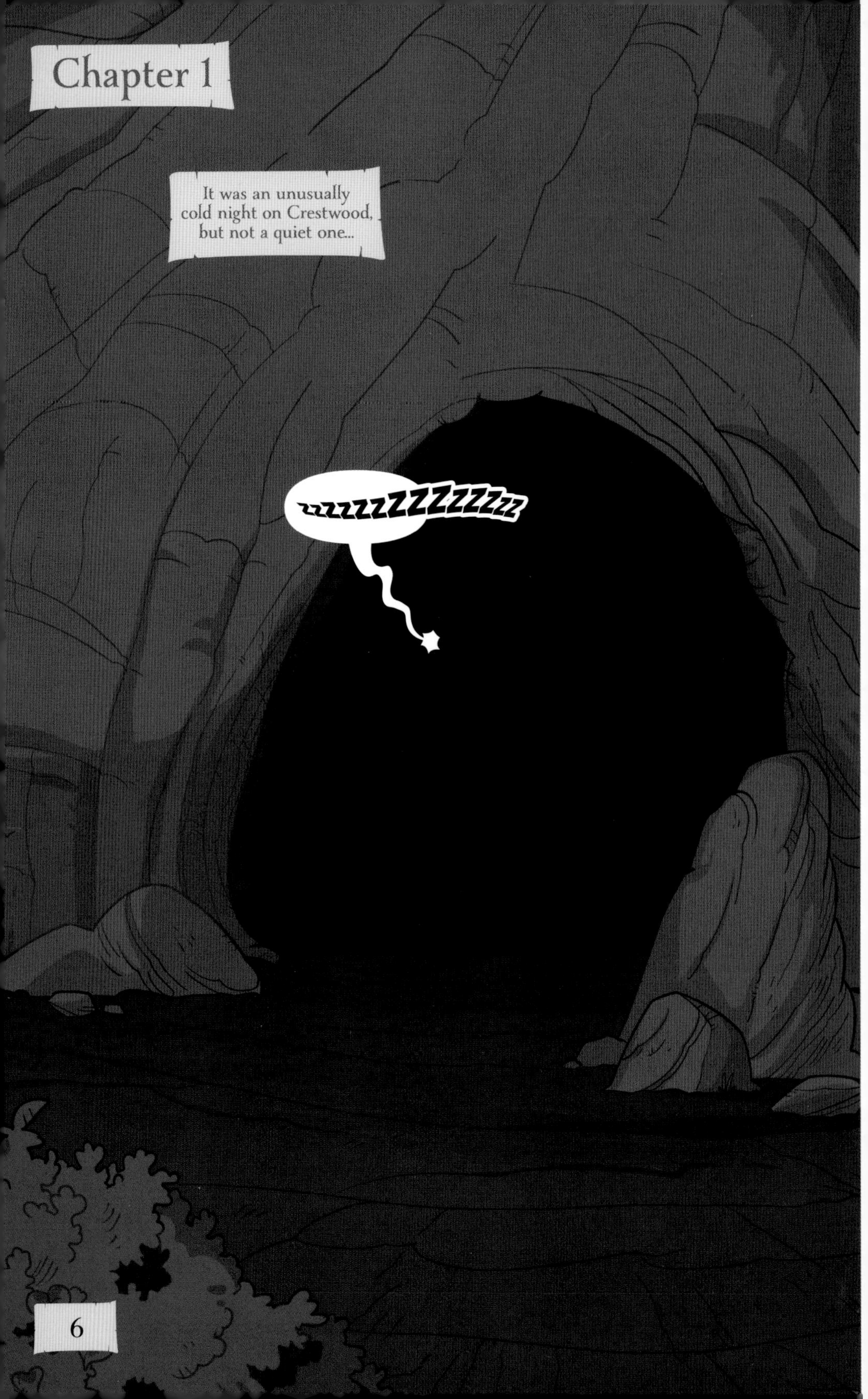
It was an unusually cold night on Crestwood, but not a quiet one...
zzzzzzZZZzzzzzz

...ZZZ...

But as cold as the cave was...

...colder **still** was the chill running down Cinder's spine.

...ZZZZZ...

...ZZZZZZZ...

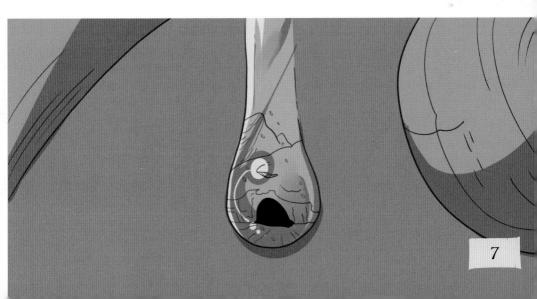

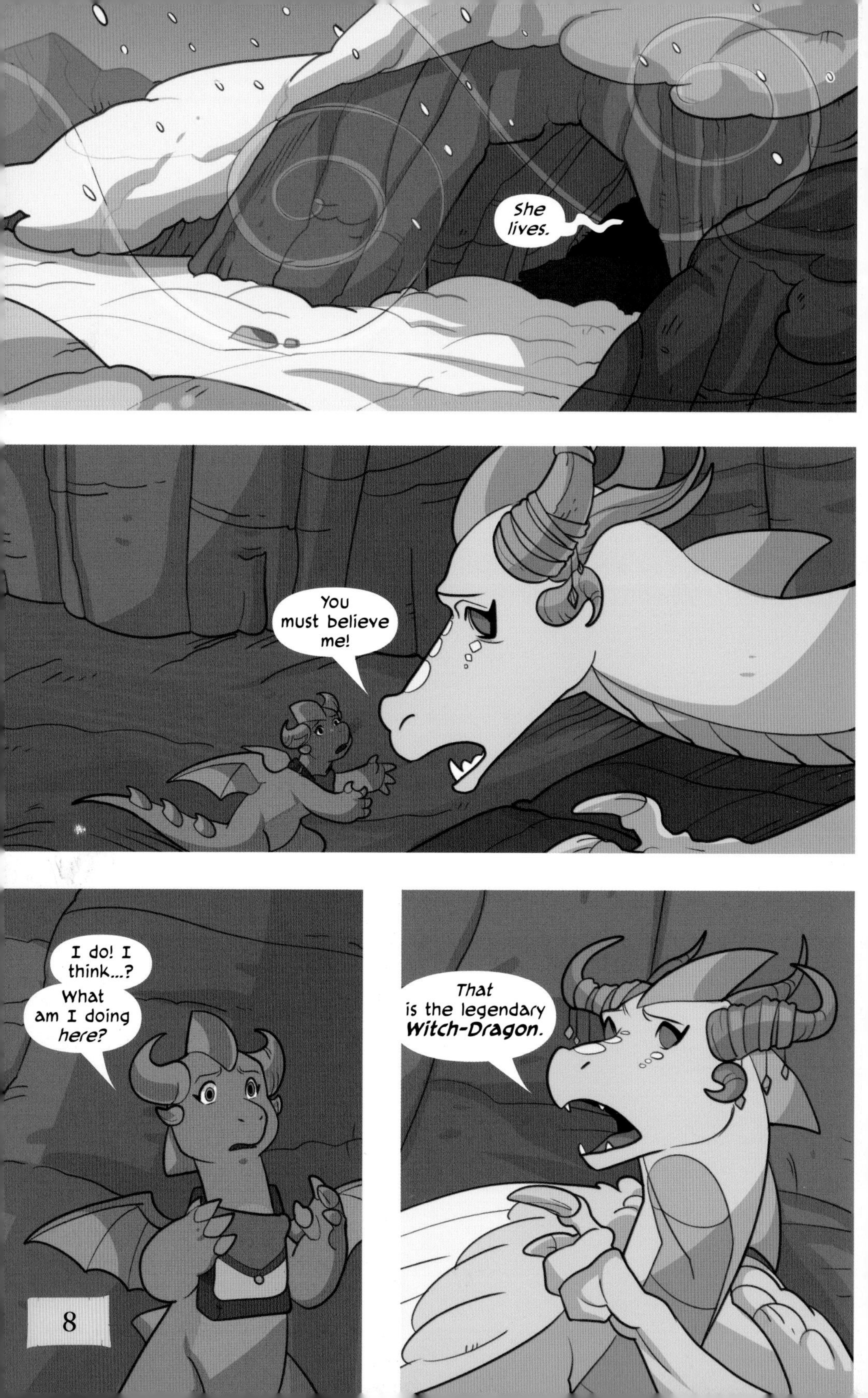
She lives.
You must believe me!
I do! I think...?
What am I doing *here?*
That is the legendary **Witch-Dragon**.

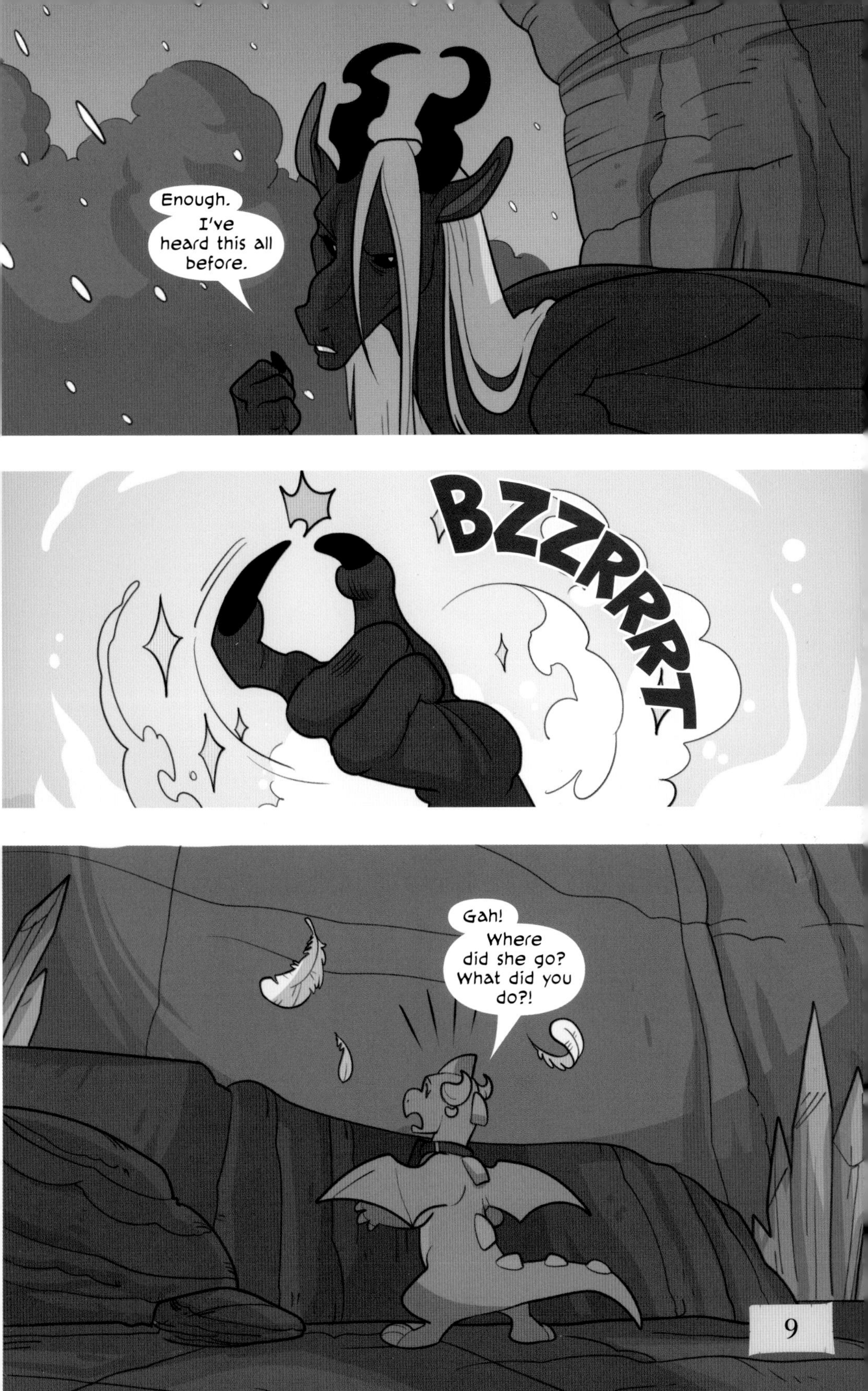
Enough. I've heard this all before.
BZZRRRT
Gah! Where did she go? What did you do?!

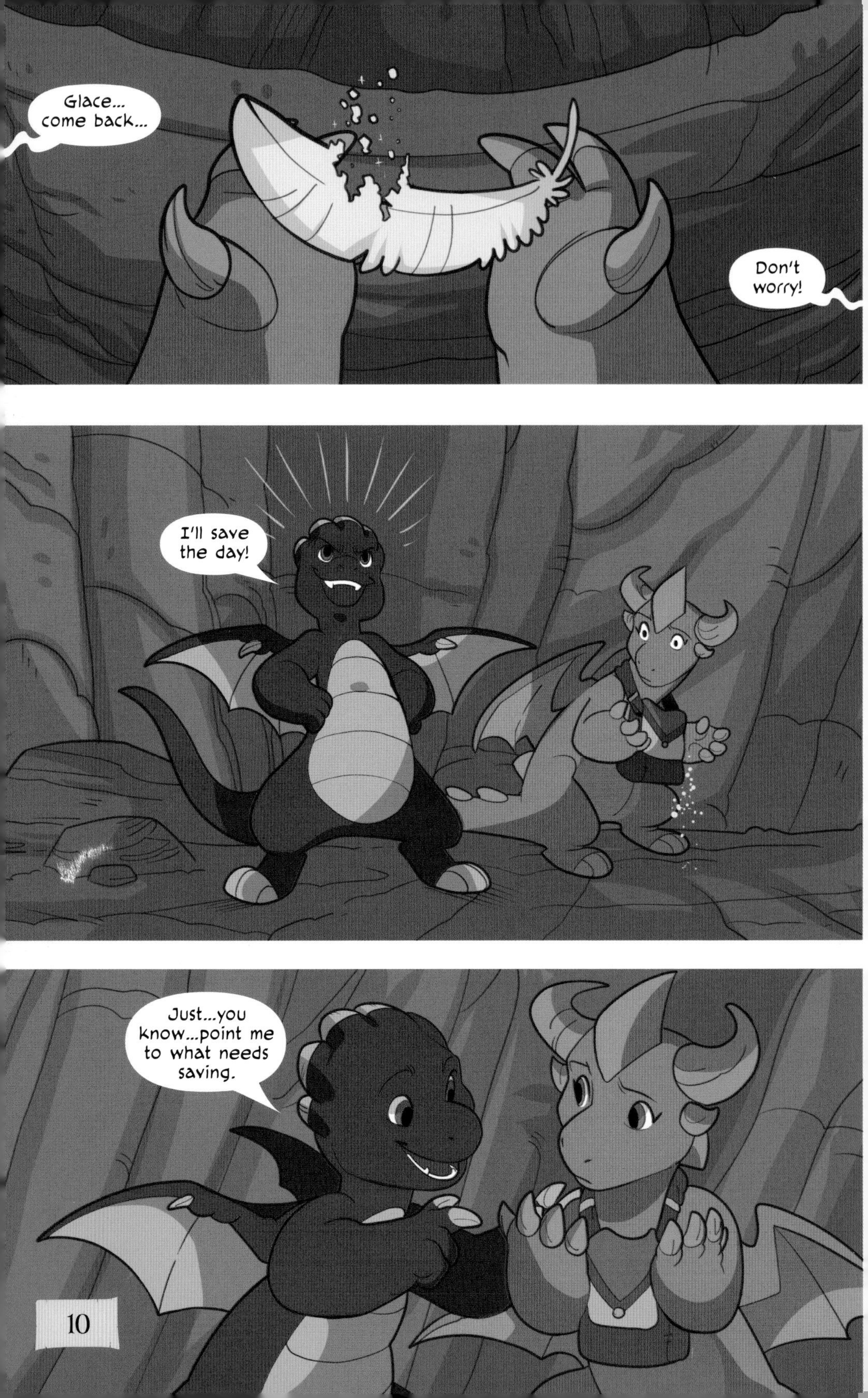
Glace...
come back...
Don't worry!
I'll save the day!
Just...you know...point me to what needs saving.

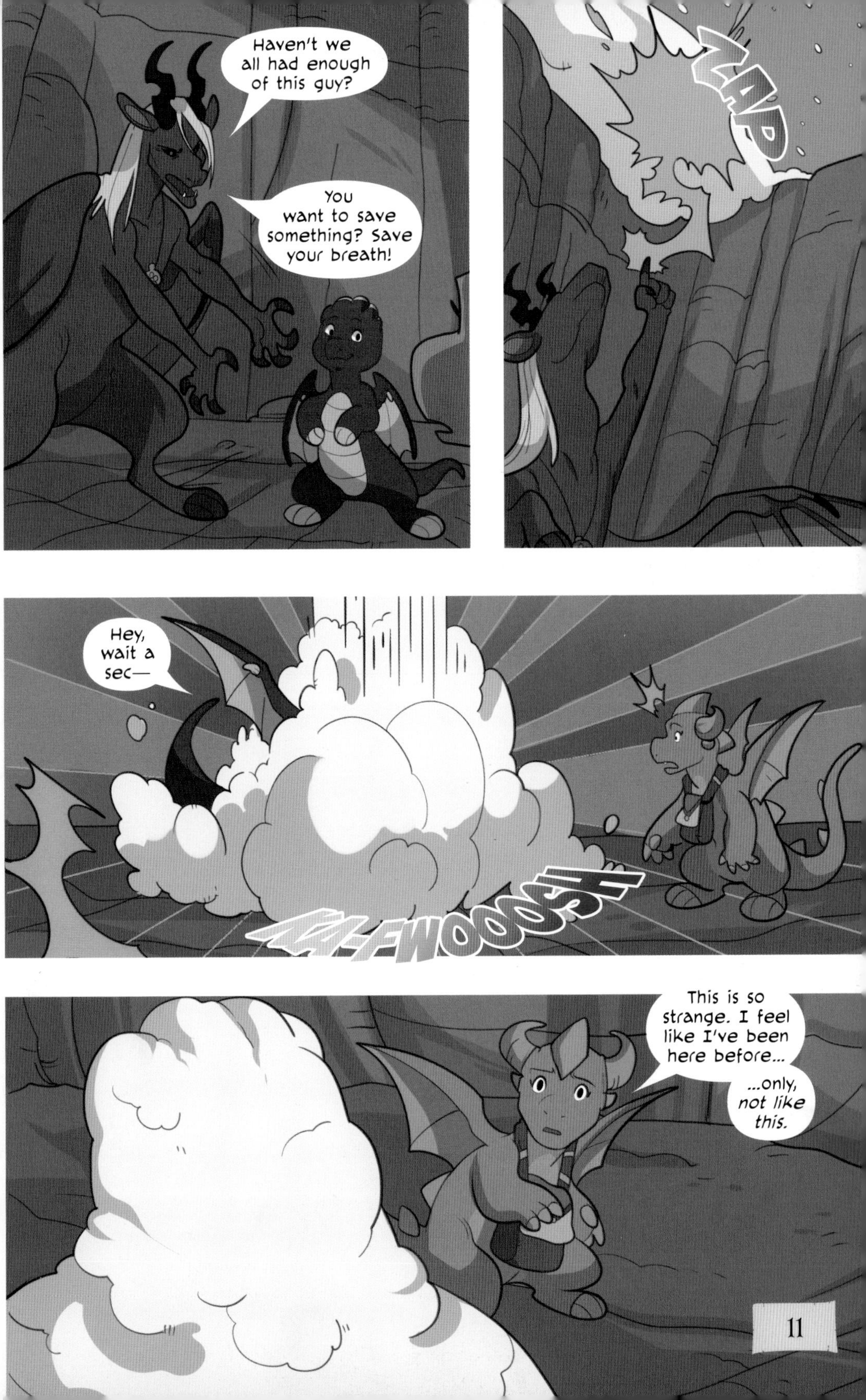
Haven't we all had enough of this guy?
You want to save something? Save your breath!
ZAP
Hey, wait a sec—
KA-FWOOOSH
This is so strange. I feel like I've been here before...
...only, *not like this.*

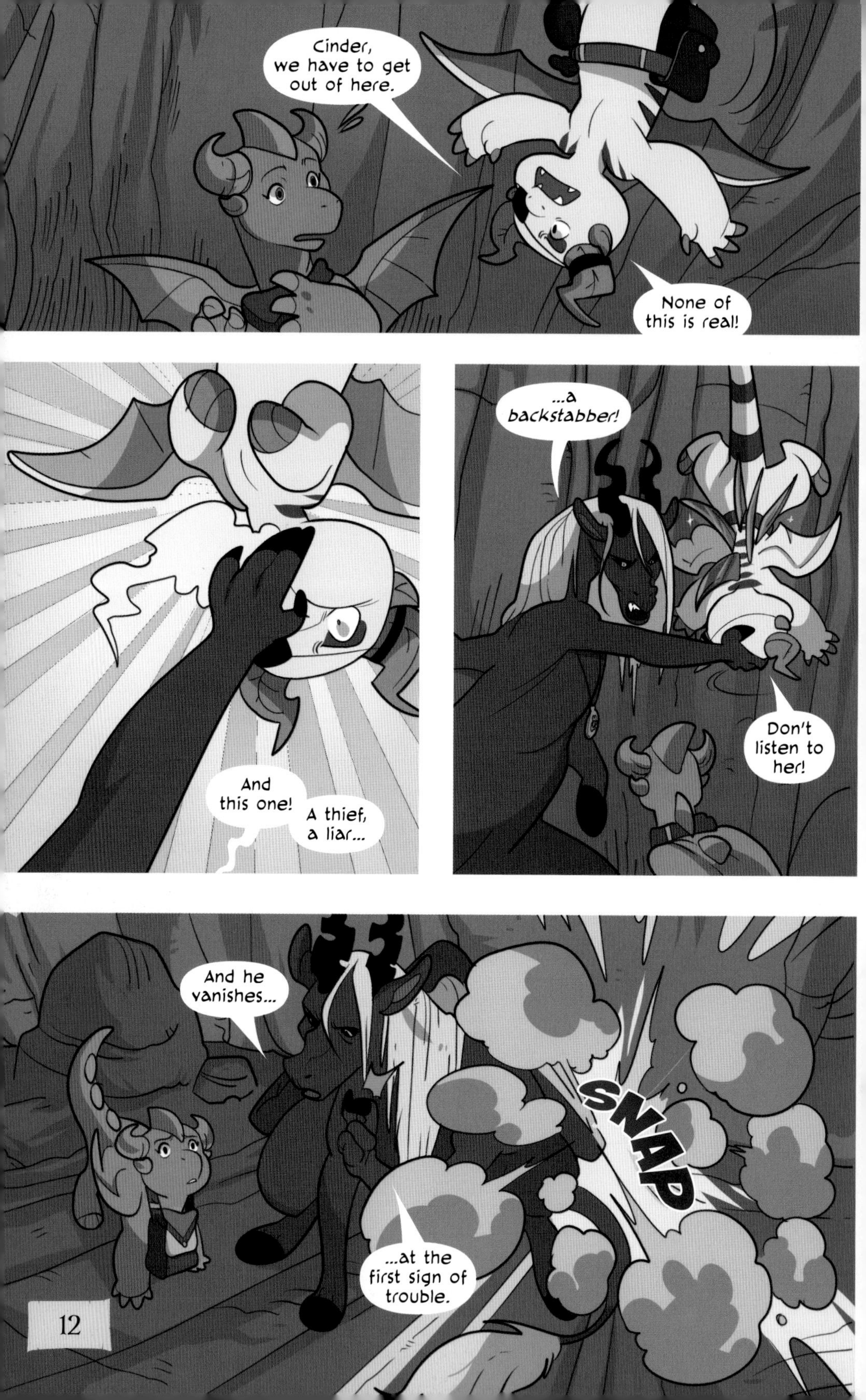
Cinder, we have to get out of here.
None of this is real!
And this one!
A thief, a liar...
...a backstabber!
Don't listen to her!
And he vanishes...
SNAP
...at the first sign of trouble.

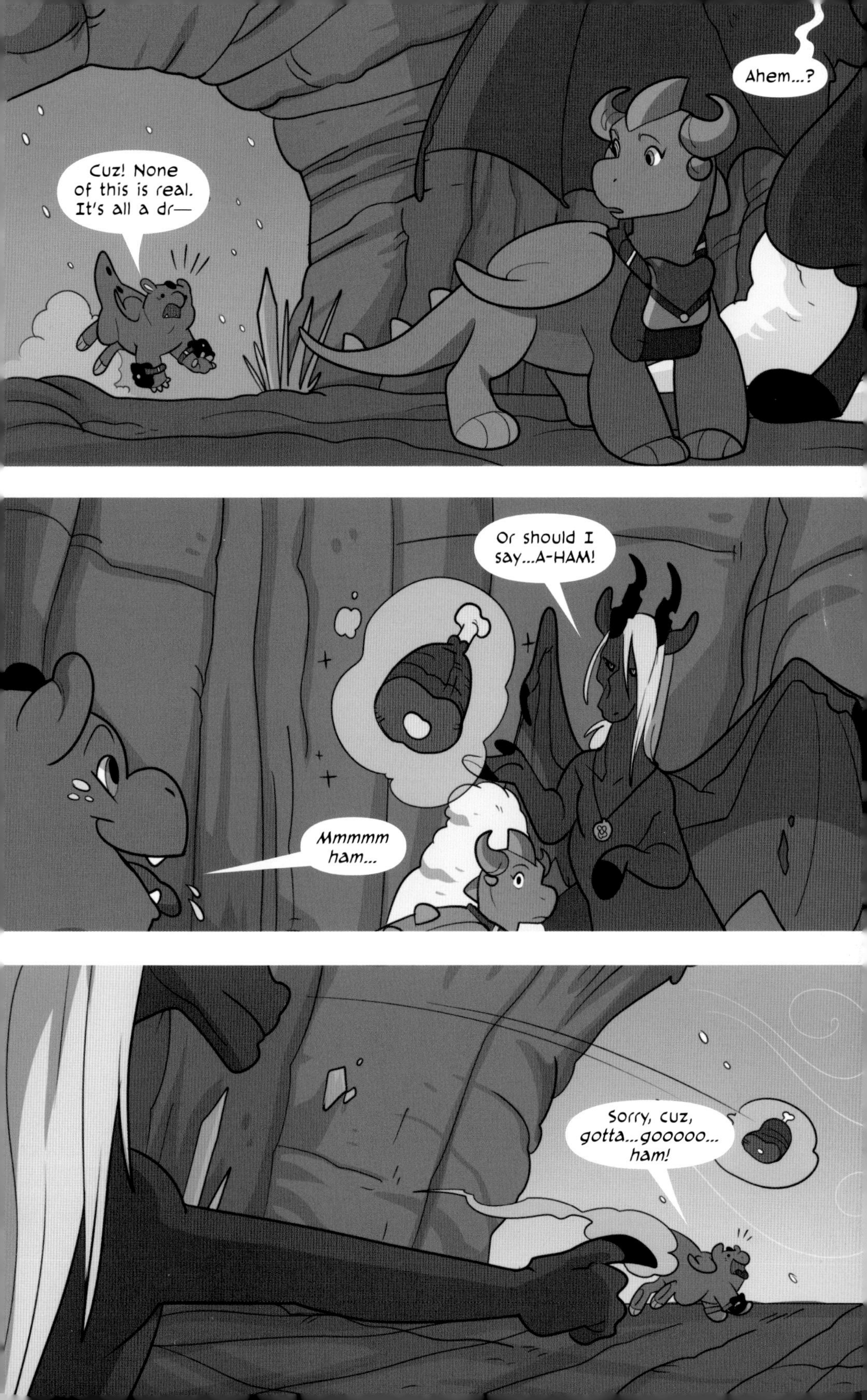
Ahem...?
Cuz! None of this is real. It's all a dr—
Or should I say...A-HAM!
Mmmmm ham...
Sorry, cuz, gotta...gooooo... ham!

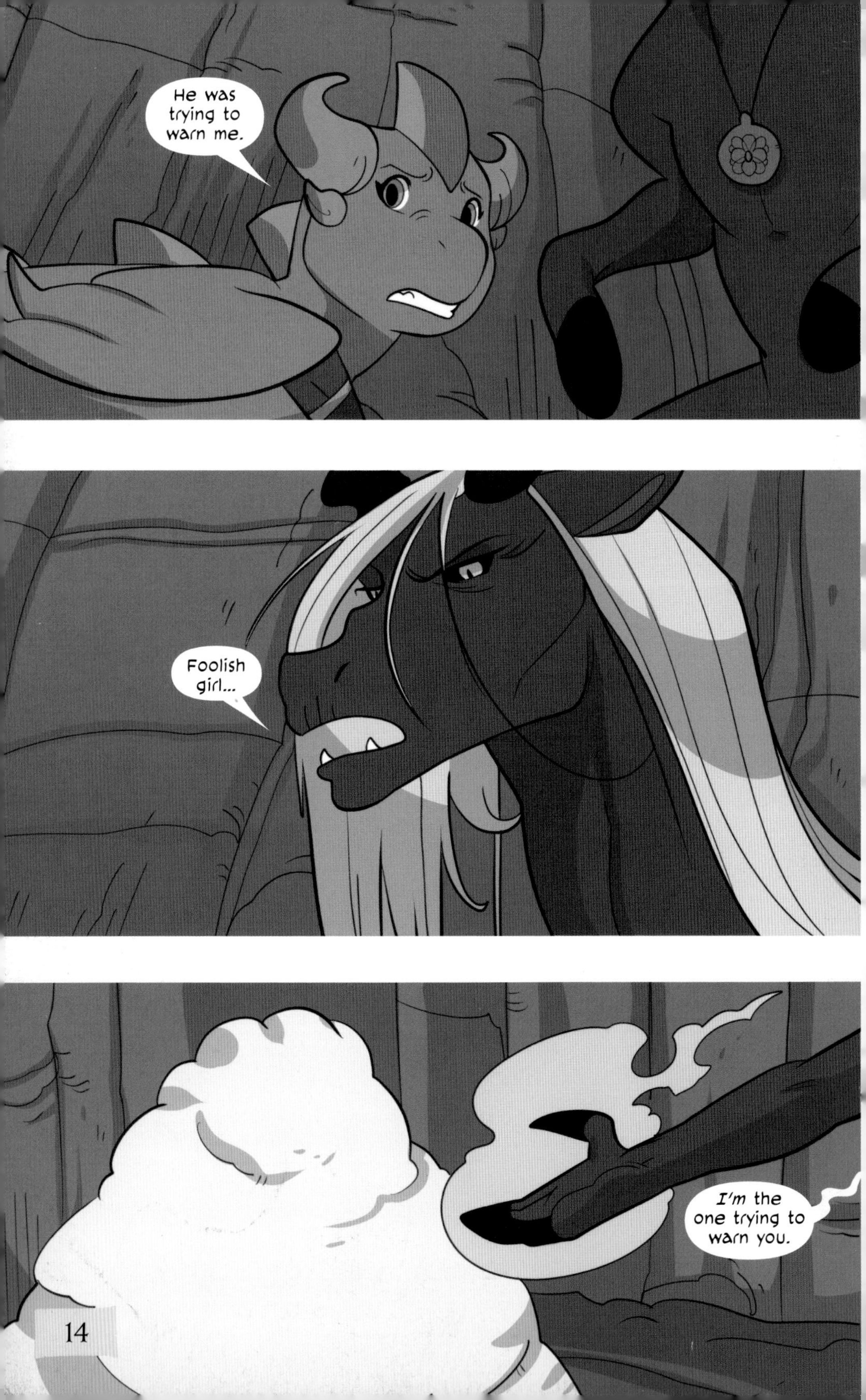
He was trying to warn me.
Foolish girl...
I'm the one trying to warn you.

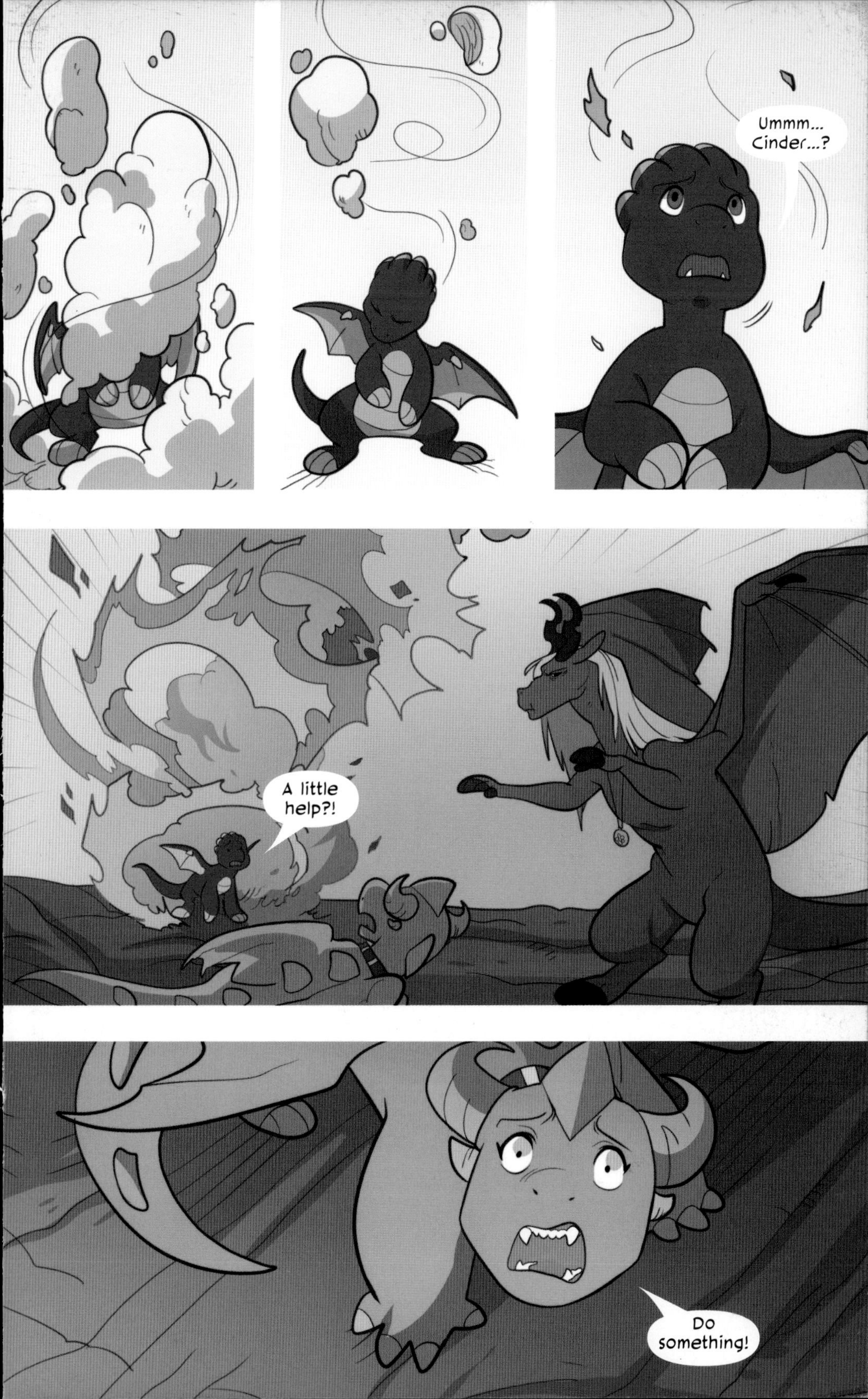
Ummm... Cinder...?
A little help?!
Do something!

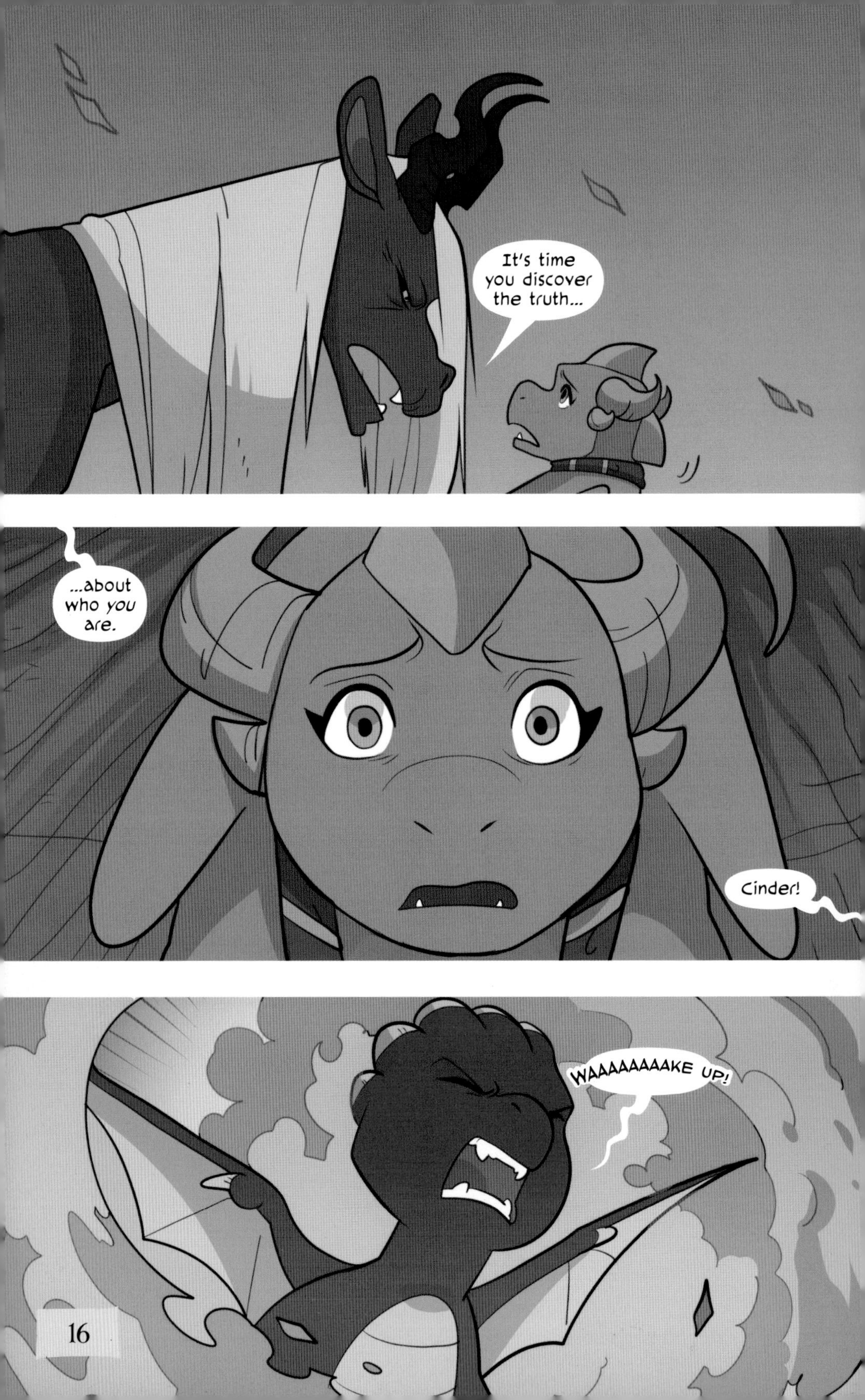
It's time you discover the truth...
...about who *you* are.
Cinder!
WAAAAAAAAKE UP!

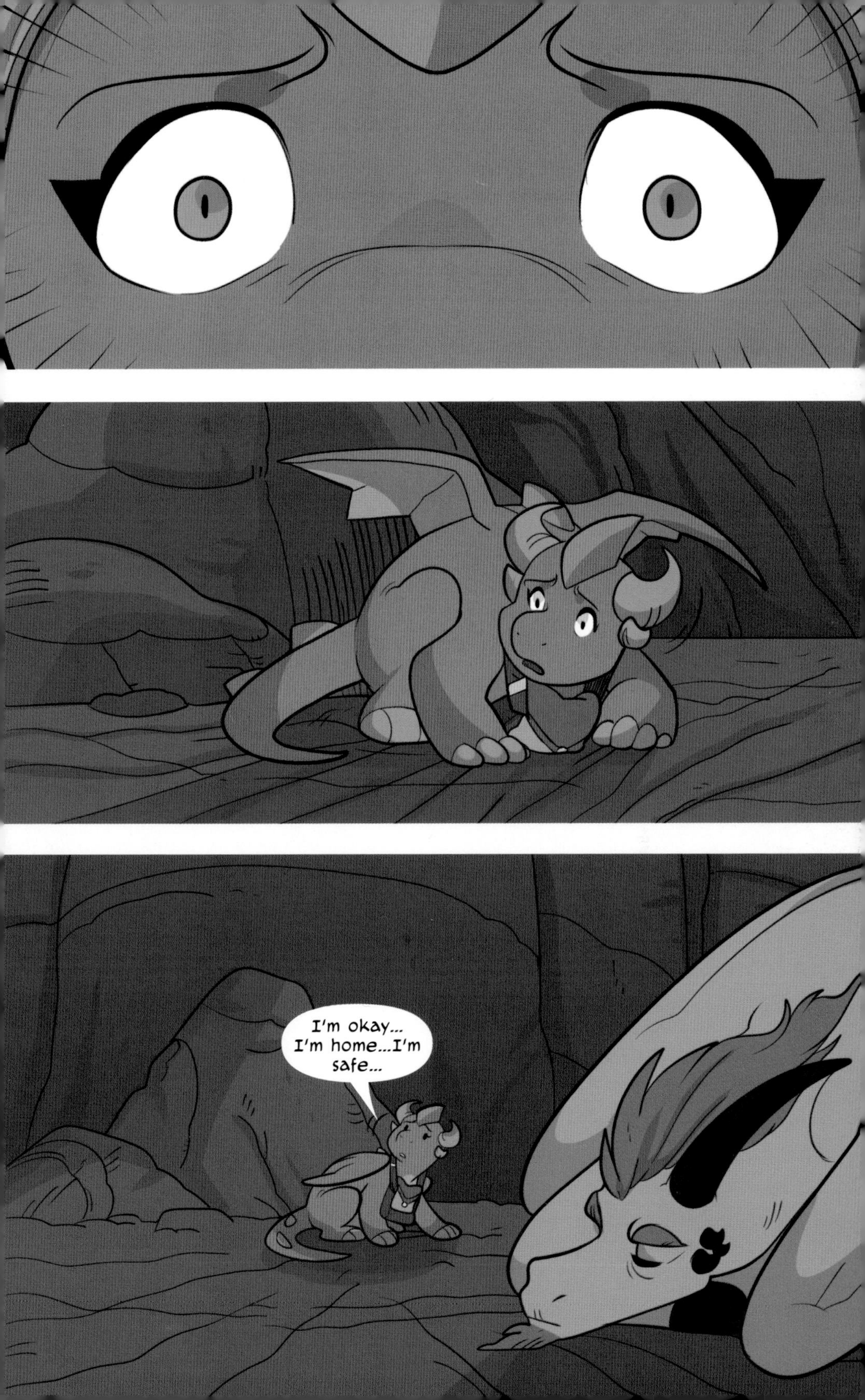
I'm okay... I'm home...I'm safe...

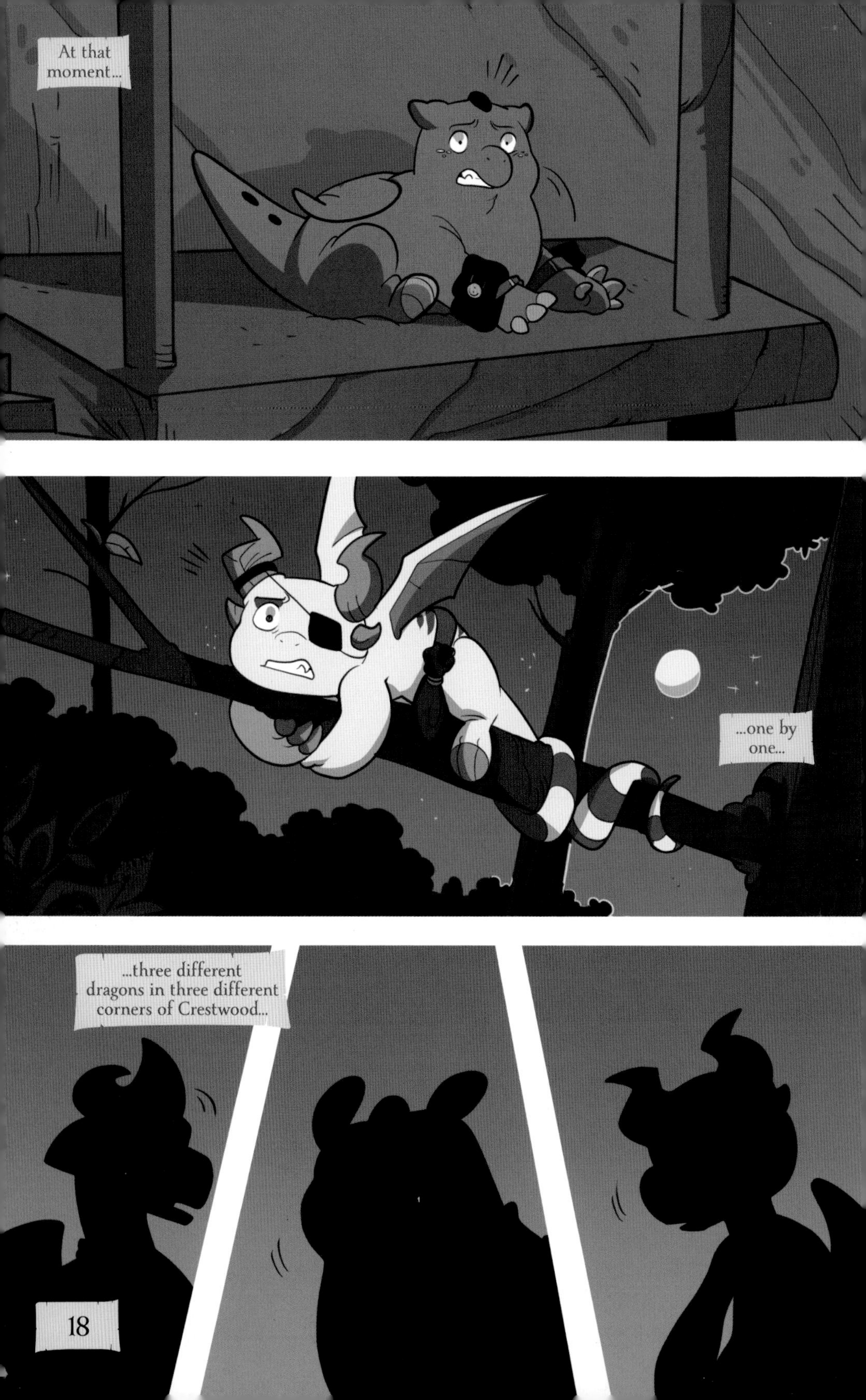
At that moment...
...one by one...
...three different dragons in three different corners of Crestwood...

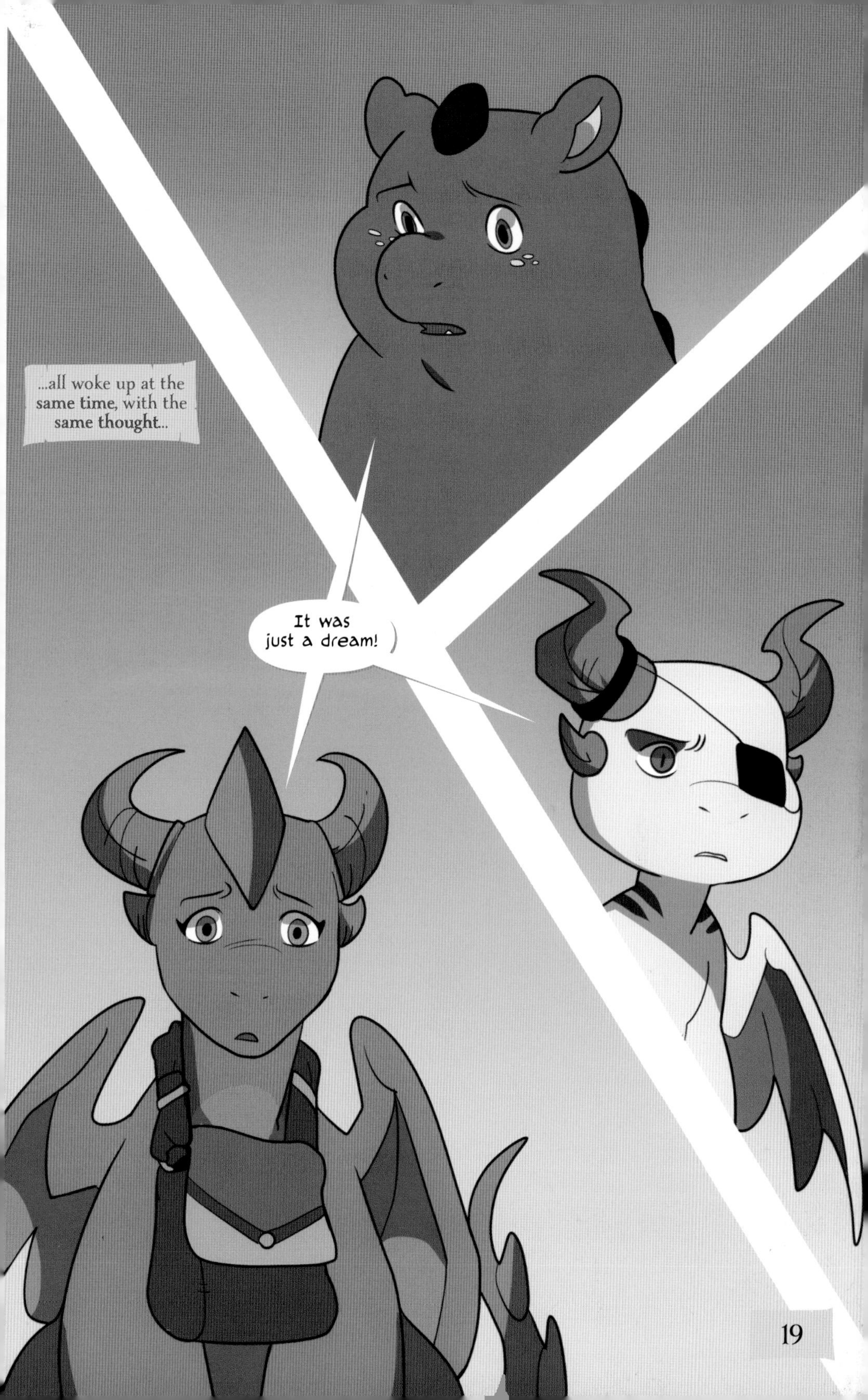
...all woke up at the same time, with the same thought...
It was just a dream!

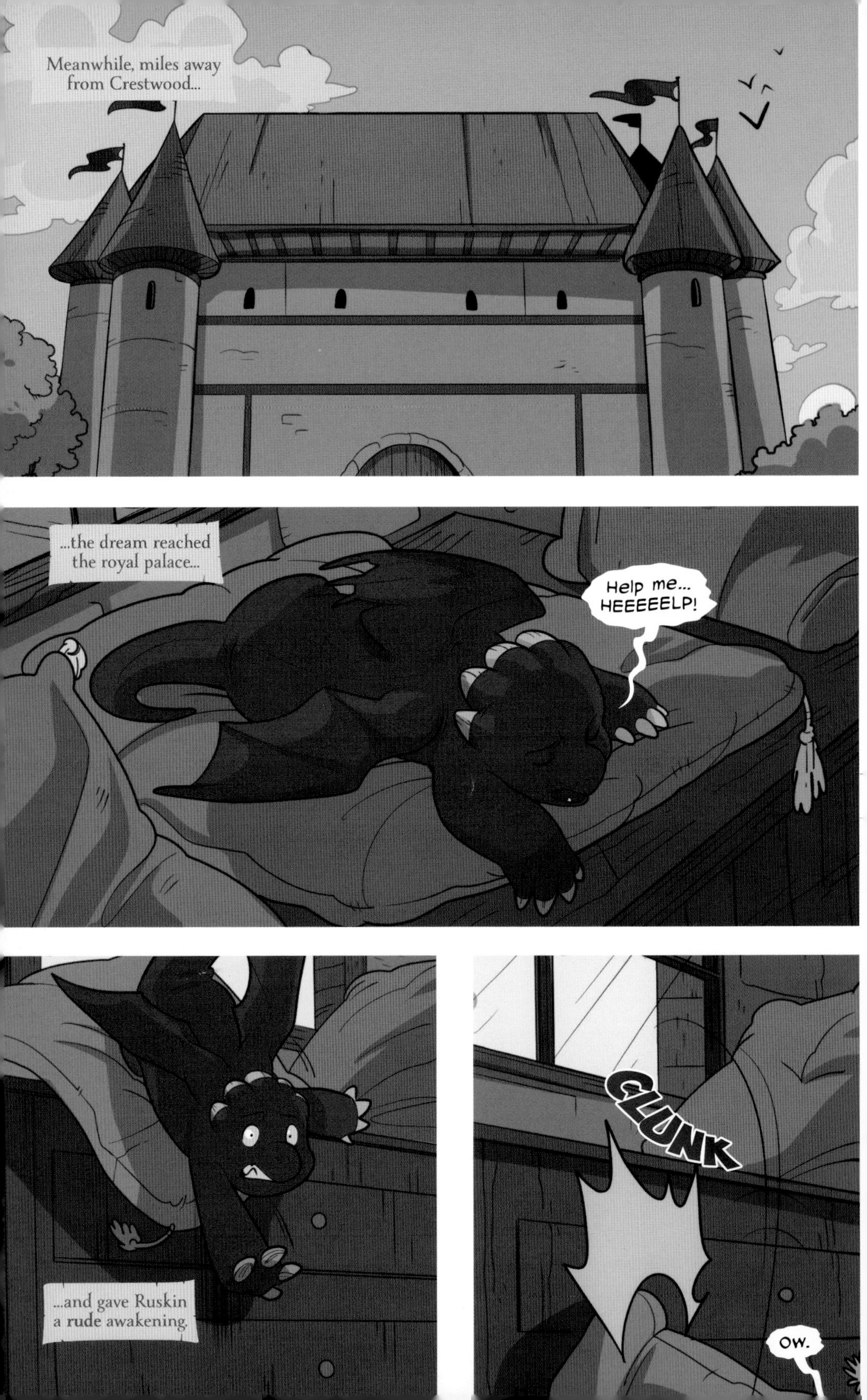
Meanwhile, miles away from Crestwood...
...the dream reached the royal palace...
Help me... HEEEEELP!
...and gave Ruskin a rude awakening.
CLUNK
OW.

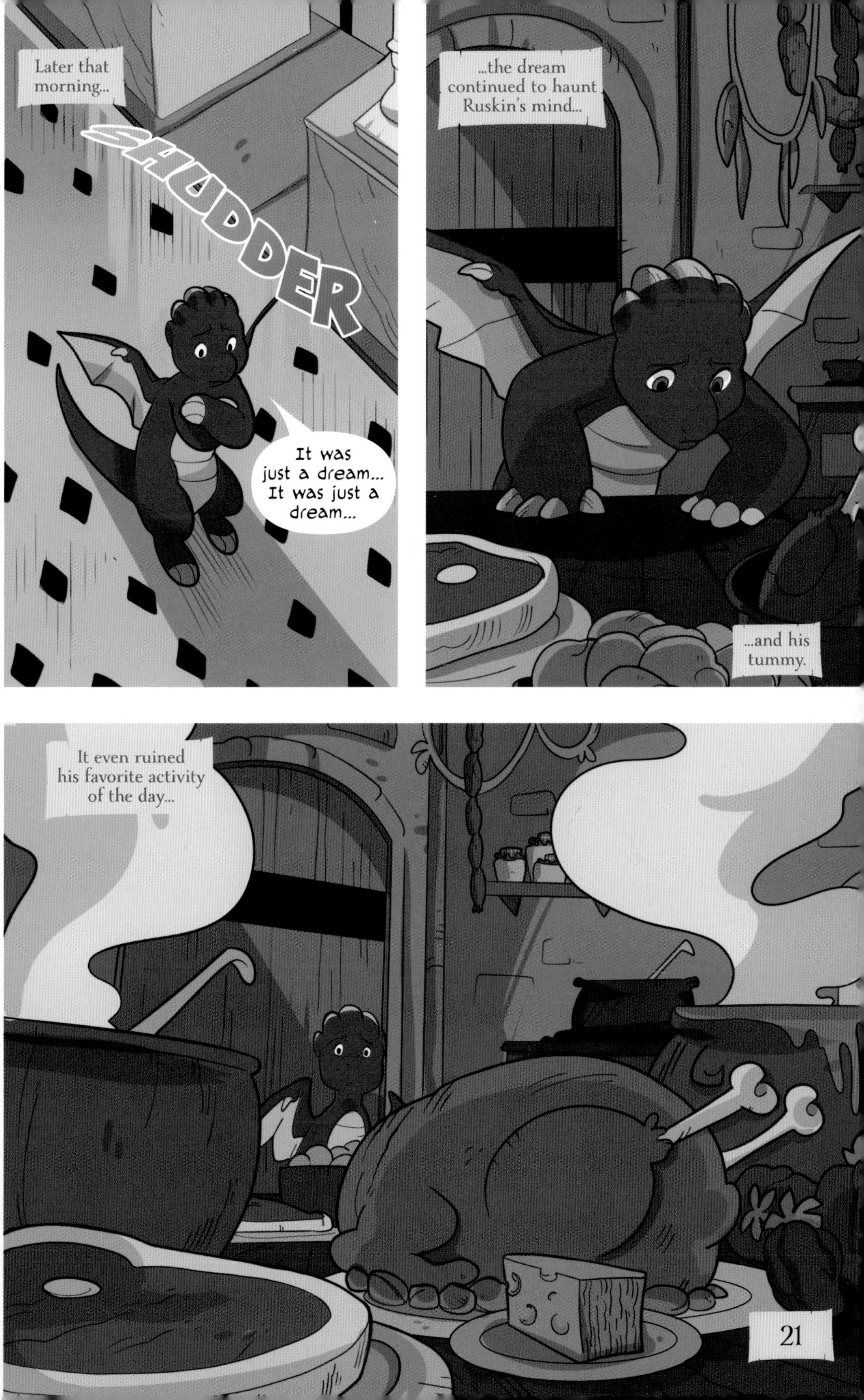

Later that morning...
SHUDDER
It was just a dream... It was just a dream...
...the dream continued to haunt Ruskin's mind...
...and his tummy.
It even ruined his favorite activity of the day...

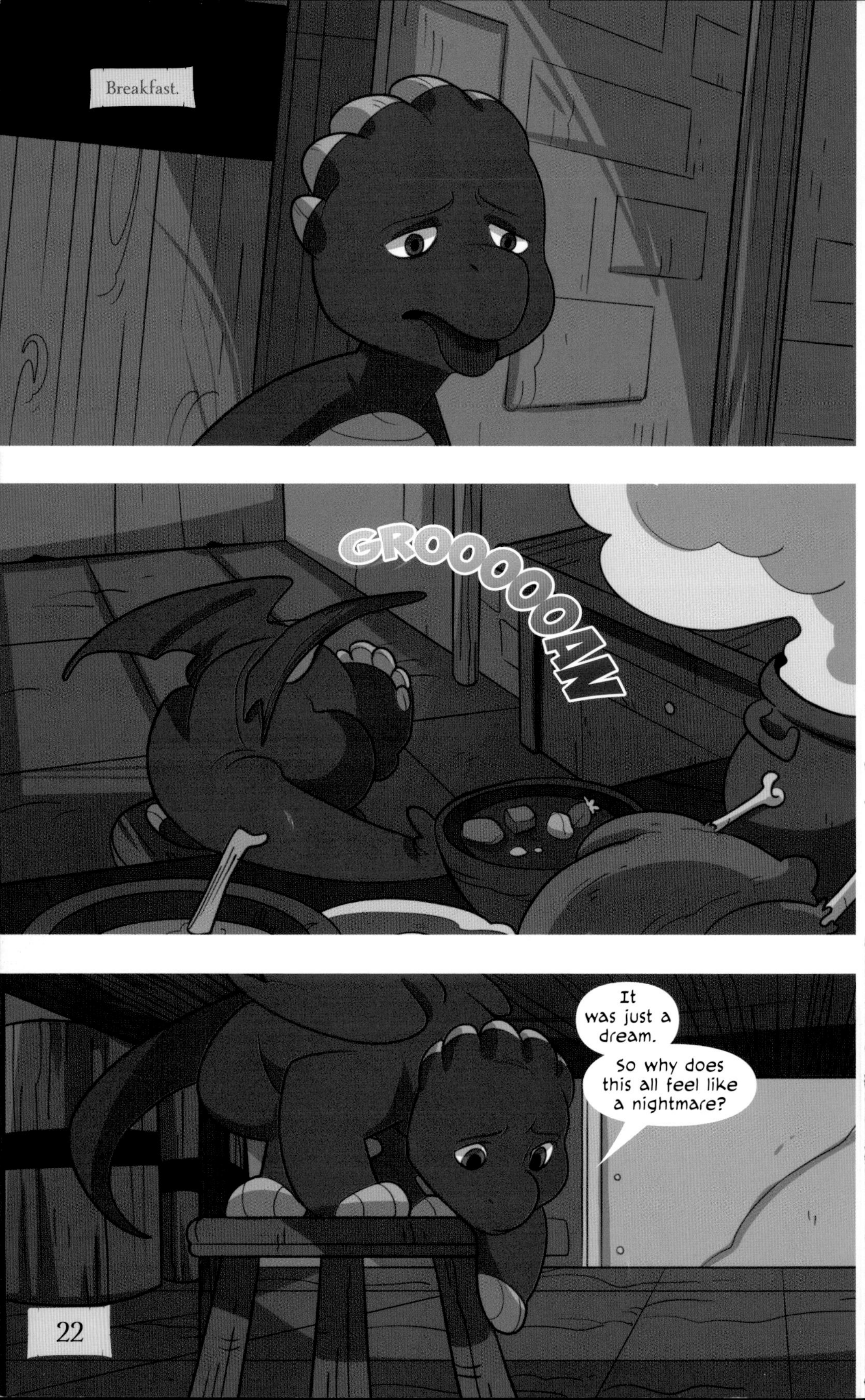

Breakfast.
GROOOOOAN
It was just a dream.
So why does this all feel like a nightmare?

Chapter 2

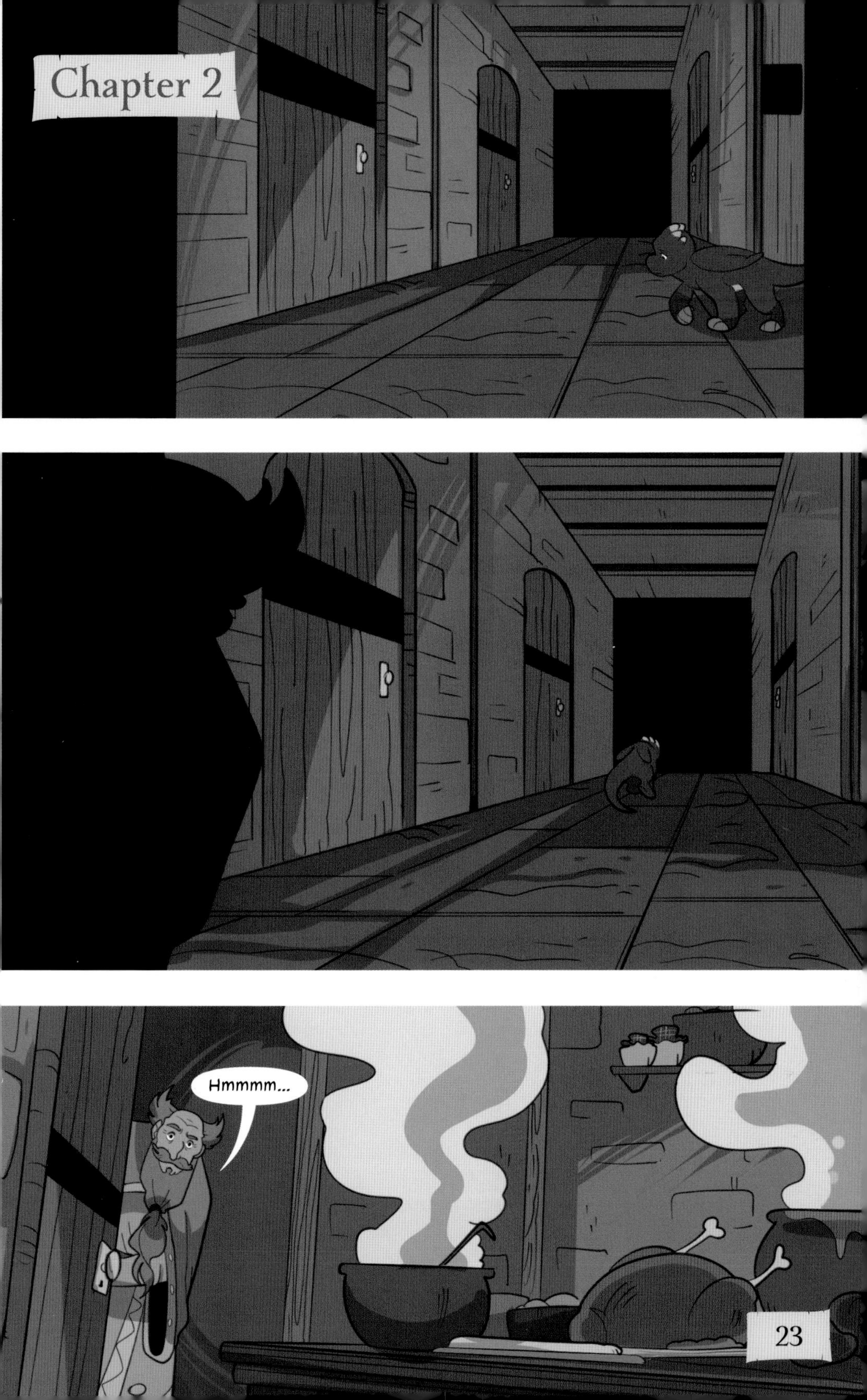
Hmmmm...

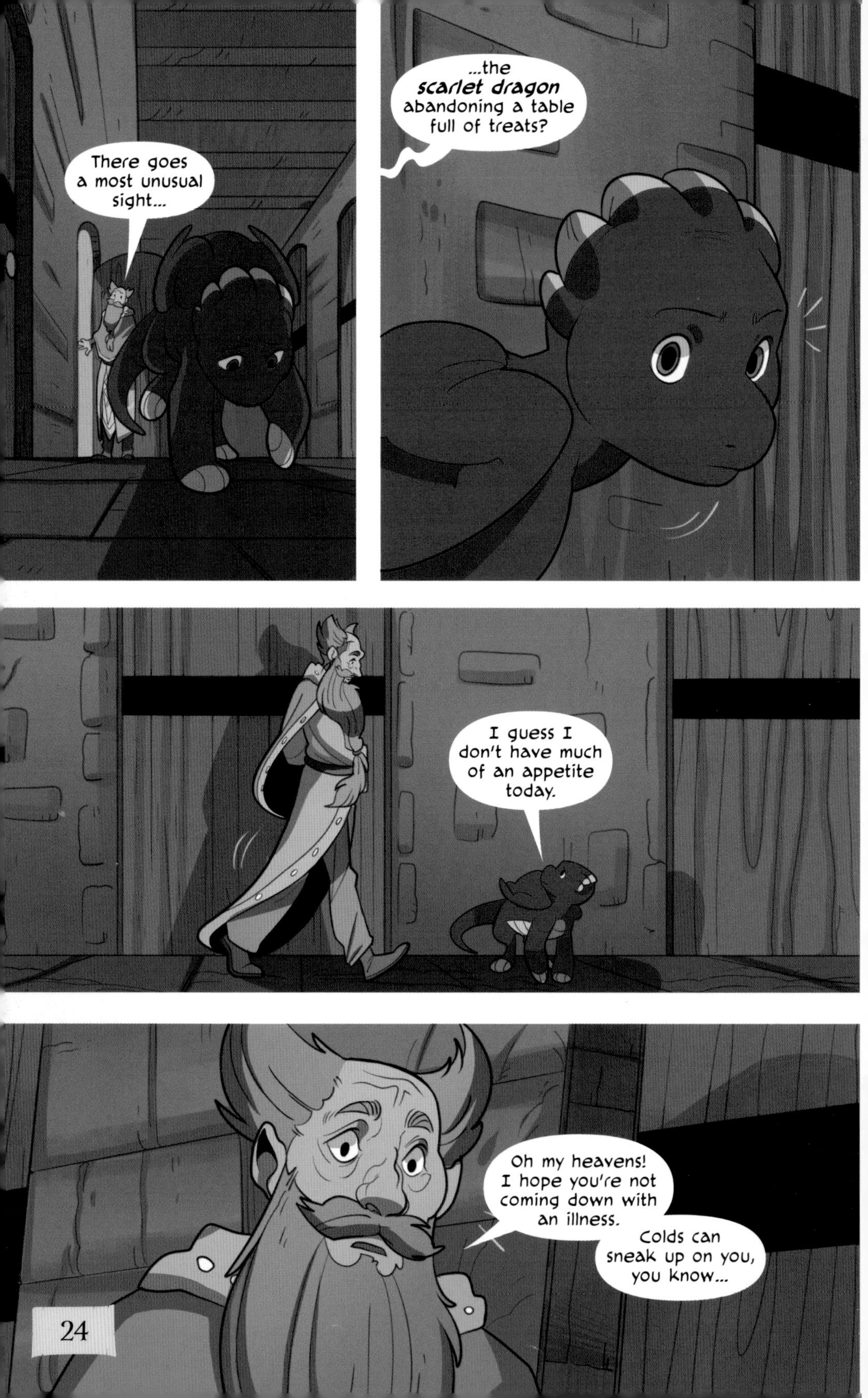

There goes a most unusual sight...
...the *scarlet dragon* abandoning a table full of treats?
I guess I don't have much of an appetite today.
Oh my heavens! I hope you're not coming down with an illness.
Colds can sneak up on you, you know...

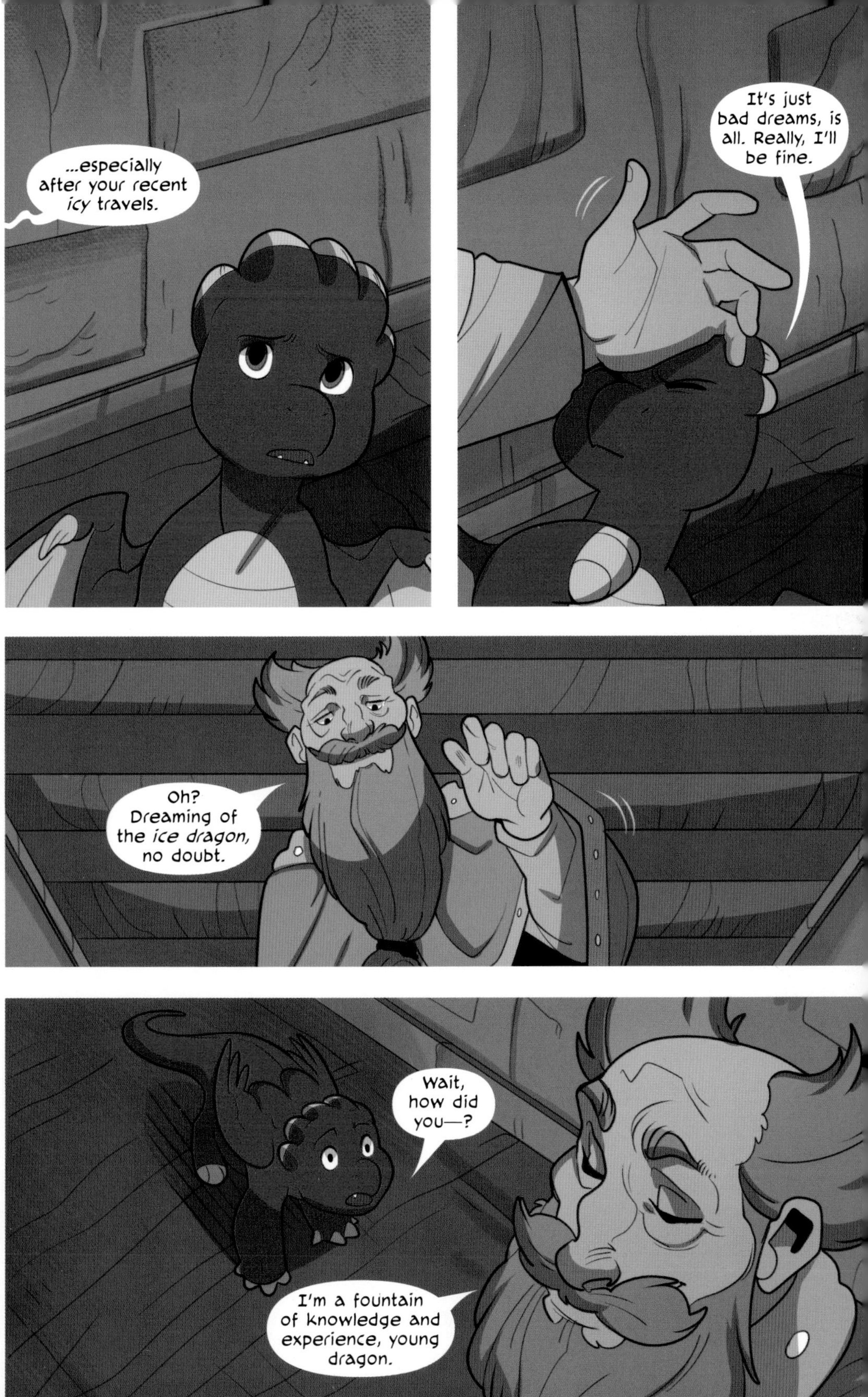
...especially after your recent *icy* travels.
It's just bad dreams, is all. Really, I'll be fine.
Oh? Dreaming of the *ice dragon,* no doubt.
Wait, how did you—?
I'm a fountain of knowledge and experience, young dragon.

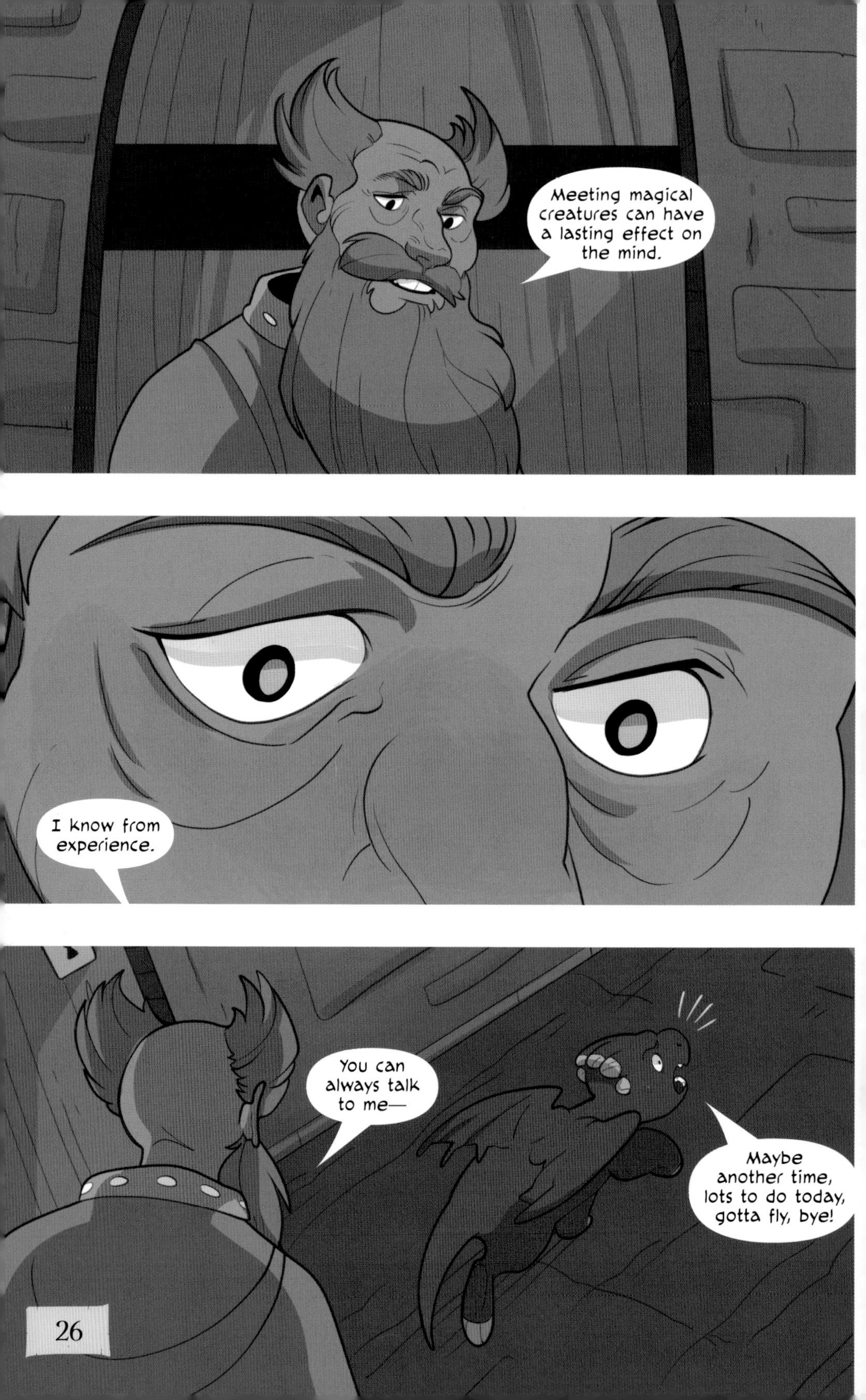
Meeting magical creatures can have a lasting effect on the mind.
I know from experience.
You can always talk to me—
Maybe another time, lots to do today, gotta fly, bye!

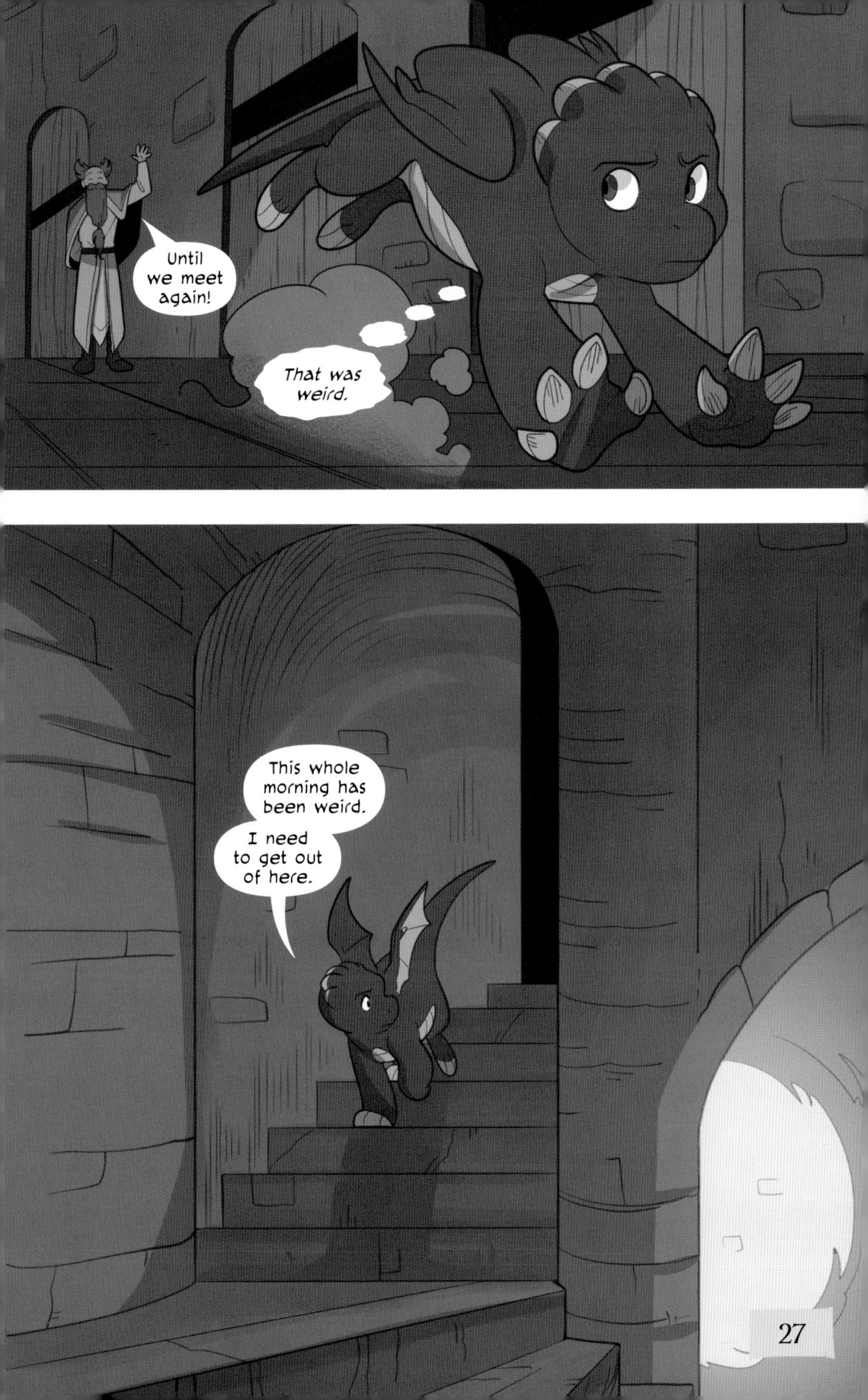
Until we meet again!
That was weird.
This whole morning has been weird.
I need to get out of here.

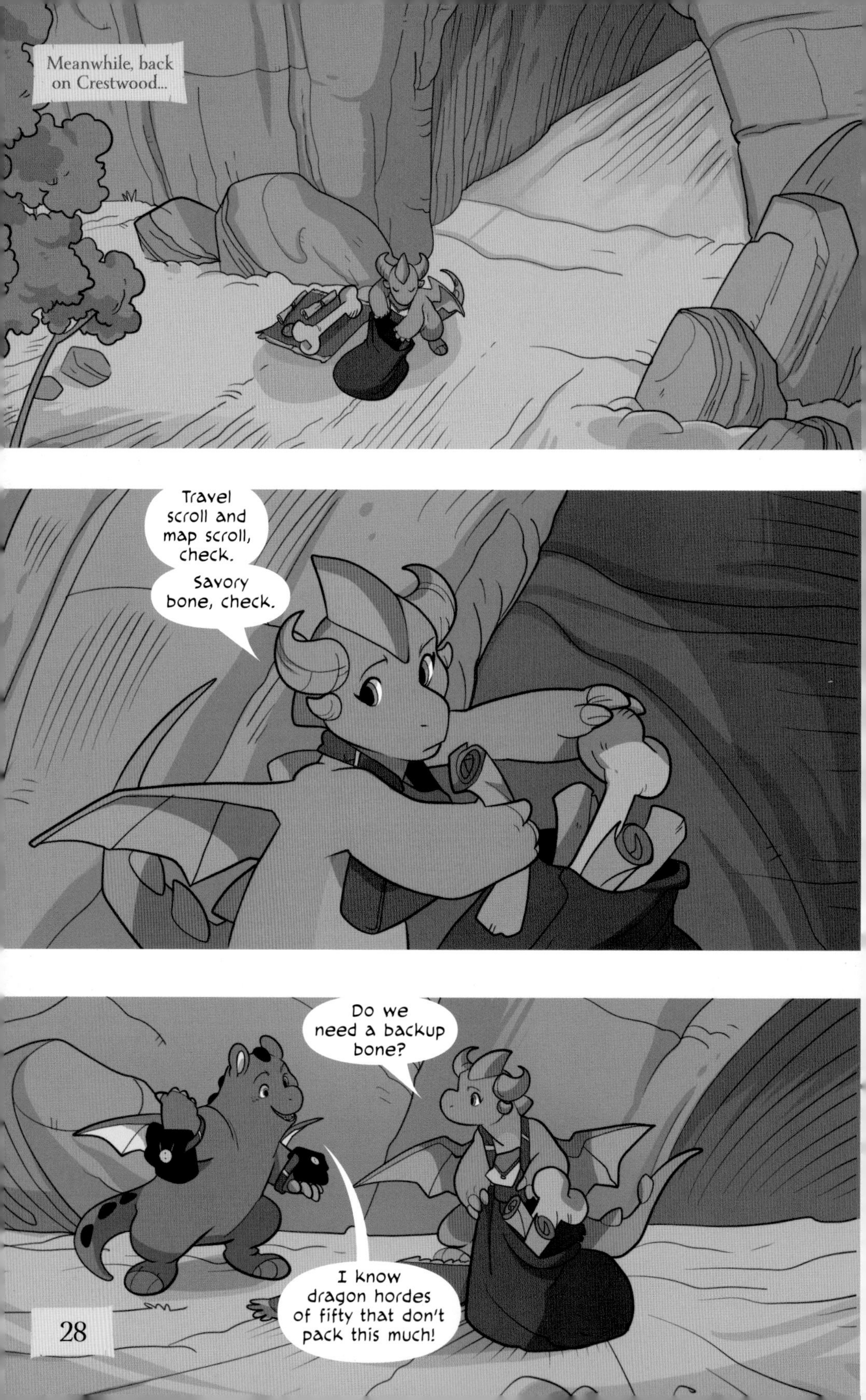
Meanwhile, back on Crestwood...
Travel scroll and map scroll, check.
Savory bone, check.
Do we need a backup bone?
I know dragon hordes of fifty that don't pack this much!

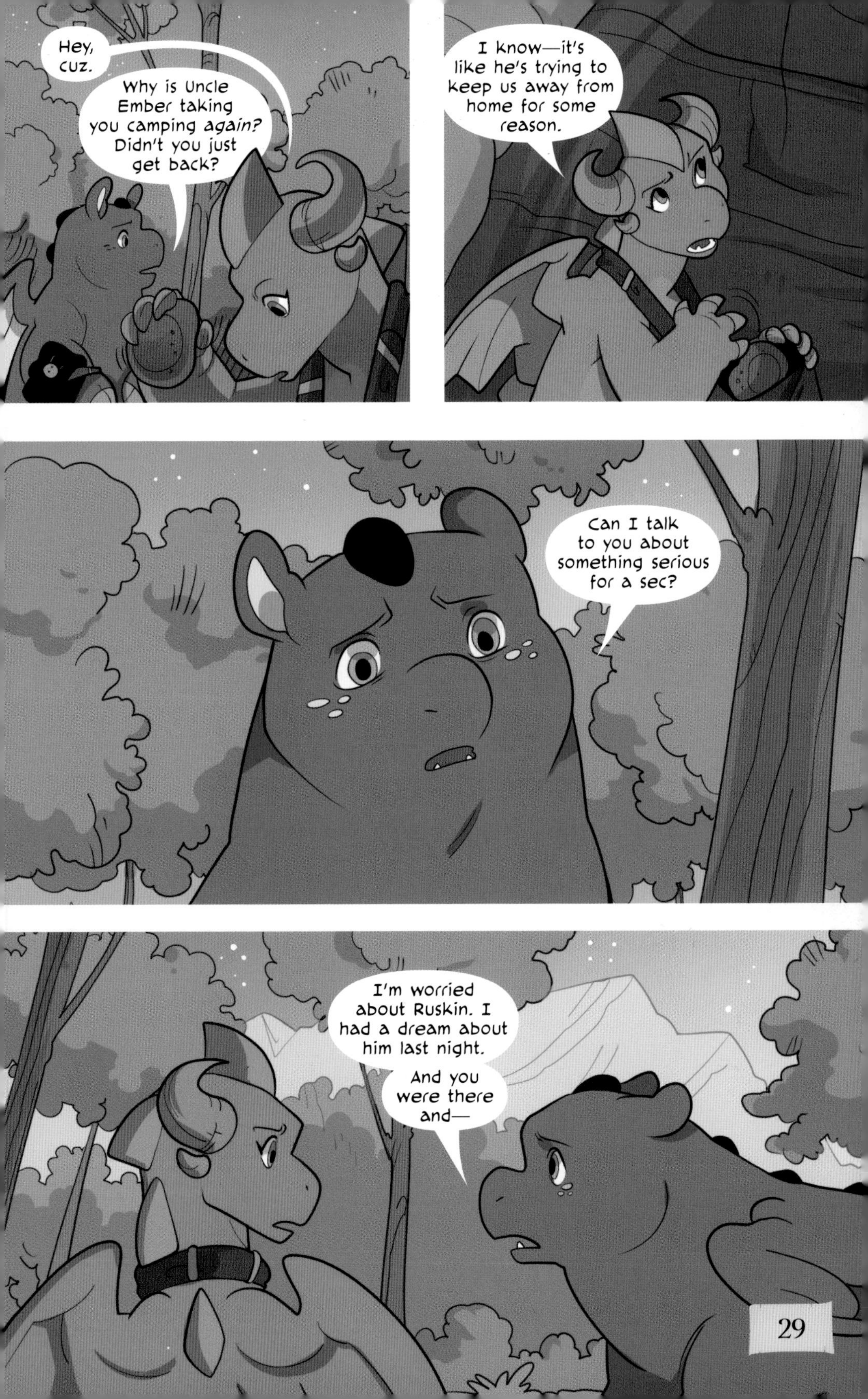
Hey, cuz.
Why is Uncle Ember taking you camping *again?* Didn't you just get back?
I know—it's like he's trying to keep us away from home for some reason.
Can I talk to you about something serious for a sec?
I'm worried about Ruskin. I had a dream about him last night.
And you were there and—

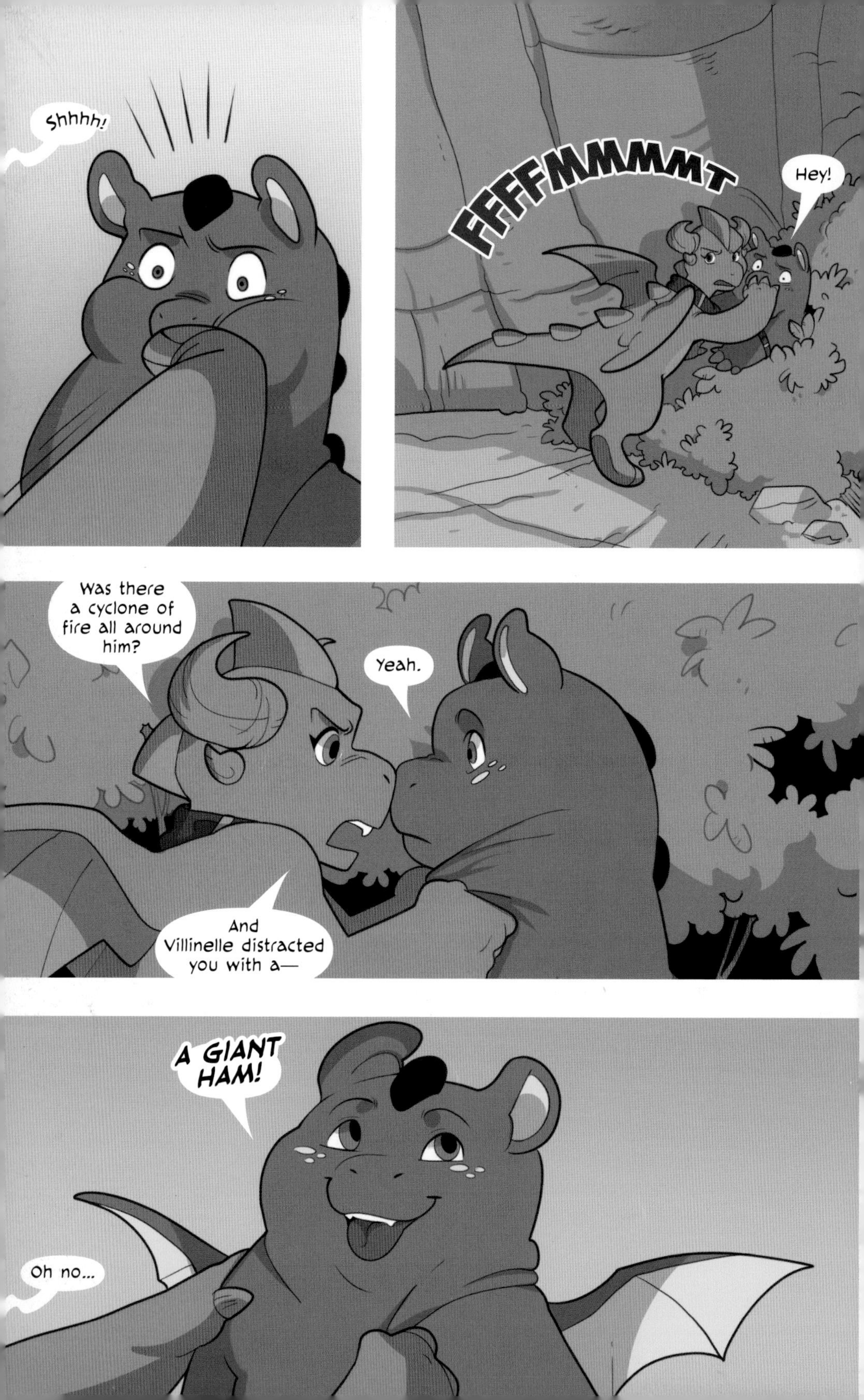
Shhhh!
FFFFMMMMMT
Hey!
Was there a cyclone of fire all around him?
Yeah.
And Villinelle distracted you with a—
A GIANT HAM!
Oh no...

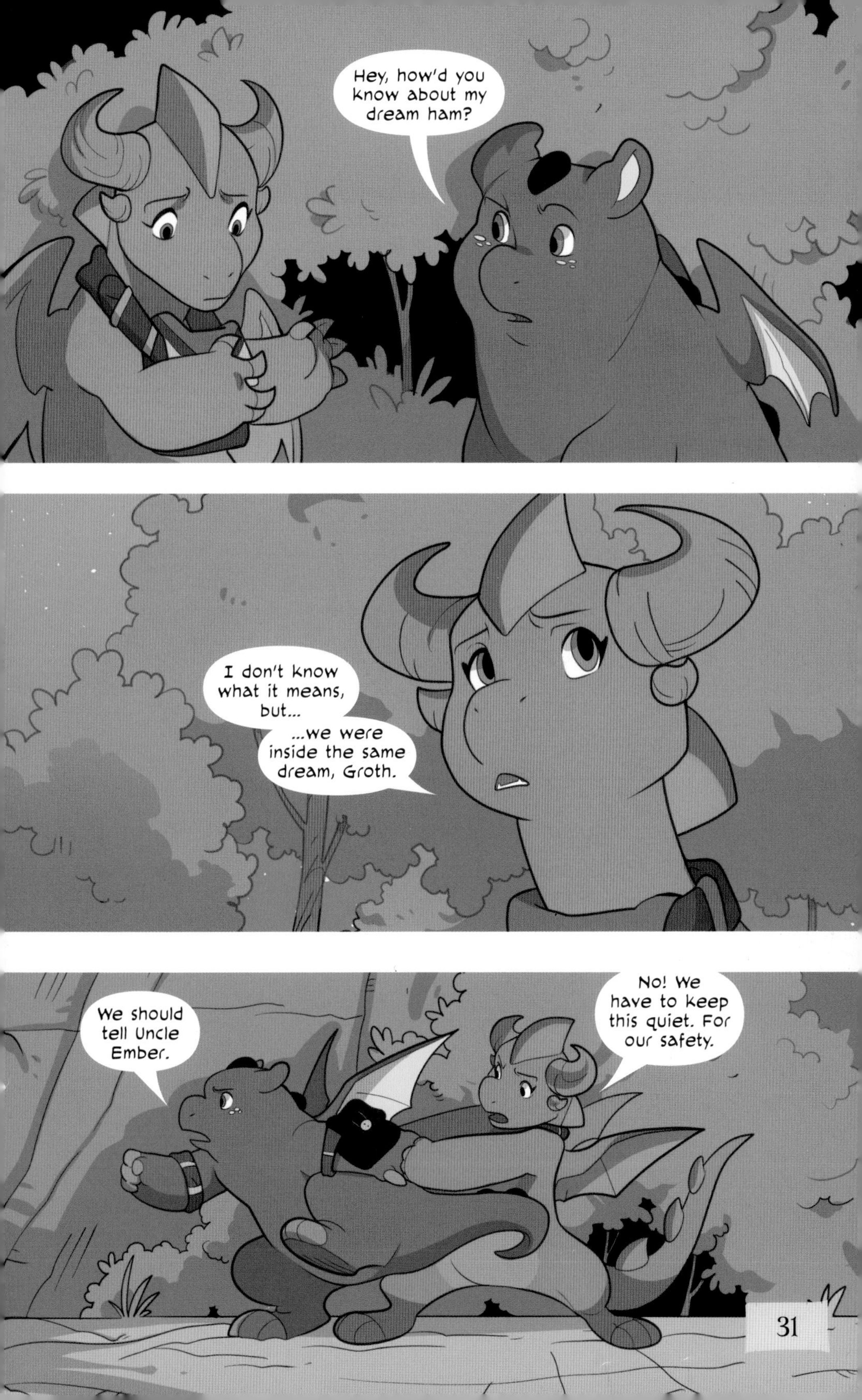
Hey, how'd you know about my dream ham?
I don't know what it means, but...
...we were inside the same dream, Groth.
We should tell Uncle Ember.
No! We have to keep this quiet. For our safety.

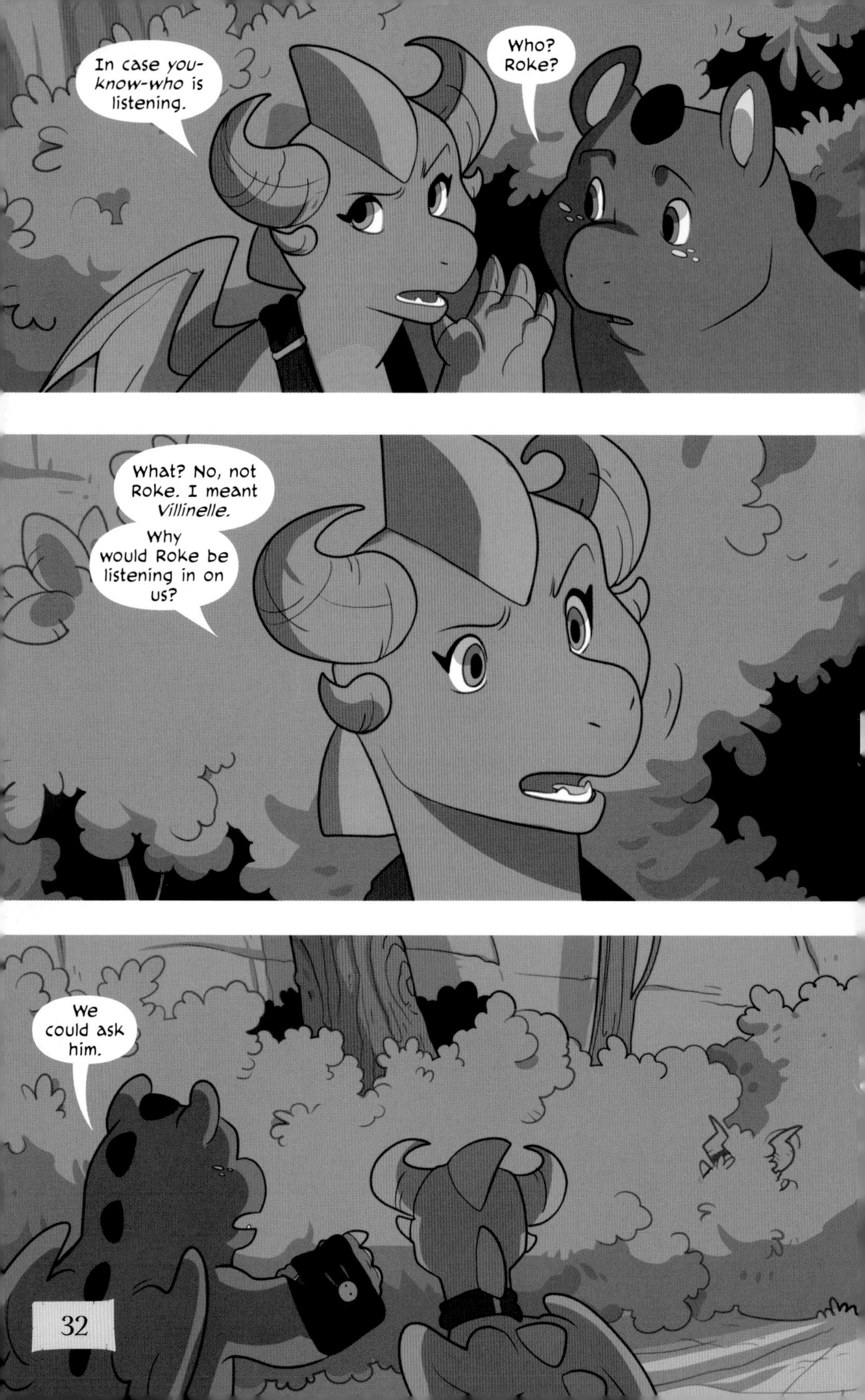

In case *you-know-who* is listening.
Who? Roke?
What? No, not Roke. I meant *Villinelle.*
Why would Roke be listening in on us?
We could ask him.

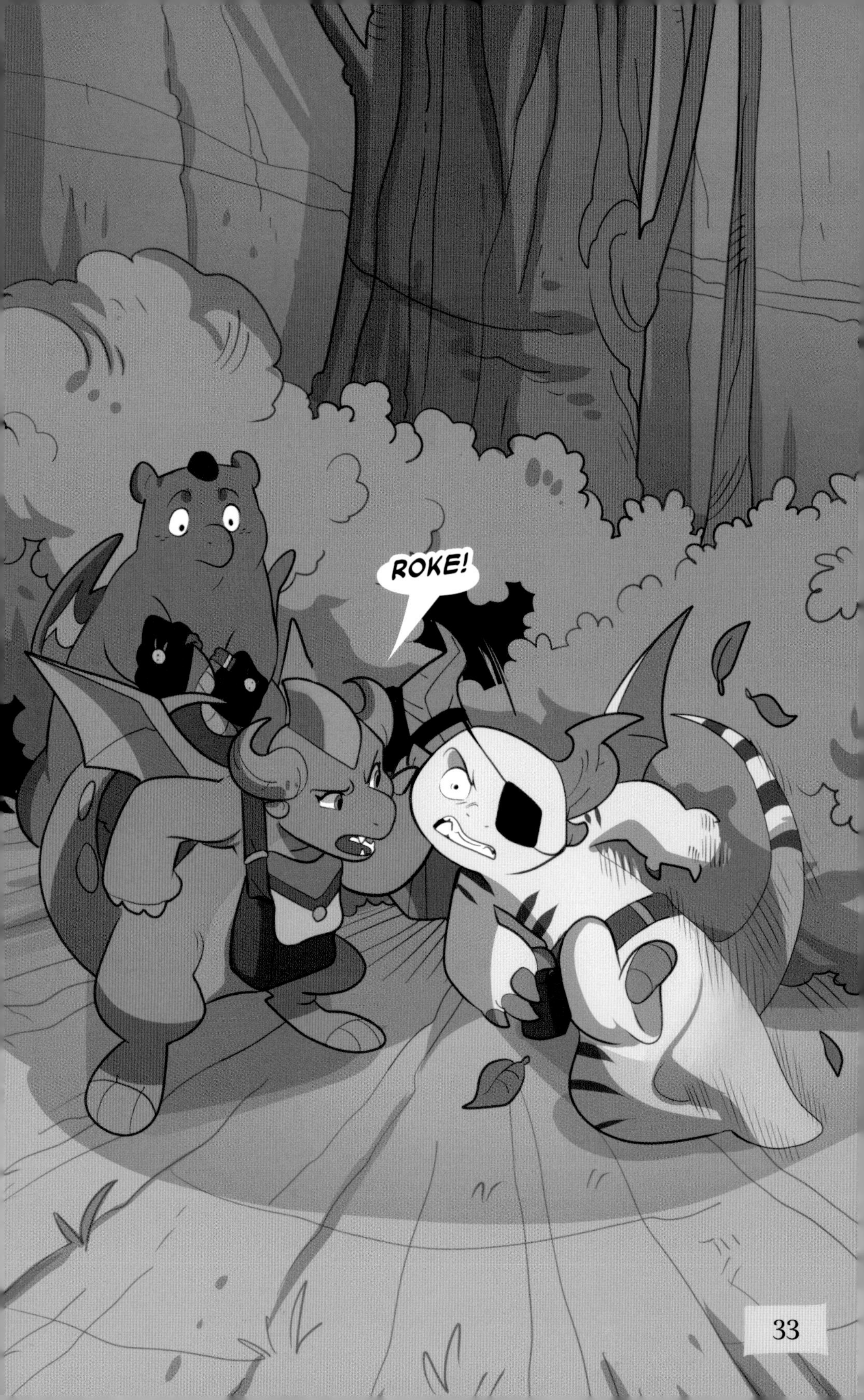
ROKE!

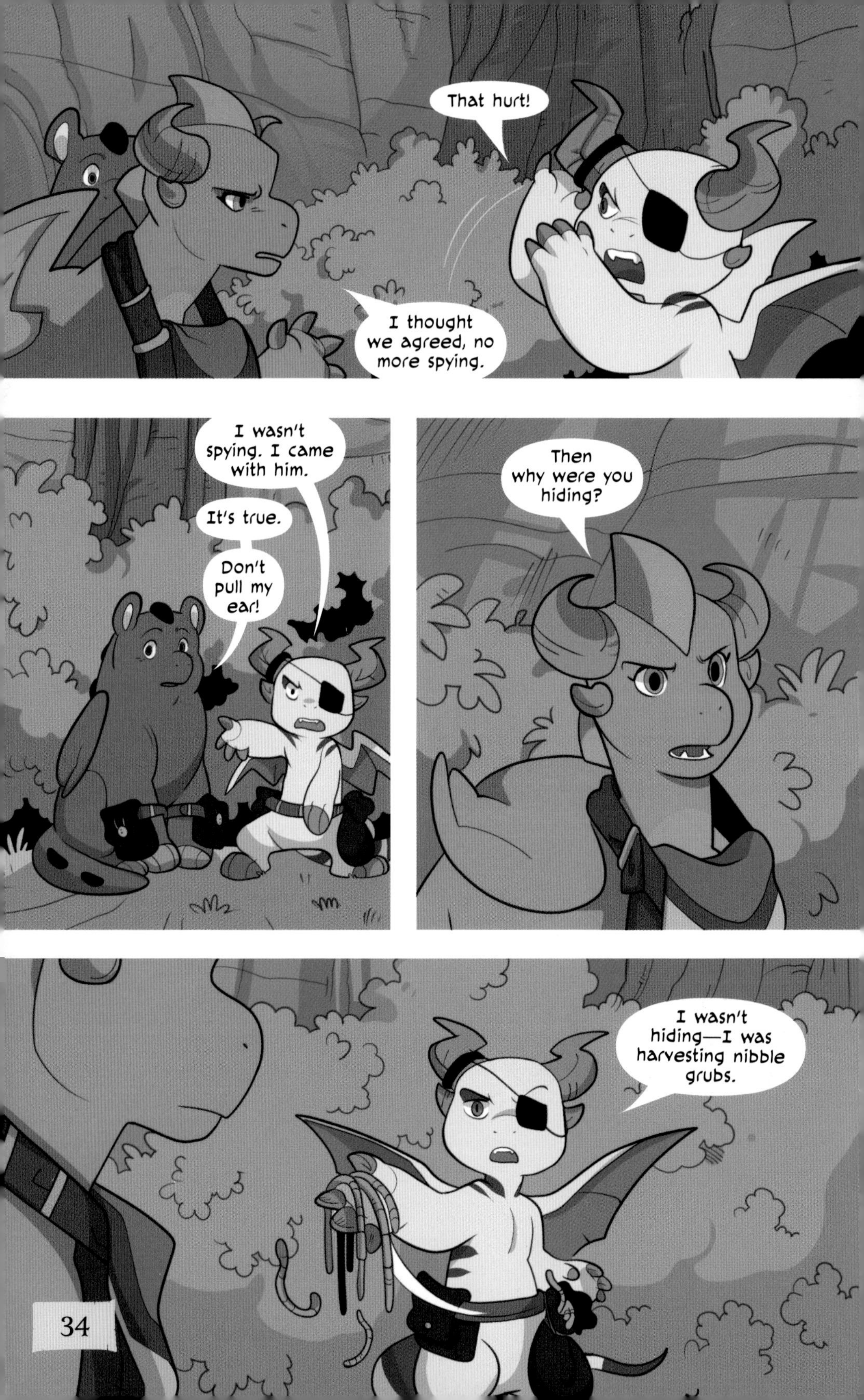
That hurt!
I thought we agreed, no more spying.
I wasn't spying. I came with him.
It's true.
Don't pull my ear!
Then why were you hiding?
I wasn't hiding—I was harvesting nibble grubs.

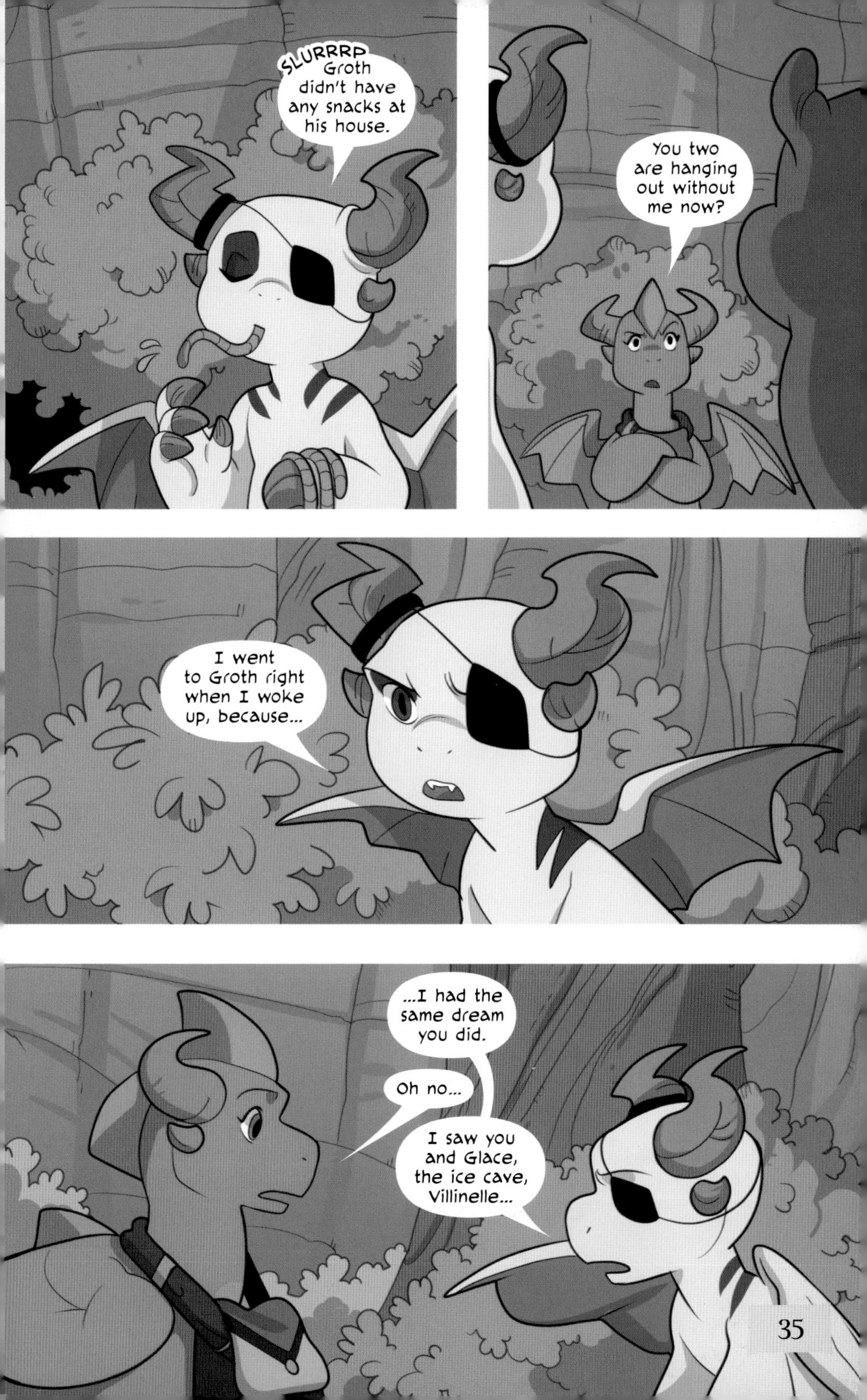
SLURRRP
Groth didn't have any snacks at his house.
You two are hanging out without me now?
I went to Groth right when I woke up, because...
...I had the same dream you did.
Oh no...
I saw you and Glace, the ice cave, Villinelle...

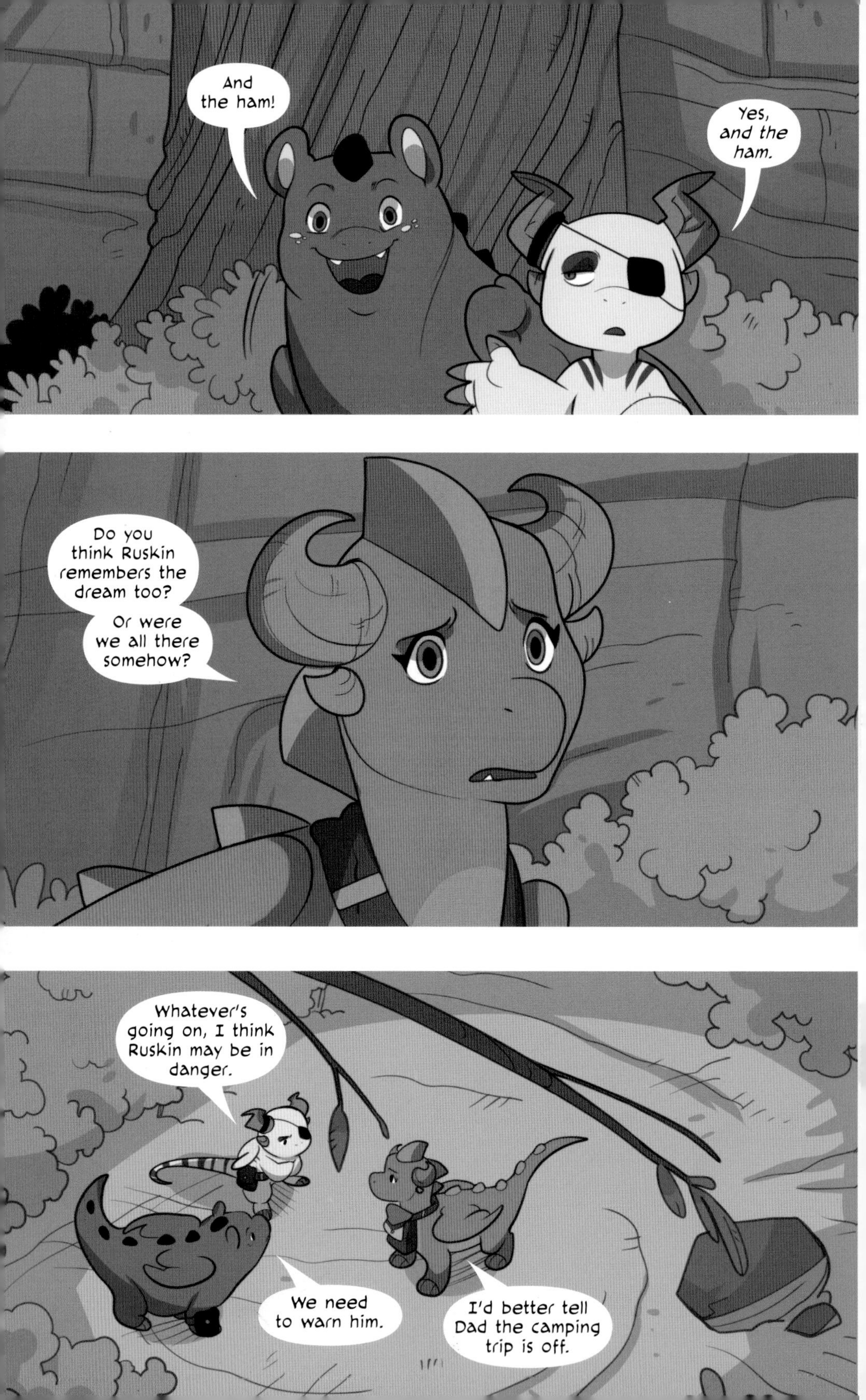
And the ham!
Yes, and the ham.
Do you think Ruskin remembers the dream too?
Or were we all there somehow?
Whatever's going on, I think Ruskin may be in danger.
We need to warn him.
I'd better tell Dad the camping trip is off.

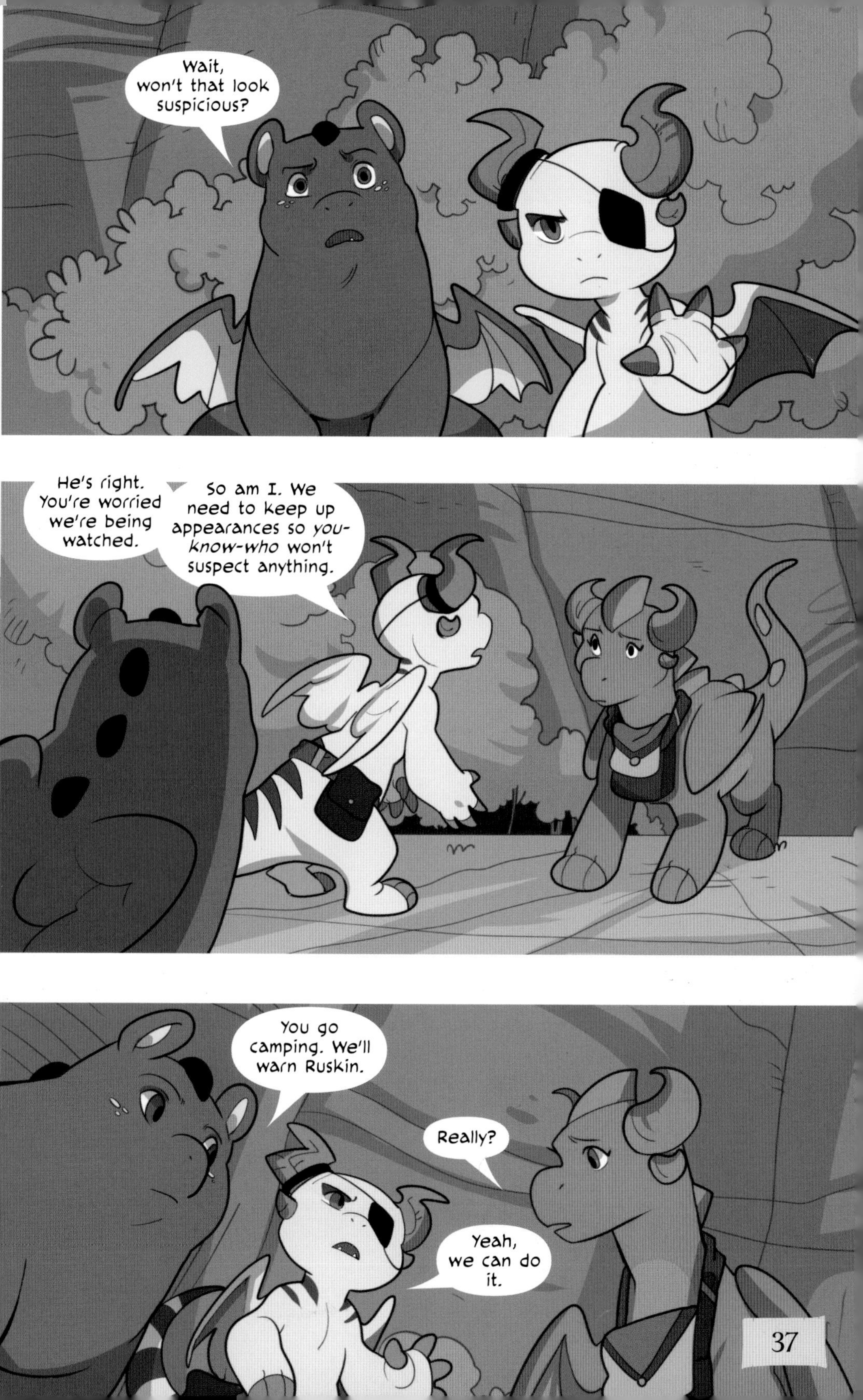
Wait, won't that look suspicious?
He's right. You're worried we're being watched.
So am I. We need to keep up appearances so *you-know-who* won't suspect anything.
You go camping. We'll warn Ruskin.
Really?
Yeah, we can do it.

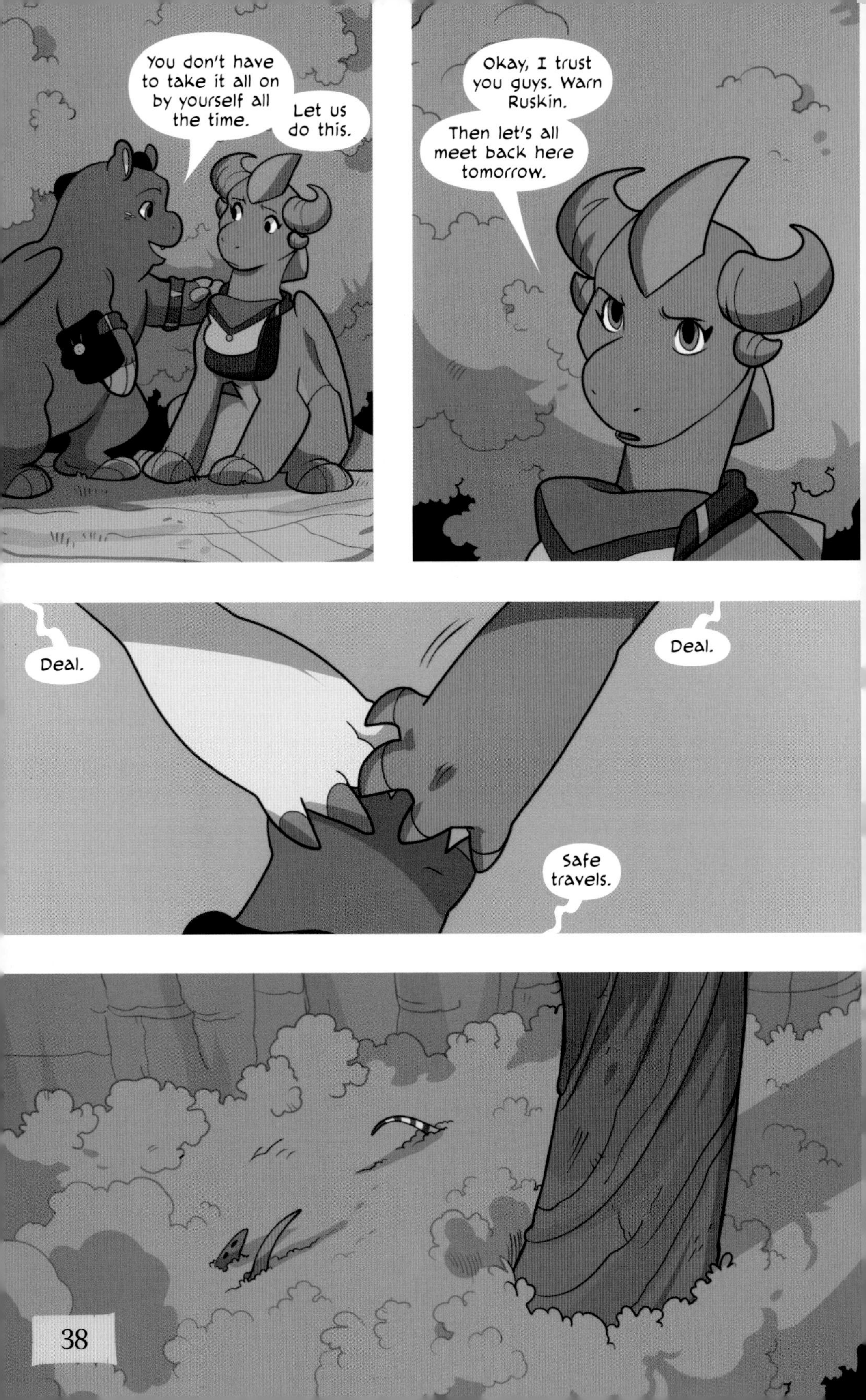

You don't have to take it all on by yourself all the time.
Let us do this.
Okay, I trust you guys. Warn Ruskin.
Then let's all meet back here tomorrow.
Deal.
Deal.
Safe travels.

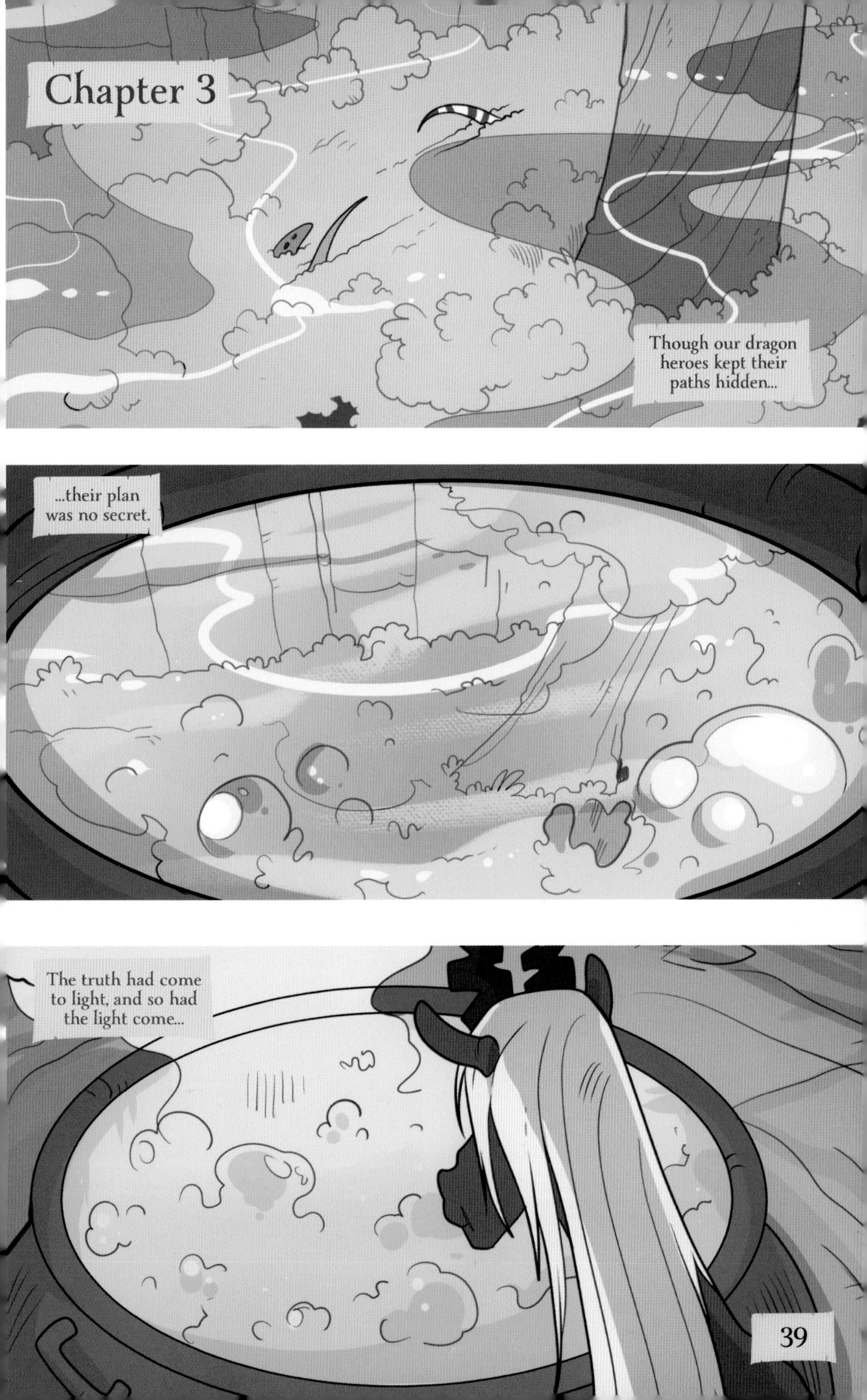
Chapter 3
Though our dragon heroes kept their paths hidden...
...their plan was no secret.
The truth had come to light, and so had the light come...

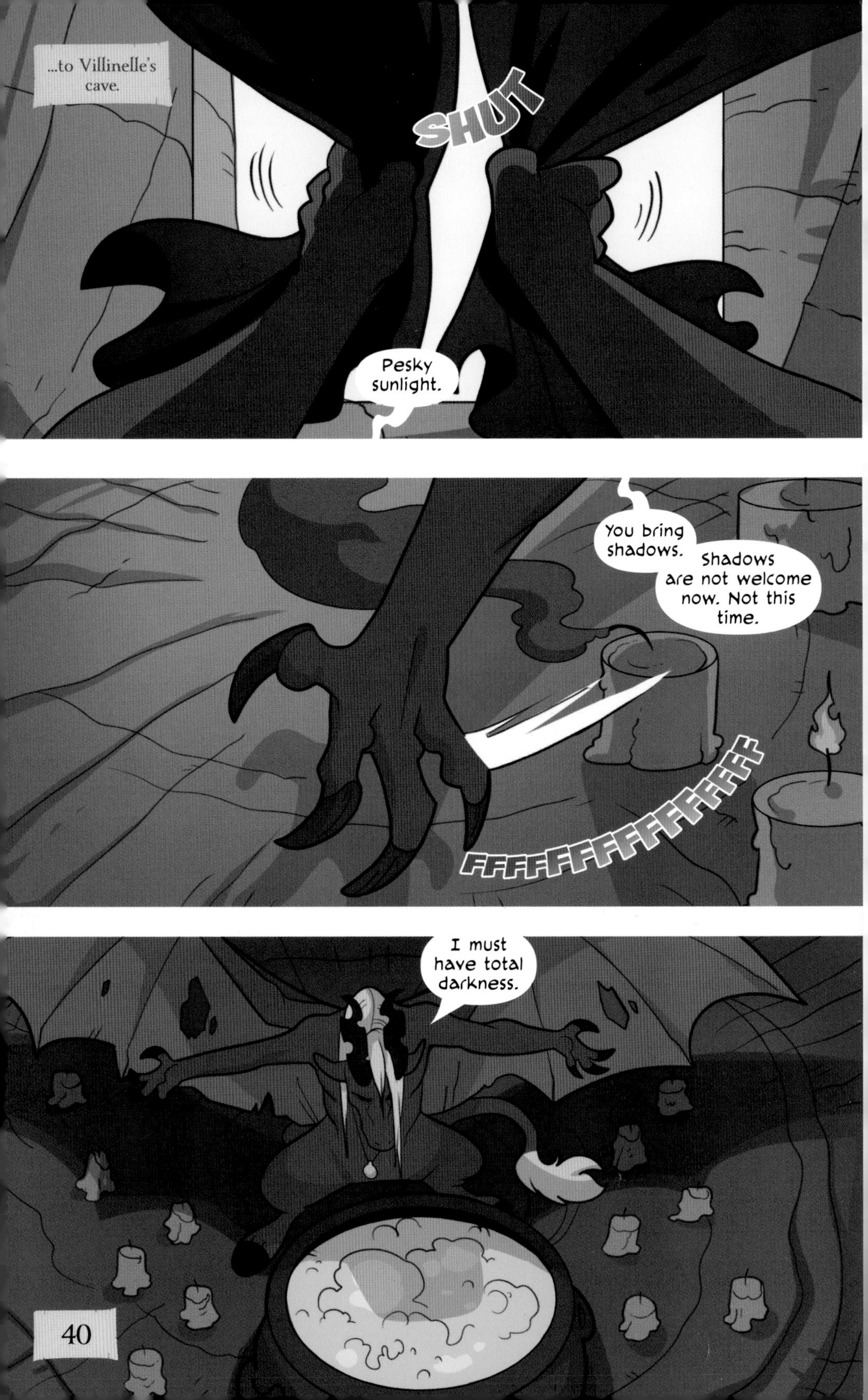
...to Villinelle's cave.
SHUT
Pesky sunlight.
You bring shadows.
Shadows are not welcome now. Not this time.
FFFFFFFFFFFFFFFF
I must have total darkness.

SSSSRR SSSSRR SSSSRR

DARKORIUM TOTALIS!

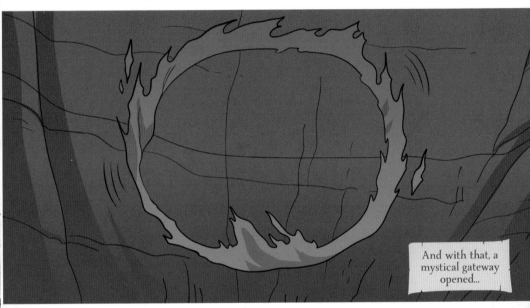

And with that, a mystical gateway opened...

...allowing Villinelle to travel beyond imagination...

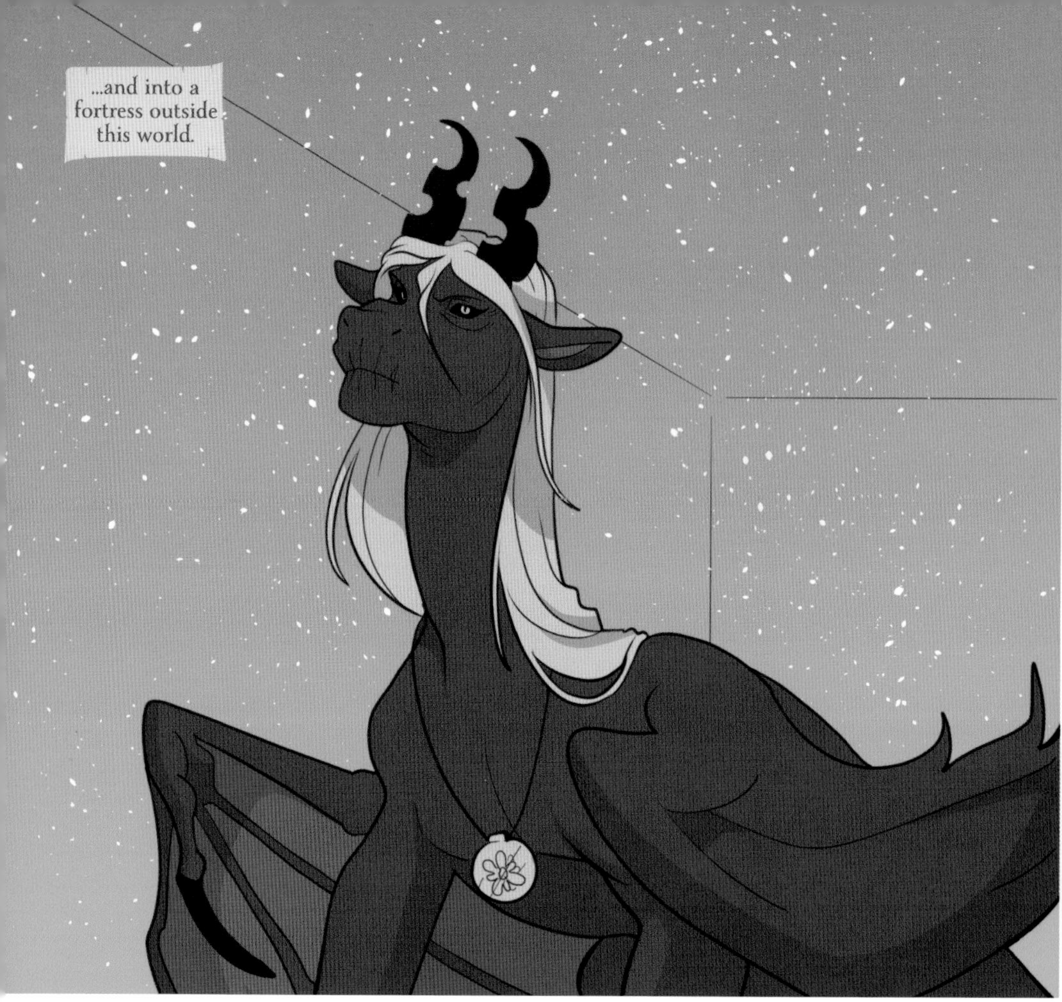
...and into a fortress outside this world.

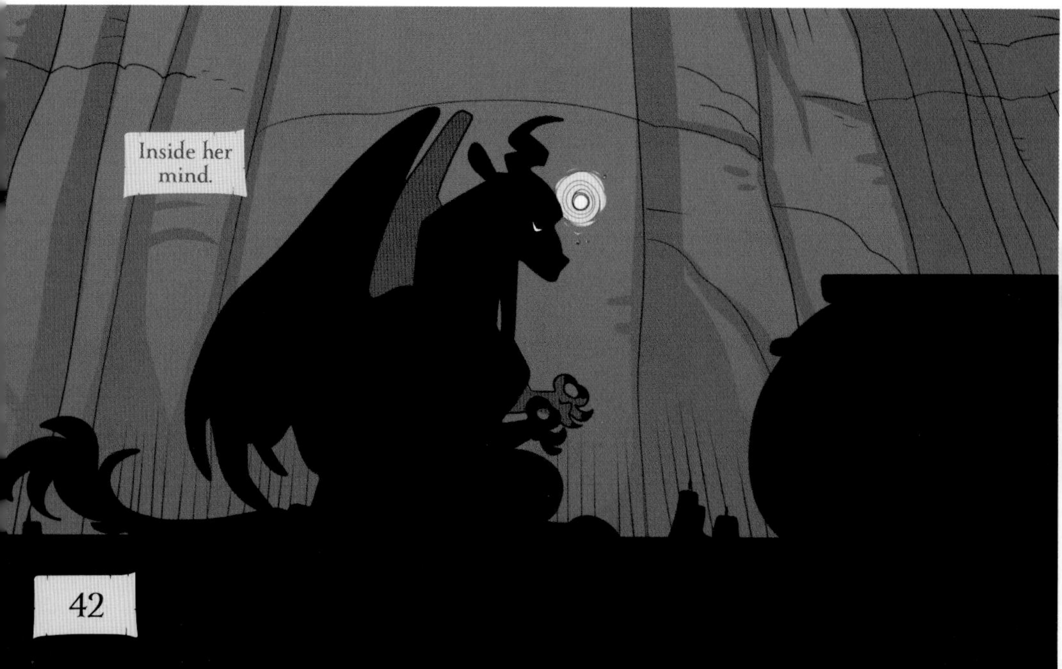
Inside her mind.

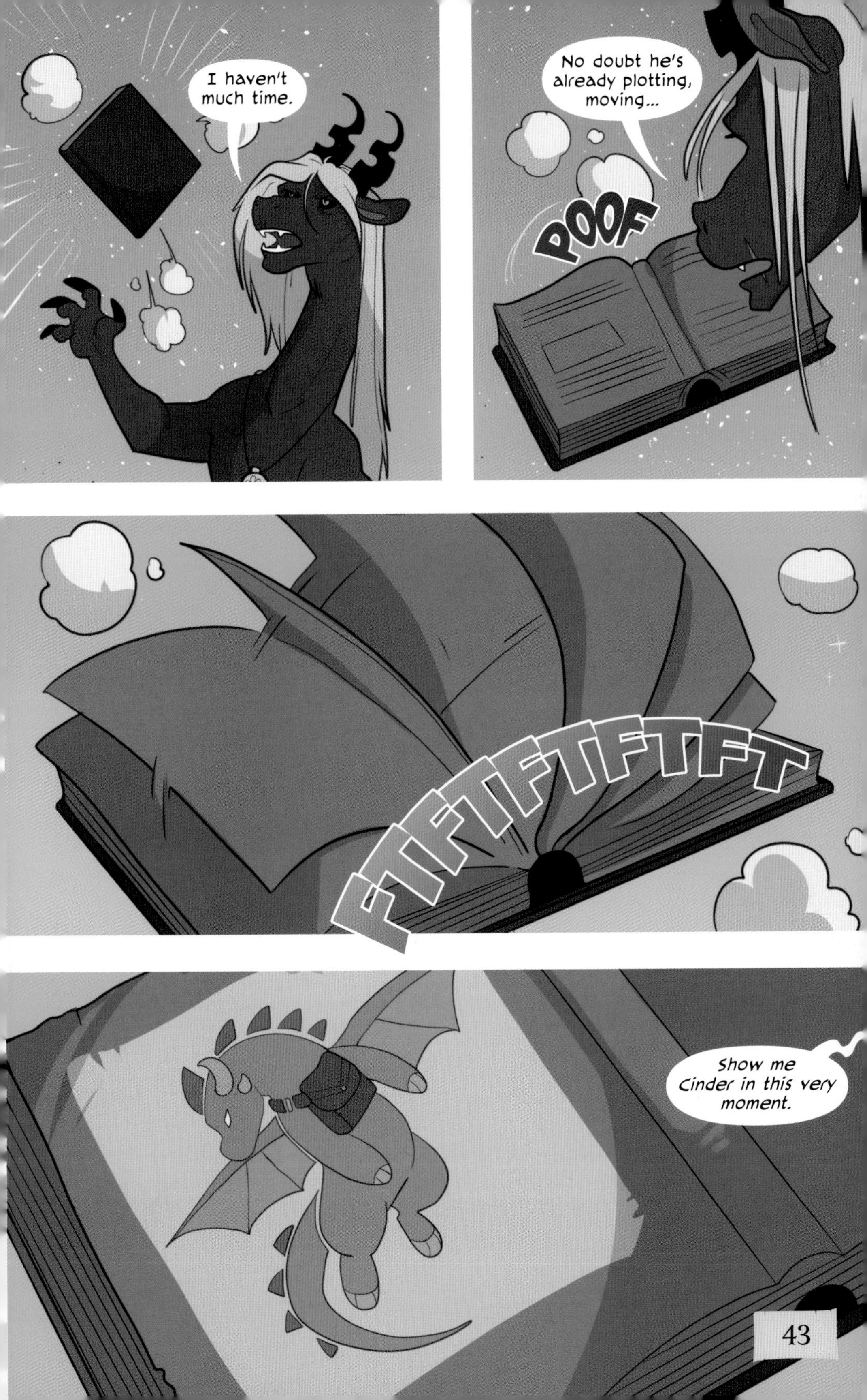
I haven't much time.
No doubt he's already plotting, moving...
POOF
FTTFTTFTTFTFT
Show me Cinder in this very moment.

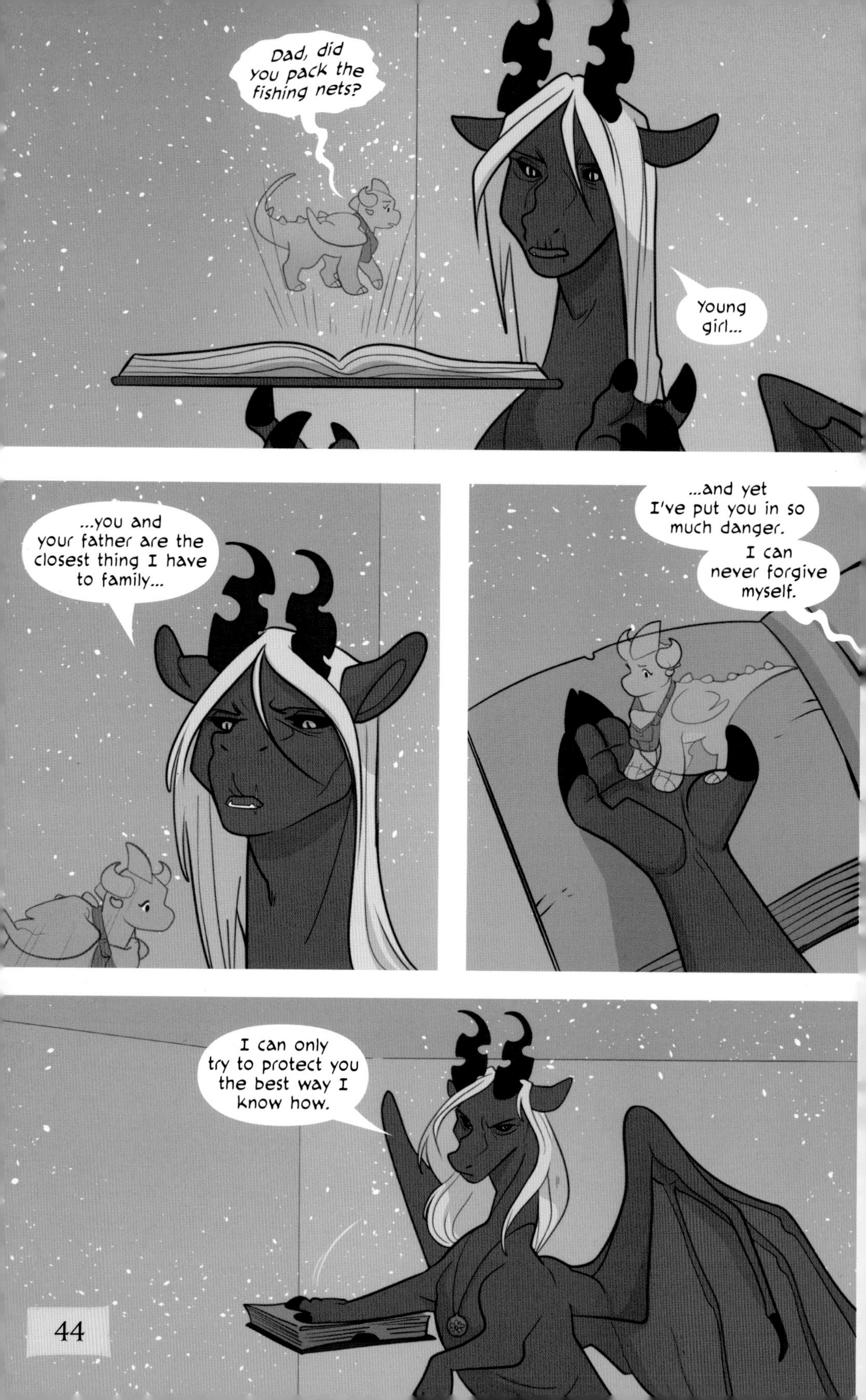
Dad, did you pack the fishing nets?
Young girl...
...you and your father are the closest thing I have to family...
...and yet I've put you in so much danger.
I can never forgive myself.
I can only try to protect you the best way I know how.

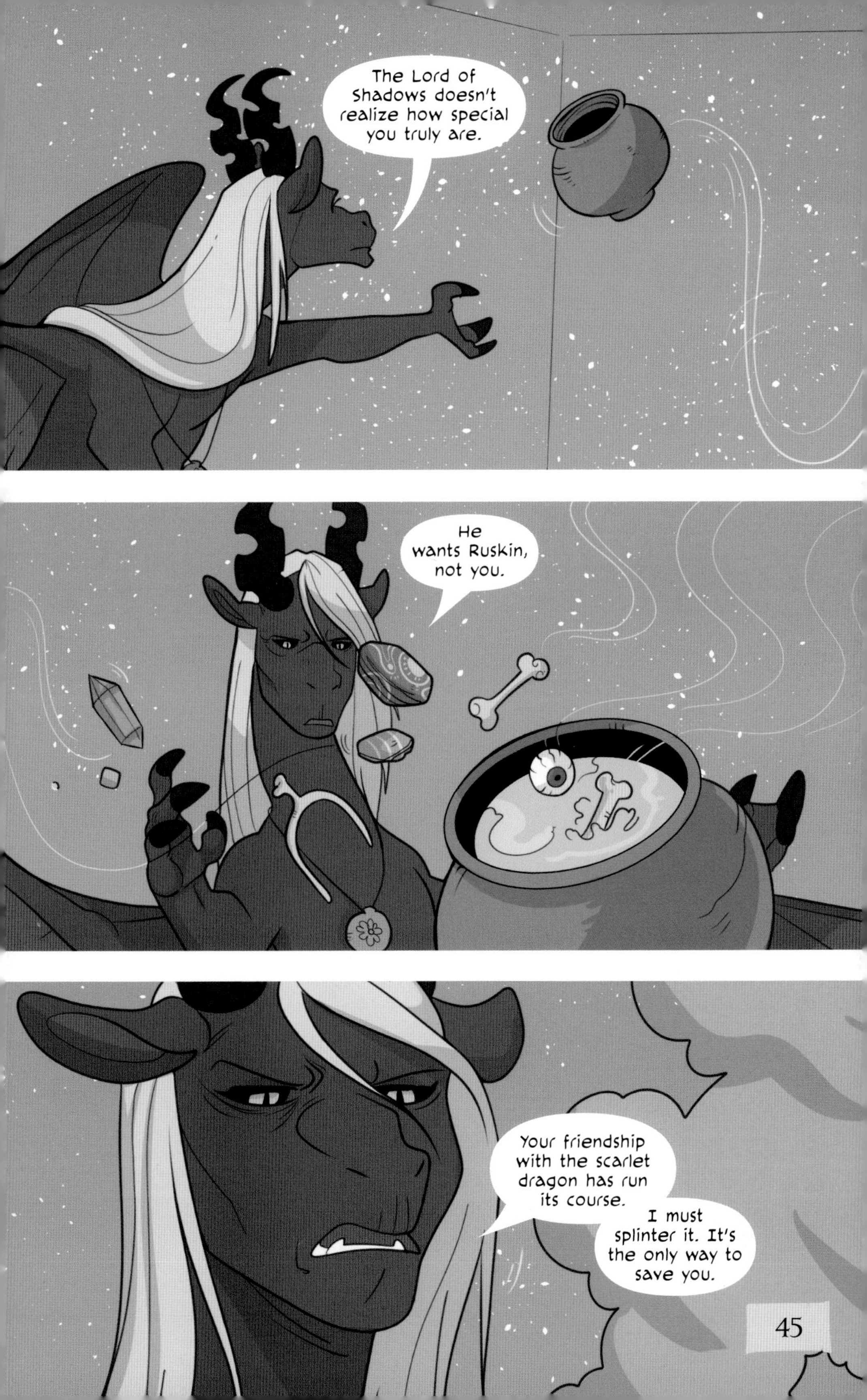
The Lord of Shadows doesn't realize how special you truly are.
He wants Ruskin, not you.
Your friendship with the scarlet dragon has run its course.
I must splinter it. It's the only way to save you.

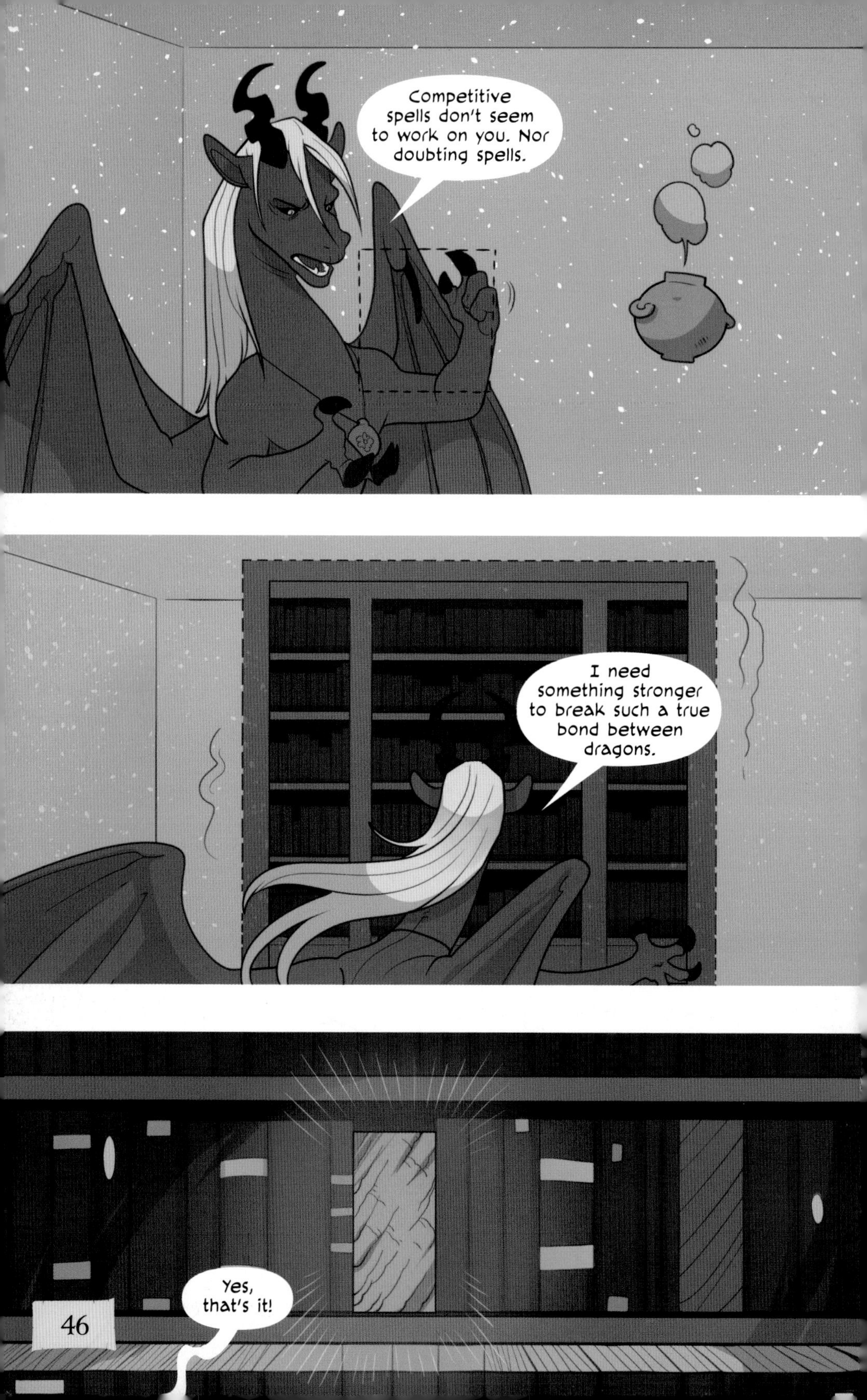
Competitive spells don't seem to work on you. Nor doubting spells.
I need something stronger to break such a true bond between dragons.
Yes, that's it!

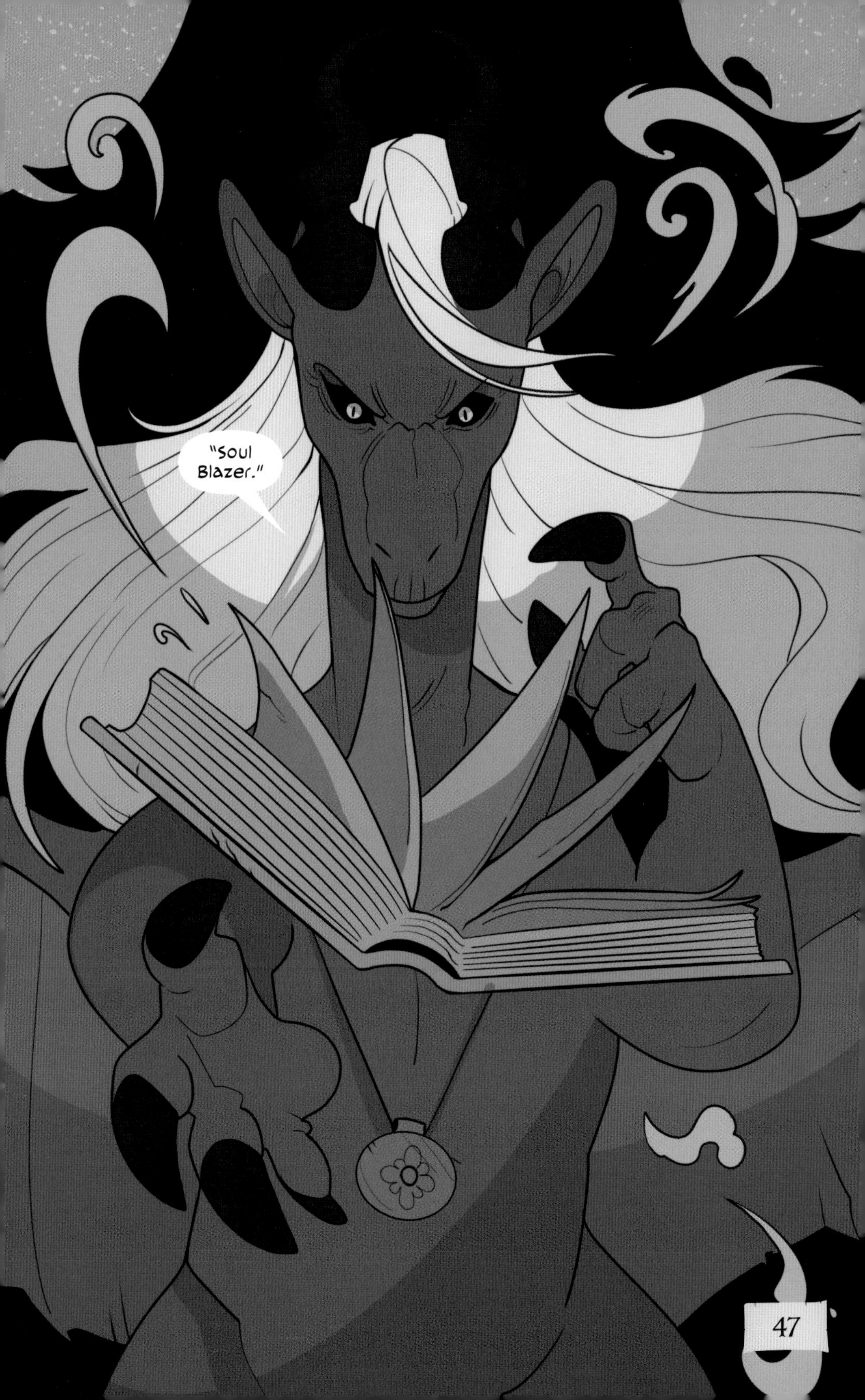
"Soul Blazer."

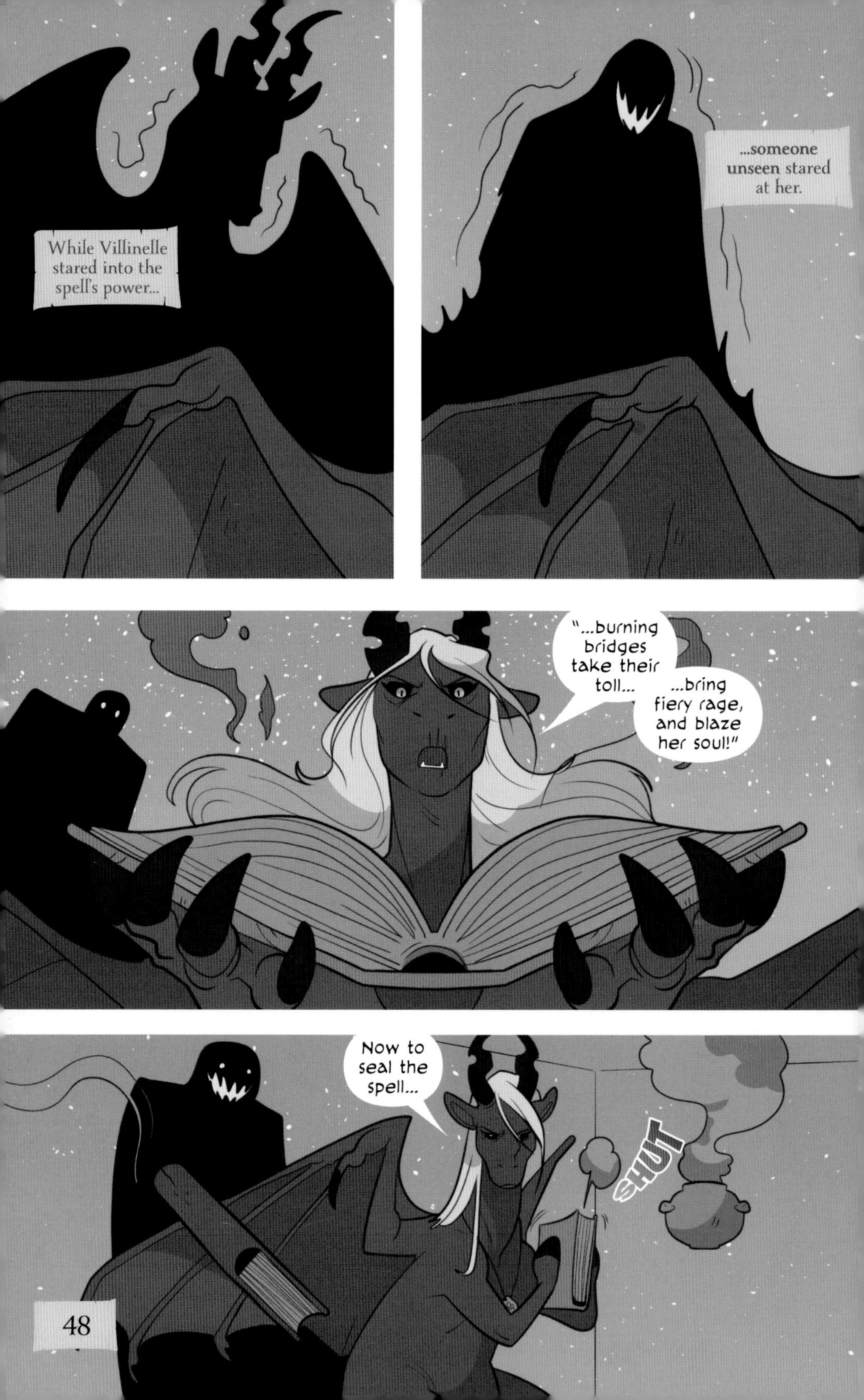
While Villinelle stared into the spell's power...
...someone unseen stared at her.
"...burning bridges take their toll...
...bring fiery rage, and blaze her soul!"
Now to seal the spell...
SHUT

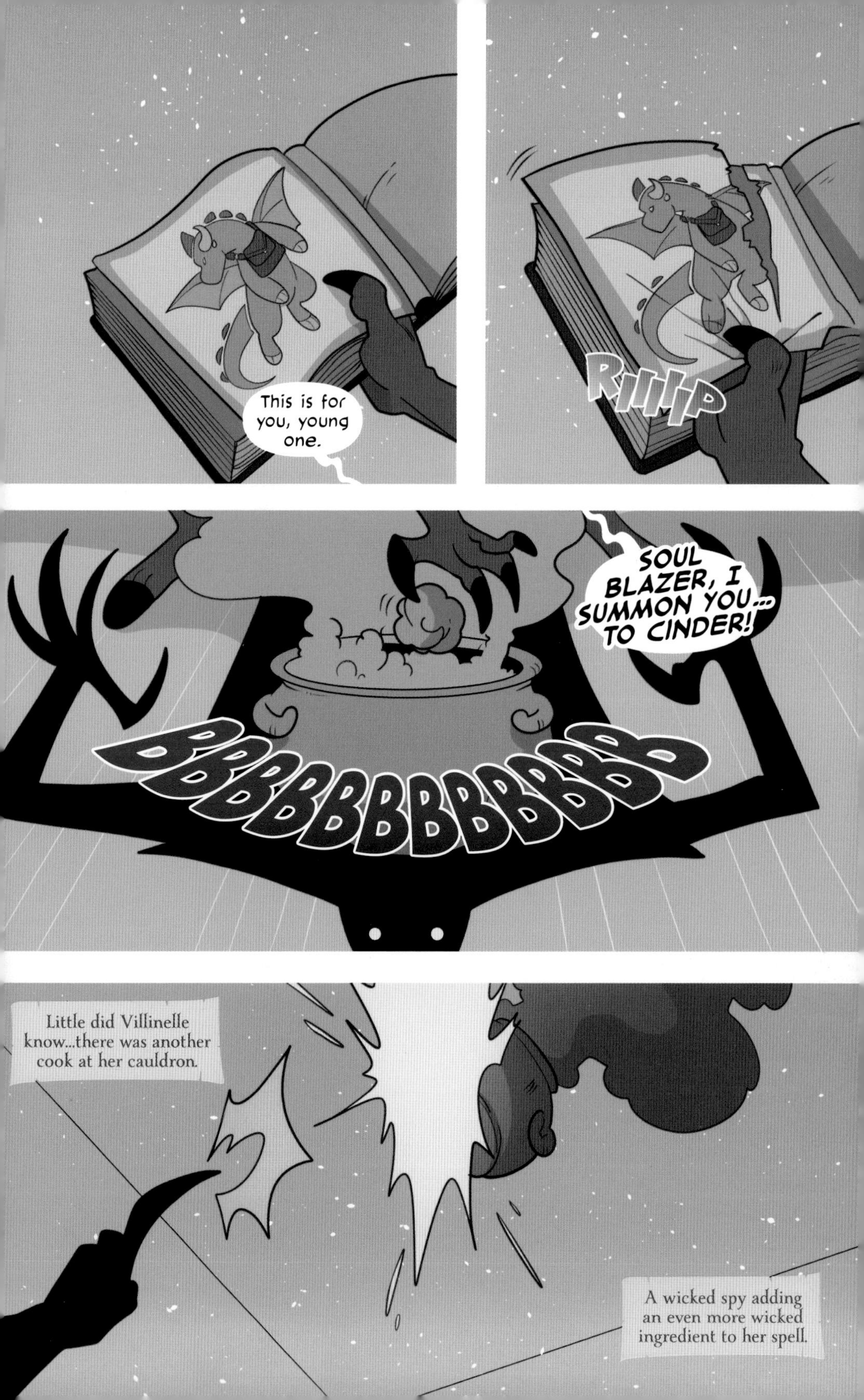
This is for you, young one.
RIIIIP
SOUL BLAZER, I SUMMON YOU... TO CINDER!
BBBBBBBBBBBBB
Little did Villinelle know...there was another cook at her cauldron.
A wicked spy adding an even more wicked ingredient to her spell.

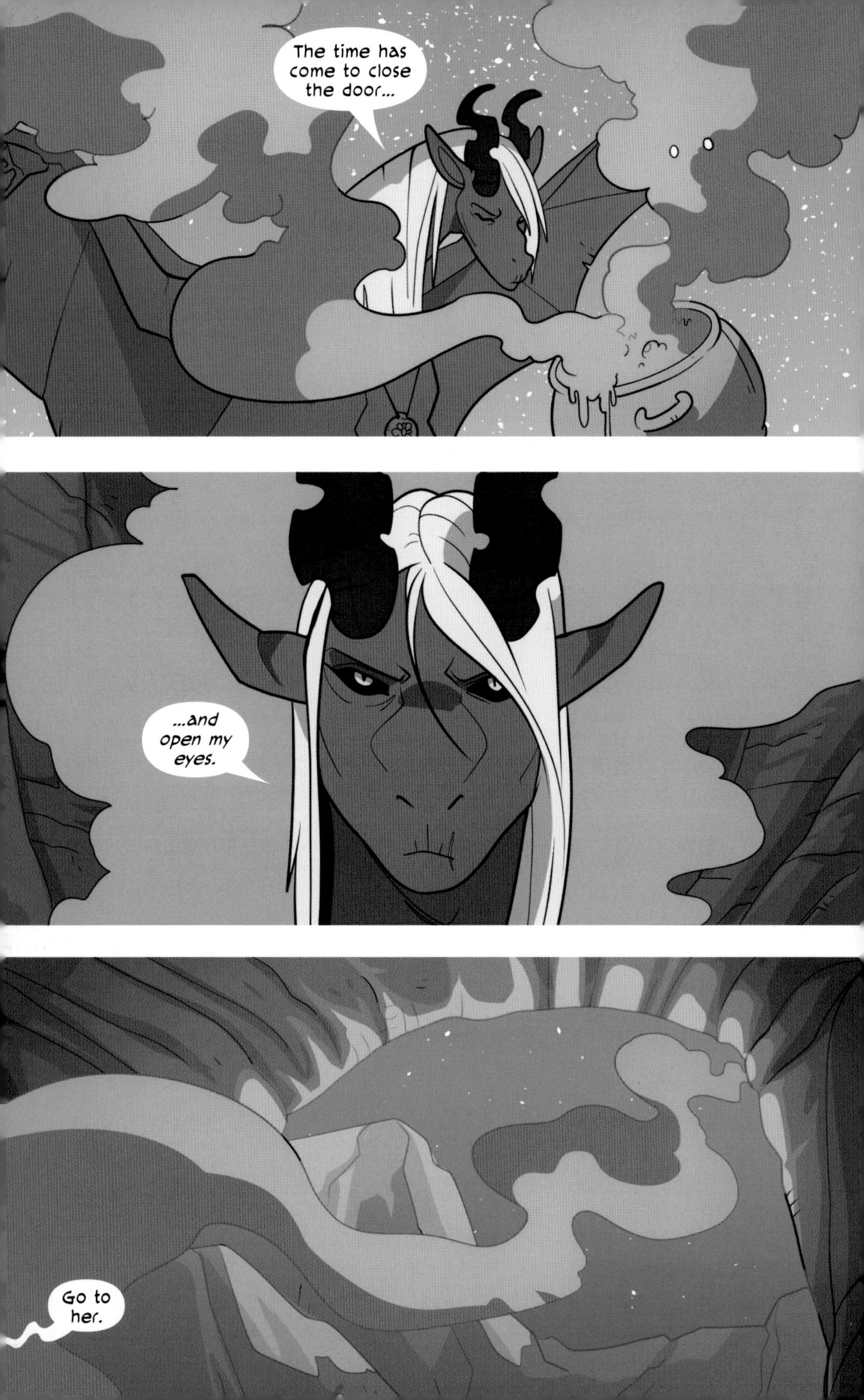
The time has come to close the door...
...and open my eyes.
Go to her.

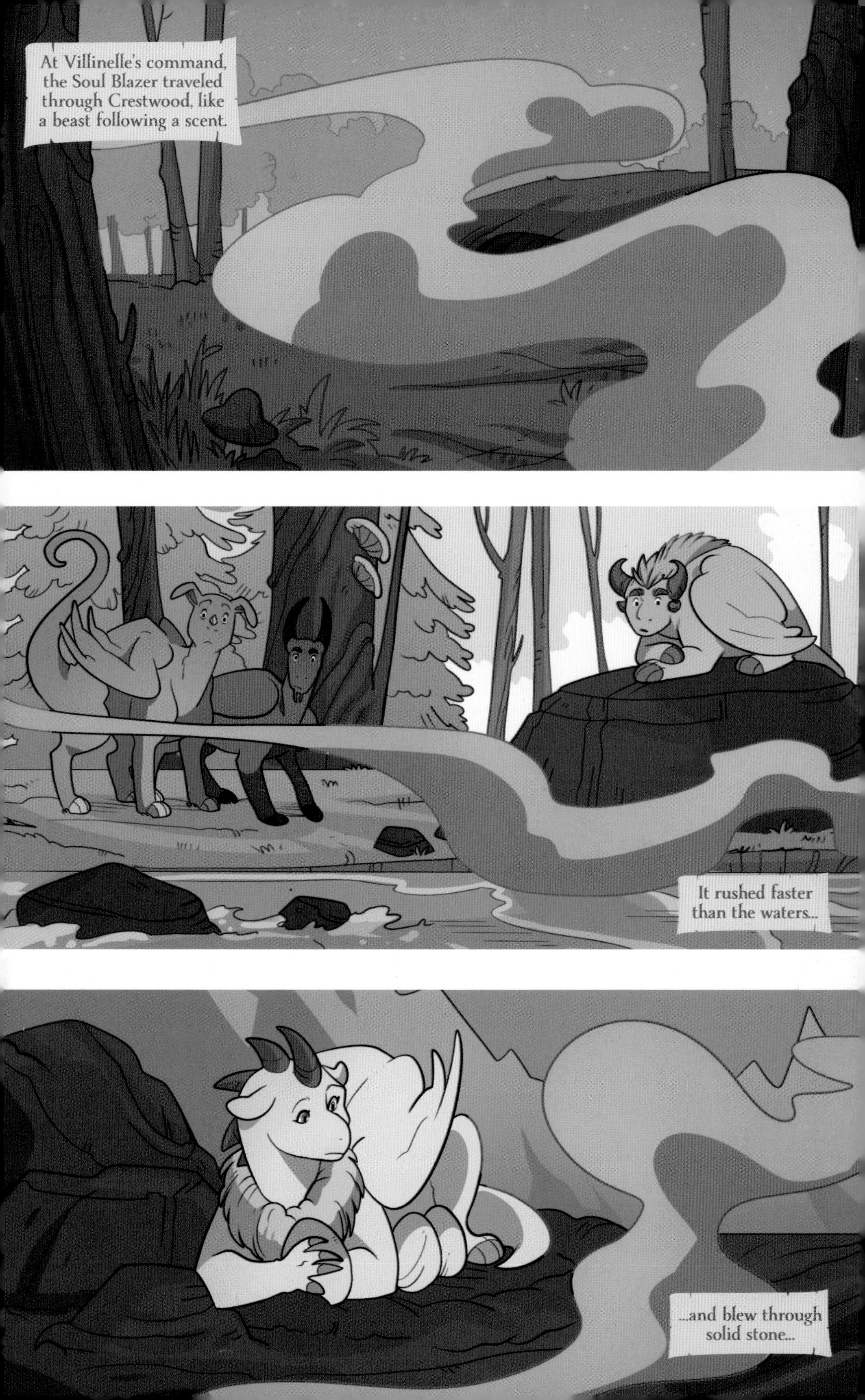
At Villinelle's command, the Soul Blazer traveled through Crestwood, like a beast following a scent.
It rushed faster than the waters...
...and blew through solid stone...

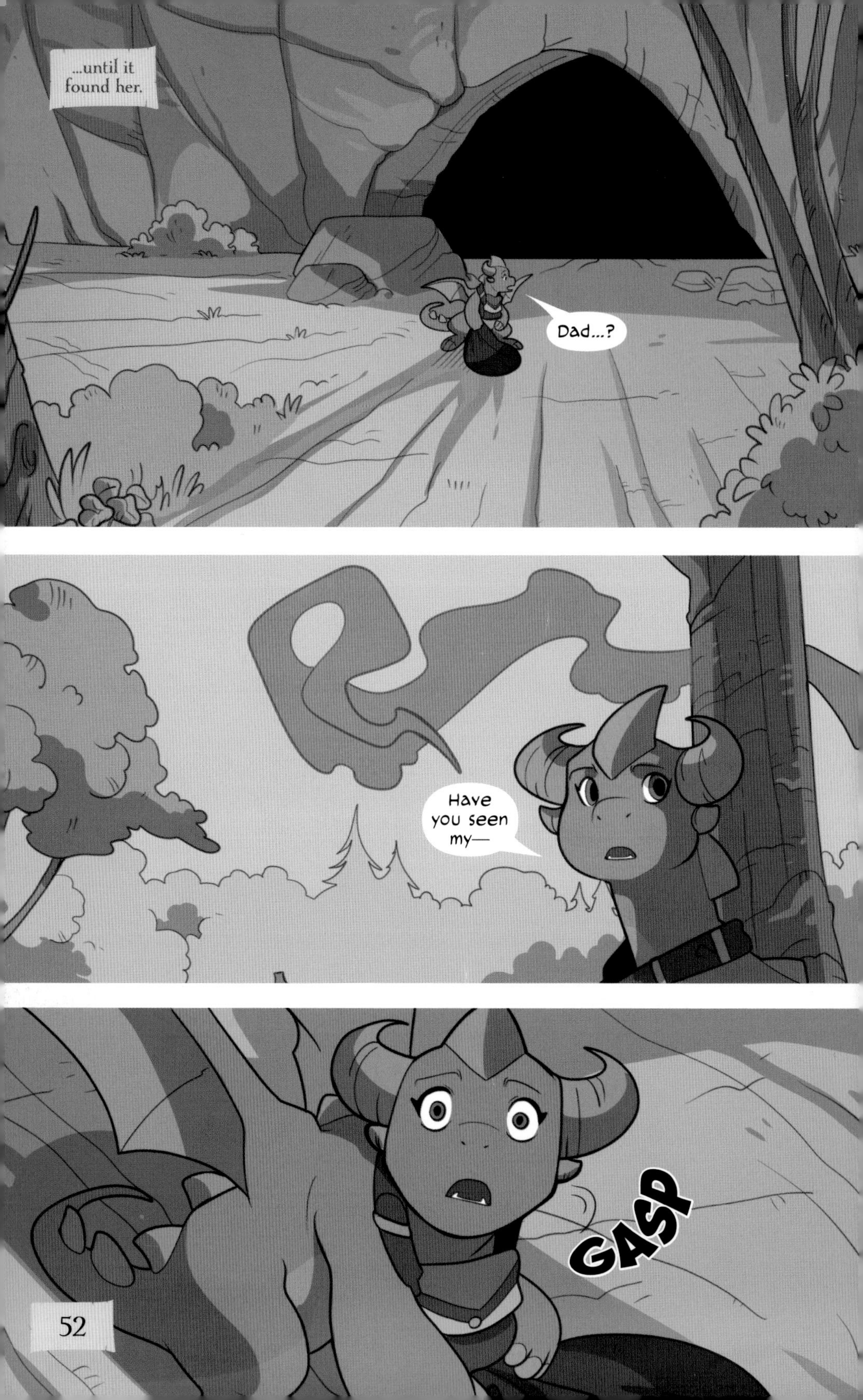
...until it found her.
Dad...?
Have you seen my—
GASP

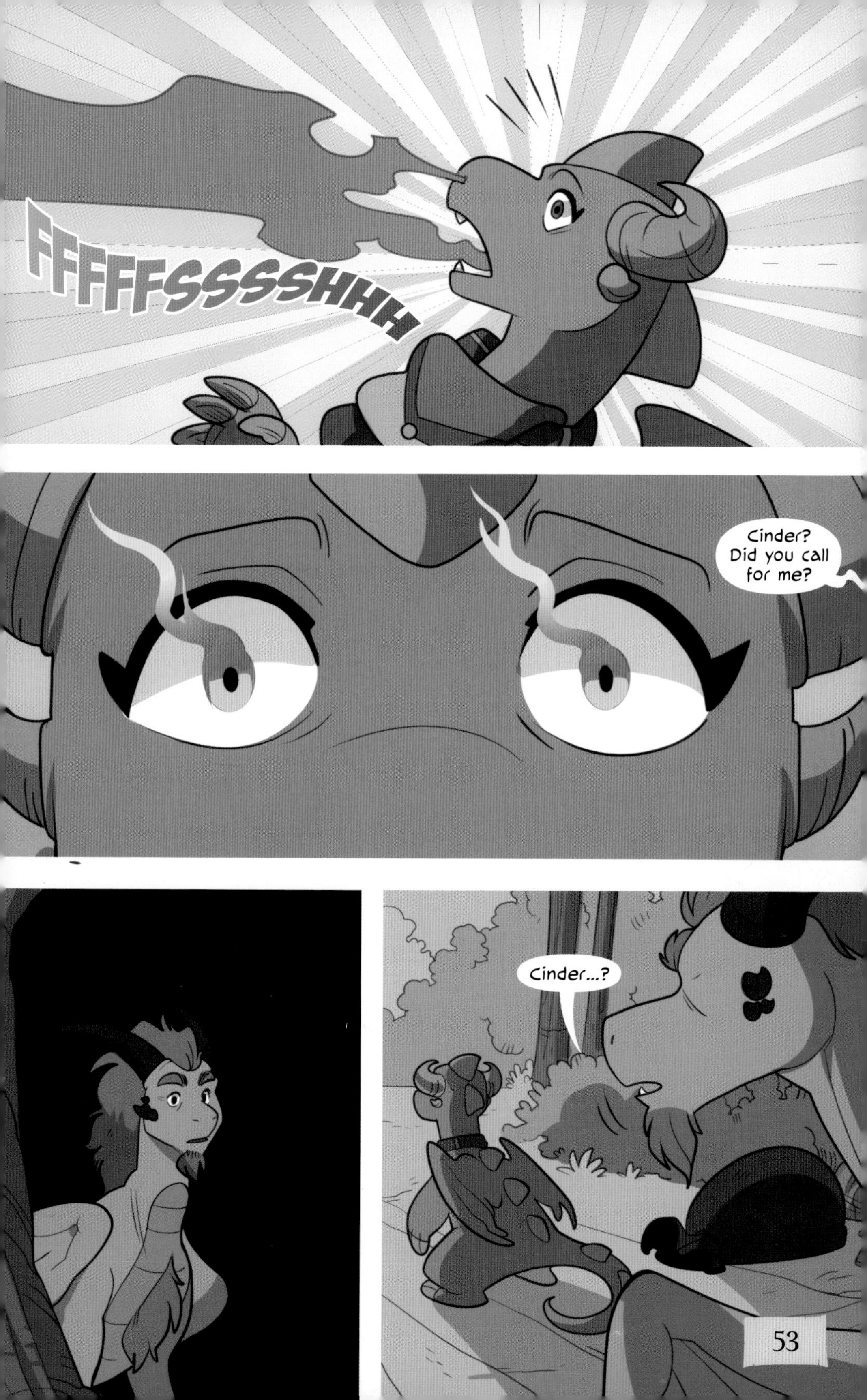
FFFFFSSSSHHH
Cinder? Did you call for me?
Cinder...?

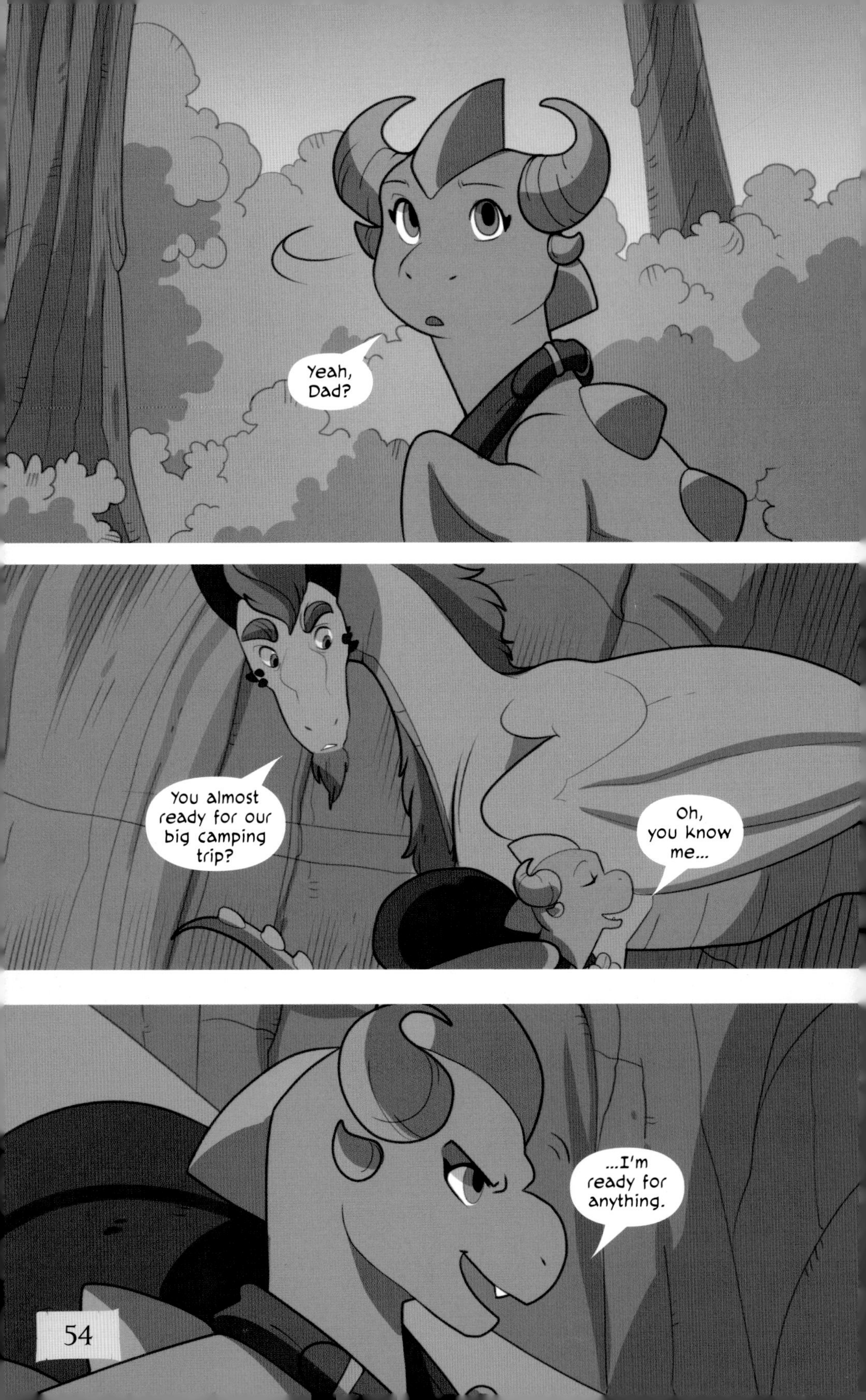
Yeah, Dad?
You almost ready for our big camping trip?
Oh, you know me...
...I'm ready for anything.

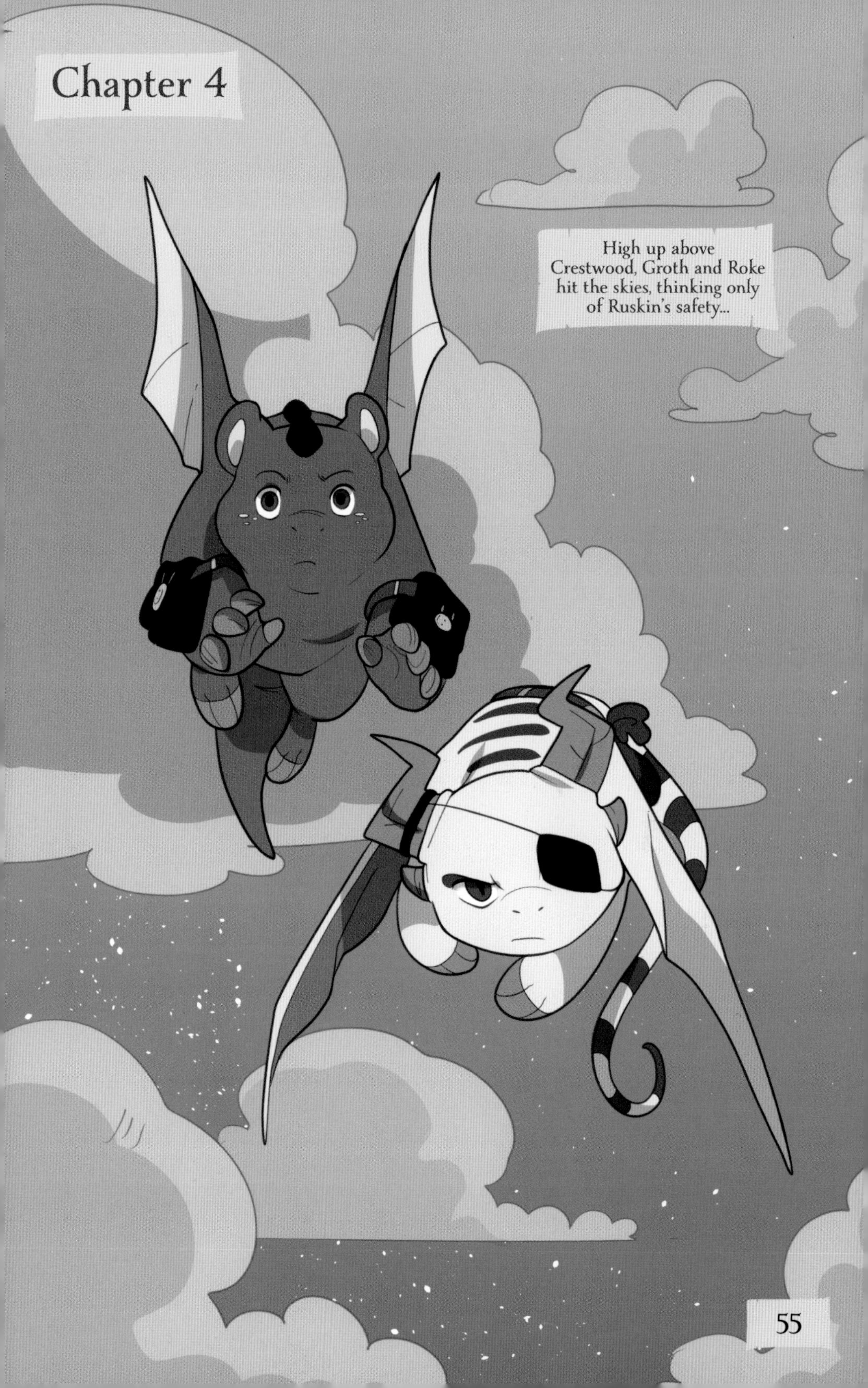
Chapter 4
High up above Crestwood, Groth and Roke hit the skies, thinking only of Ruskin's safety...

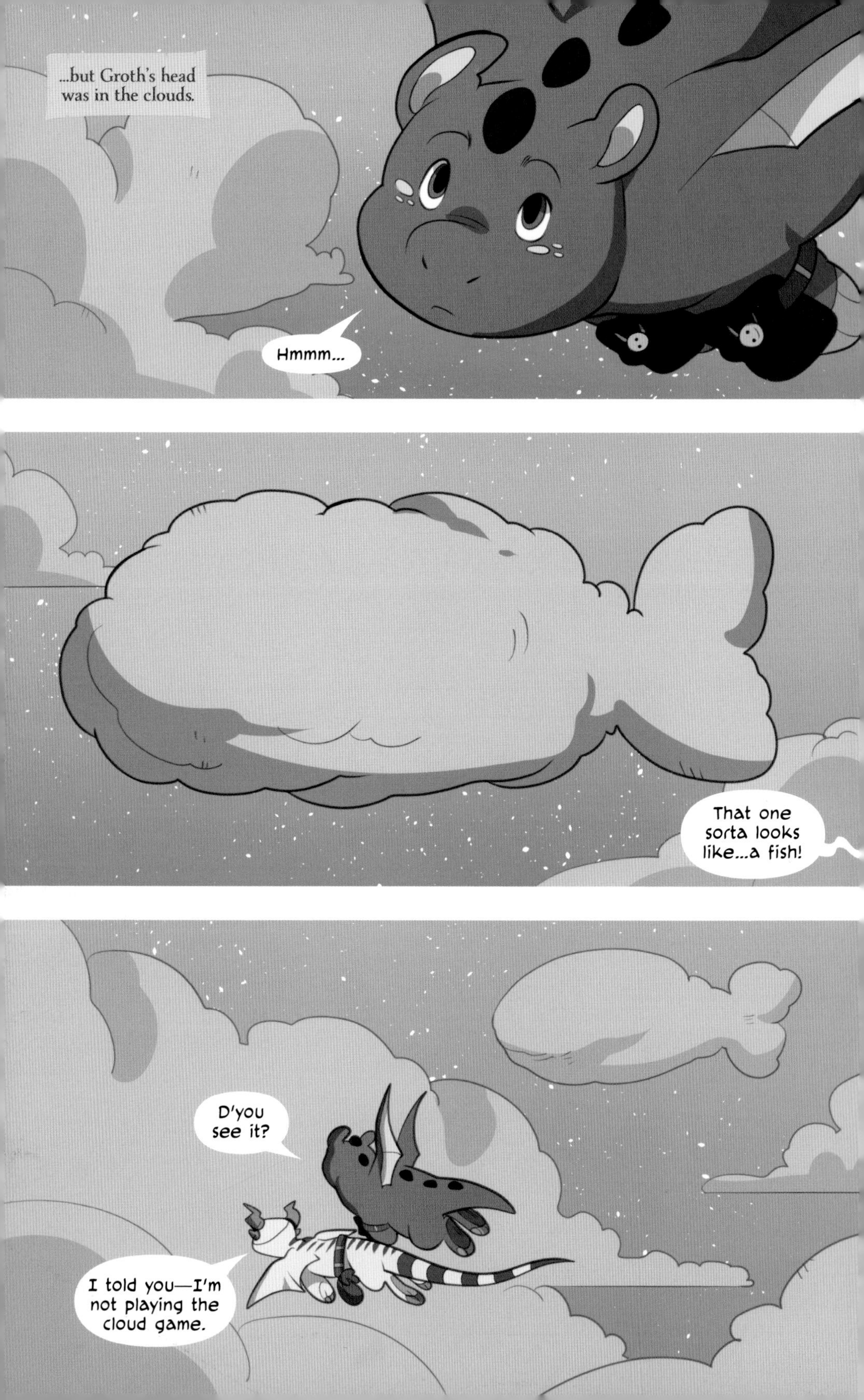
...but Groth's head was in the clouds.
Hmmm...
That one sorta looks like...a fish!
D'you see it?
I told you—I'm not playing the cloud game.

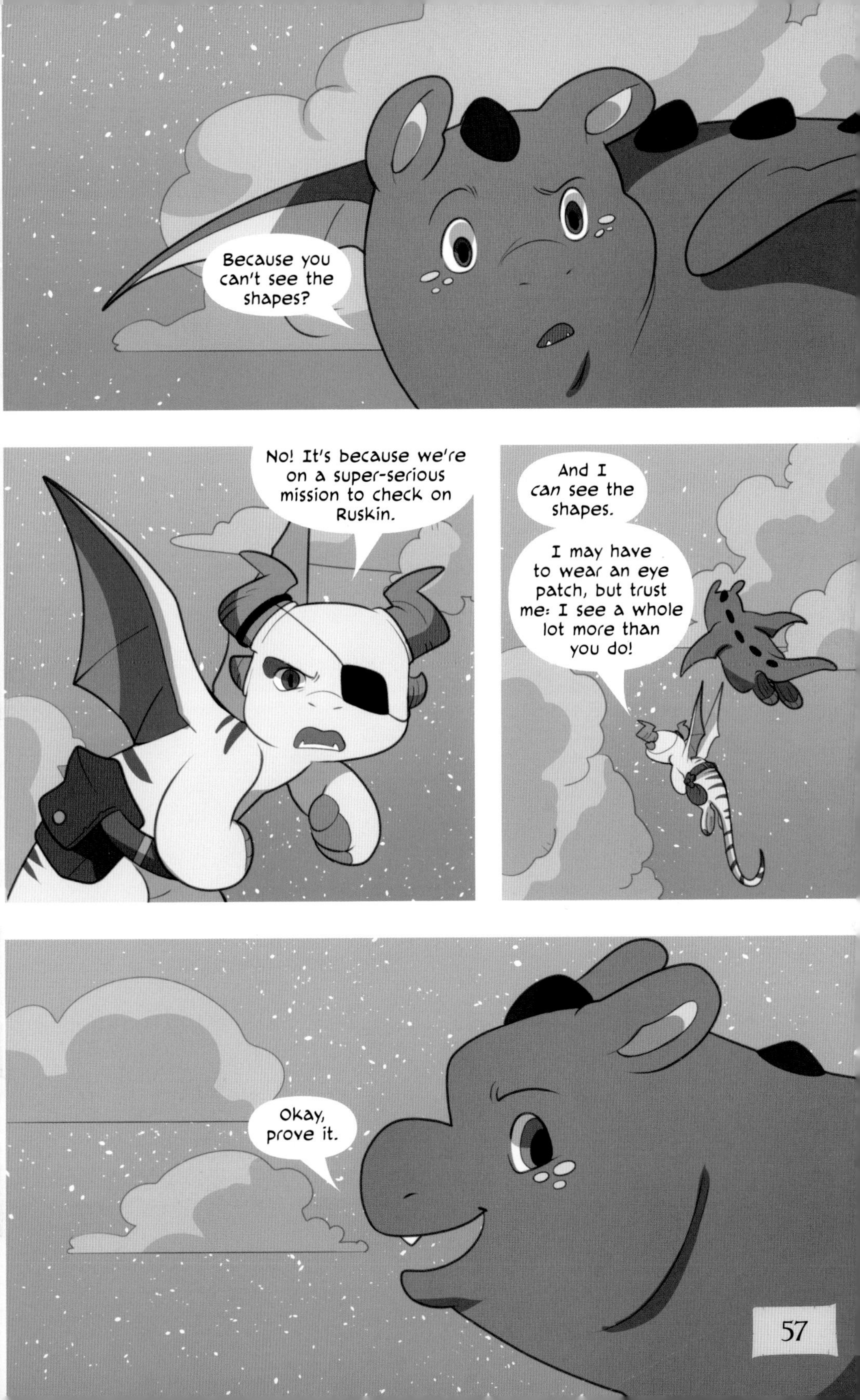
Because you can't see the shapes?
No! It's because we're on a super-serious mission to check on Ruskin.
And I *can* see the shapes.
I may have to wear an eye patch, but trust me: I see a whole lot more than you do!
Okay, prove it.

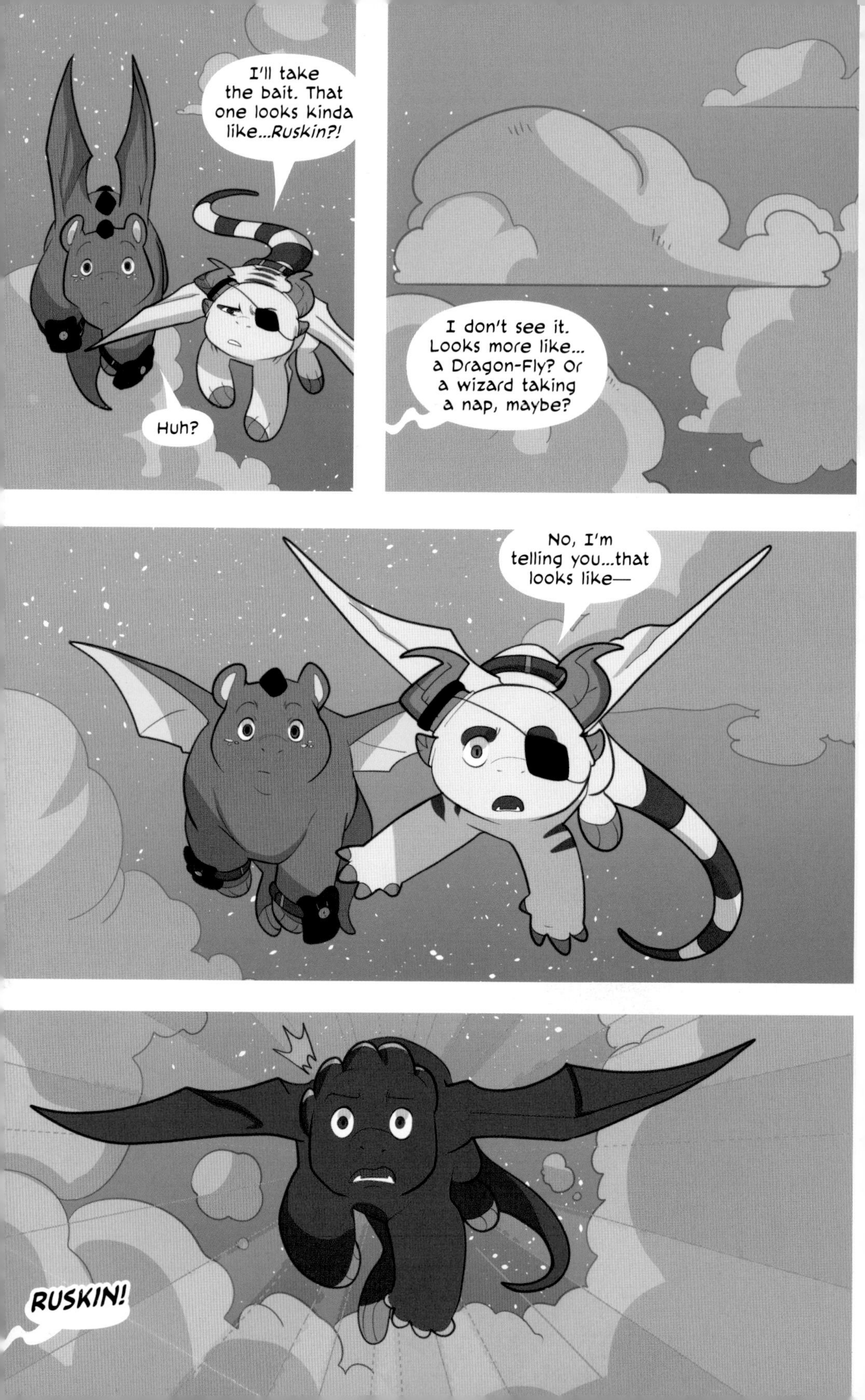
I'll take the bait. That one looks kinda like...*Ruskin?!*
Huh?
I don't see it. Looks more like... a Dragon-Fly? Or a wizard taking a nap, maybe?
No, I'm telling you...that looks like—
RUSKIN!

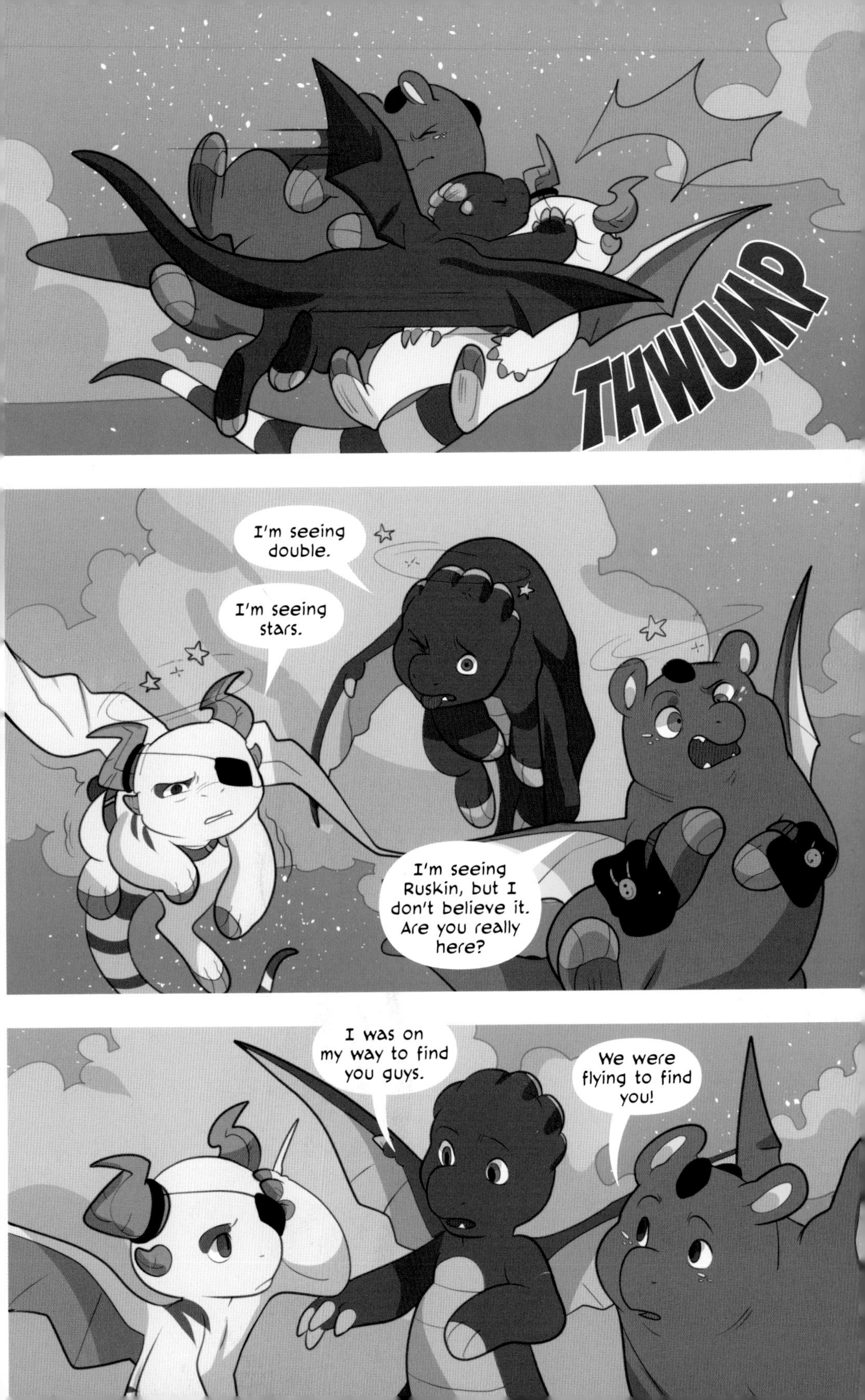
THWUMP
I'm seeing double.
I'm seeing stars.
I'm seeing Ruskin, but I don't believe it. Are you really here?
I was on my way to find you guys.
We were flying to find you!

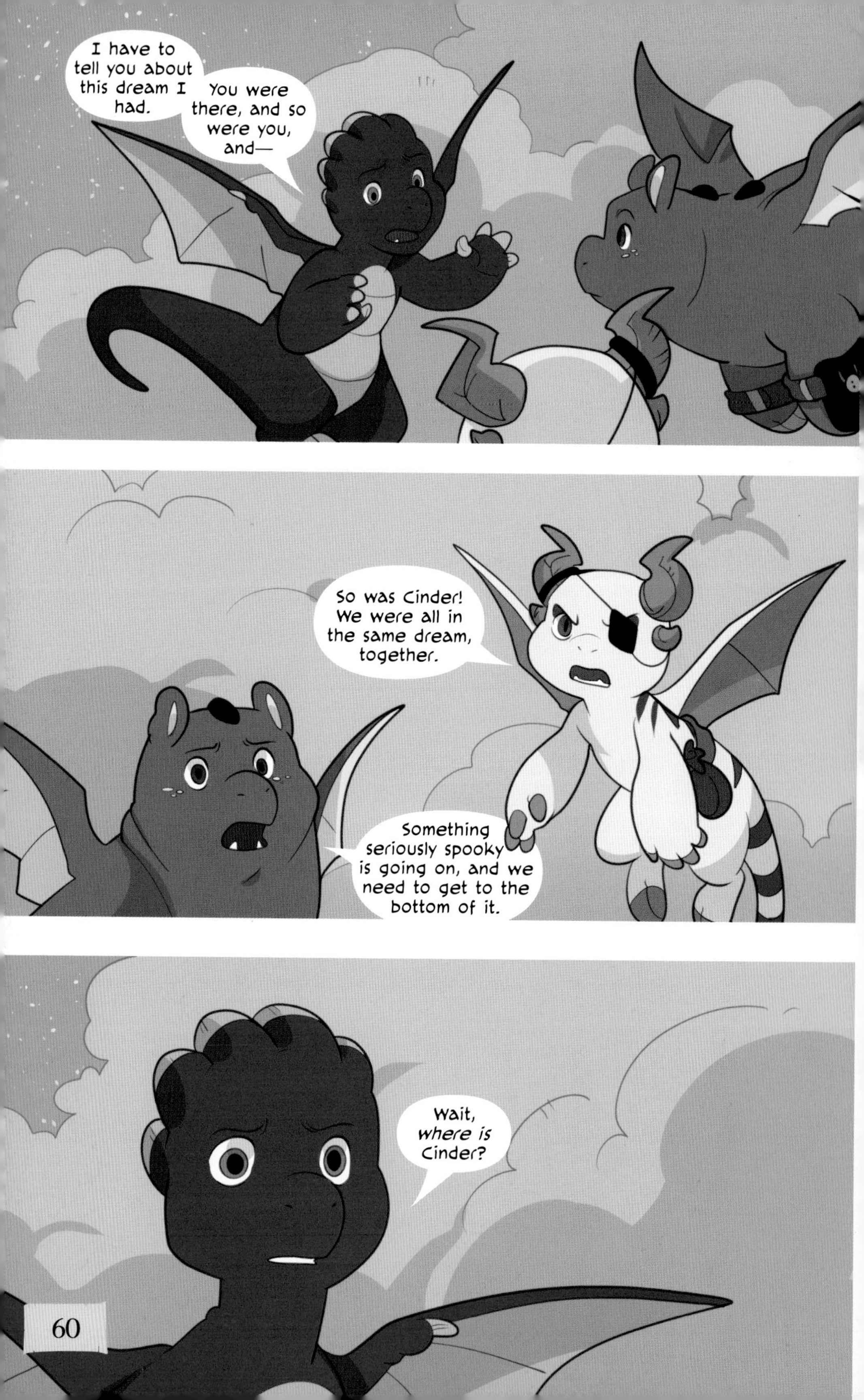
I have to tell you about this dream I had.
You were there, and so were you, and—
So was Cinder! We were all in the same dream, together.
Something seriously spooky is going on, and we need to get to the bottom of it.
Wait, *where is* Cinder?

C'mon, you stupid thing, stay tied!

...Cinder's camping trip was about to be turned upside down.

Just then, back on Crestwood...

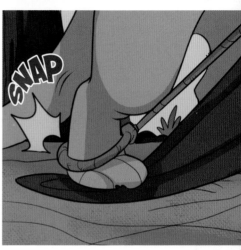

SNAP

GAAAAH!

Whoa, Cinder!

Grrrrr...
stupidtentthingIhatethis...
I HATE EVERYTHING!

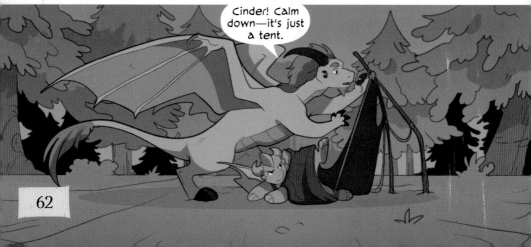

Cinder! Calm down—it's just a tent.

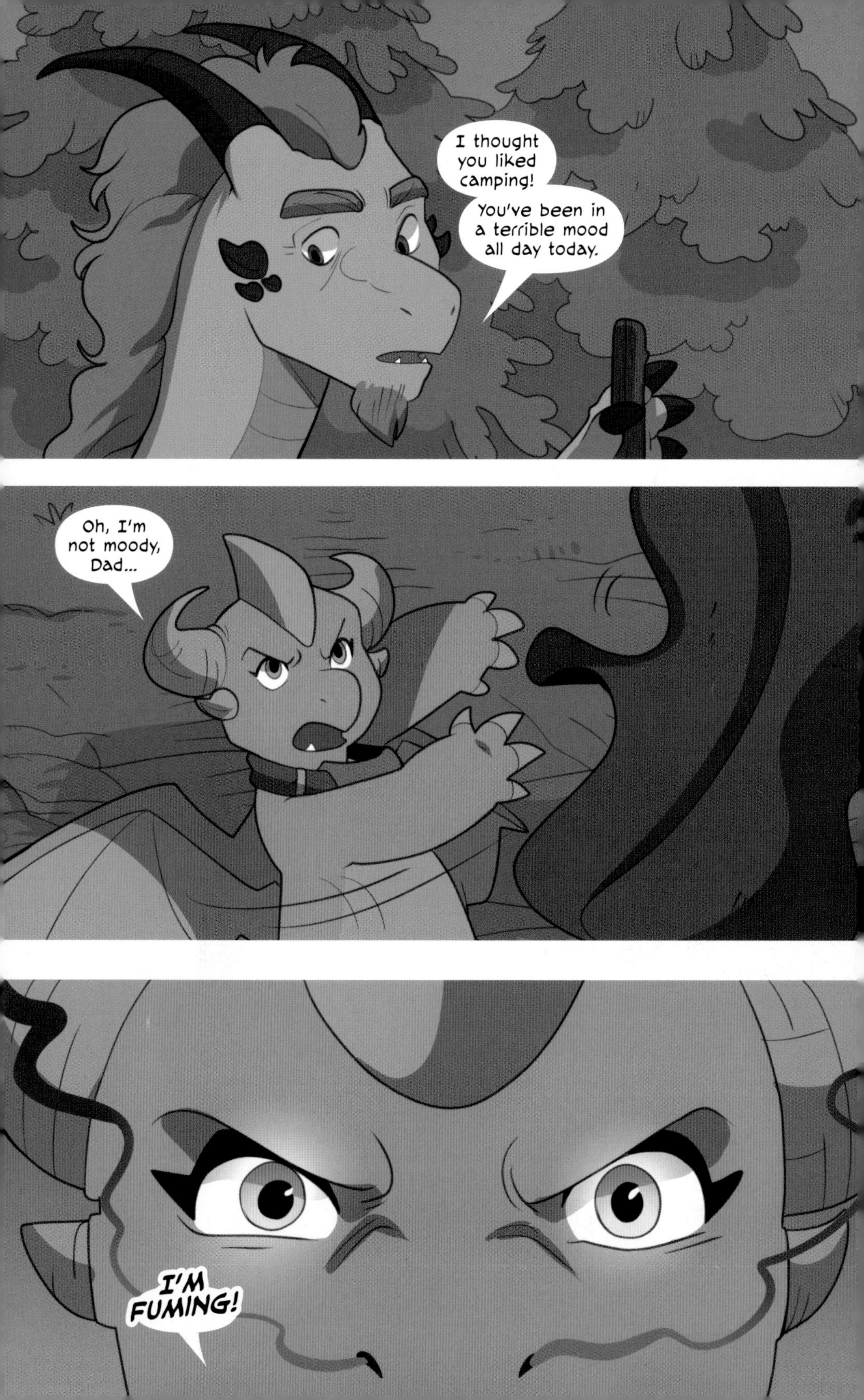
I thought you liked camping!
You've been in a terrible mood all day today.
Oh, I'm not moody, Dad...
I'M FUMING!

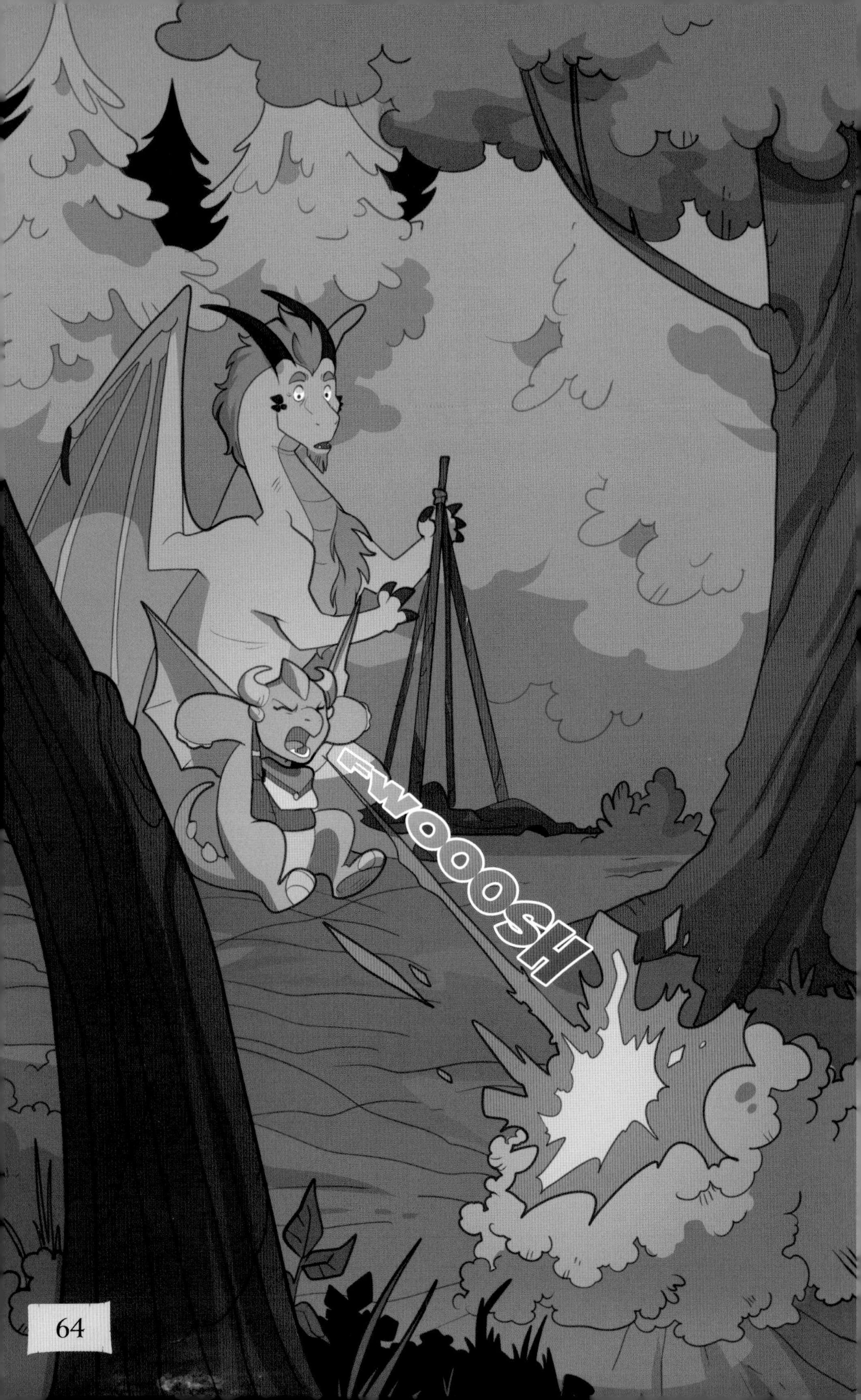
FWOOOSH

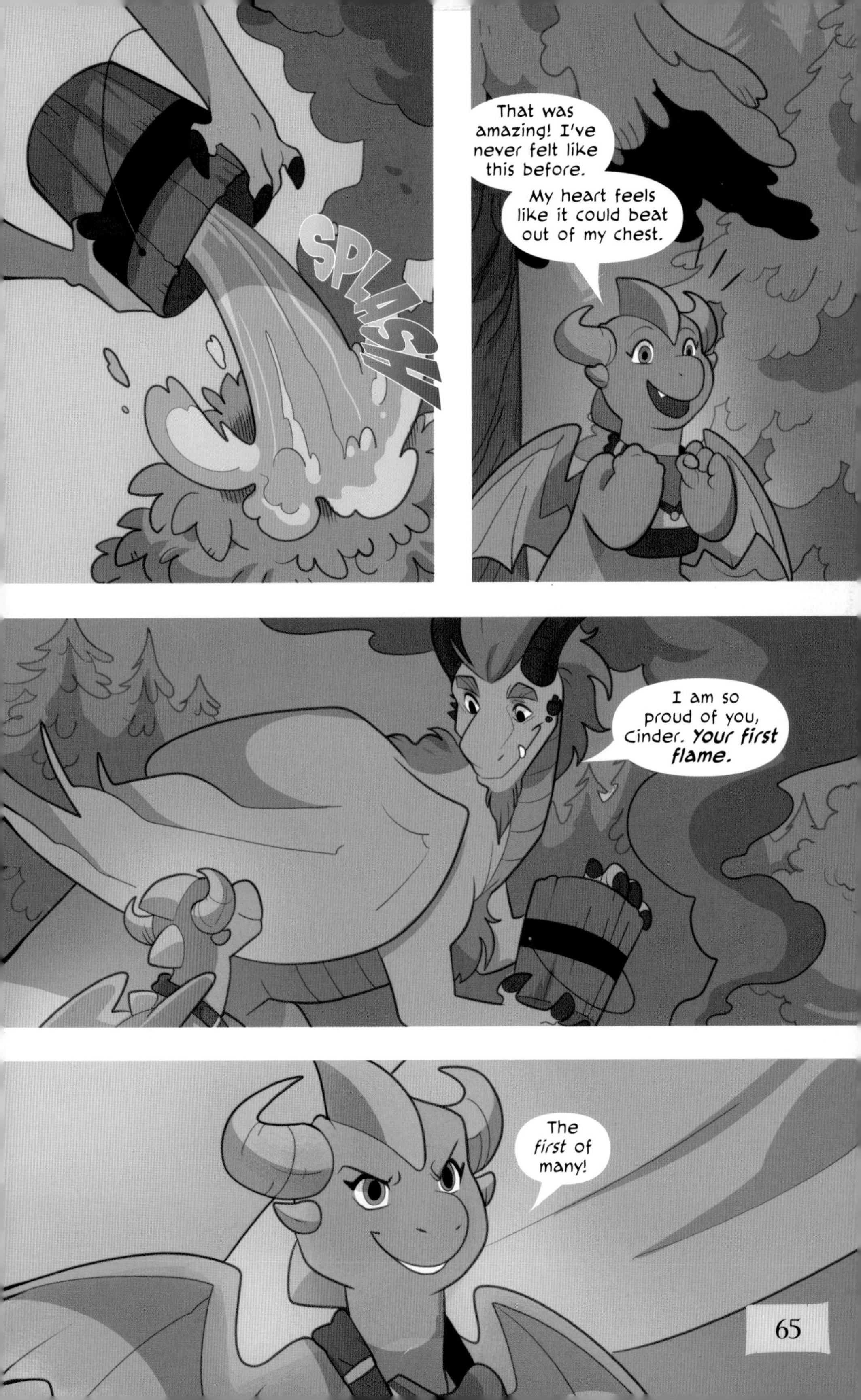
SPLASH
That was amazing! I've never felt like this before.
My heart feels like it could beat out of my chest.
I am so proud of you, Cinder. *Your first flame.*
The *first* of many!

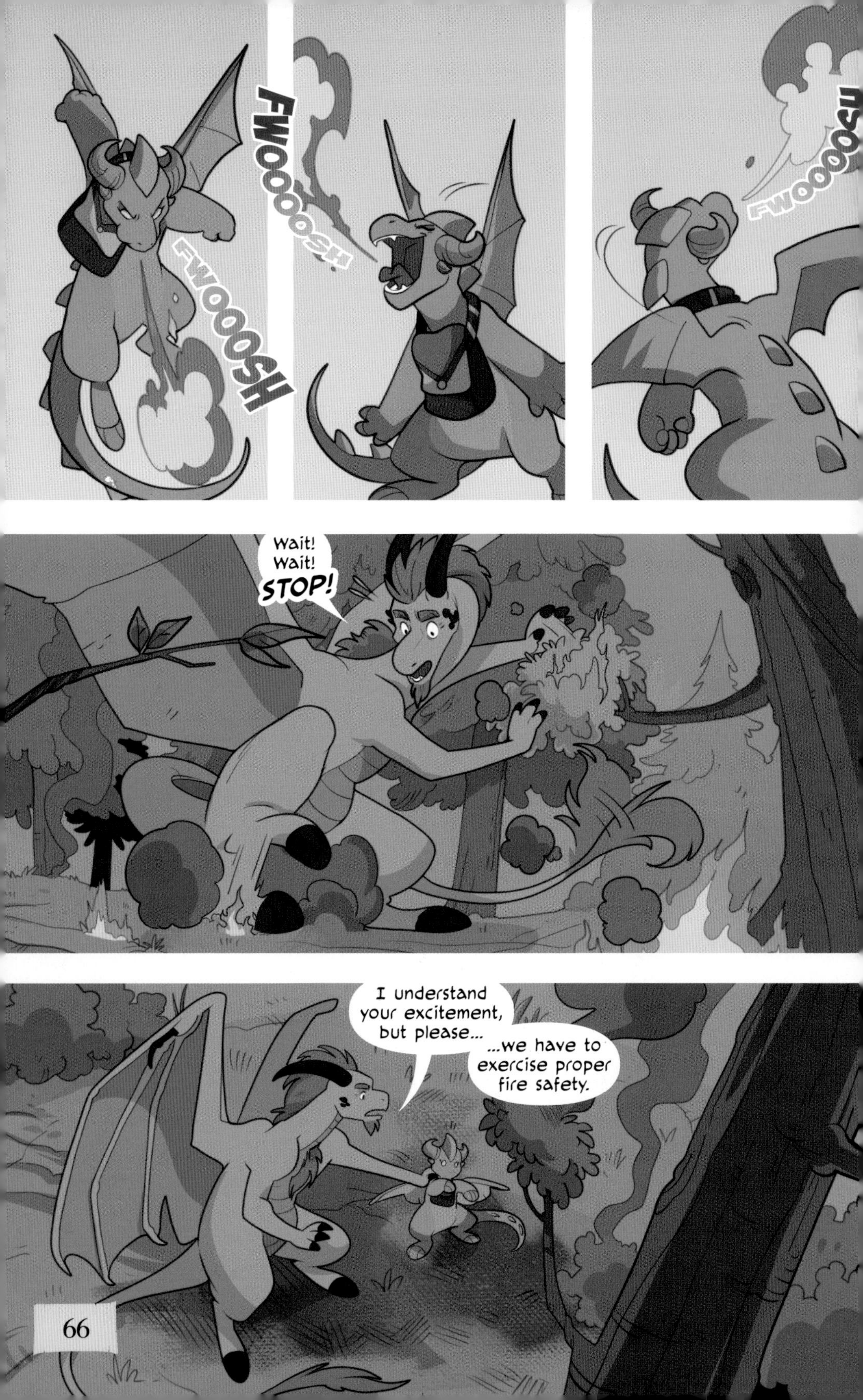
FWOOOOSH
FWOOOOSH!
FWOOOOSH
Wait! Wait! STOP!
I understand your excitement, but please...
...we have to exercise proper fire safety.

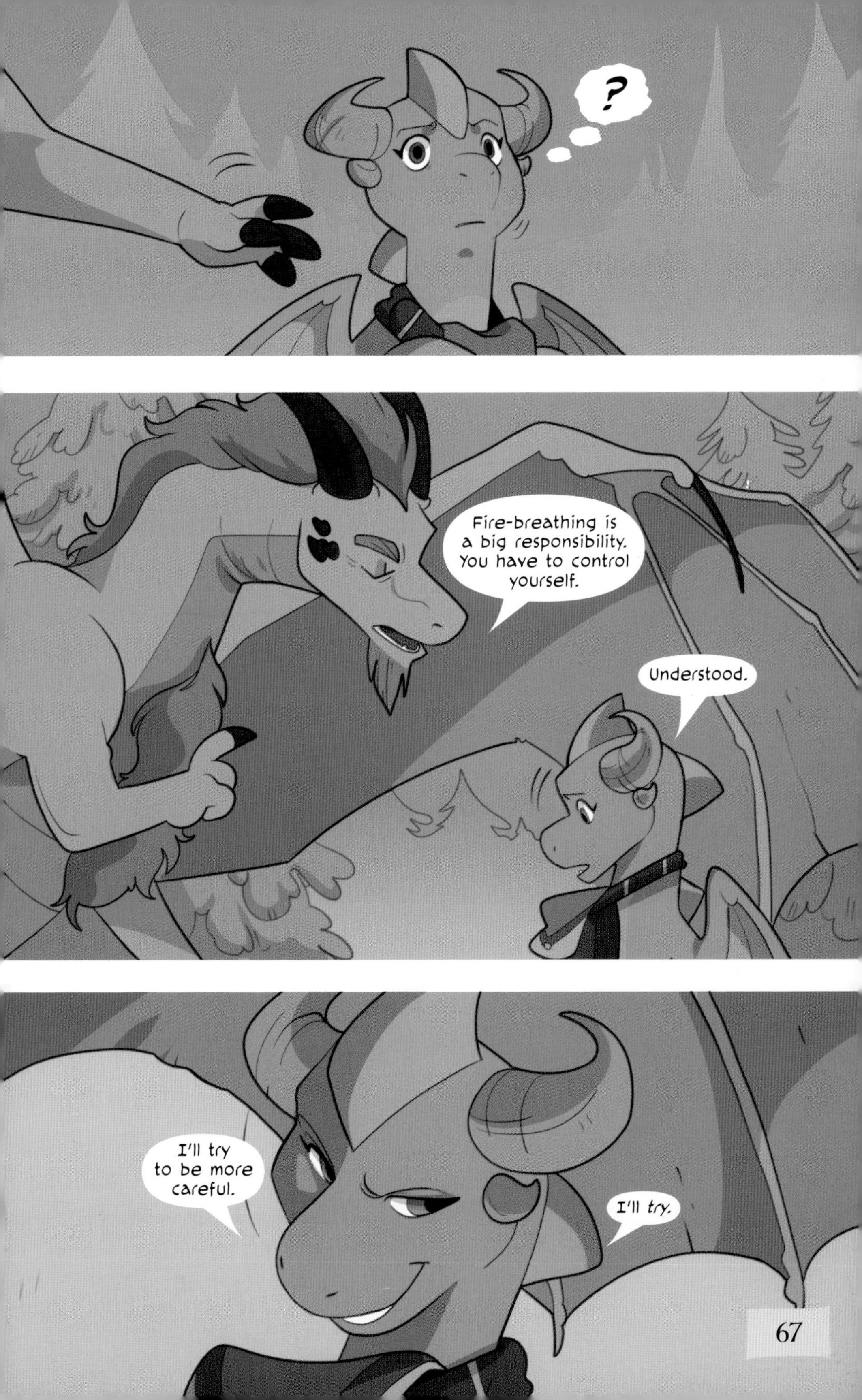
?
Fire-breathing is a big responsibility. You have to control yourself.
Understood.
I'll try to be more careful.
I'll *try*.

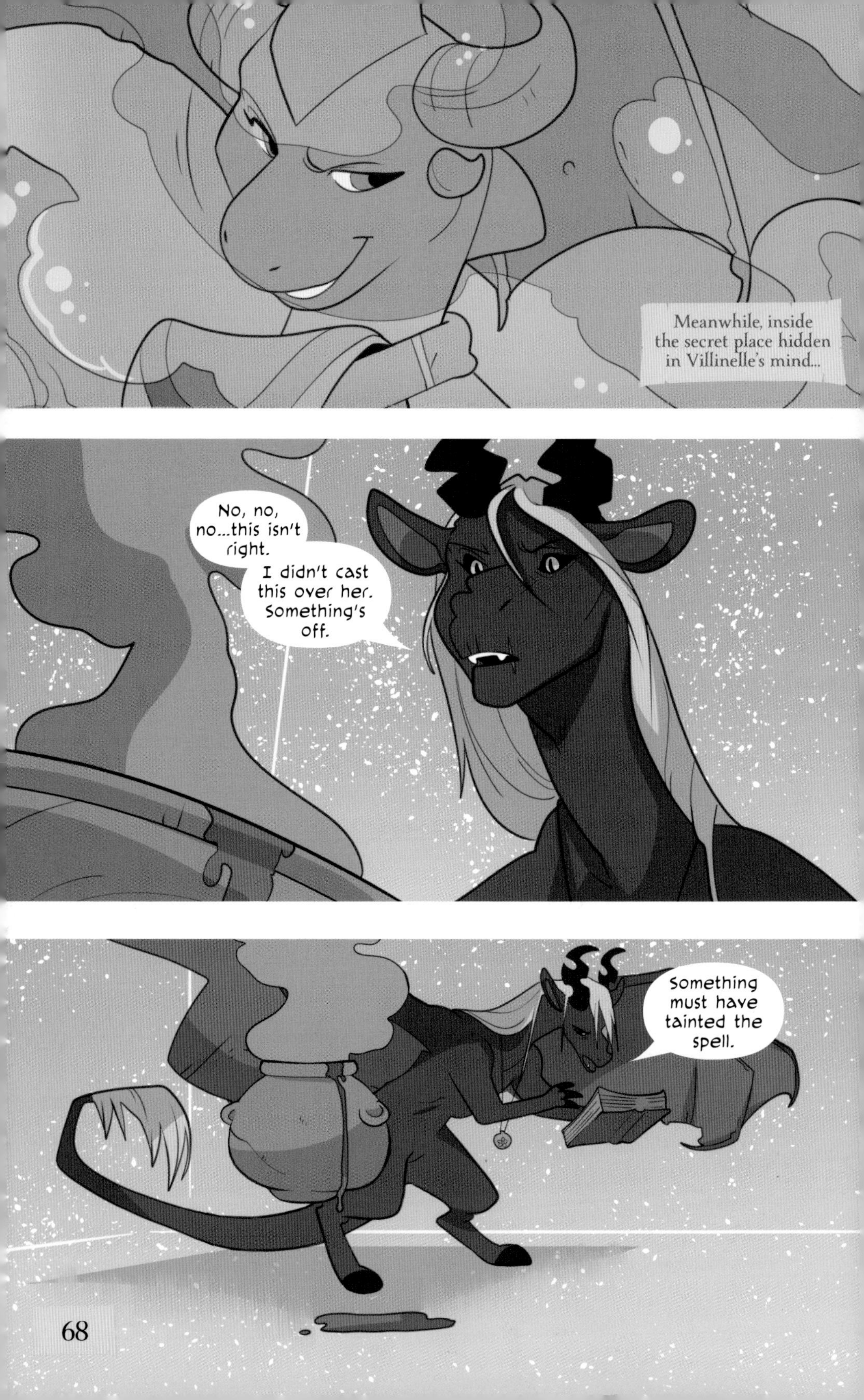
Meanwhile, inside the secret place hidden in Villinelle's mind...
No, no, no...this isn't right.
I didn't cast this over her. Something's off.
Something must have tainted the spell.

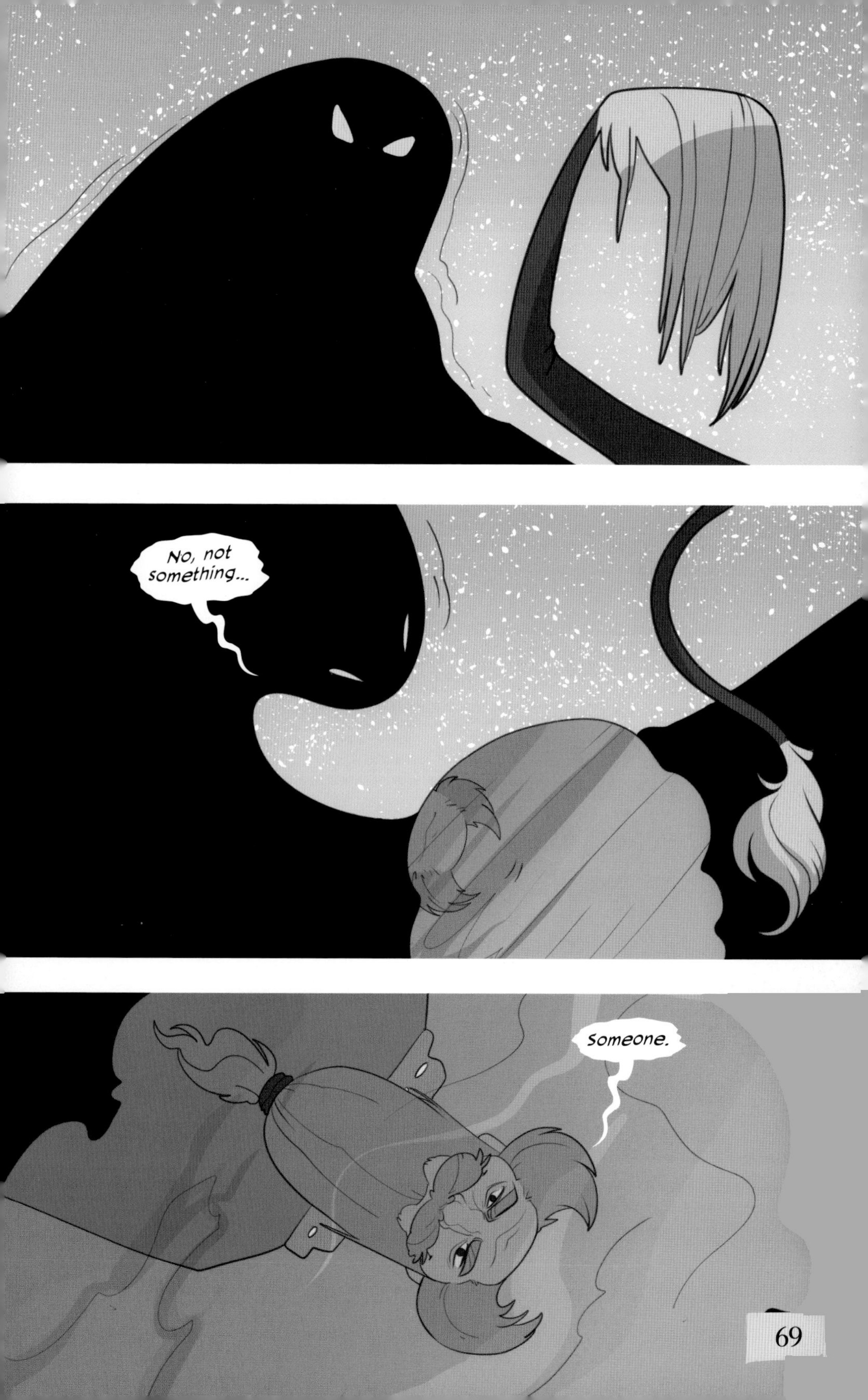
No, not something...
Someone.

Chapter 5

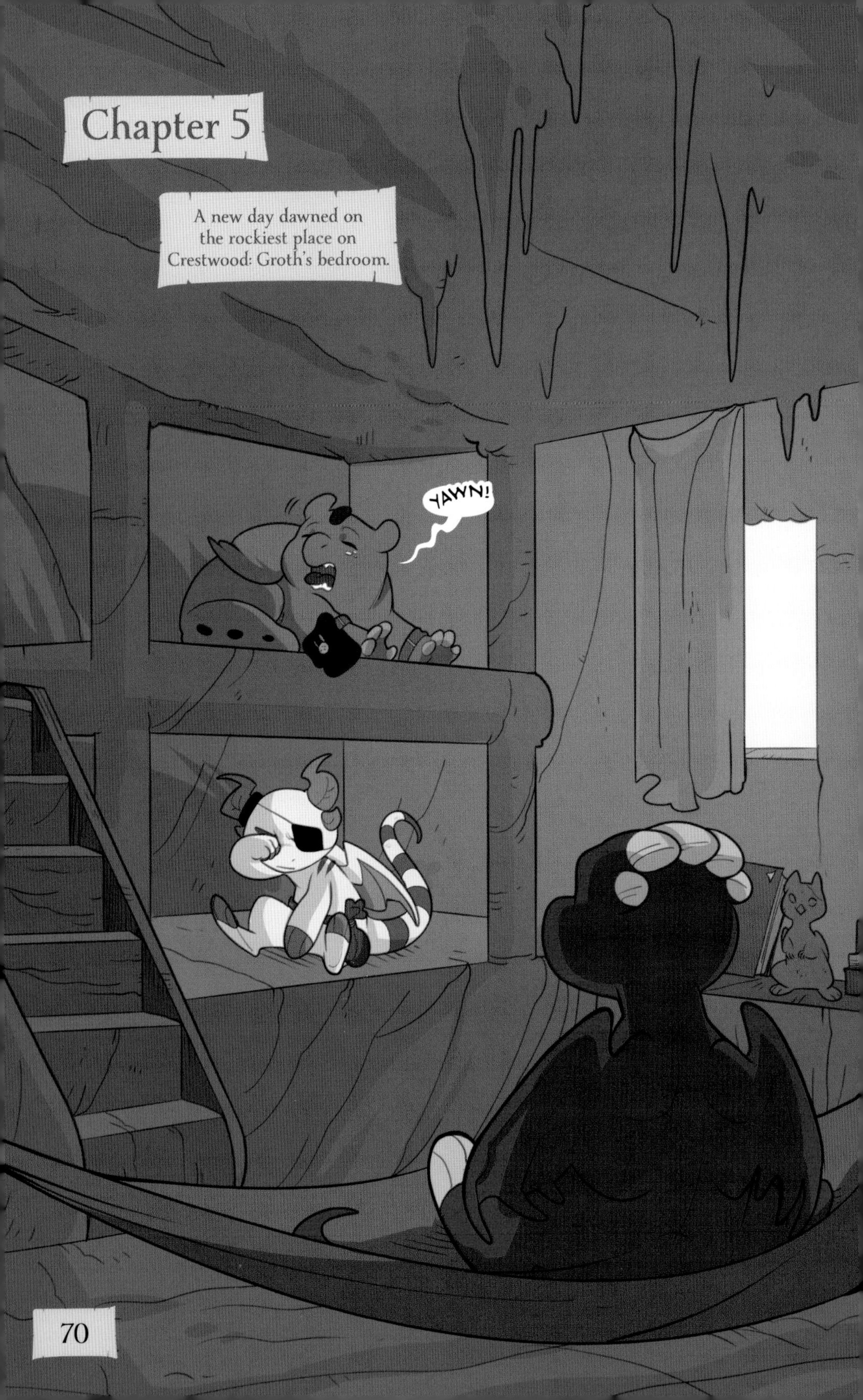
A new day dawned on the rockiest place on Crestwood: Groth's bedroom.
YAWN!

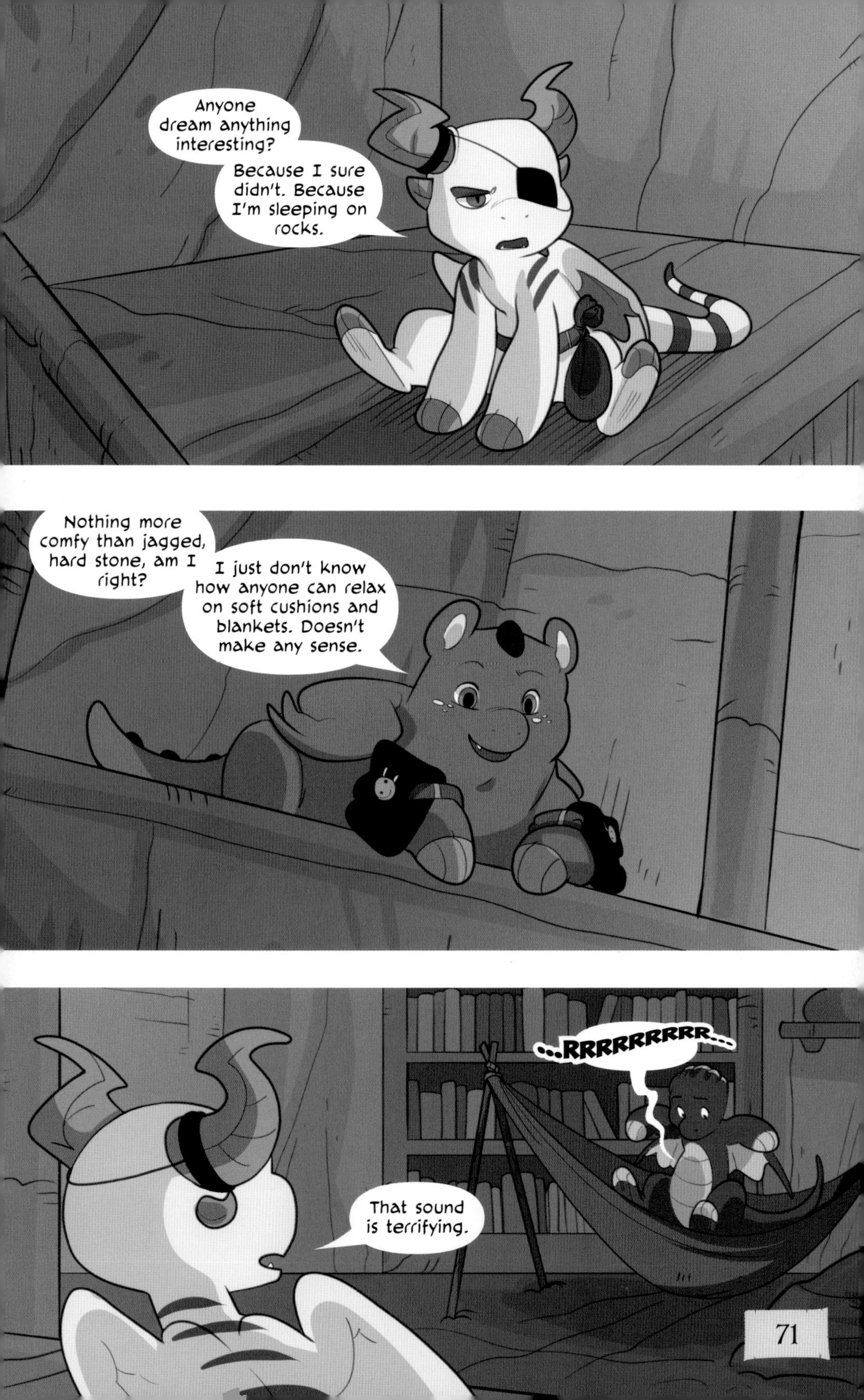
Anyone dream anything interesting?
Because I sure didn't. Because I'm sleeping on rocks.
Nothing more comfy than jagged, hard stone, am I right?
I just don't know how anyone can relax on soft cushions and blankets. Doesn't make any sense.
...RRRRRRRRR...
That sound is terrifying.

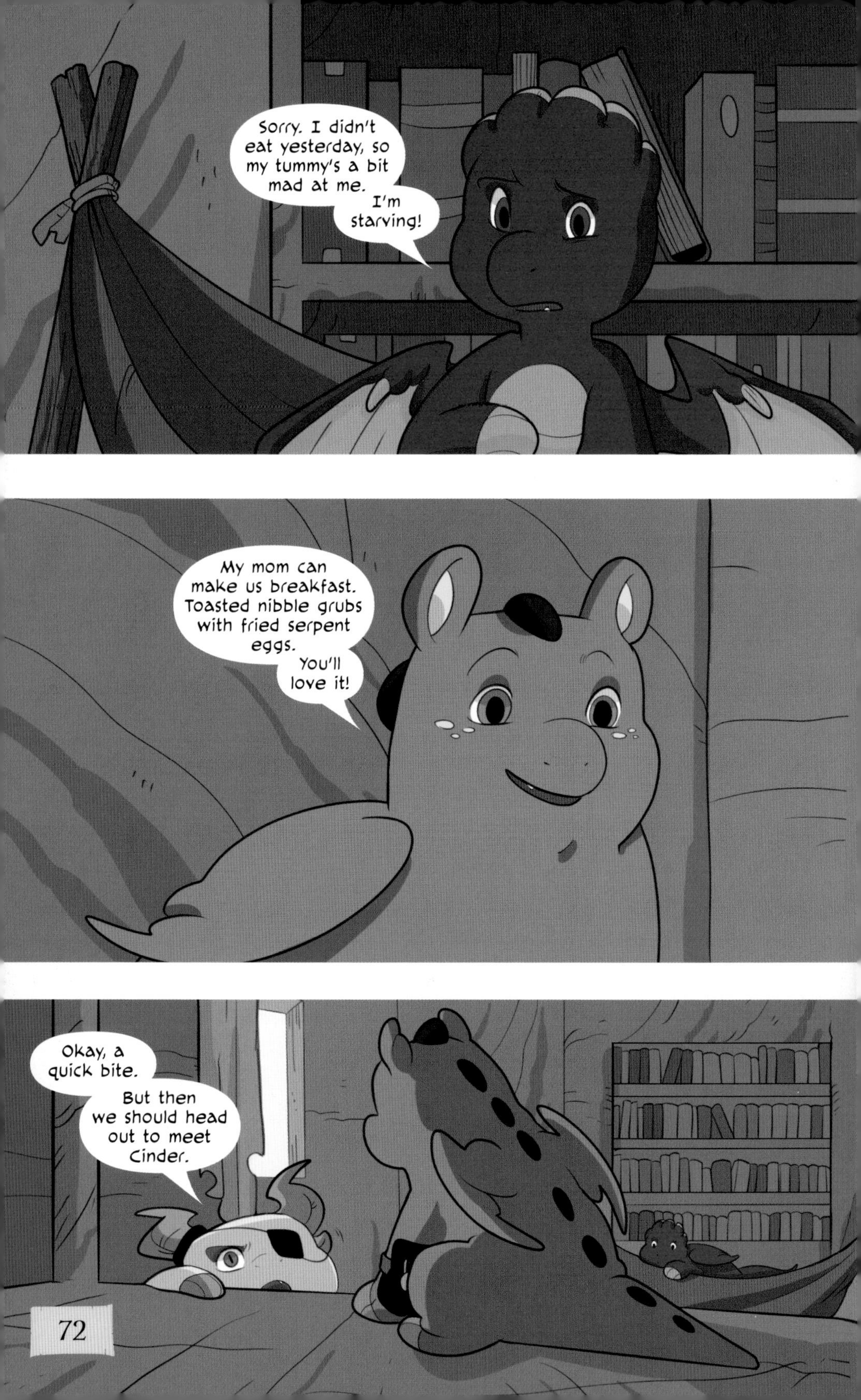
Sorry. I didn't eat yesterday, so my tummy's a bit mad at me.
I'm starving!
My mom can make us breakfast. Toasted nibble grubs with fried serpent eggs.
You'll love it!
Okay, a quick bite.
But then we should head out to meet Cinder.

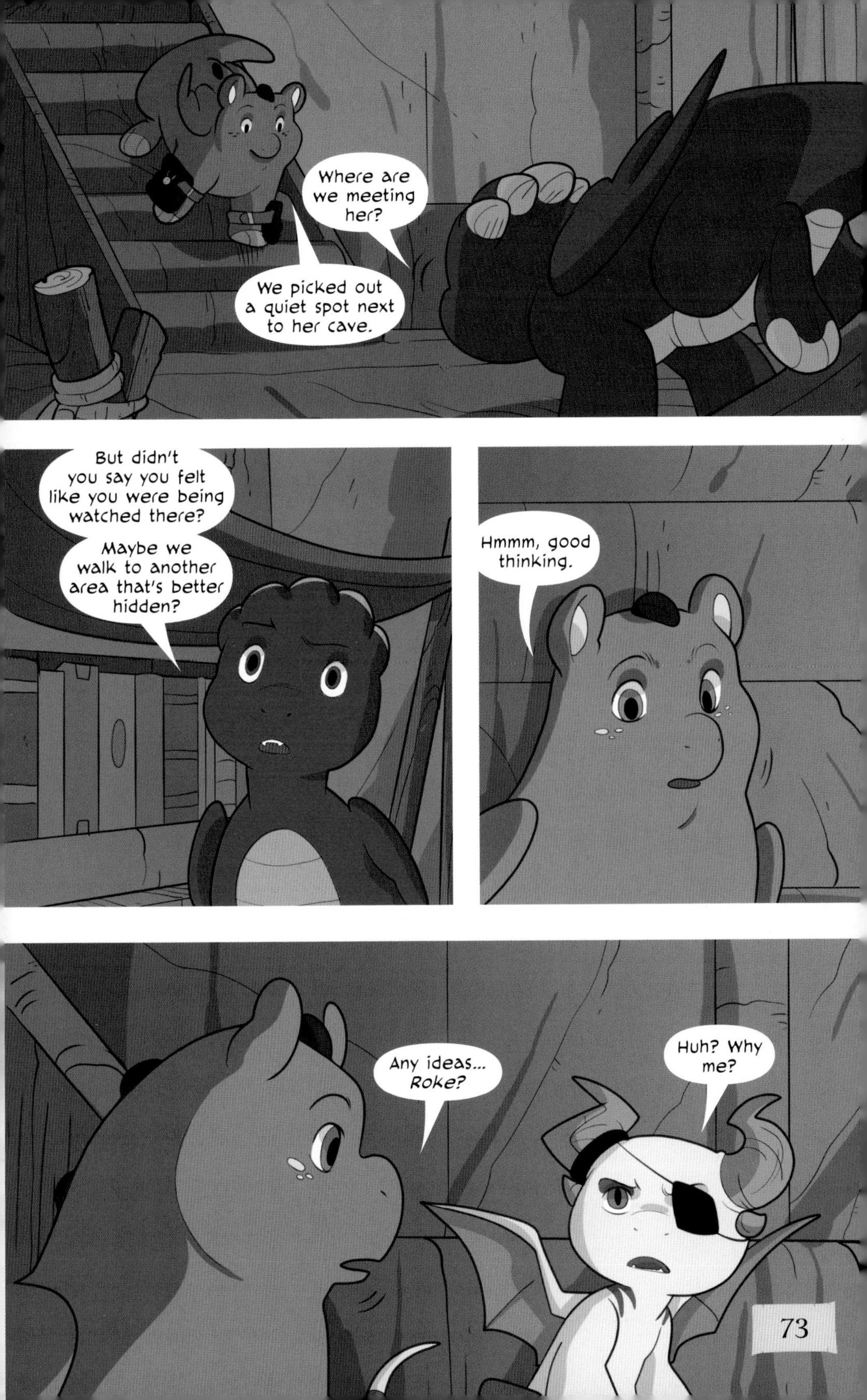
Where are we meeting her?
We picked out a quiet spot next to her cave.
But didn't you say you felt like you were being watched there?
Maybe we walk to another area that's better hidden?
Hmmm, good thinking.
Any ideas... *Roke?*
Huh? Why me?

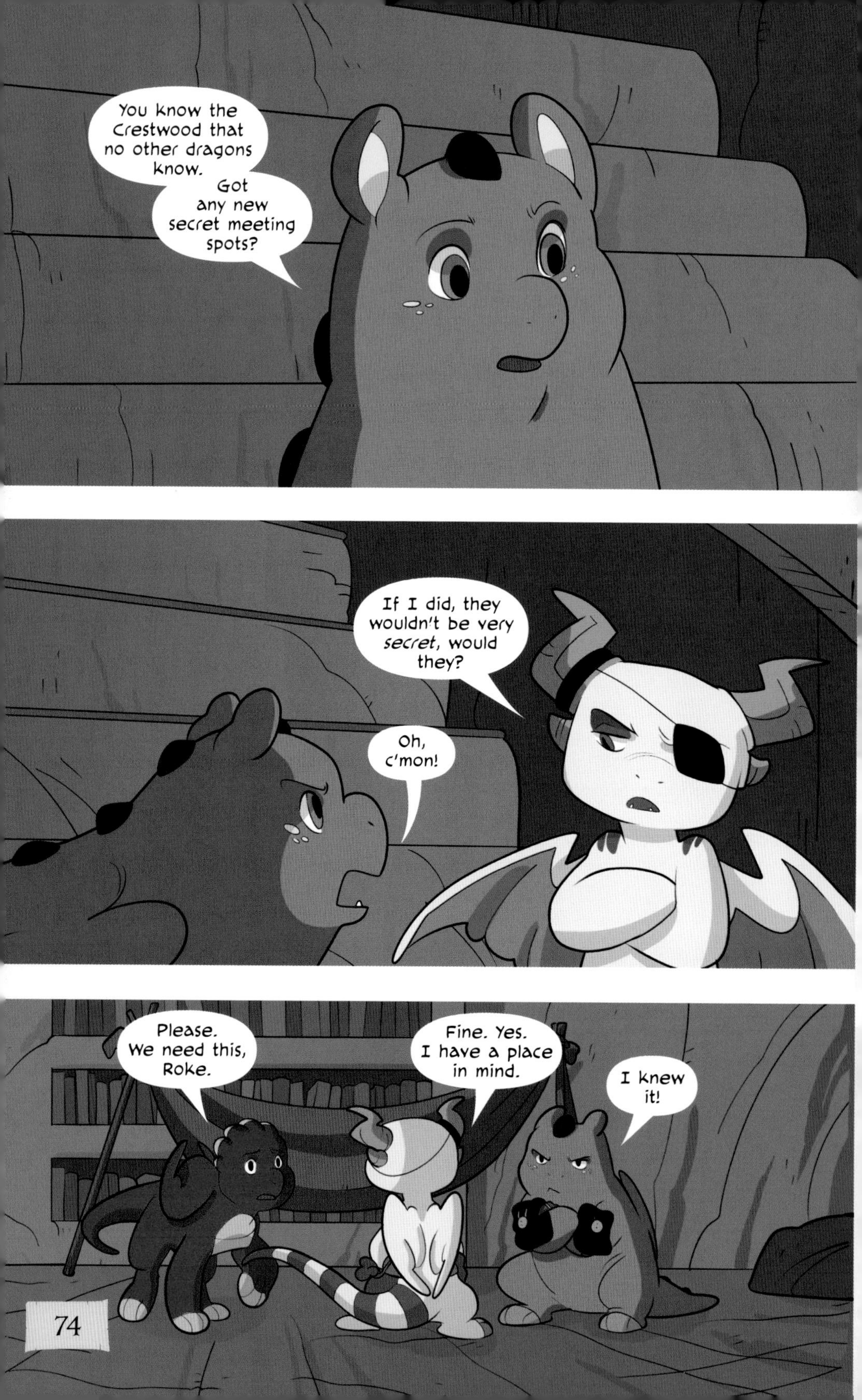

You know the Crestwood that no other dragons know.
Got any new secret meeting spots?
If I did, they wouldn't be very *secret*, would they?
Oh, c'mon!
Please. We need this, Roke.
Fine. Yes. I have a place in mind.
I knew it!

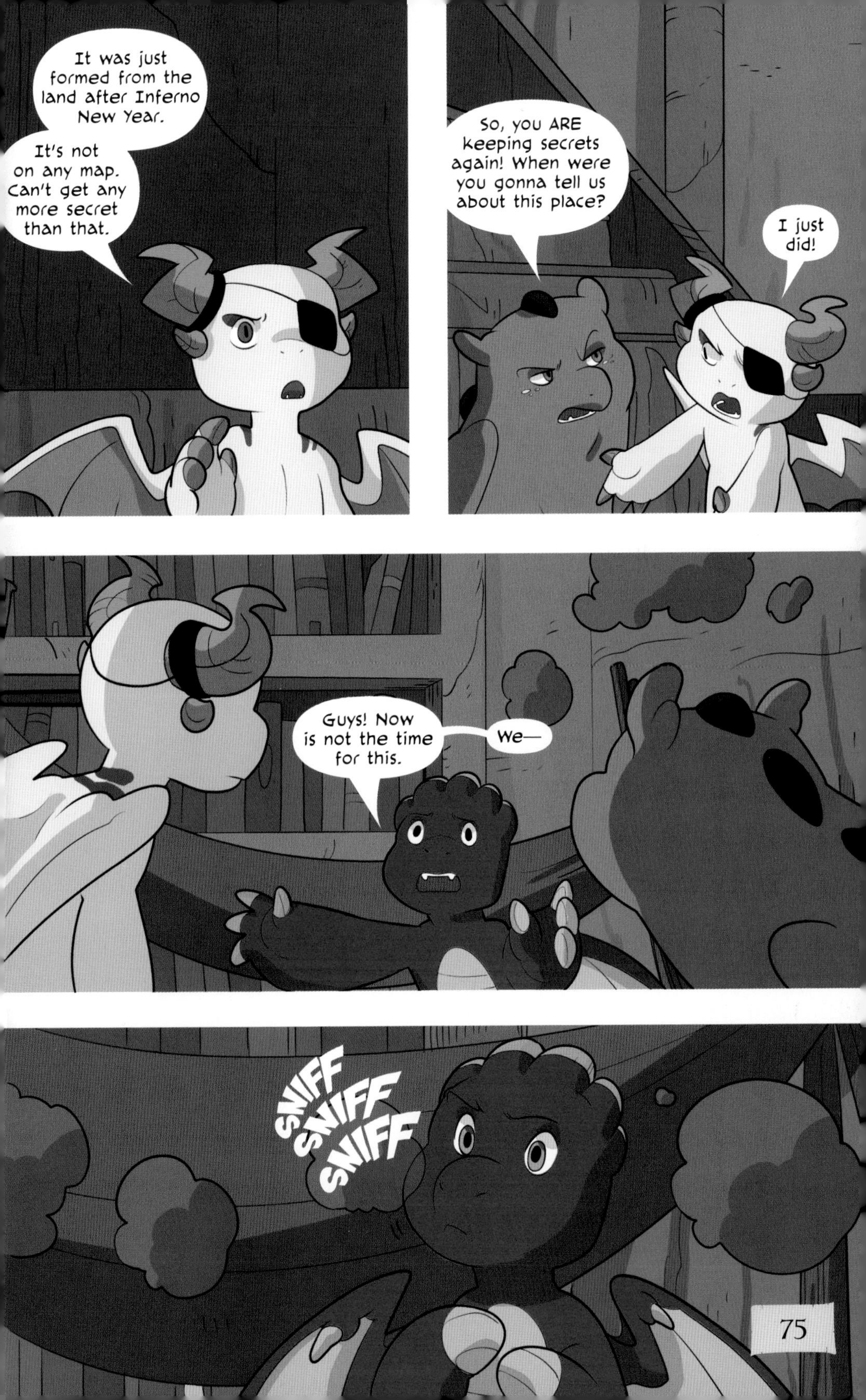
It was just formed from the land after Inferno New Year.
It's not on any map. Can't get any more secret than that.
So, you ARE keeping secrets again! When were you gonna tell us about this place?
I just did!
Guys! Now is not the time for this.
We—
SNIFF SNIFF SNIFF

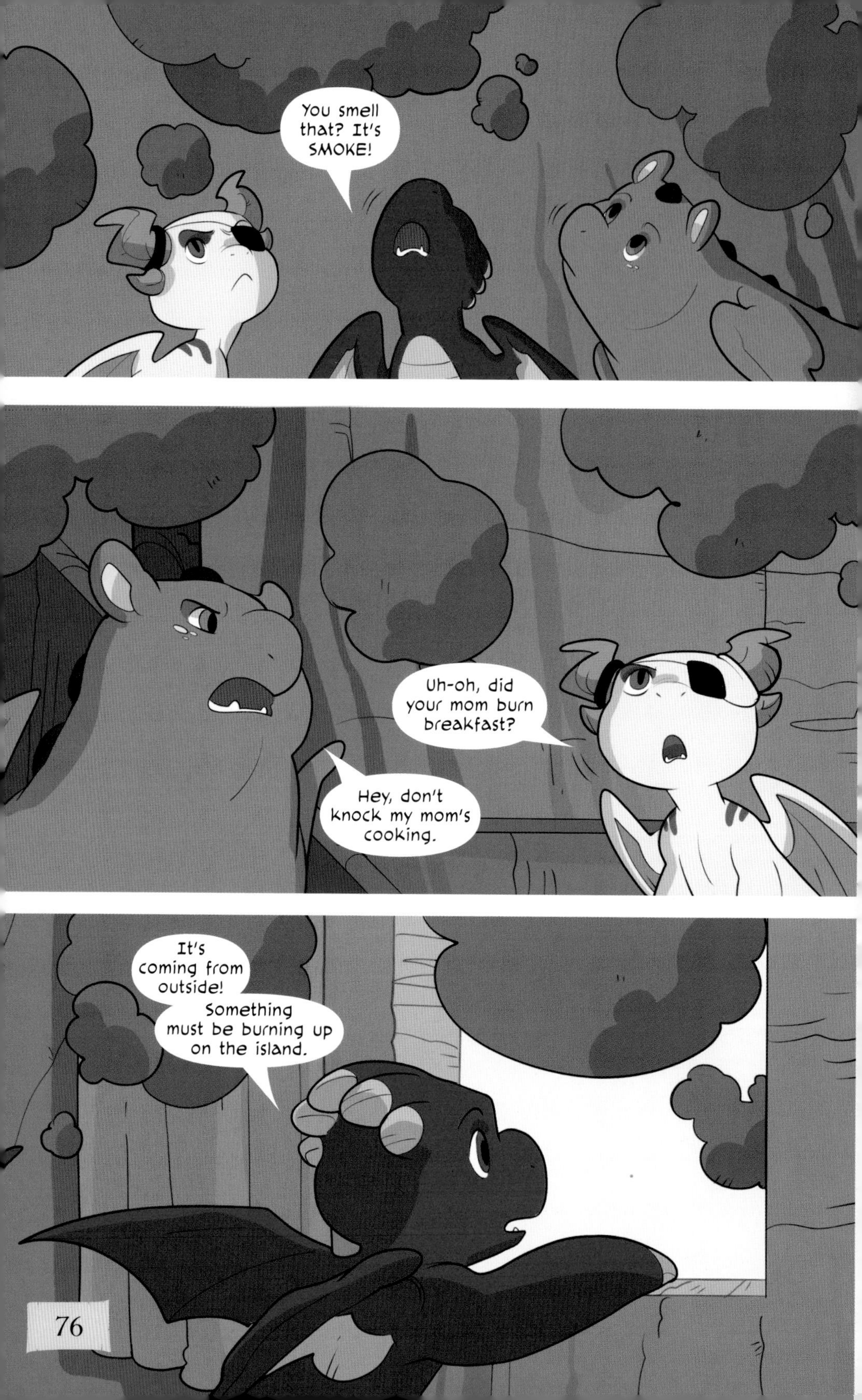
You smell that? It's SMOKE!
Uh-oh, did your mom burn breakfast?
Hey, don't knock my mom's cooking.
It's coming from outside!
Something must be burning up on the island.

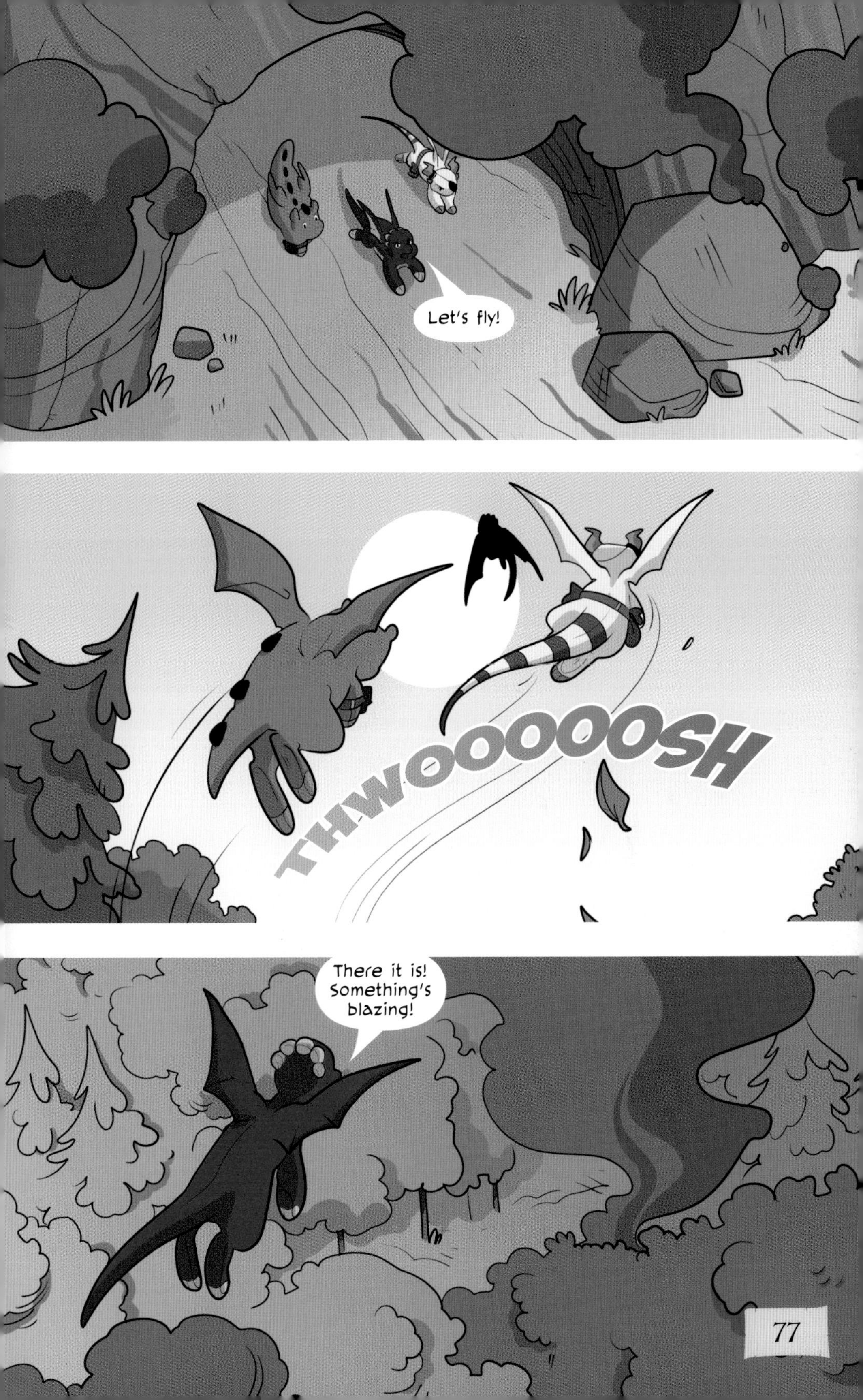
Let's fly!
THWOOOOOSH
There it is! Something's blazing!

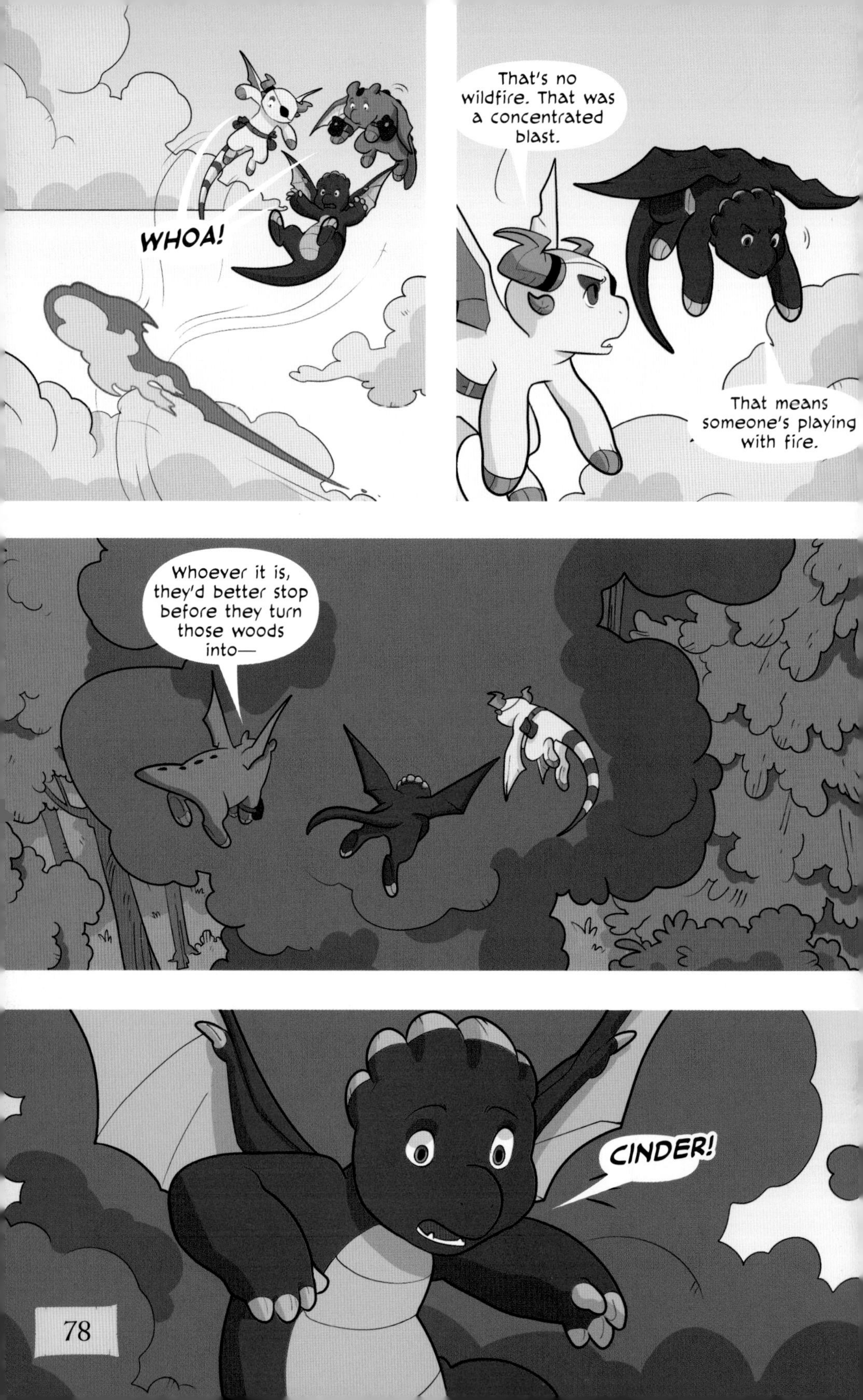
WHOA!
That's no wildfire. That was a concentrated blast.
That means someone's playing with fire.
Whoever it is, they'd better stop before they turn those woods into—
CINDER!

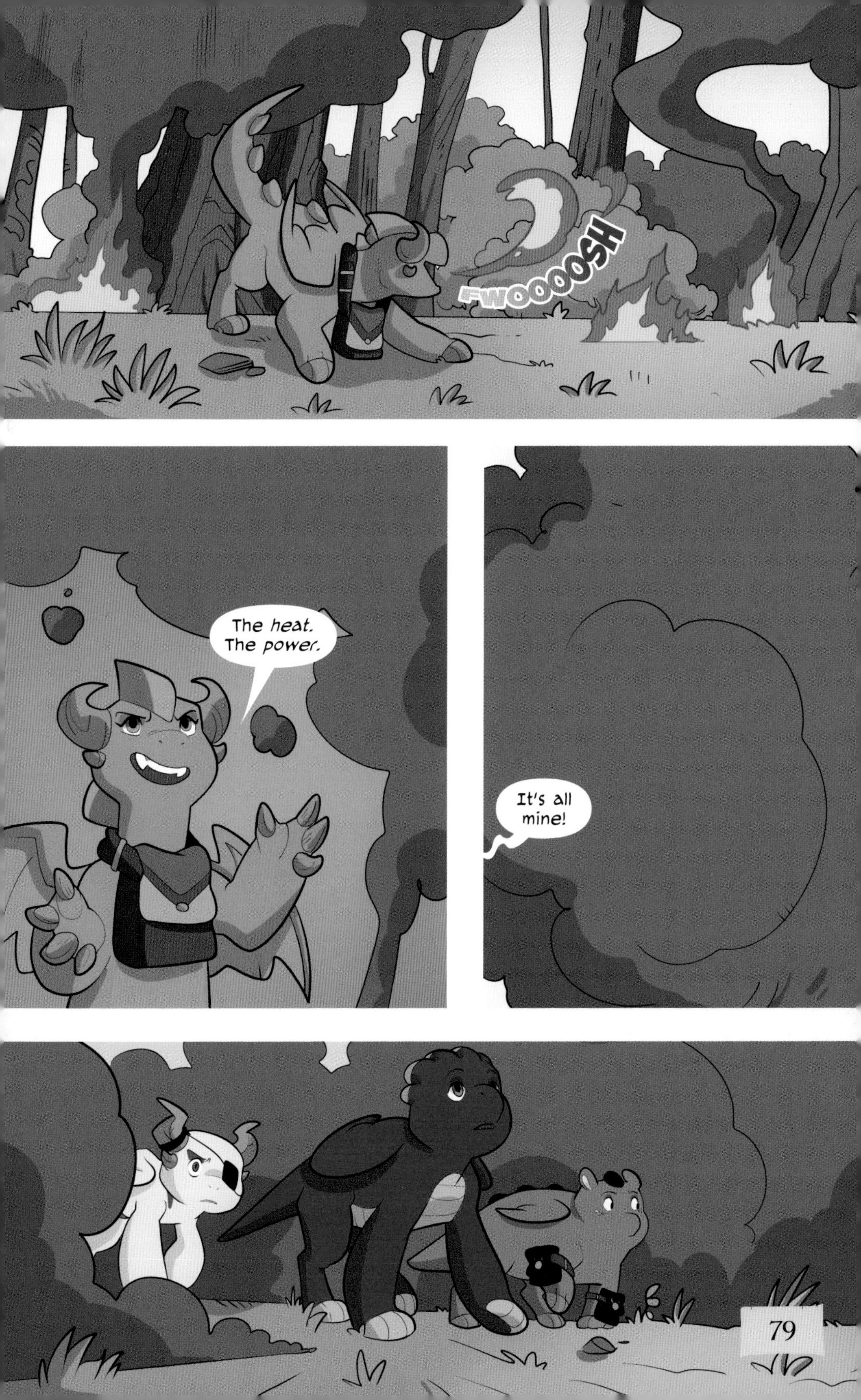
FWOOOOSH!
The *heat.* The *power.*
It's all mine!

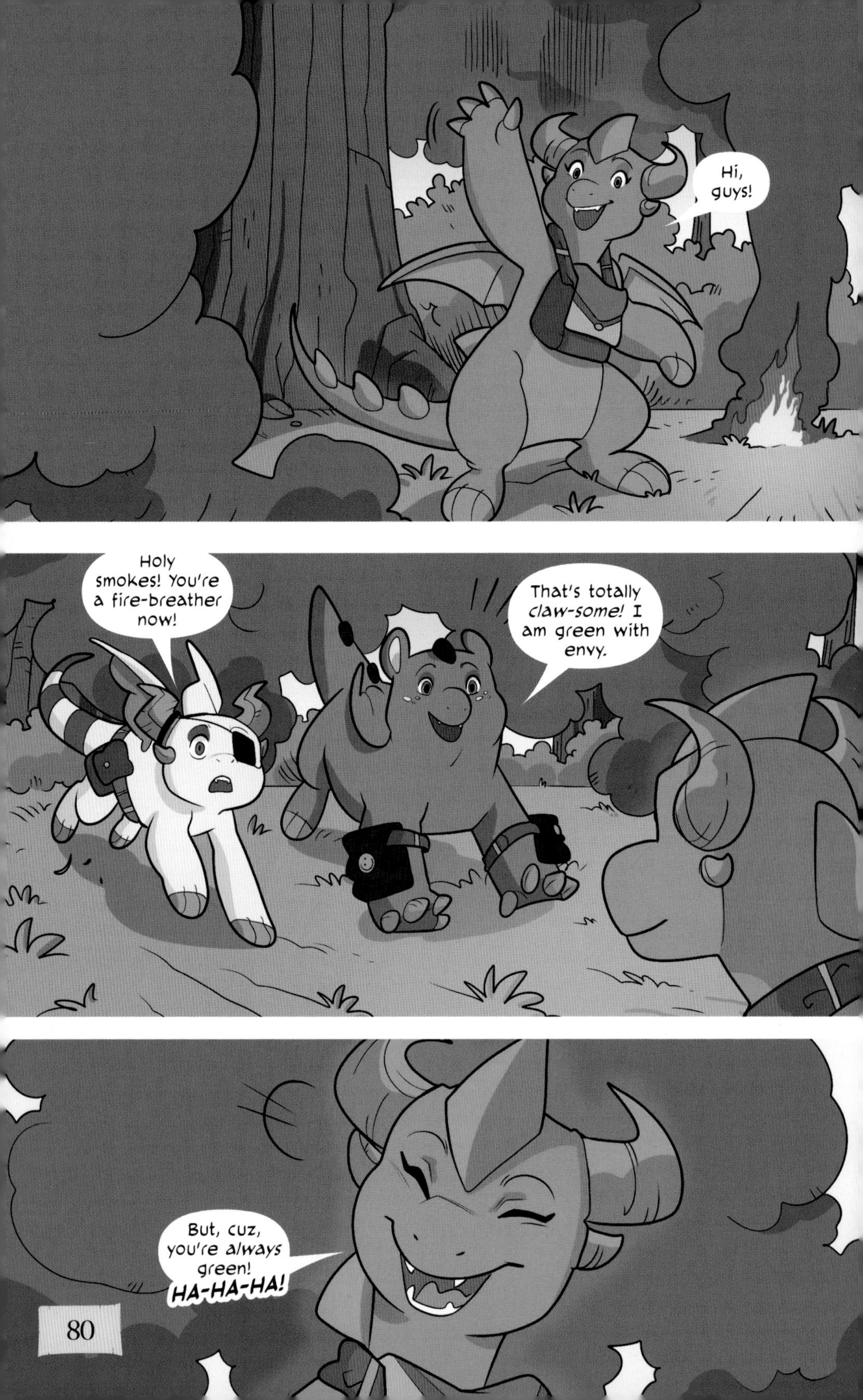

Hi, guys!
Holy smokes! You're a fire-breather now!
That's totally *claw-some!* I am green with envy.
But, cuz, you're always green! **HA-HA-HA!**

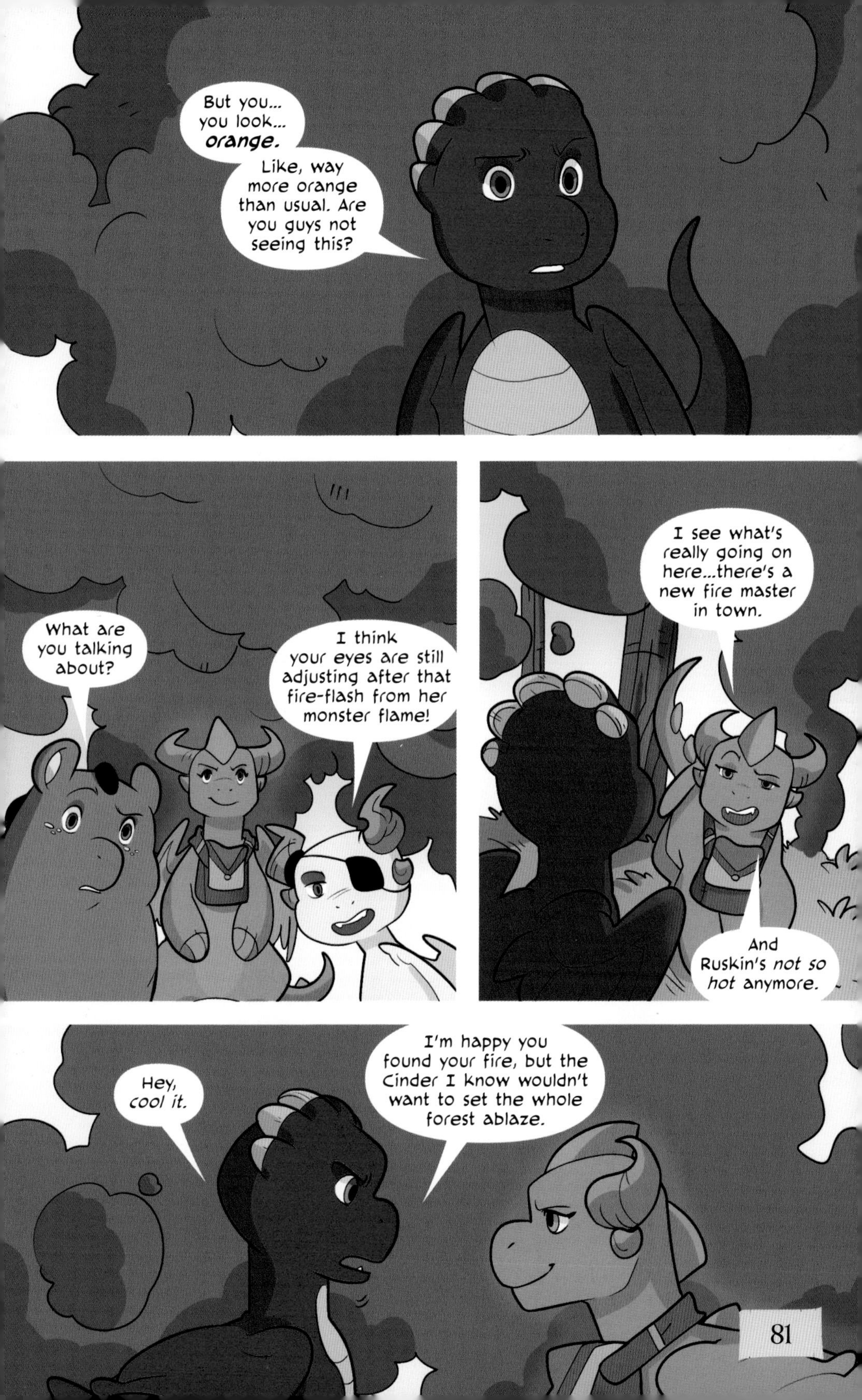
But you... you look... ***orange.***
Like, way more orange than usual. Are you guys not seeing this?
What are you talking about?
I think your eyes are still adjusting after that fire-flash from her monster flame!
I see what's really going on here...there's a new fire master in town.
And Ruskin's *not so hot* anymore.
Hey, *cool it.*
I'm happy you found your fire, but the Cinder I know wouldn't want to set the whole forest ablaze.

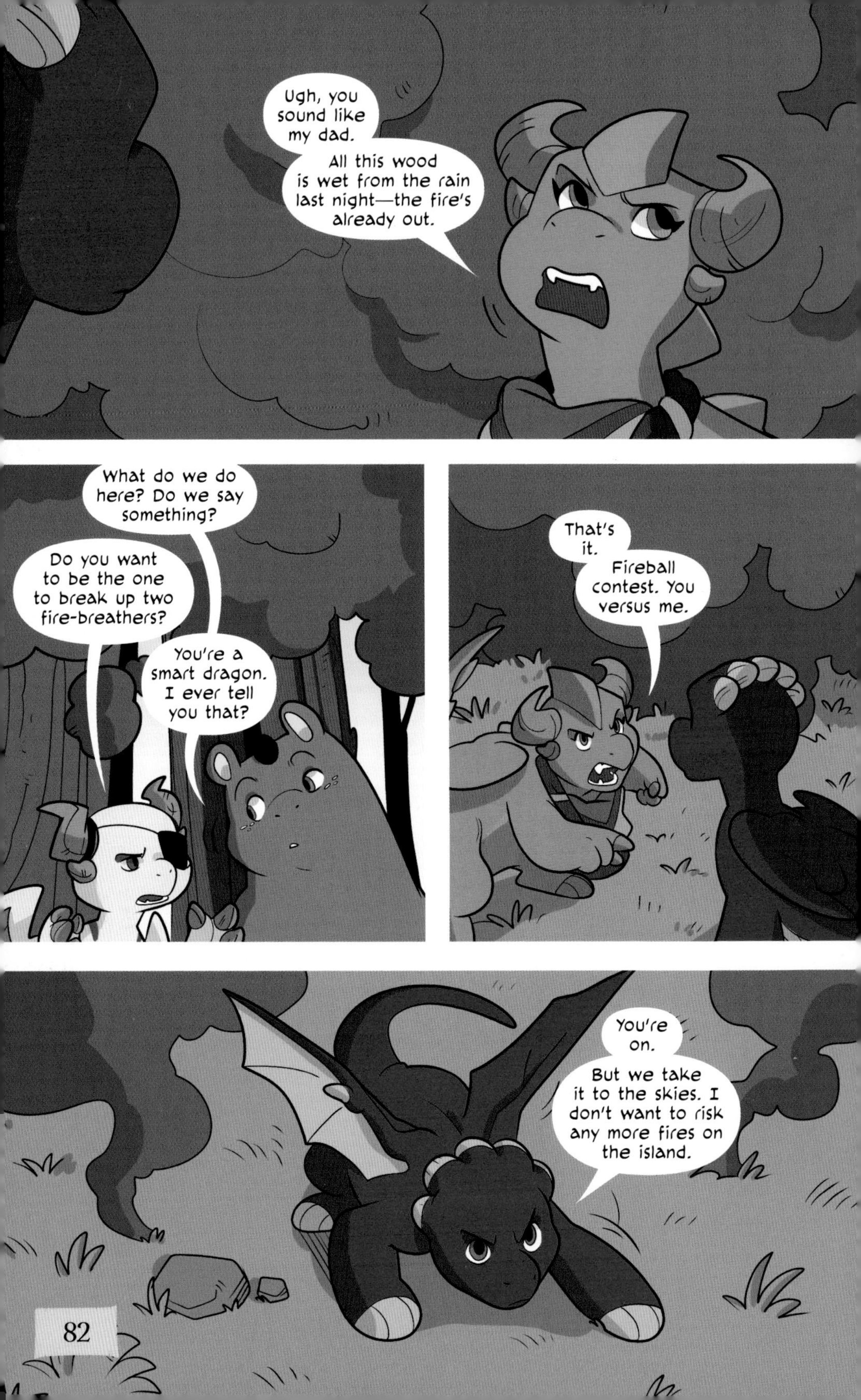
Ugh, you sound like my dad.
All this wood is wet from the rain last night—the fire's already out.
What do we do here? Do we say something?
Do you want to be the one to break up two fire-breathers?
You're a smart dragon. I ever tell you that?
That's it.
Fireball contest. You versus me.
You're on.
But we take it to the skies. I don't want to risk any more fires on the island.

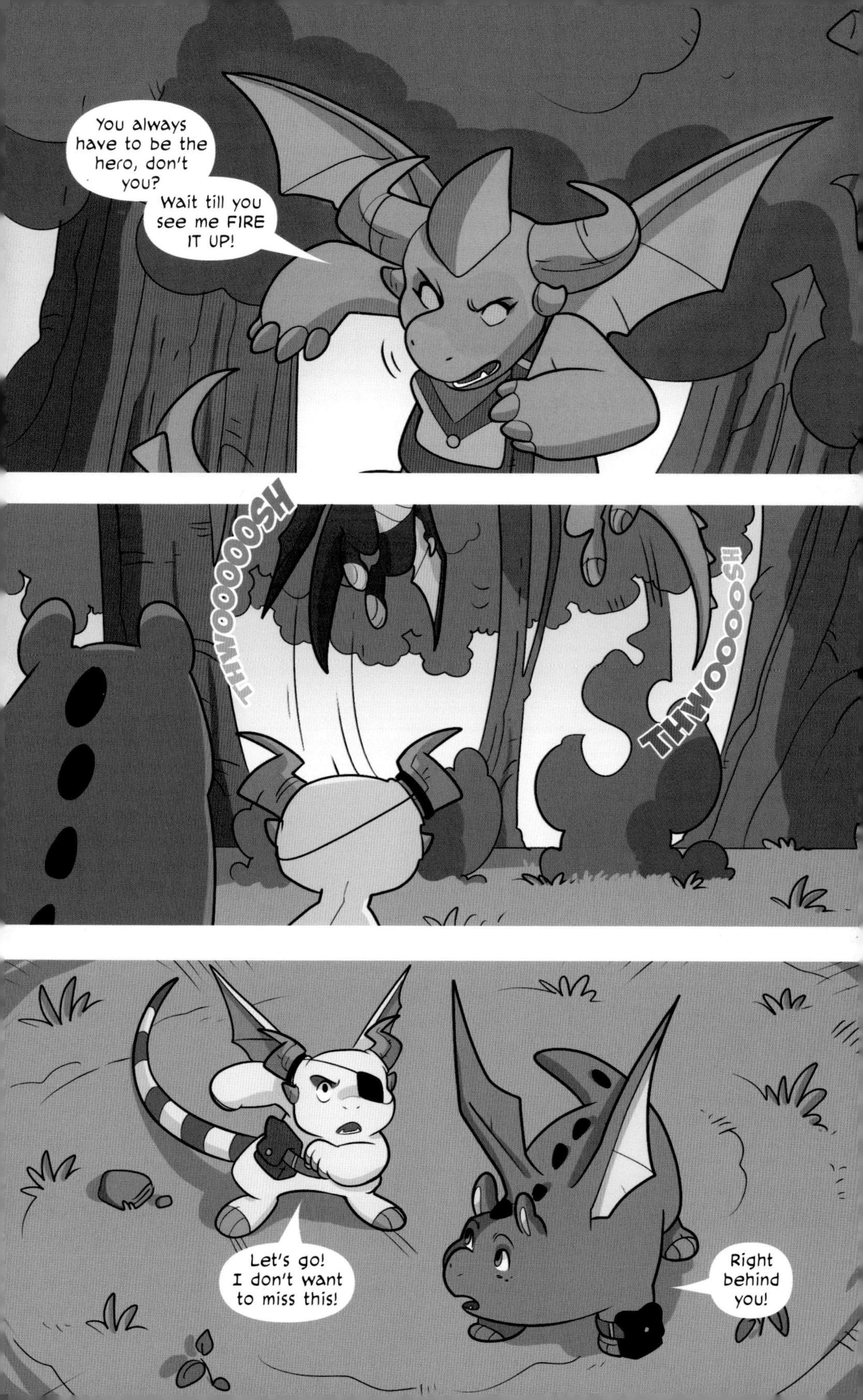
You always have to be the hero, don't you?
Wait till you see me FIRE IT UP!
THWOOOOOSH
THWOOOOSH
Let's go! I don't want to miss this!
Right behind you!

Chapter 6

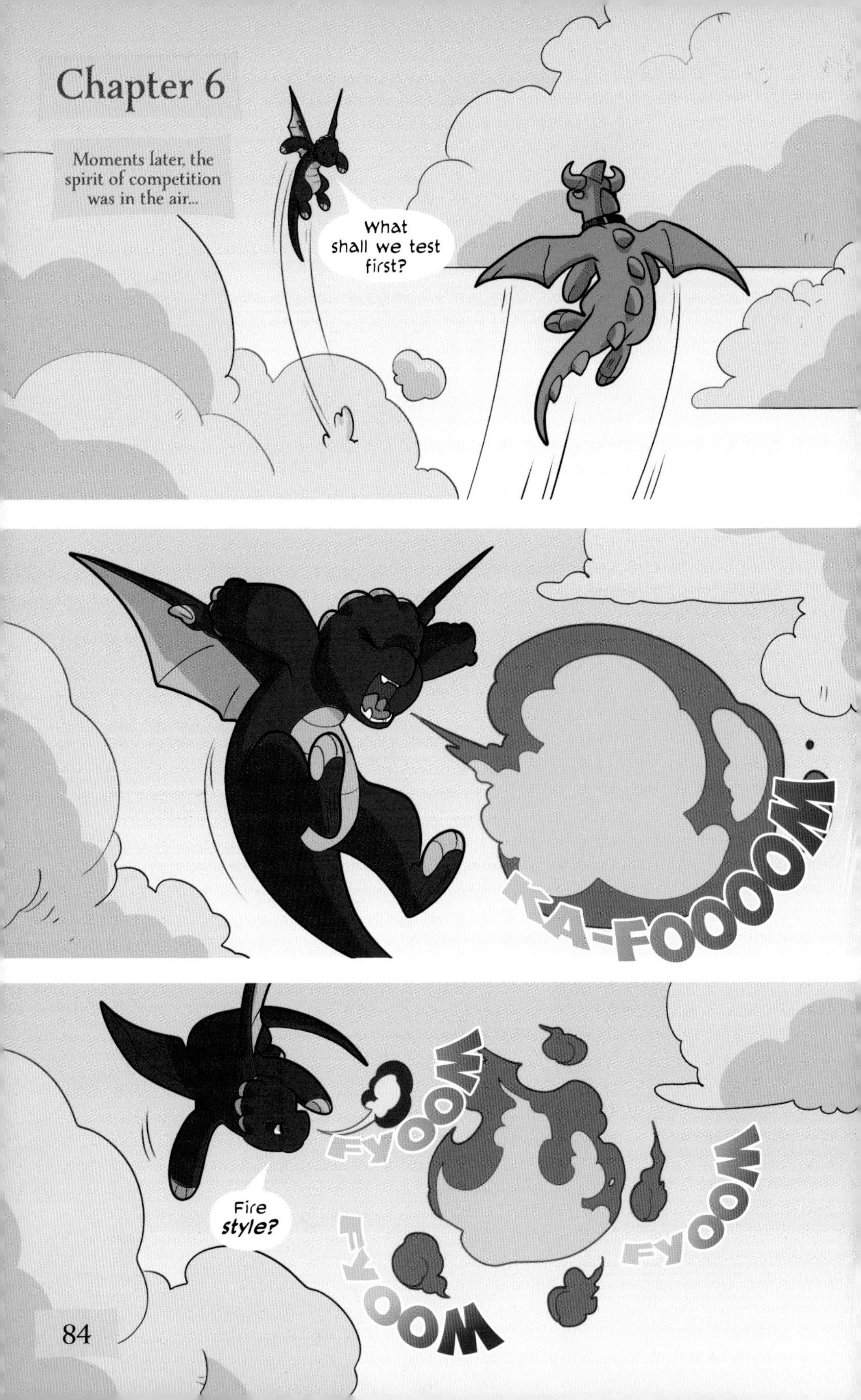
Moments later, the spirit of competition was in the air...
What shall we test first?
KA-FOOOOOM
Fire *style?*
FYOOOM
FYOOOM
FYOOOM

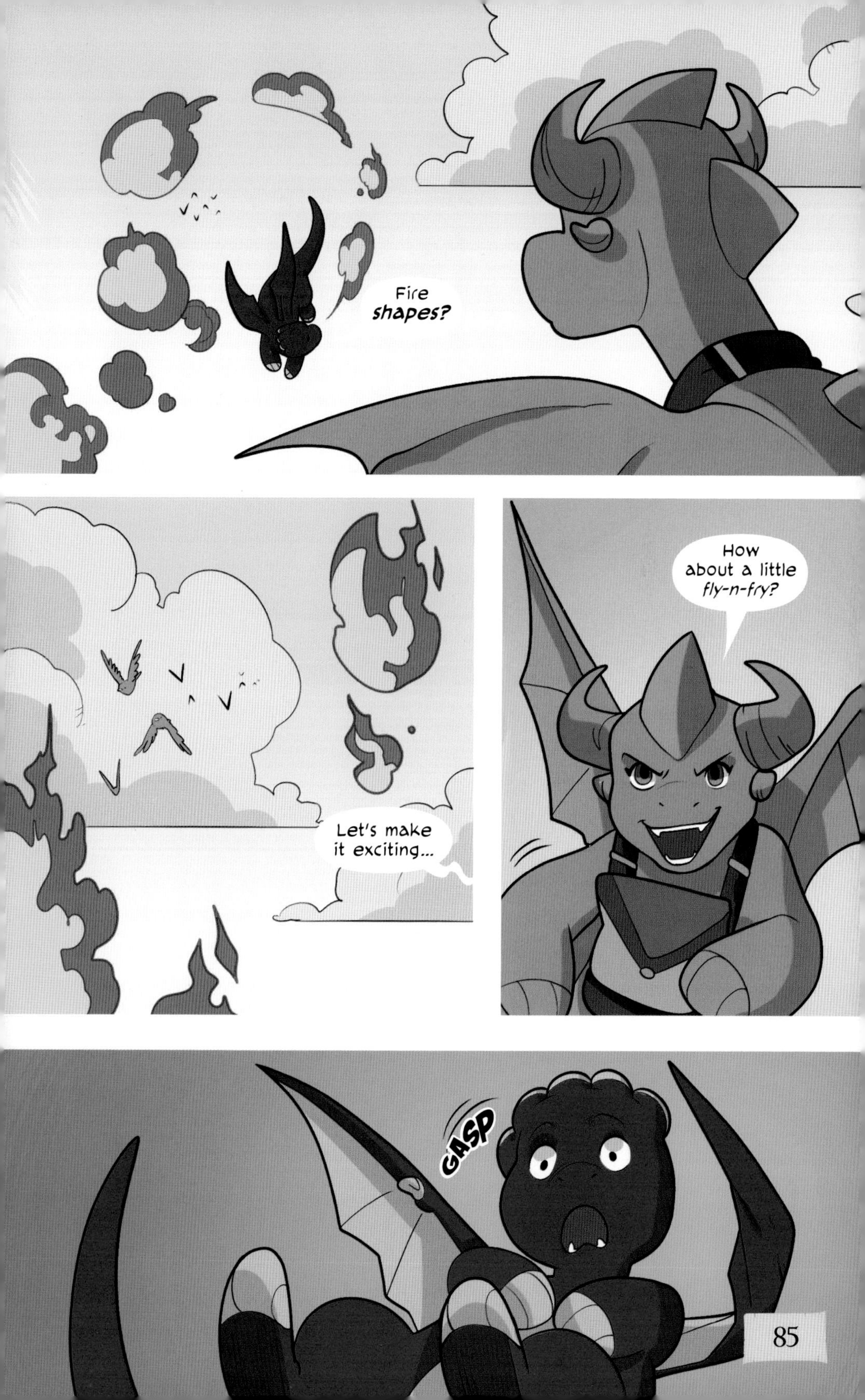
Fire shapes?
Let's make it exciting...
How about a little fly-n-fry?
GASP

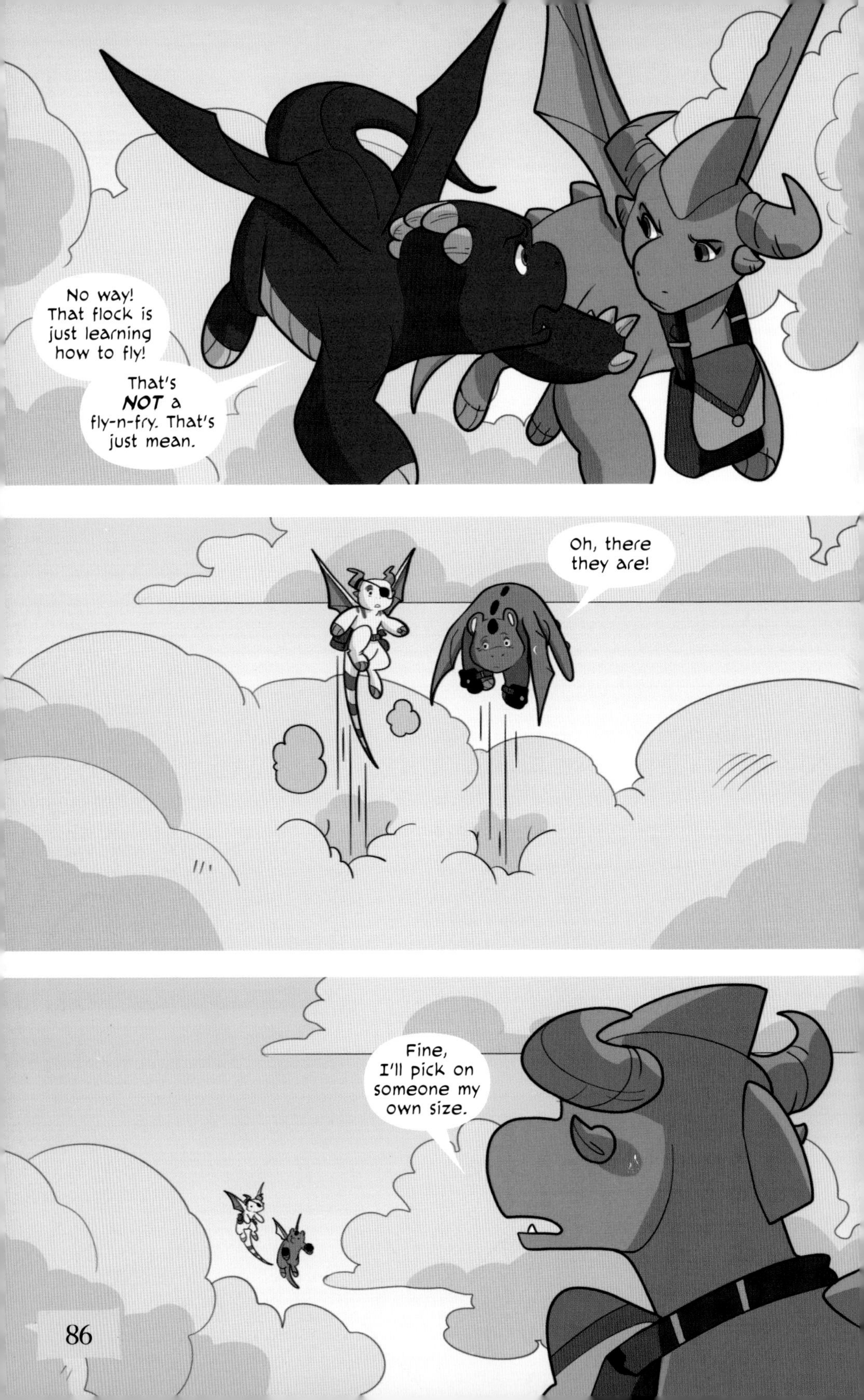
No way! That flock is just learning how to fly!
That's **NOT** a fly-n-fry. That's just mean.
Oh, there they are!
Fine, I'll pick on someone my own size.

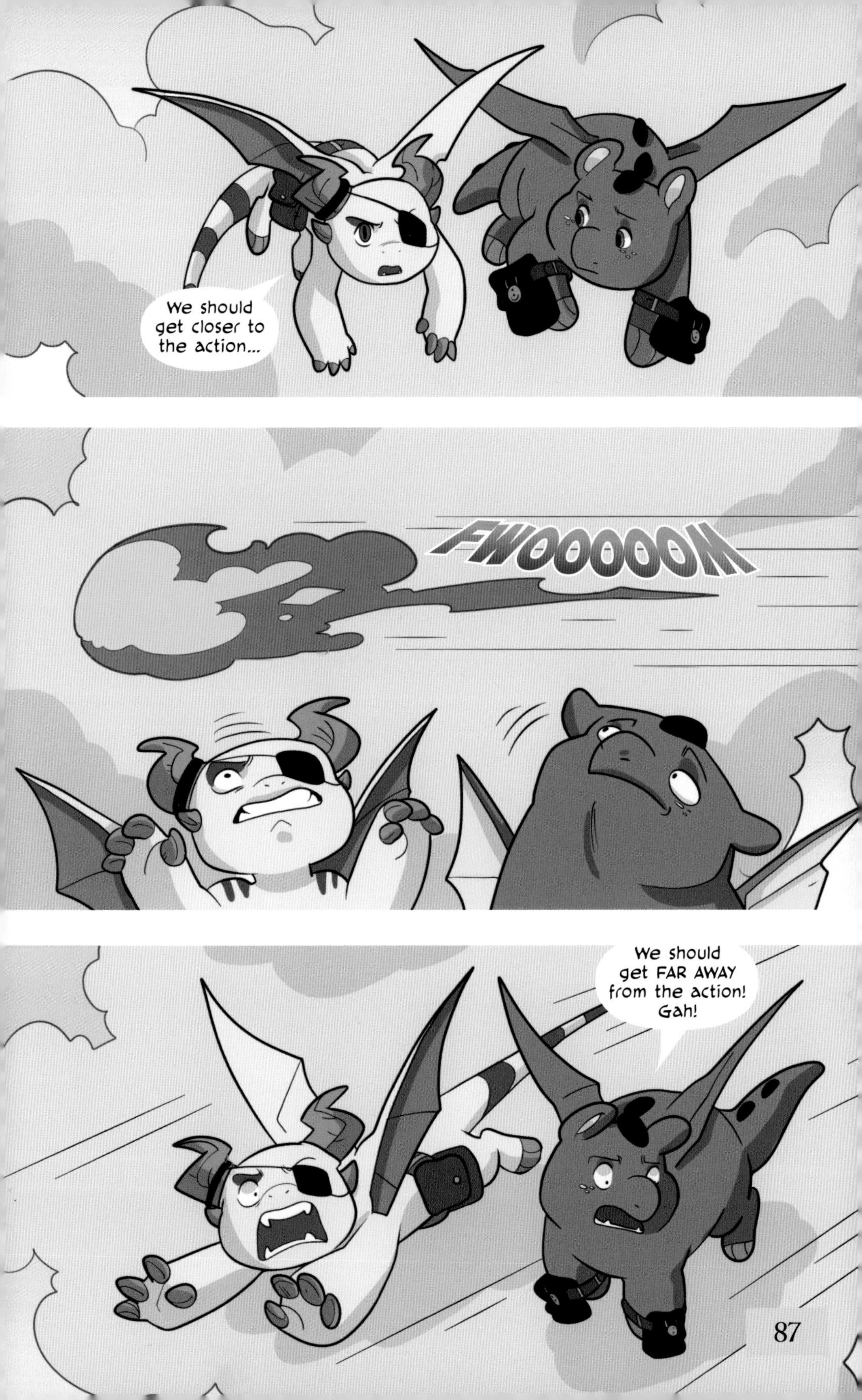
We should get closer to the action...
FWOOOOOM
We should get FAR AWAY from the action! Gah!

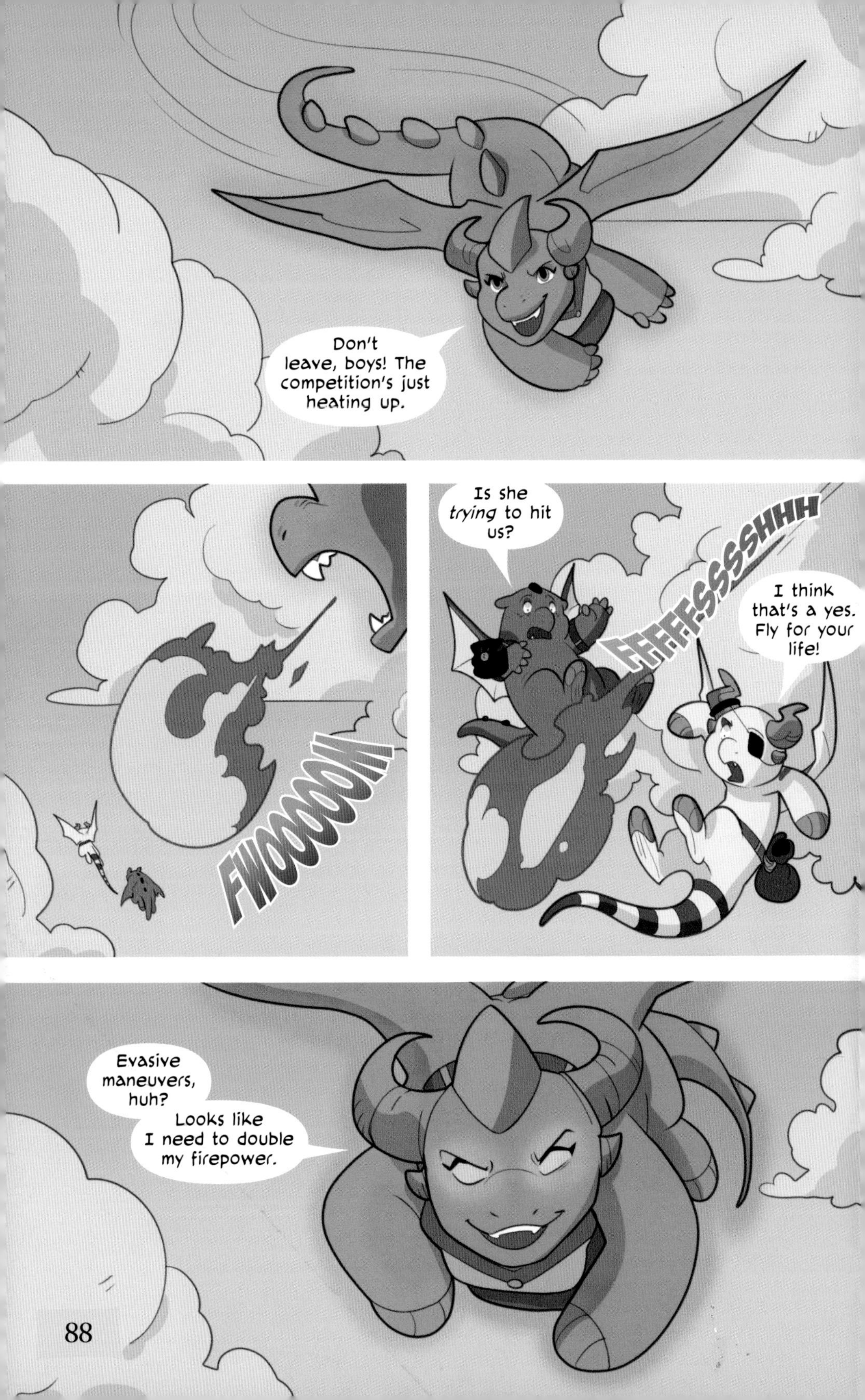

Don't leave, boys! The competition's just heating up.
FWOOOOOOM
Is she *trying* to hit us?
FFFFFSSSSHHH
I think that's a yes. Fly for your life!
Evasive maneuvers, huh?
Looks like I need to double my firepower.

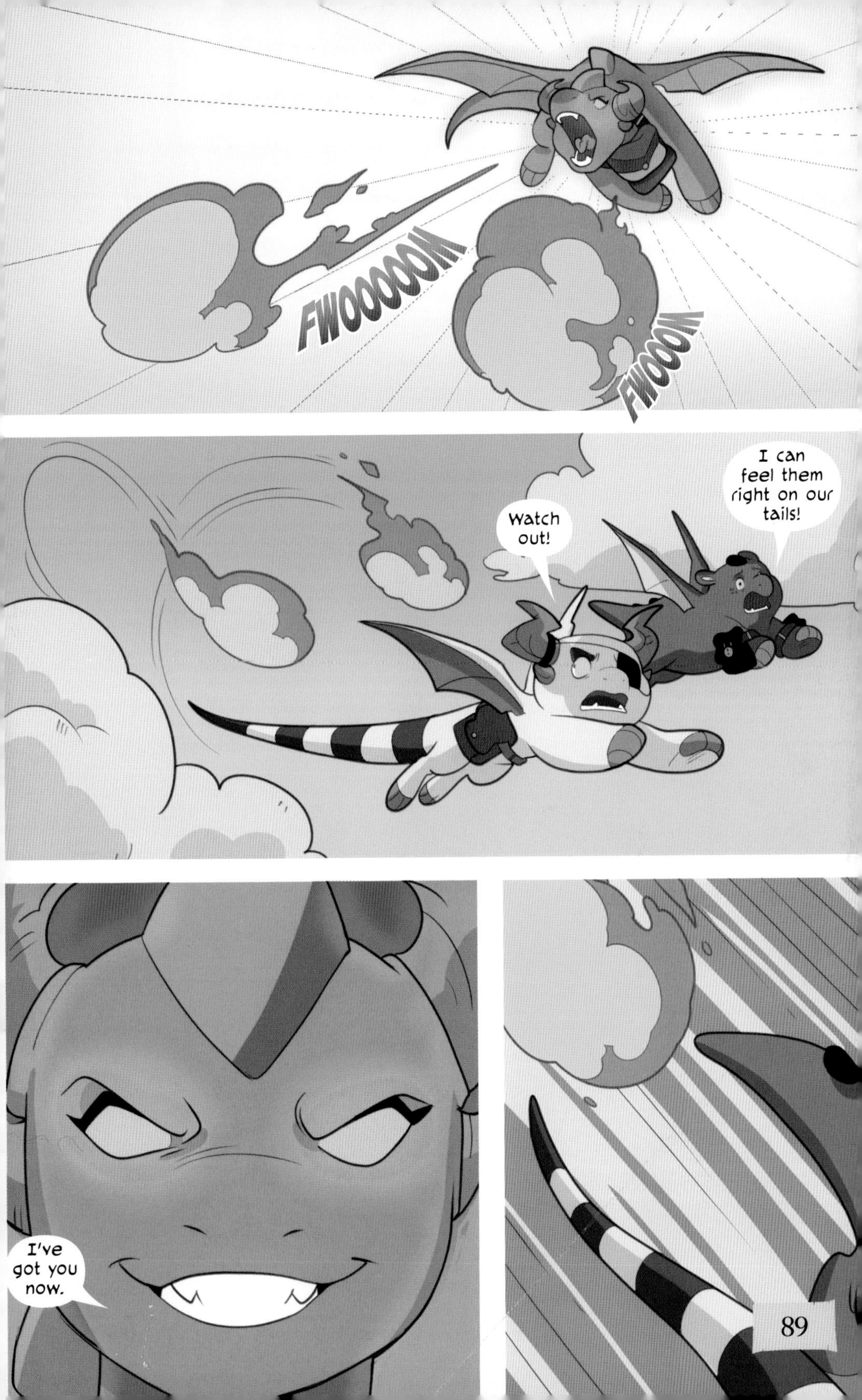
FWOOOOOM
FWOOOM
Watch out!
I can feel them right on our tails!
I've got you now.

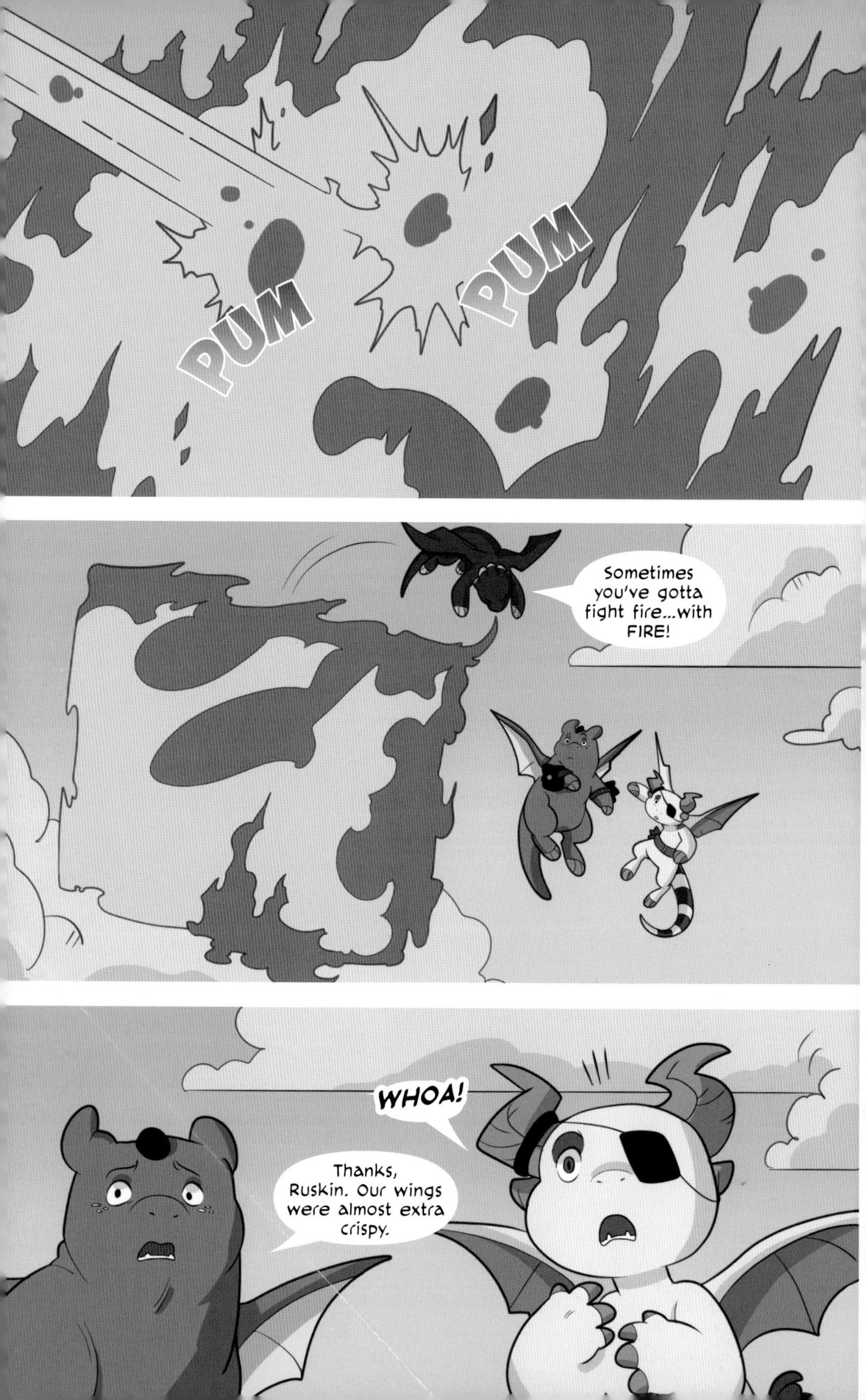
PUM
PUM
Sometimes you've gotta fight fire...with FIRE!
WHOA!
Thanks, Ruskin. Our wings were almost extra crispy.

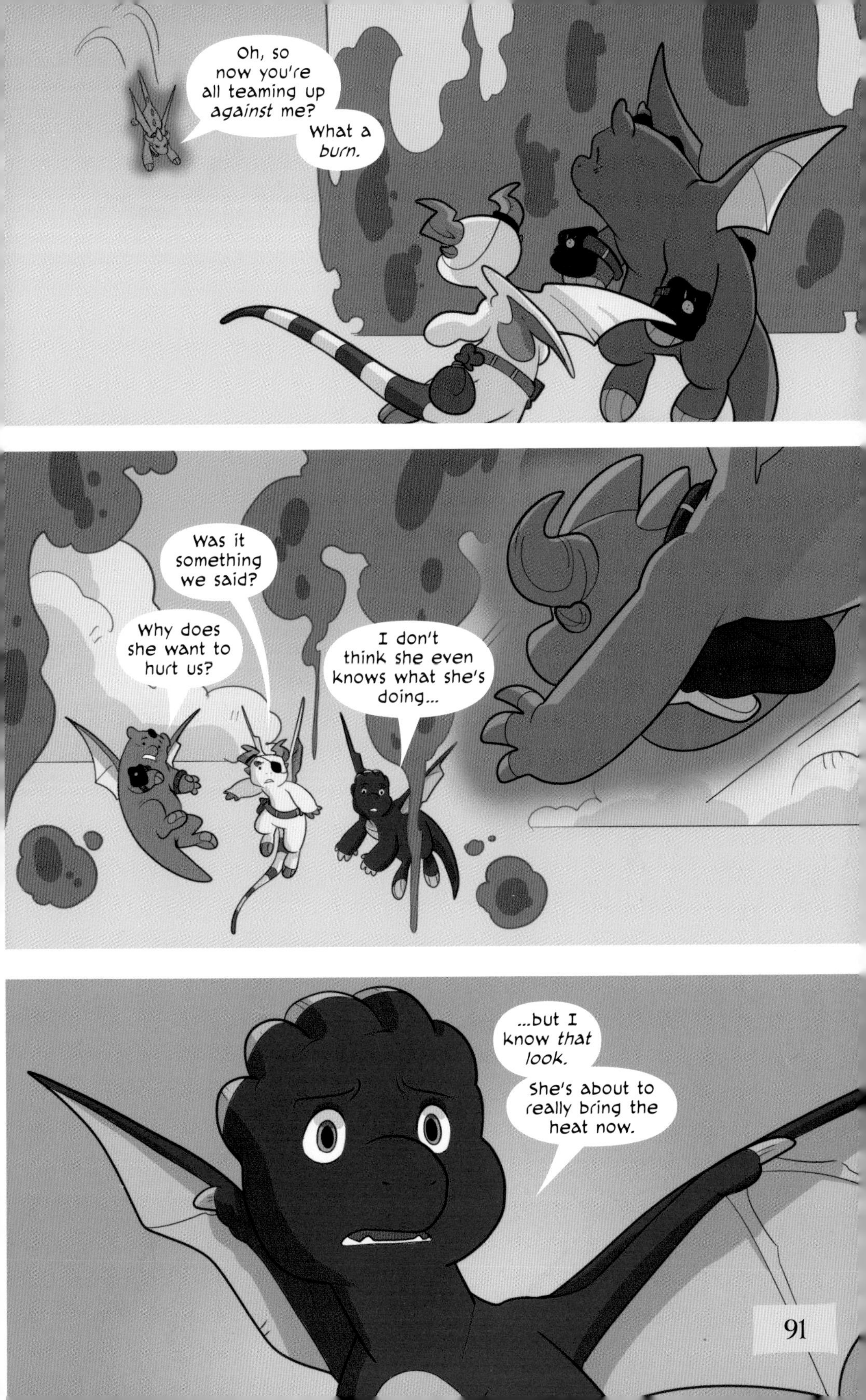

Oh, so now you're all teaming up *against* me?
What a *burn.*
Why does she want to hurt us?
Was it something we said?
I don't think she even knows what she's doing...
...but I know *that* look.
She's about to really bring the heat now.

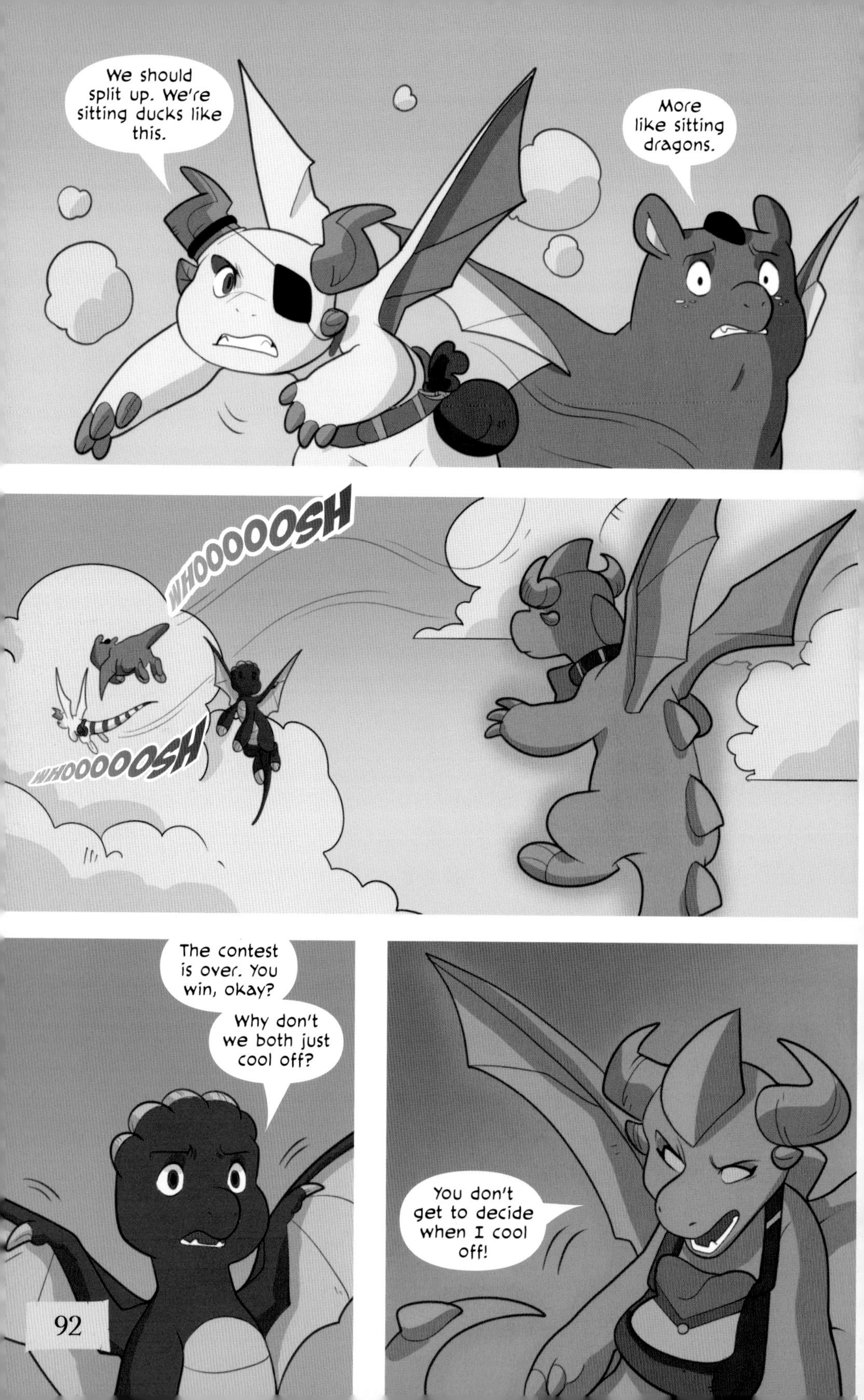
We should split up. We're sitting ducks like this.
More like sitting dragons.
WHOOOOOOSH
WHOOOOOOSH
The contest is over. You win, okay?
Why don't we both just cool off?
You don't get to decide when I cool off!

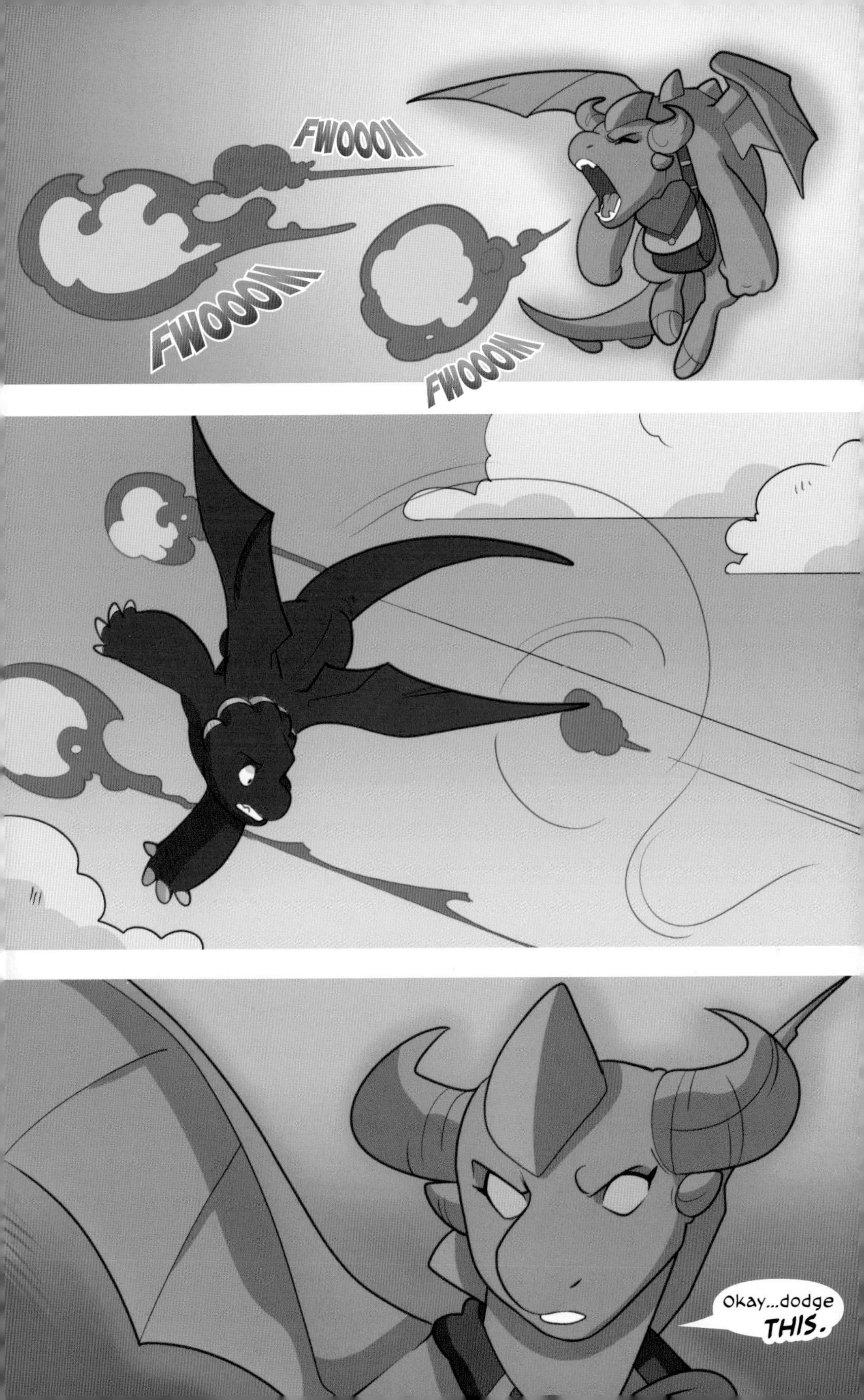
FWOOOM
FWOOOM
FWOOOM
Okay...dodge THIS.

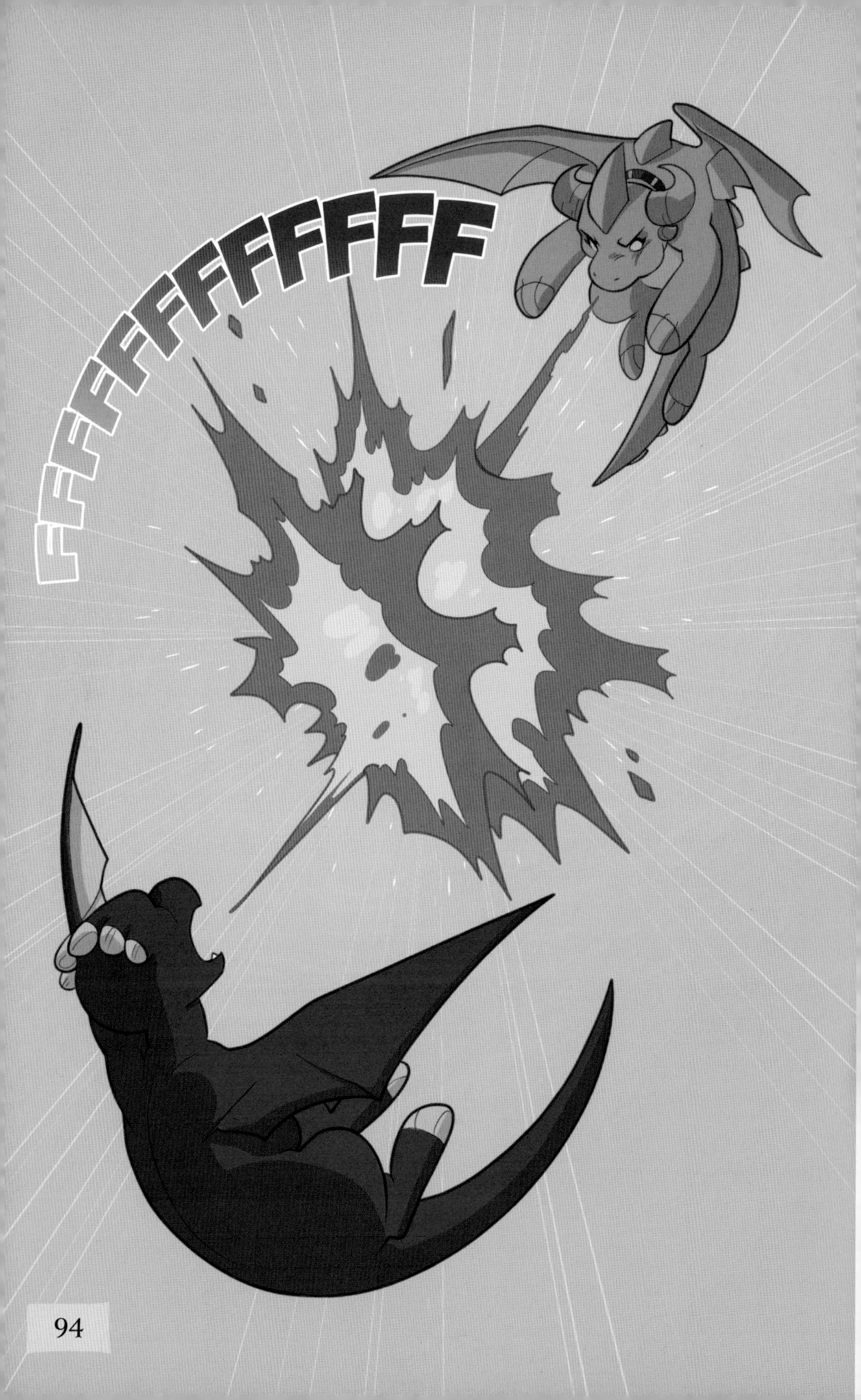
FFFFFFFFFFFF

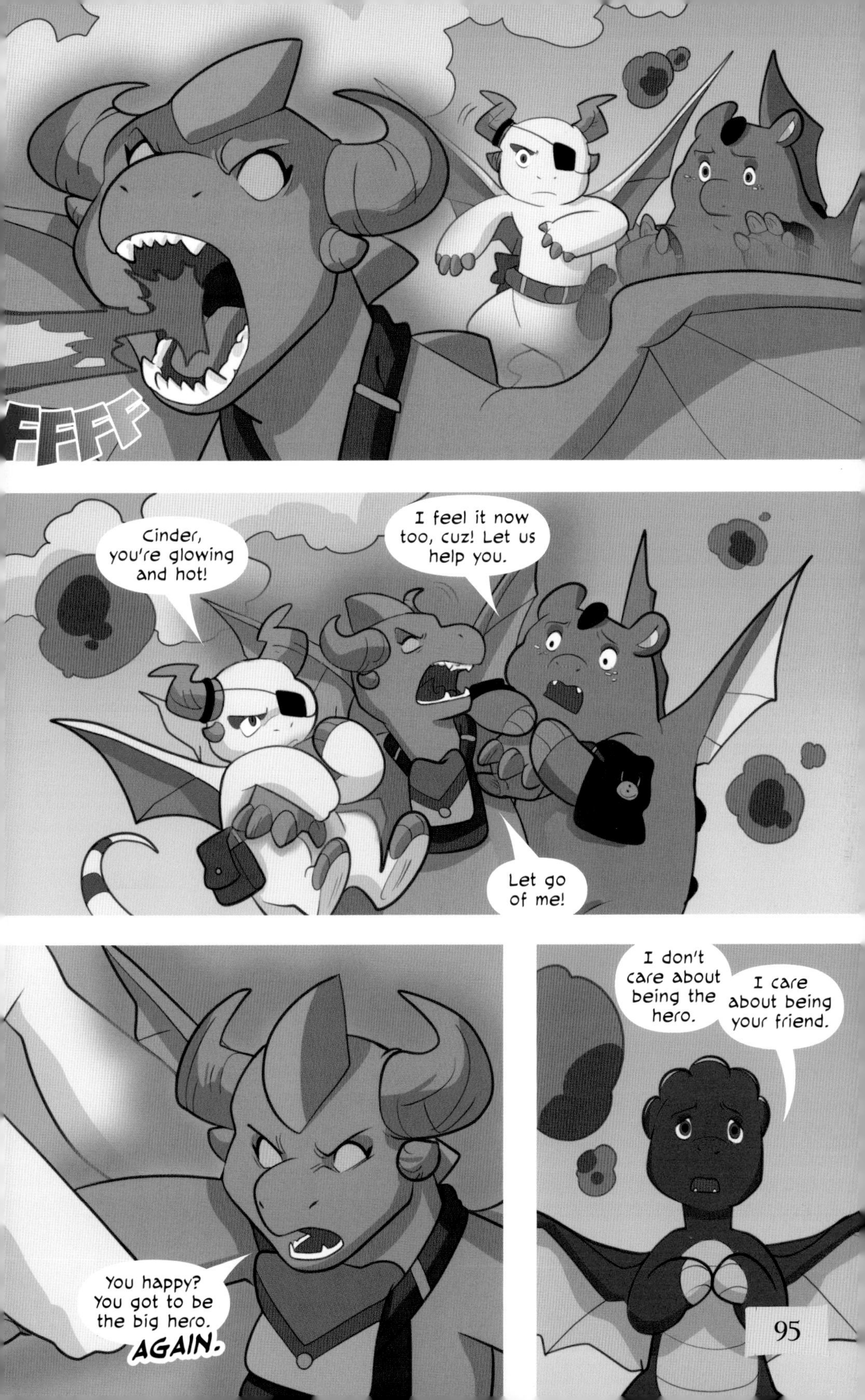
FFFF
Cinder, you're glowing and hot!
I feel it now too, cuz! Let us help you.
Let go of me!
You happy? You got to be the big hero. AGAIN.
I don't care about being the hero.
I care about being your friend.

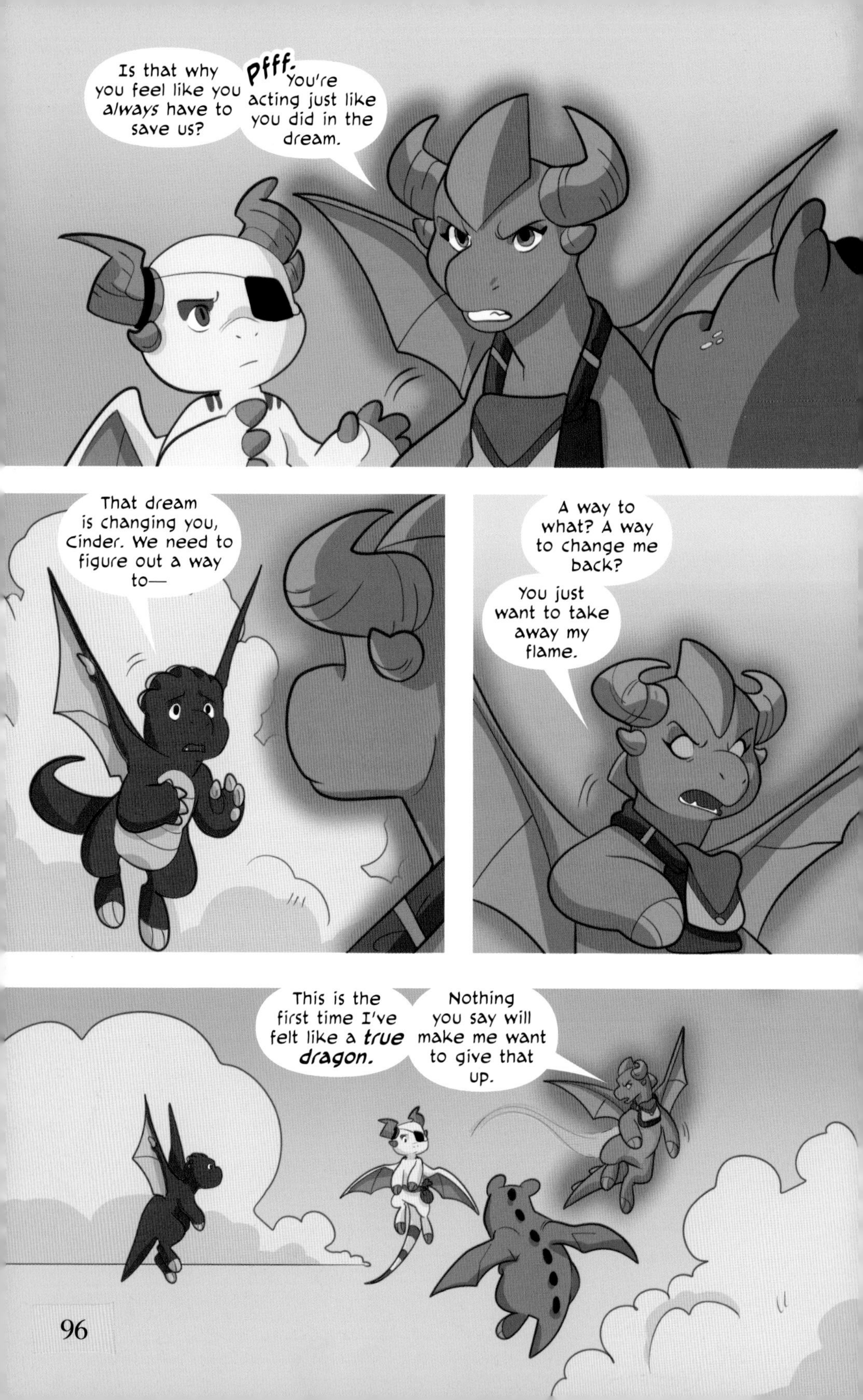
Is that why you feel like you *always* have to save us?
Pfff. You're acting just like you did in the dream.
That dream is changing you, Cinder. We need to figure out a way to—
A way to what? A way to change me back?
You just want to take away my flame.
This is the first time I've felt like a ***true dragon.***
Nothing you say will make me want to give that up.

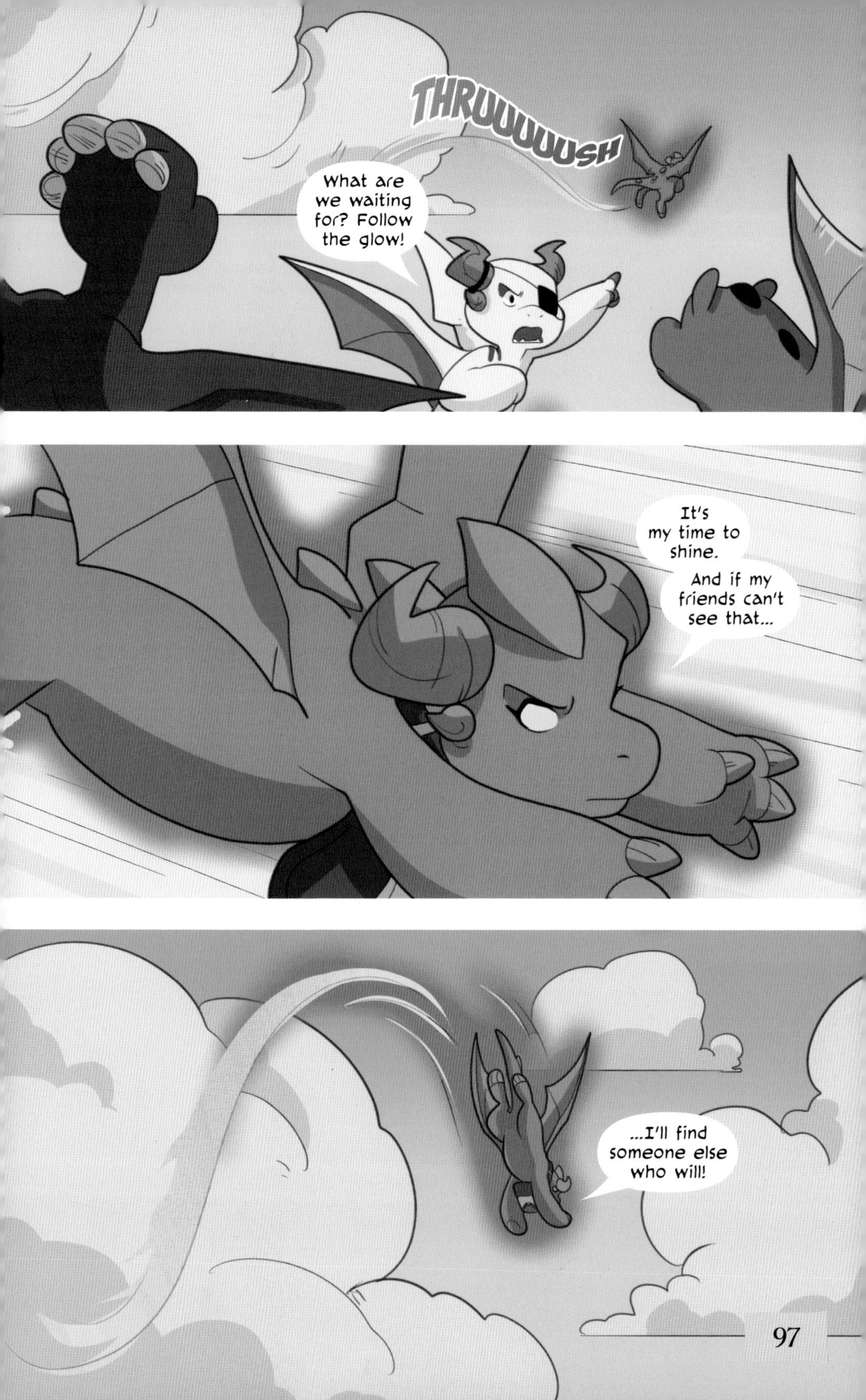
THRUUUUUUSH
What are we waiting for? Follow the glow!
It's my time to shine.
And if my friends can't see that...
...I'll find someone else who will!

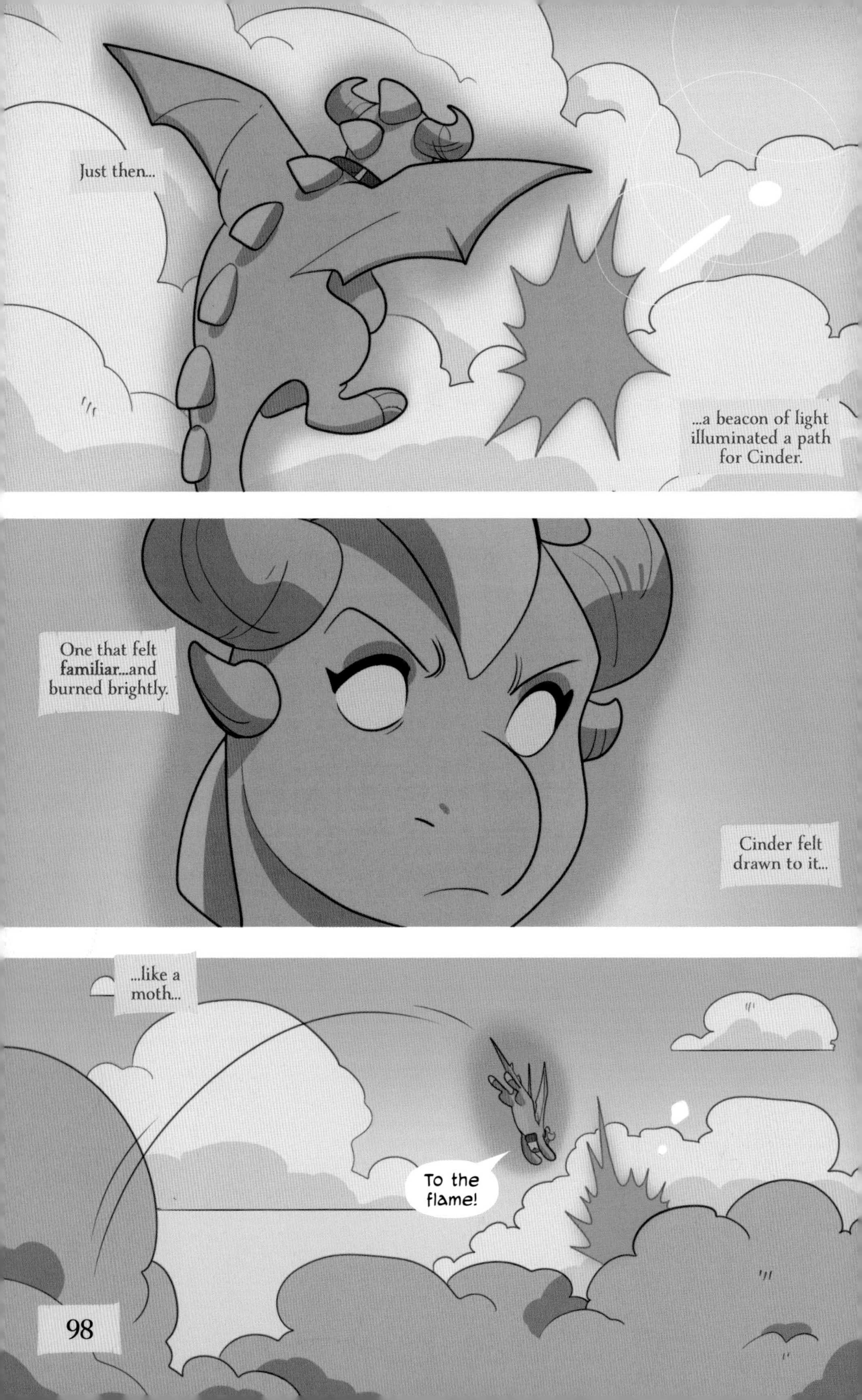
Just then...
...a beacon of light illuminated a path for Cinder.
One that felt familiar...and burned brightly.
Cinder felt drawn to it...
...like a moth...
To the flame!

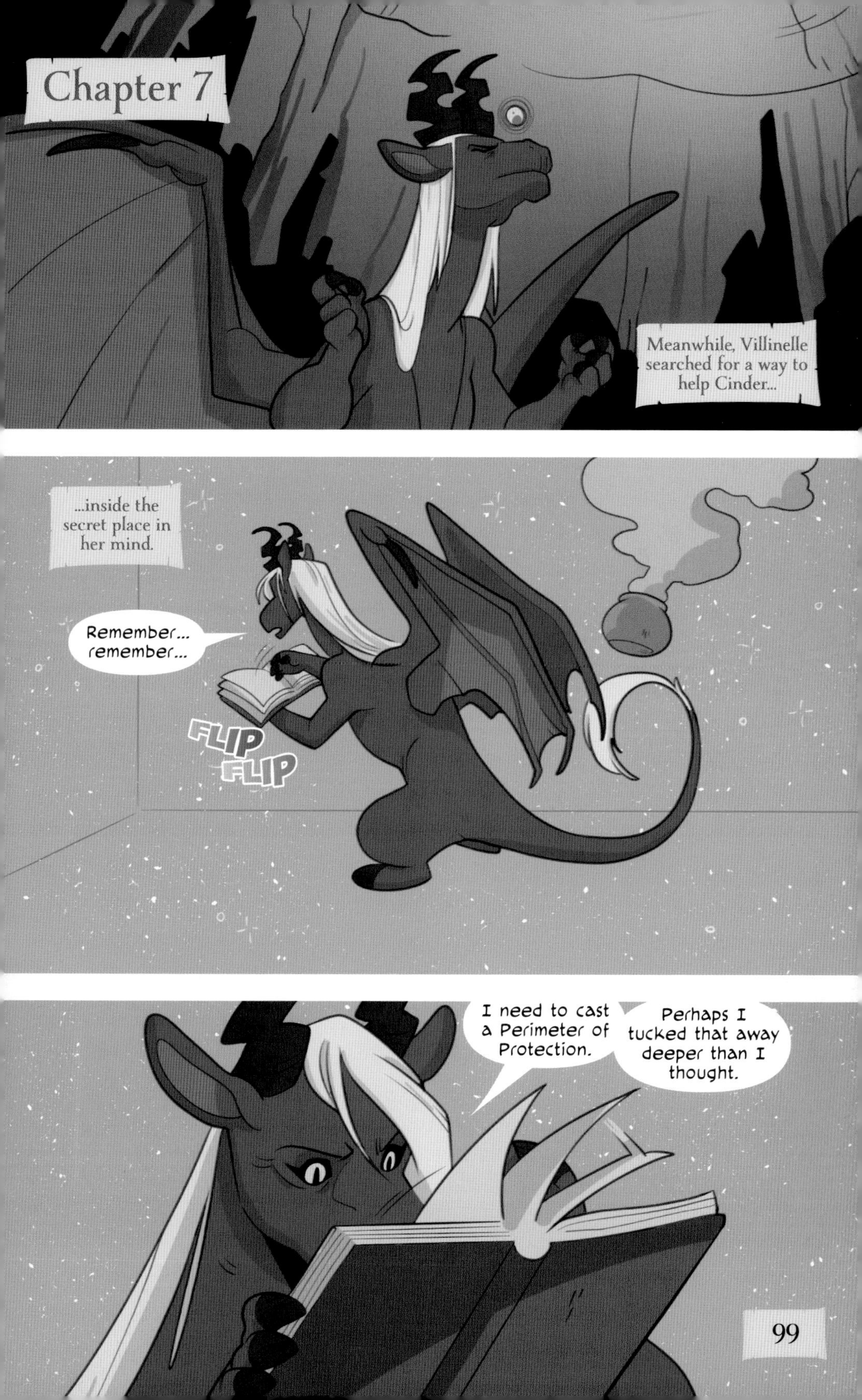
Chapter 7
Meanwhile, Villinelle searched for a way to help Cinder...
...inside the secret place in her mind.
Remember... remember...
FLIP FLIP
I need to cast a Perimeter of Protection.
Perhaps I tucked that away deeper than I thought.

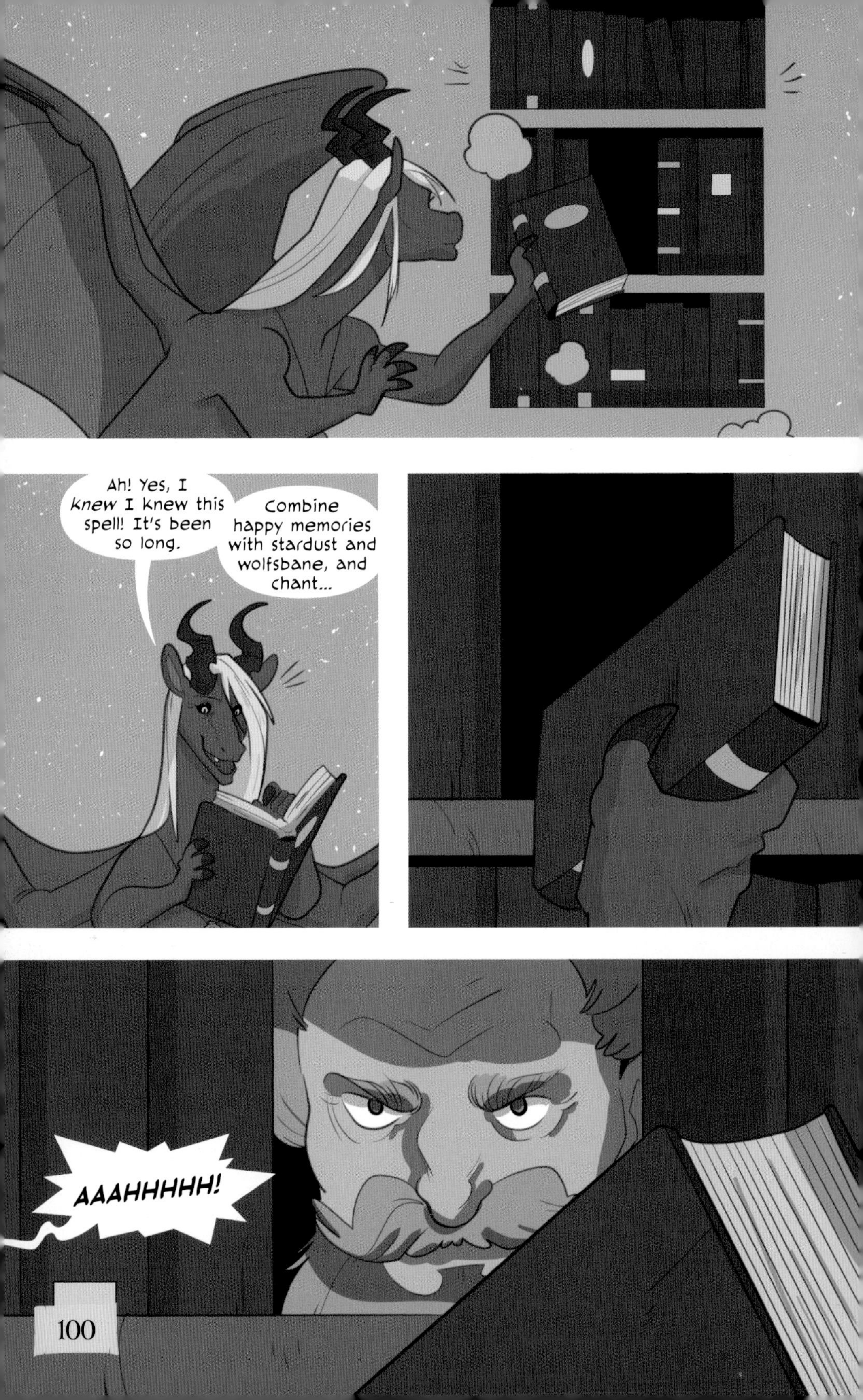

Ah! Yes, I *knew* I knew this spell! It's been so long.
Combine happy memories with stardust and wolfsbane, and chant...
AAAHHHHH!

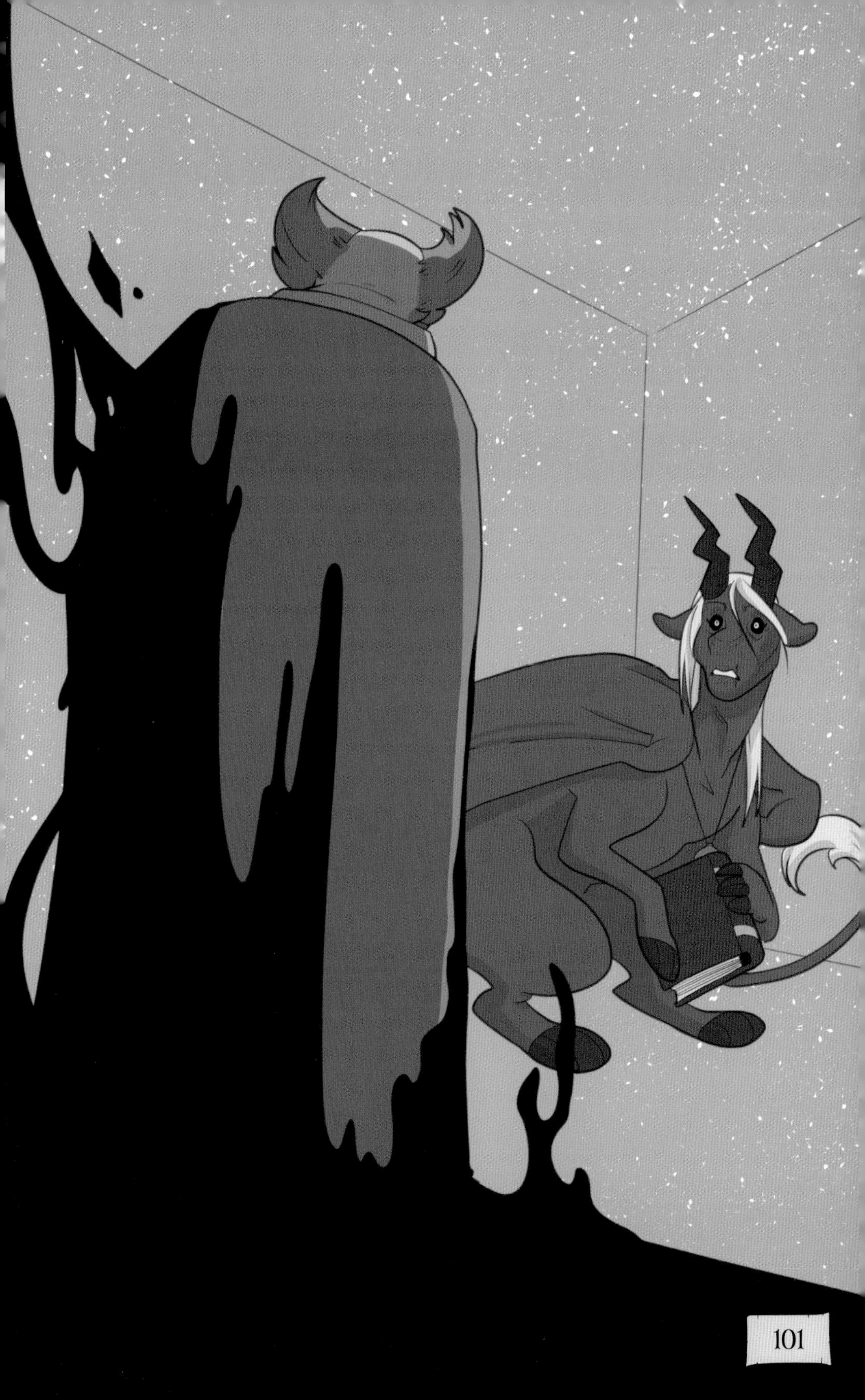

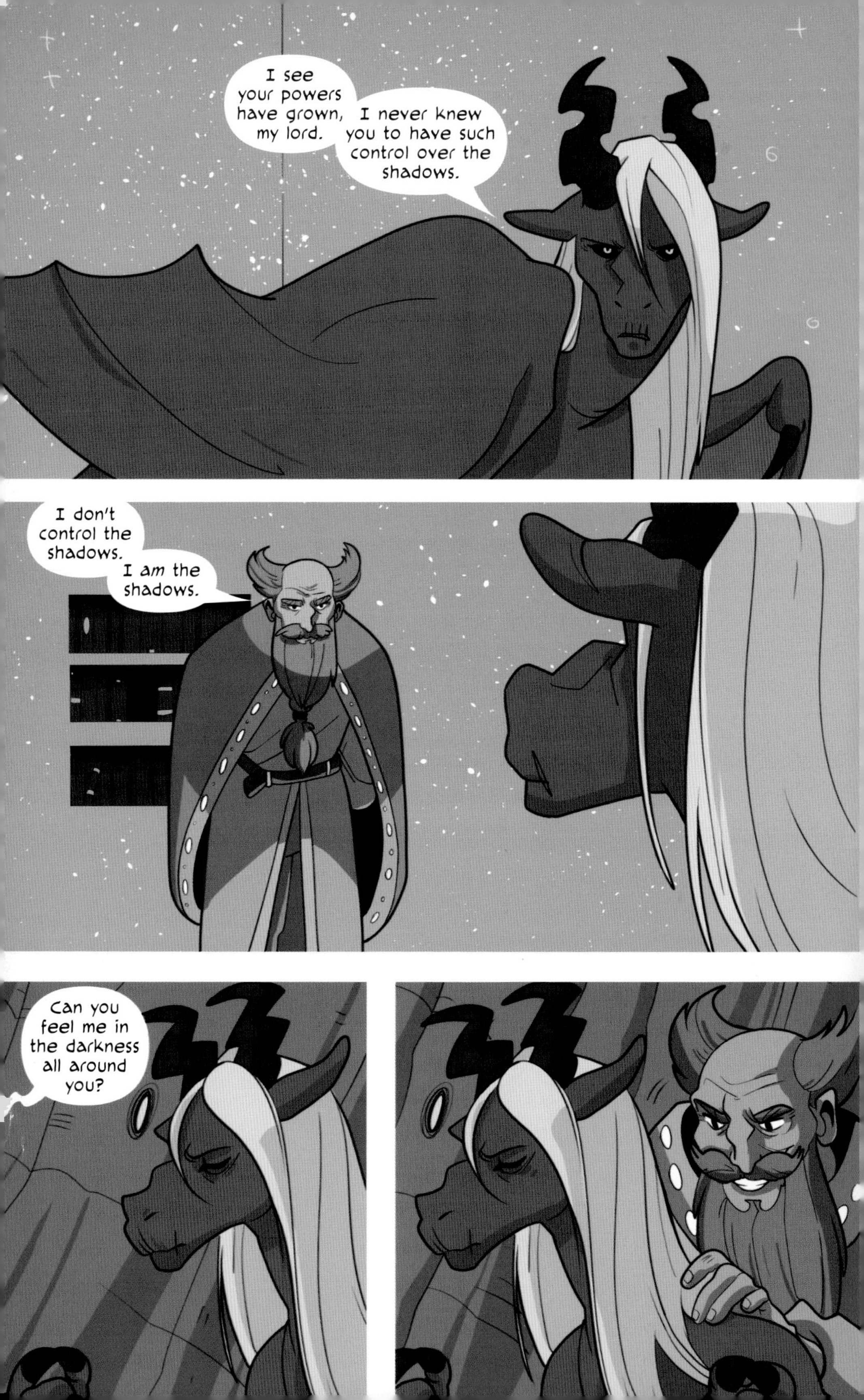
I see your powers have grown, my lord.
I never knew you to have such control over the shadows.
I don't control the shadows.
I *am* the shadows.
Can you feel me in the darkness all around you?

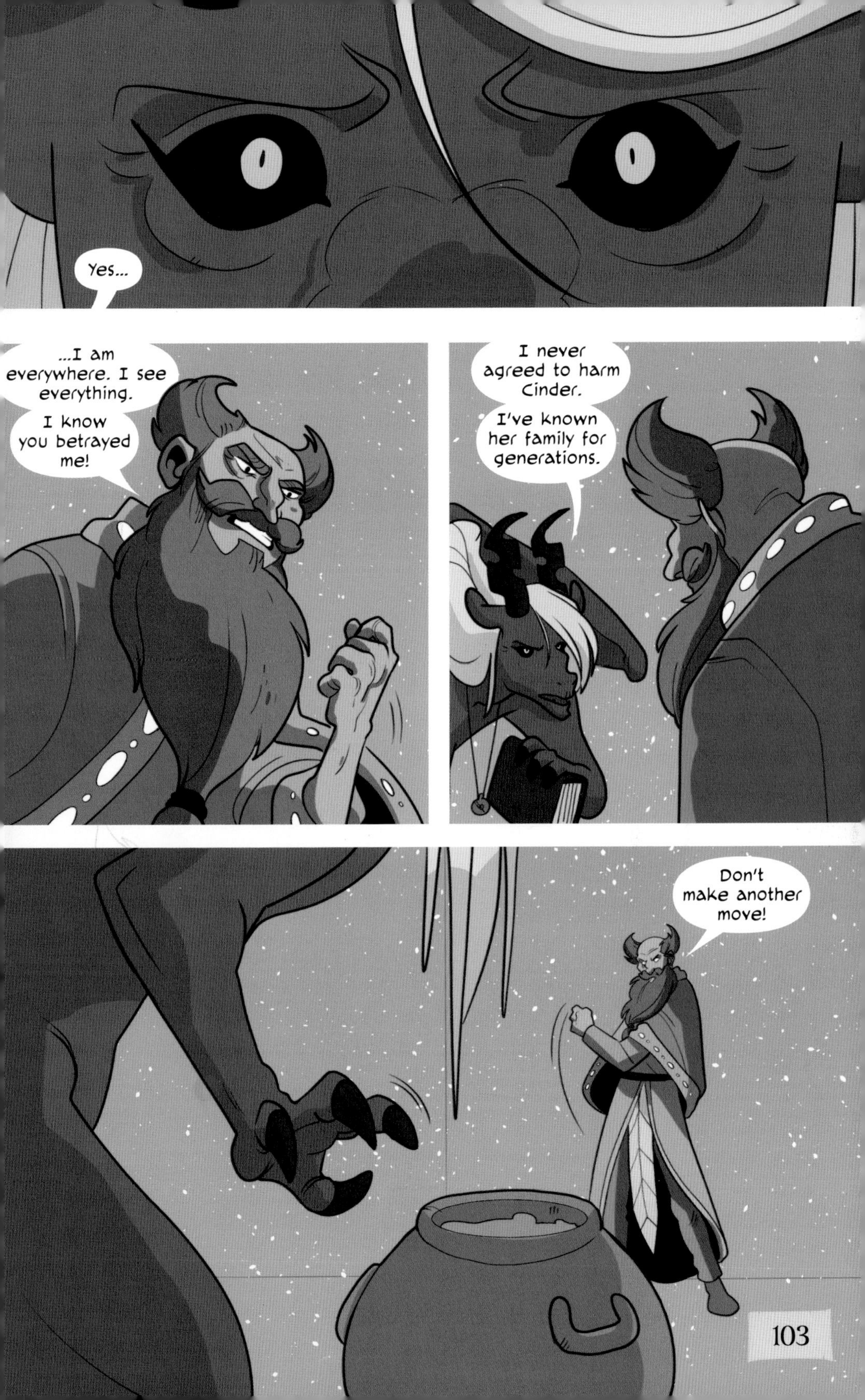

Yes...
...I am everywhere. I see everything.
I know you betrayed me!
I never agreed to harm Cinder.
I've known her family for generations.
Don't make another move!

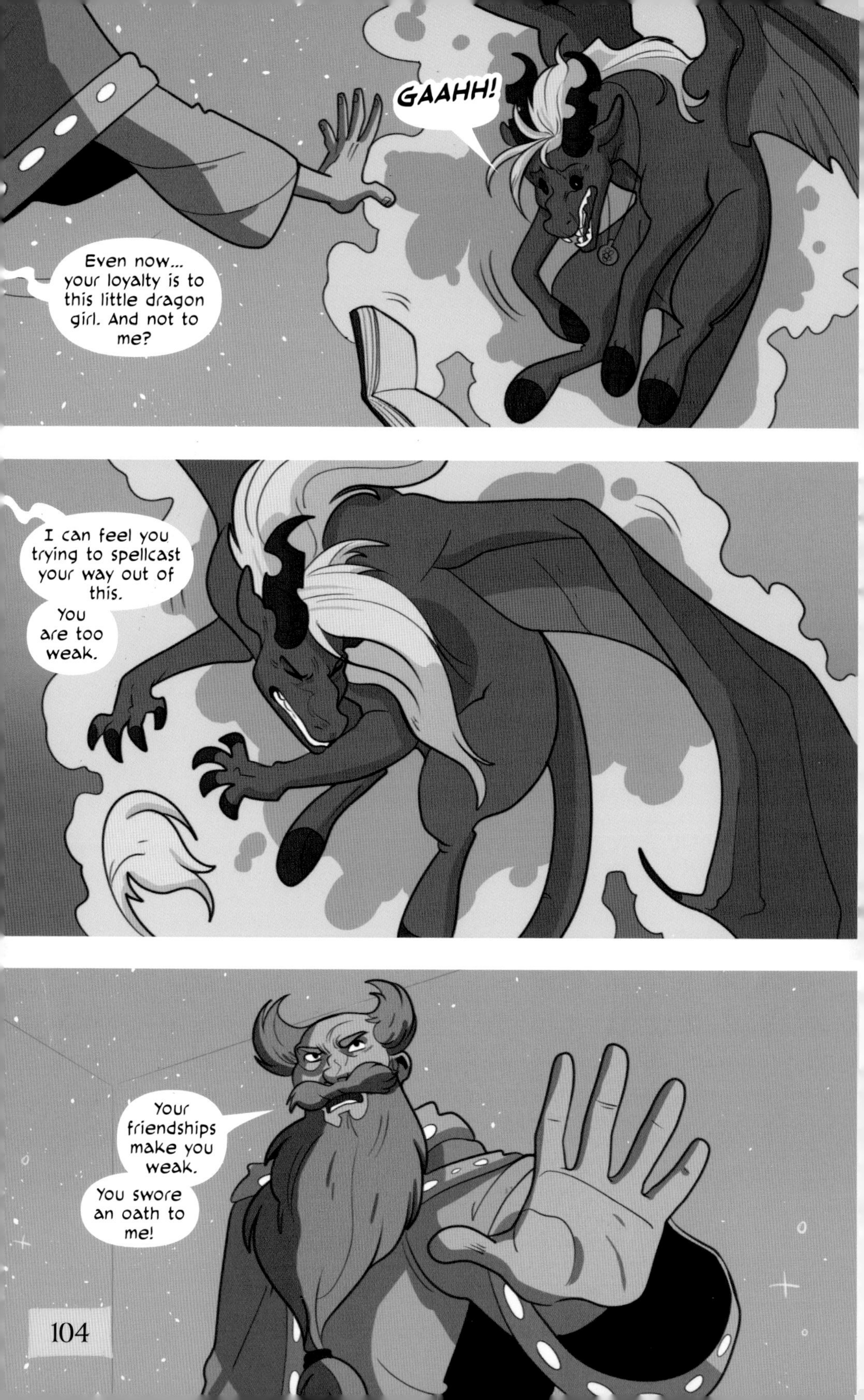
GAAHH!
Even now... your loyalty is to this little dragon girl. And not to me?
I can feel you trying to spellcast your way out of this.
You are too weak.
Your friendships make you weak.
You swore an oath to me!

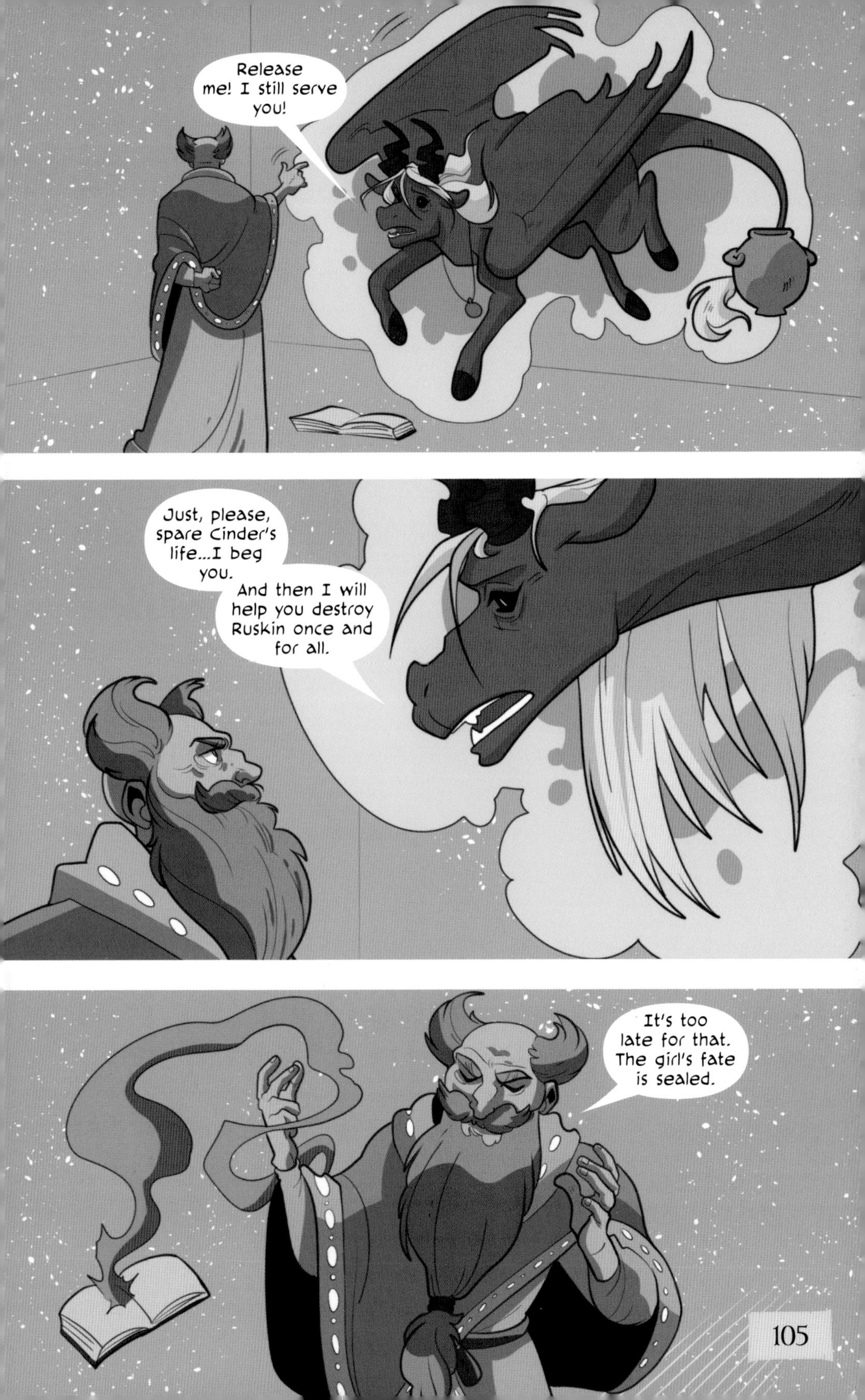
Release me! I still serve you!
Just, please, spare Cinder's life...I beg you.
And then I will help you destroy Ruskin once and for all.
It's too late for that. The girl's fate is sealed.

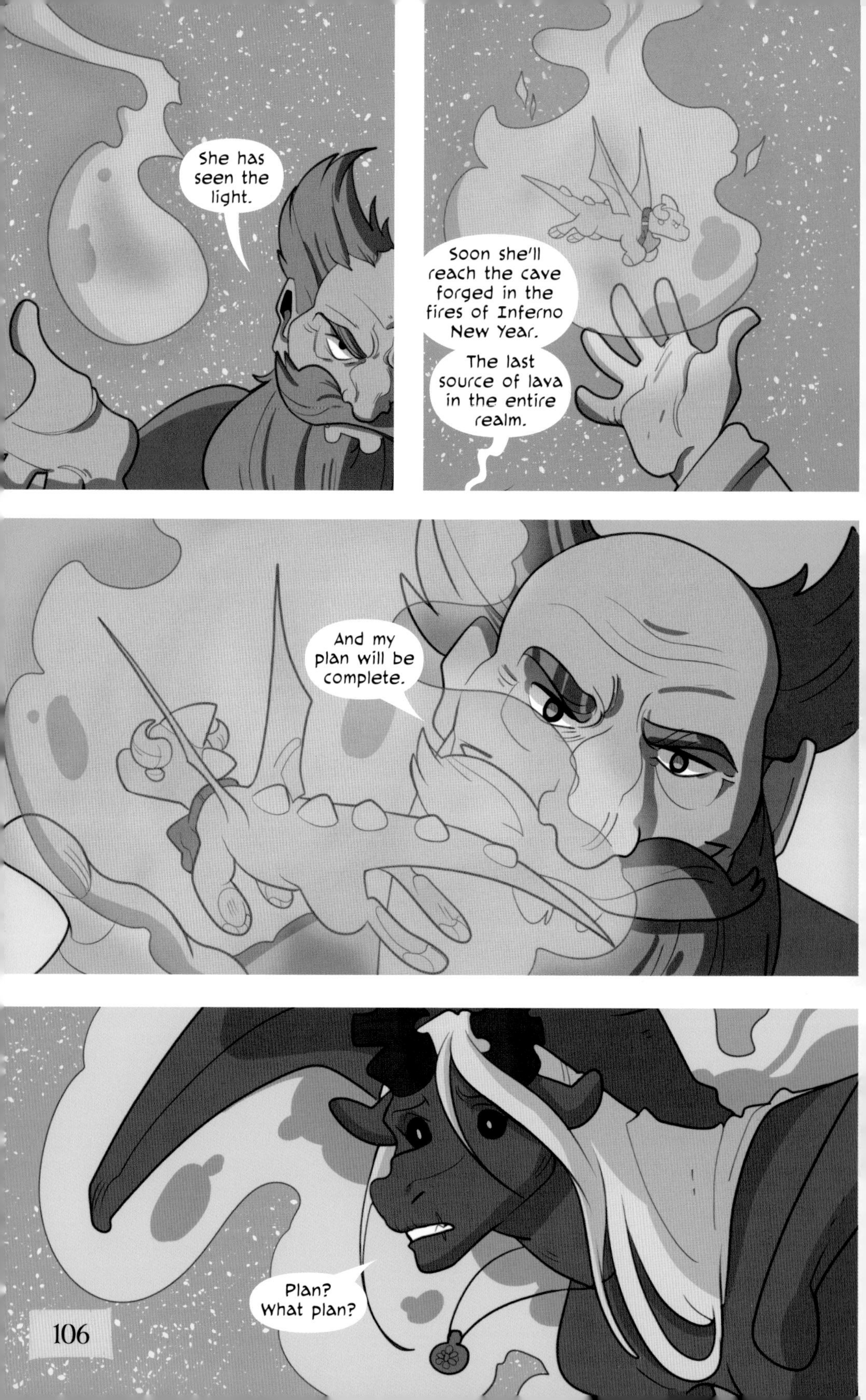
She has seen the light.
Soon she'll reach the cave forged in the fires of Inferno New Year.
The last source of lava in the entire realm.
And my plan will be complete.
Plan? What plan?

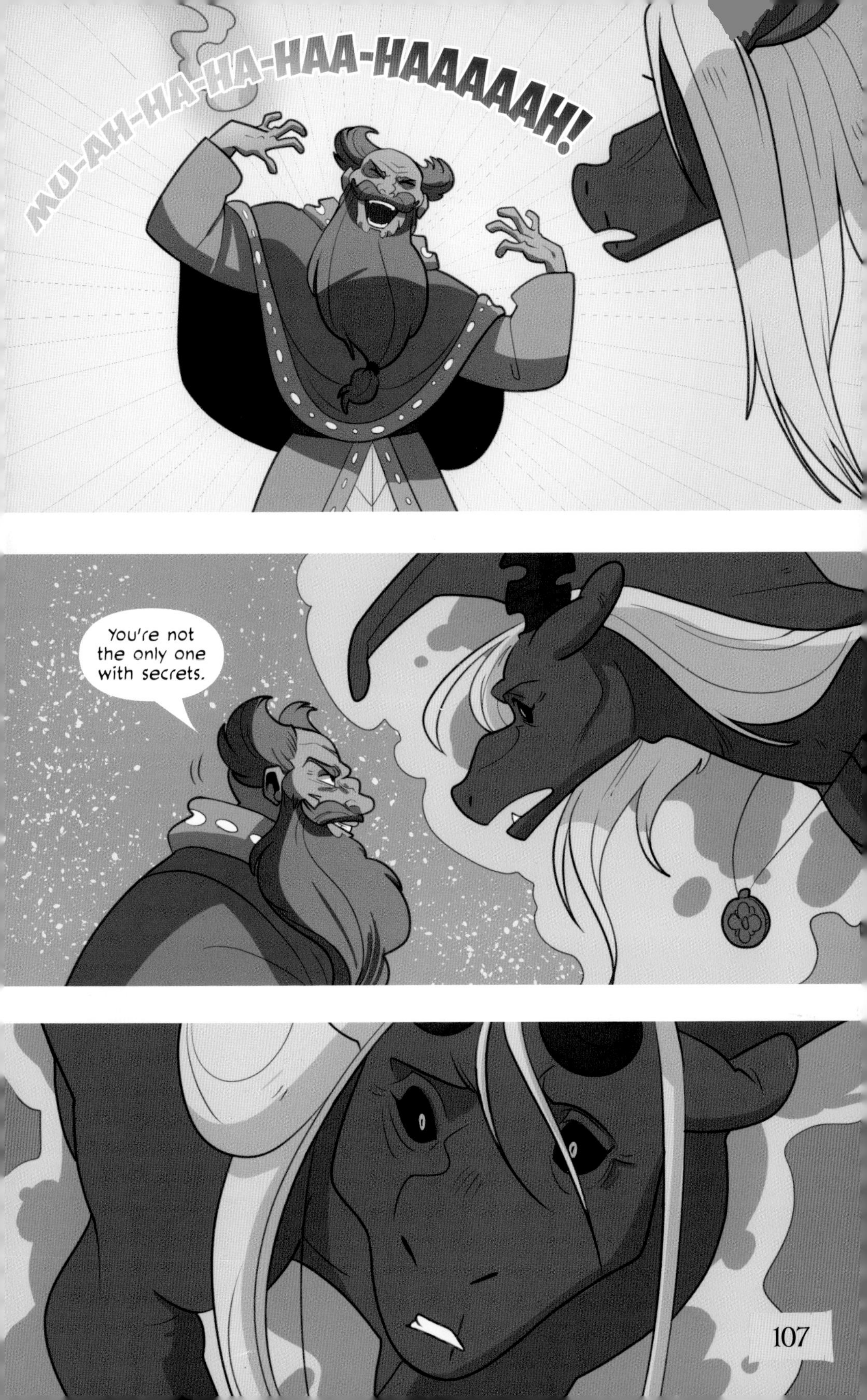
MU-AH-HA-HA-HAA-HAAAAAAH!
You're not the only one with secrets.

Chapter 8

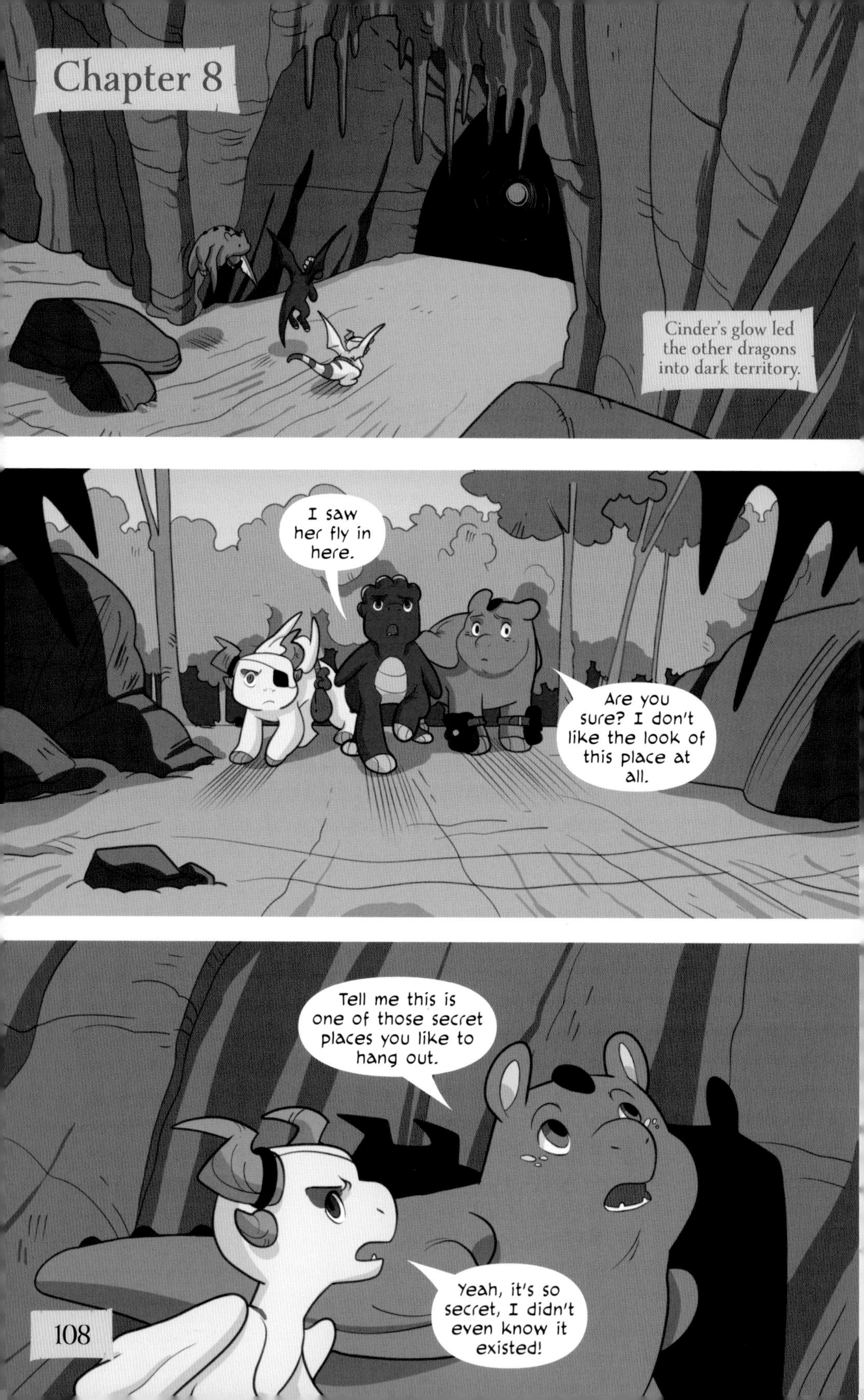
Cinder's glow led the other dragons into dark territory.
I saw her fly in here.
Are you sure? I don't like the look of this place at all.
Tell me this is one of those secret places you like to hang out.
Yeah, it's so secret, I didn't even know it existed!

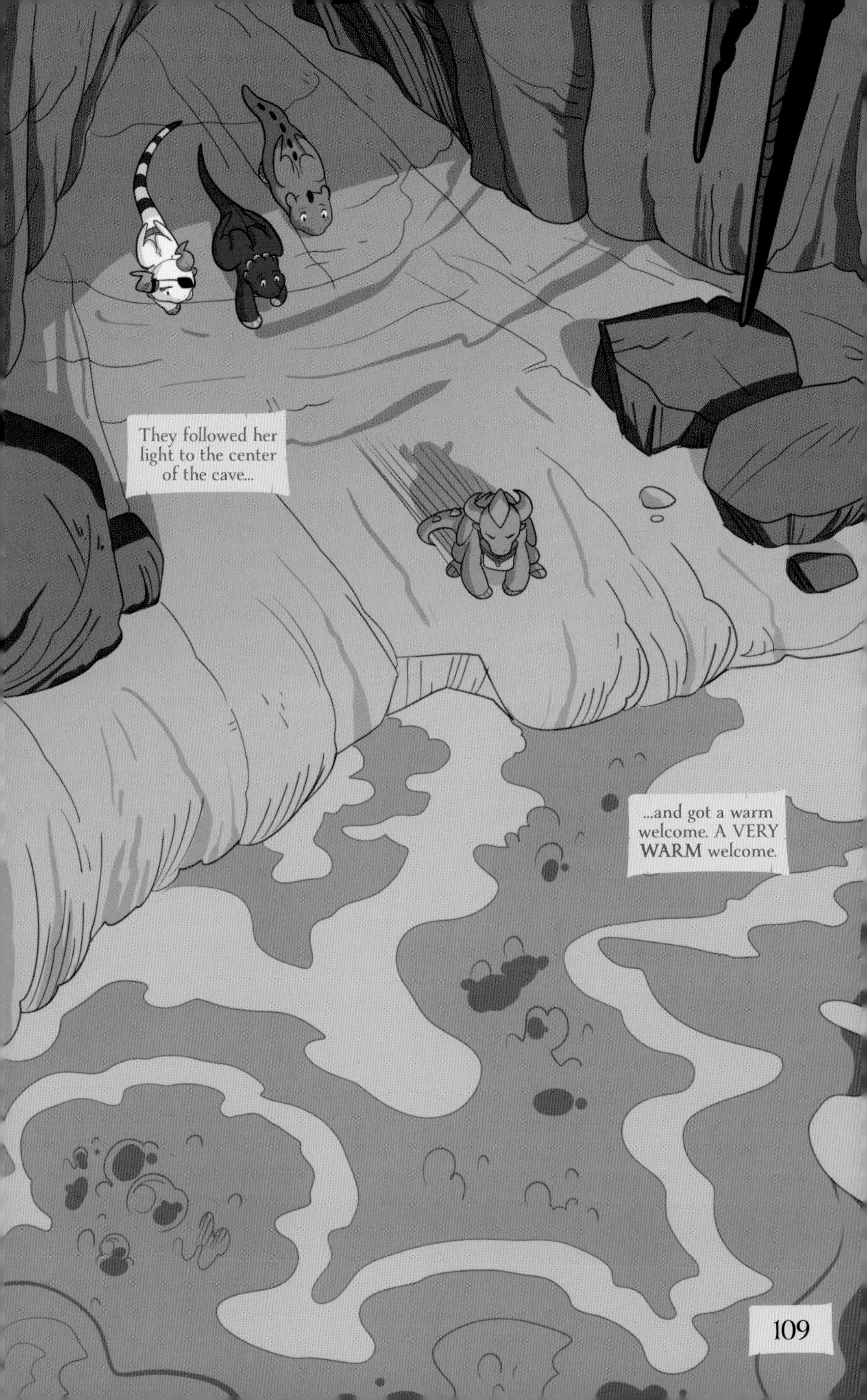
They followed her light to the center of the cave...
...and got a warm welcome. A VERY WARM welcome.

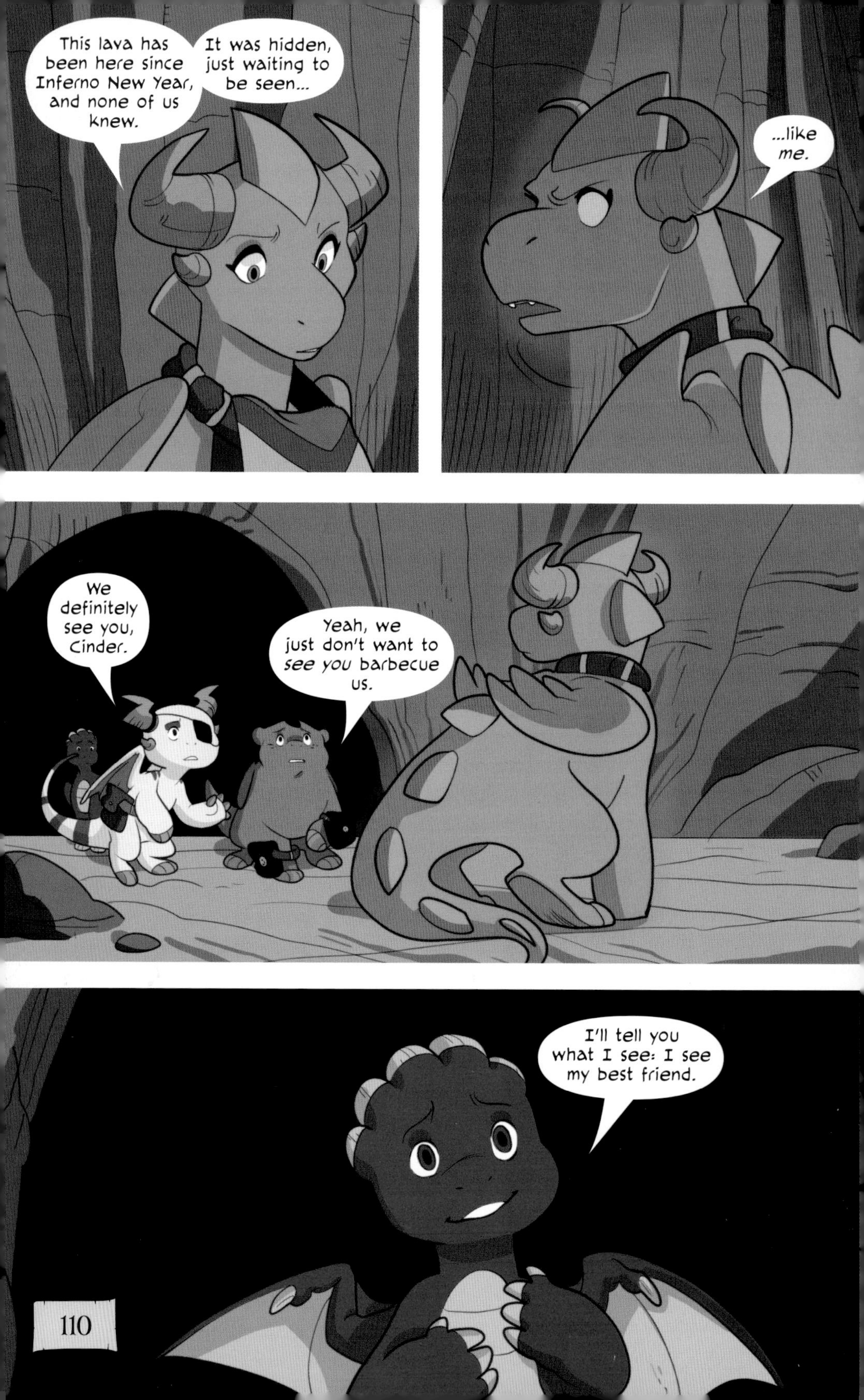
This lava has been here since Inferno New Year, and none of us knew.
It was hidden, just waiting to be seen...
...like *me.*
We definitely see you, Cinder.
Yeah, we just don't want to *see you* barbecue us.
I'll tell you what I see: I see my best friend.

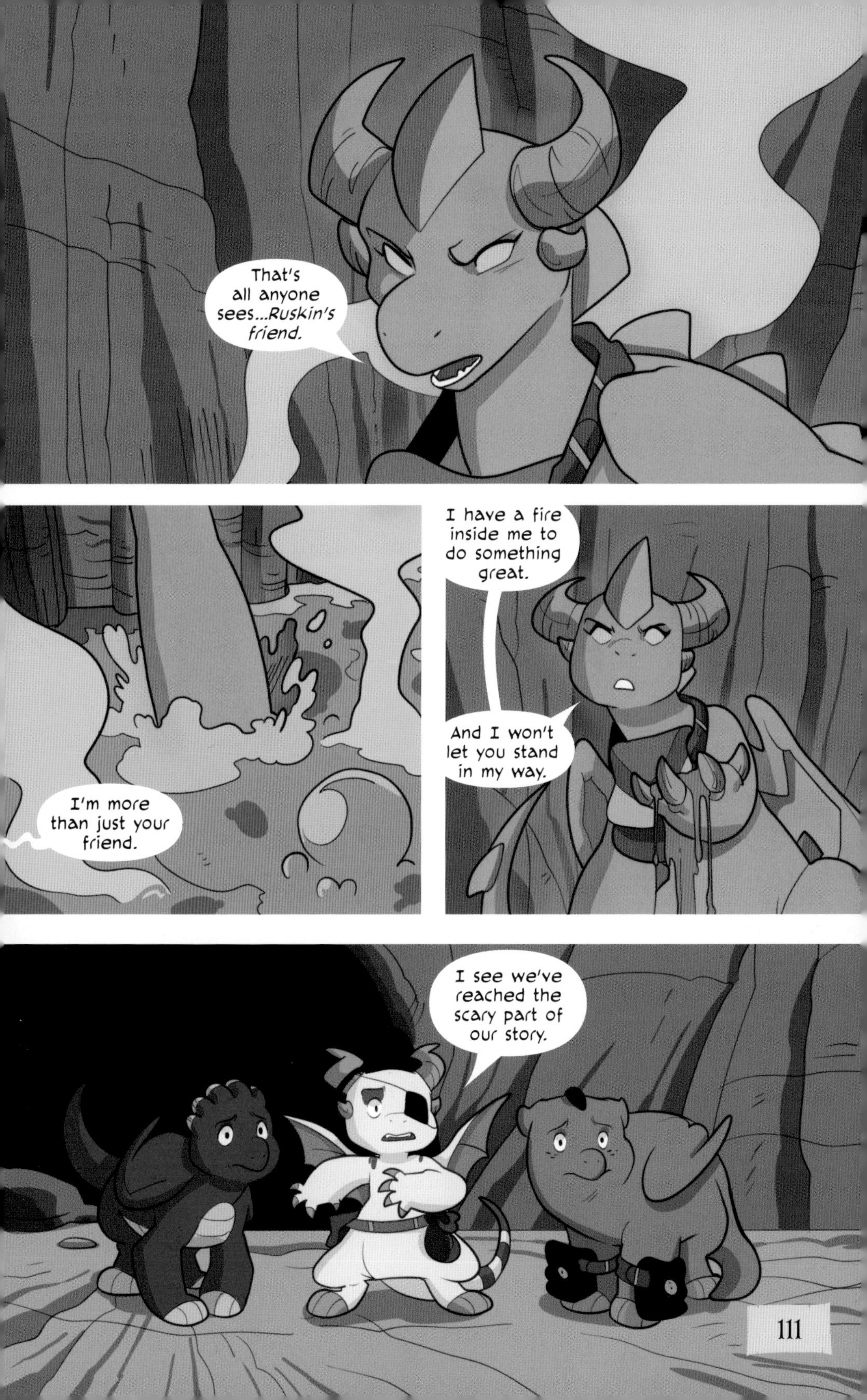
That's all anyone sees...*Ruskin's friend.*
I'm more than just your friend.
I have a fire inside me to do something great.
And I won't let you stand in my way.
I see we've reached the scary part of our story.

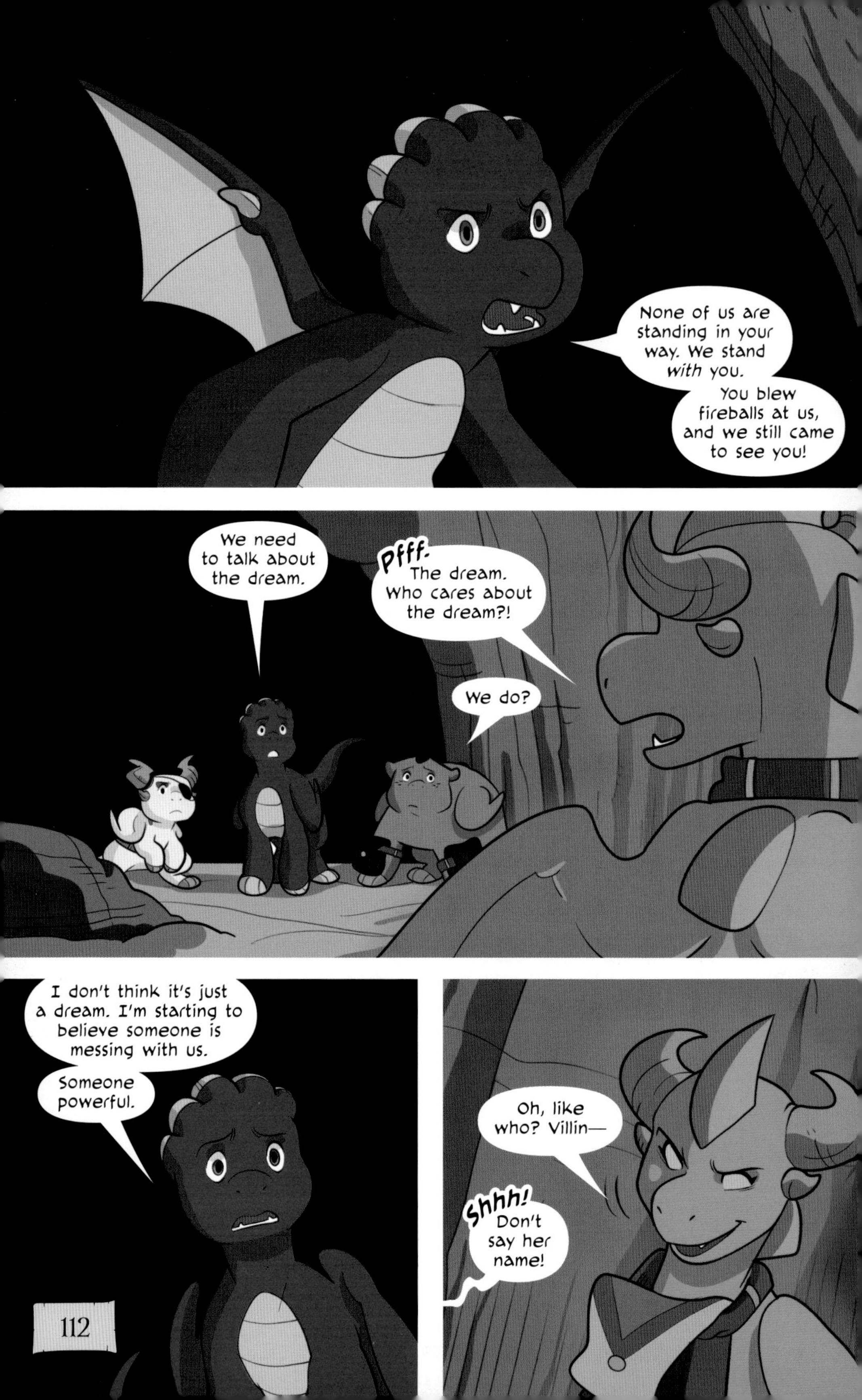
None of us are standing in your way. We stand *with* you.
You blew fireballs at us, and we still came to see you!
We need to talk about the dream.
Pfff. The dream. Who cares about the dream?!
We do?
I don't think it's just a dream. I'm starting to believe someone is messing with us.
Someone powerful.
Oh, like who? Villin—
Shhh! Don't say her name!

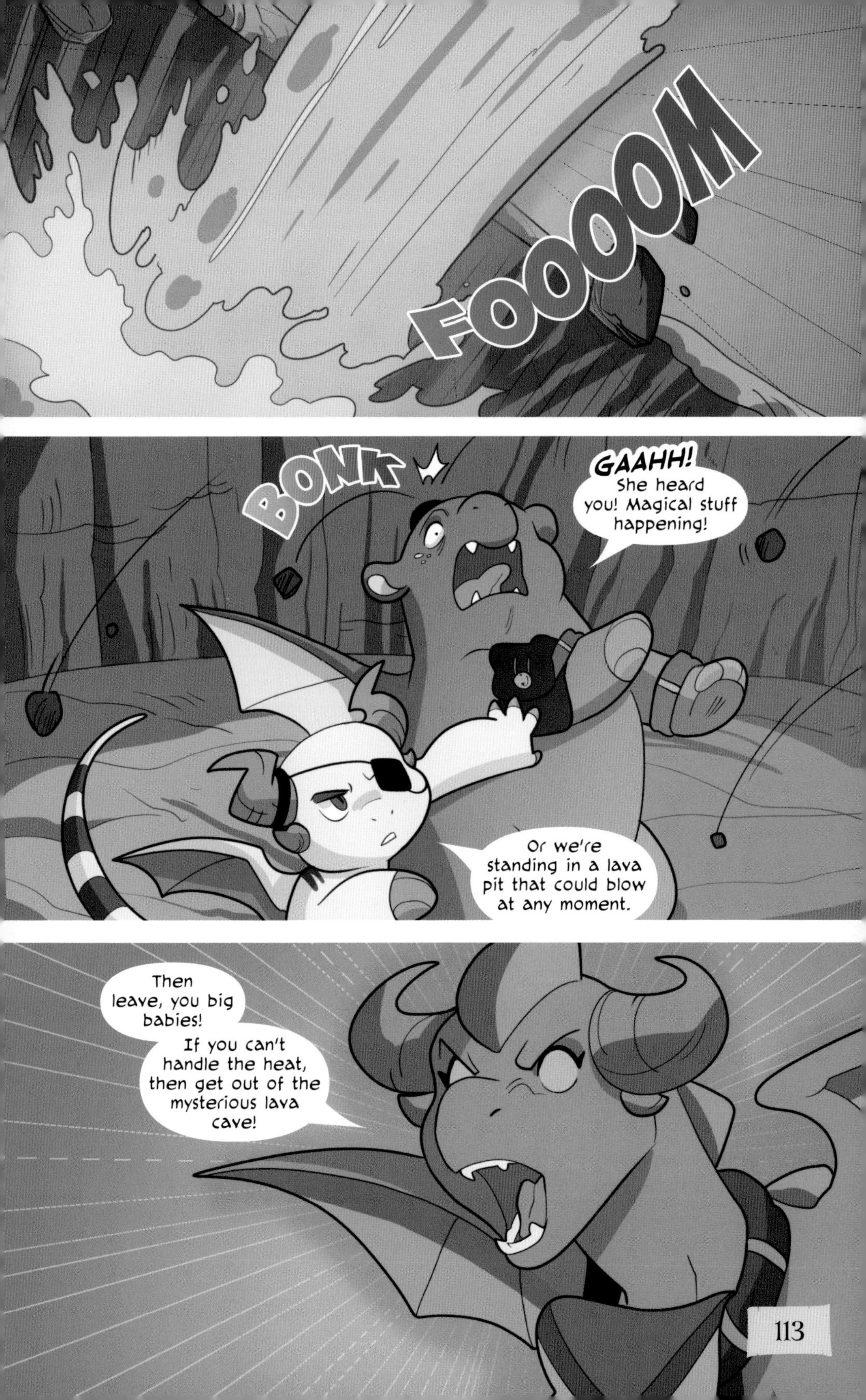
FOOOOOM
BONK
GAAHH!
She heard you! Magical stuff happening!
Or we're standing in a lava pit that could blow at any moment.
Then leave, you big babies!
If you can't handle the heat, then get out of the mysterious lava cave!

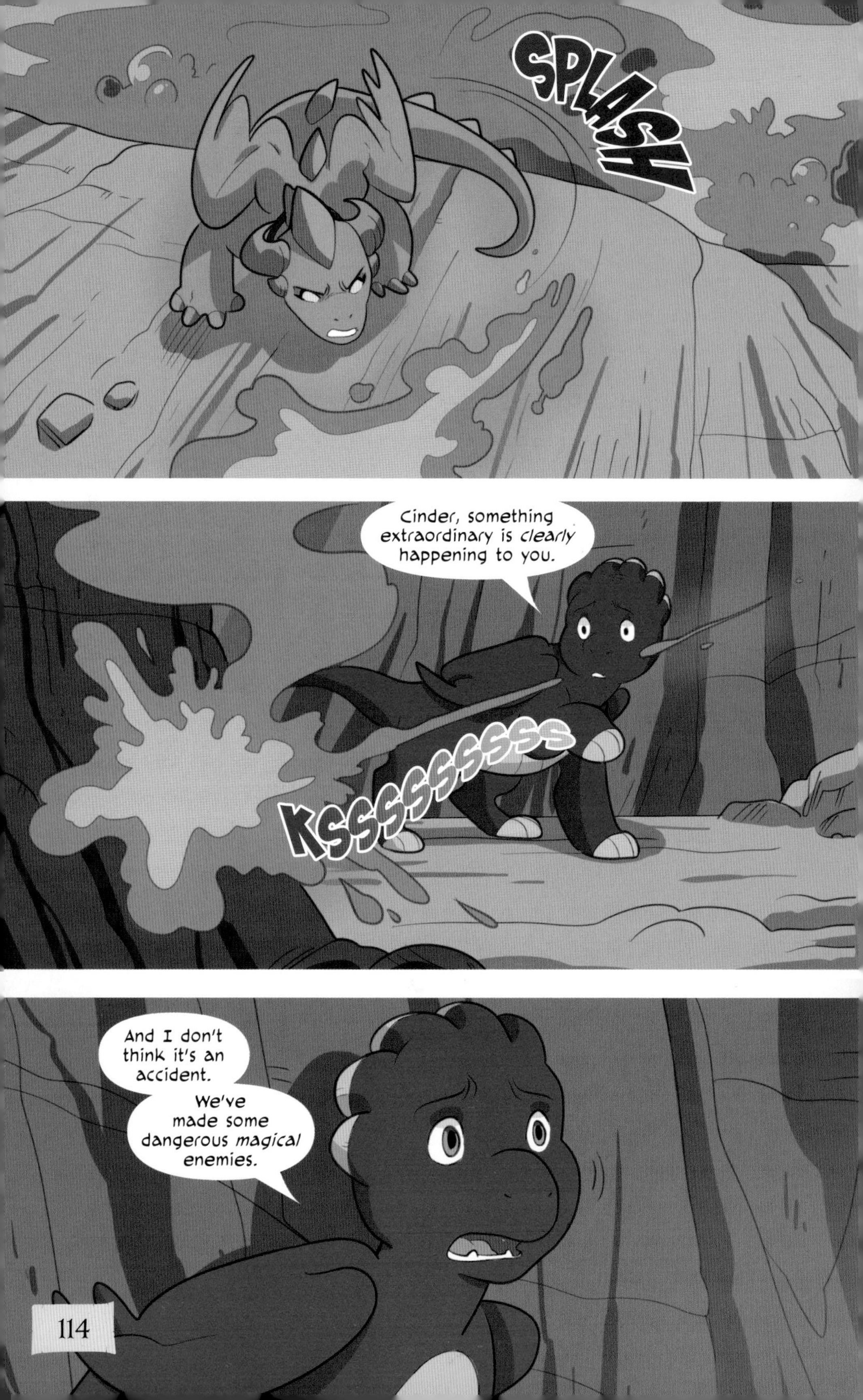
SPLASH
Cinder, something extraordinary is *clearly* happening to you.
KSSSSSSSSSS
And I don't think it's an accident.
We've made some dangerous *magical* enemies.

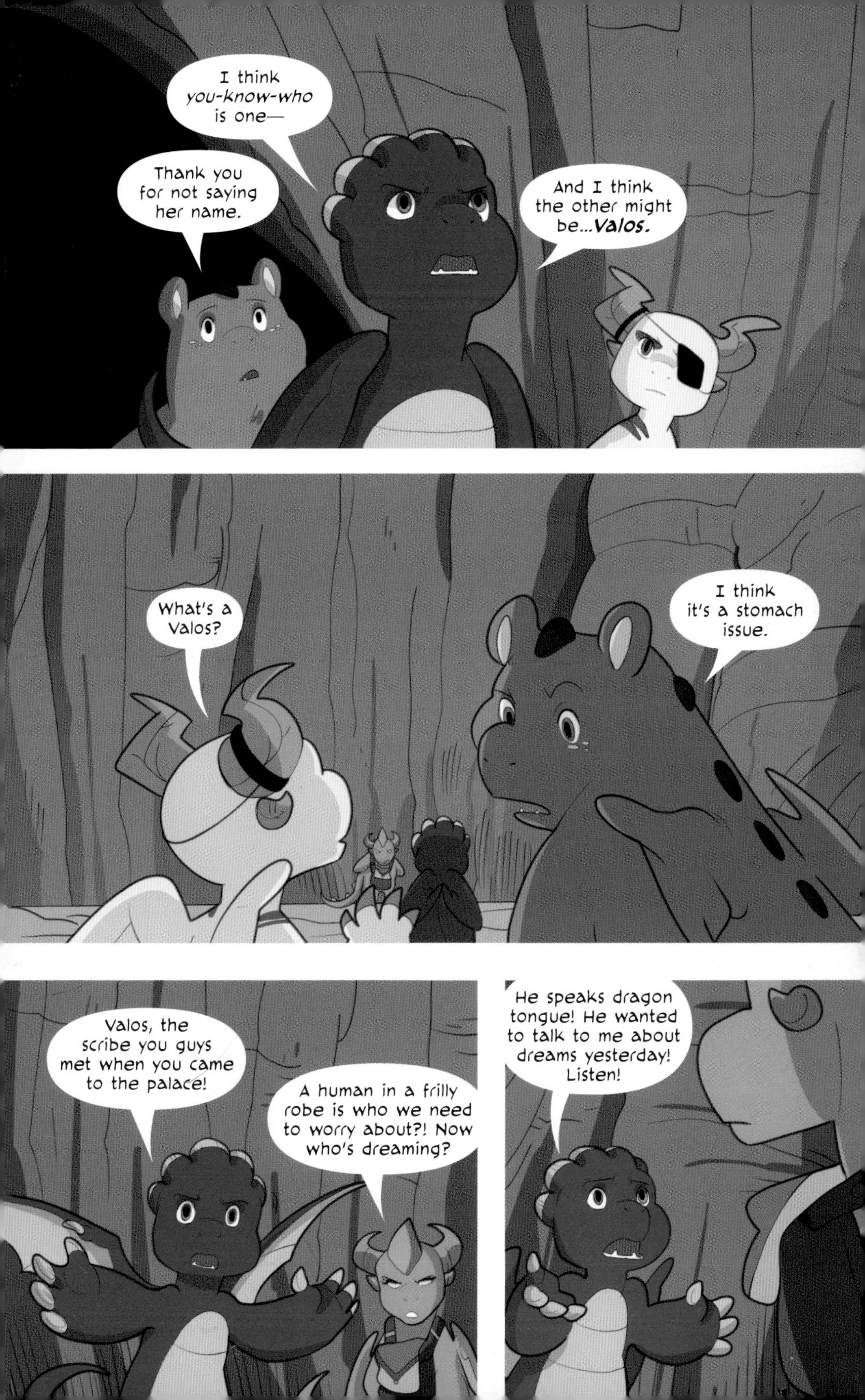
Thank you for not saying her name.
I think *you-know-who* is one—
And I think the other might be...**Valos.**
What's a Valos?
I think it's a stomach issue.
Valos, the scribe you guys met when you came to the palace!
A human in a frilly robe is who we need to worry about?! Now who's dreaming?
He speaks dragon tongue! He wanted to talk to me about dreams yesterday! Listen!

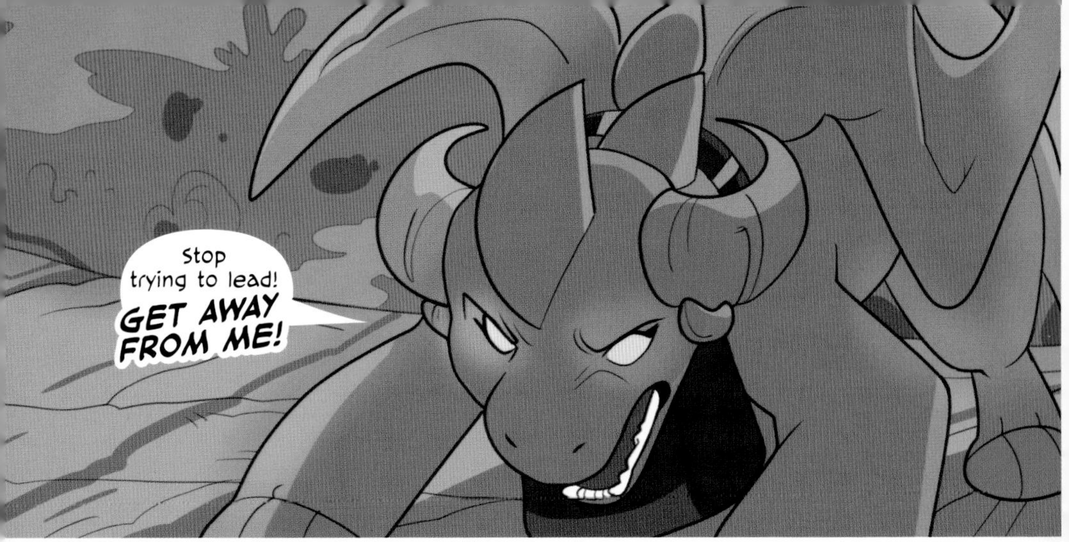
Stop trying to lead! GET AWAY FROM ME!

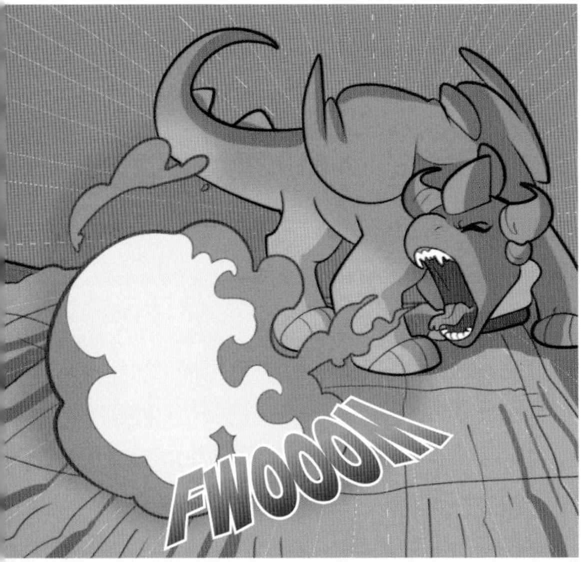
FWOOOM

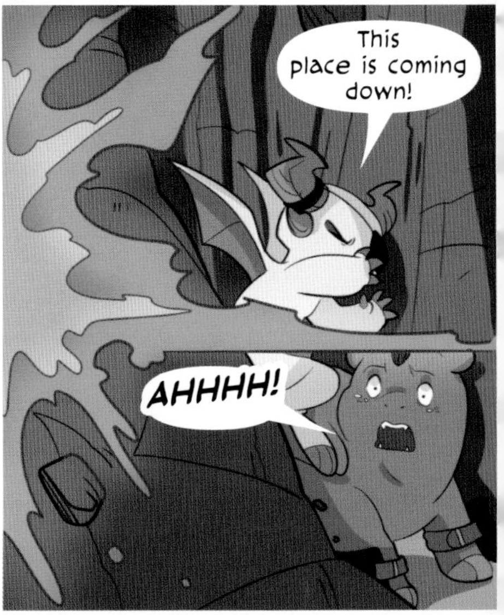
This place is coming down!
AHHHH!

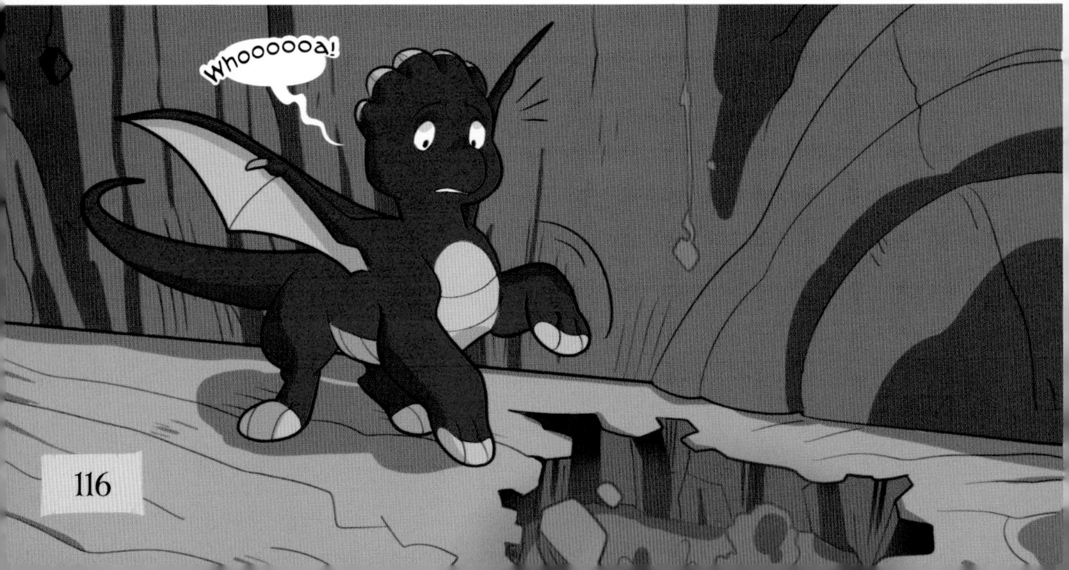
Whoooooa!

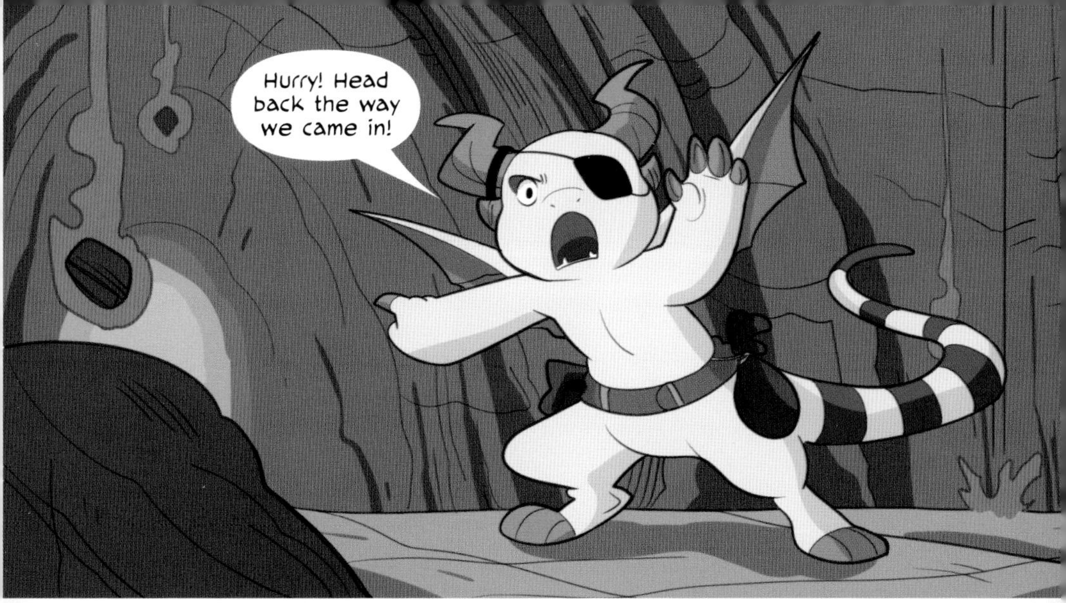
Hurry! Head back the way we came in!

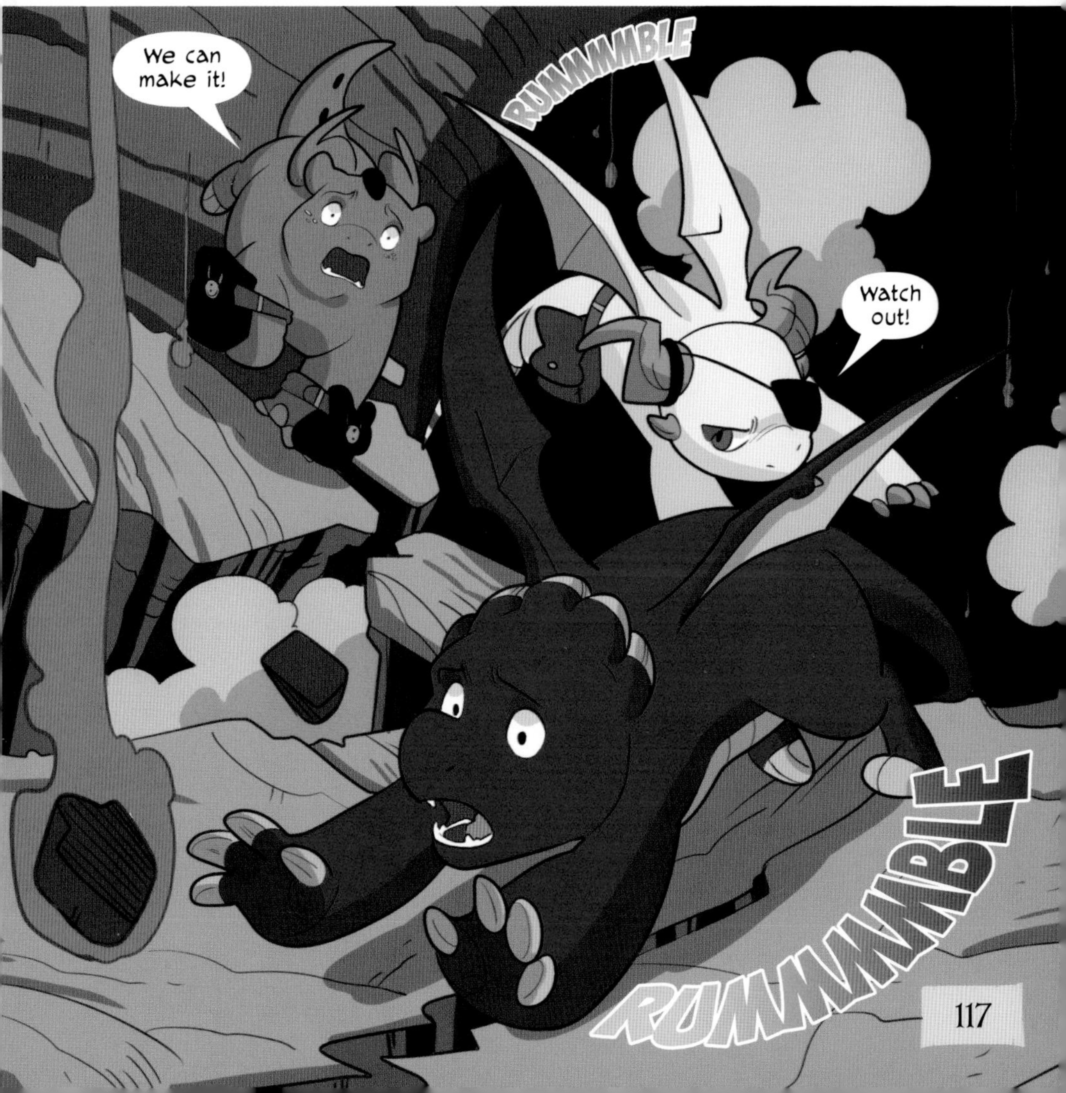
We can make it!
RUMMMMBLE
Watch out!
RUMMMMBLE

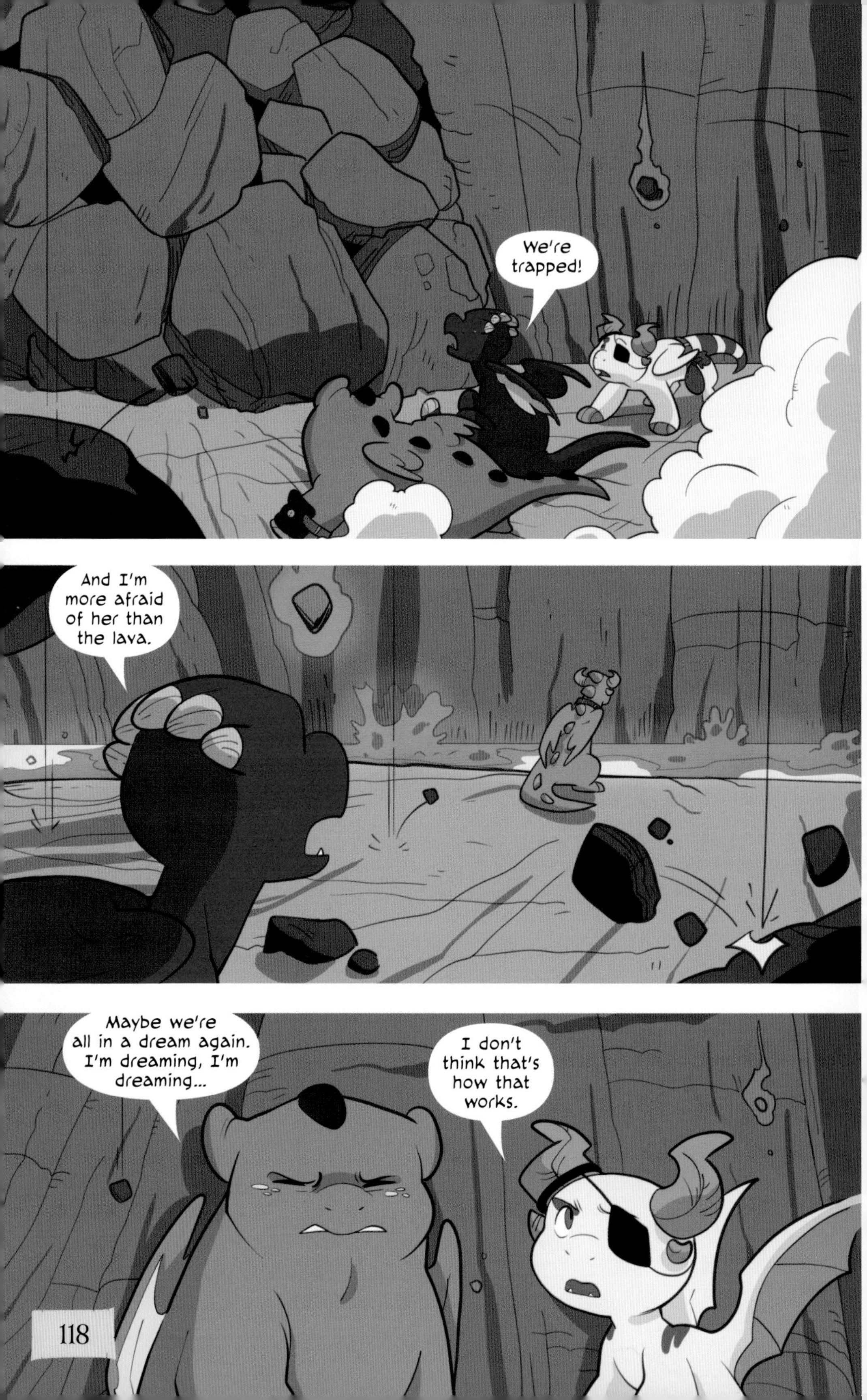
We're trapped!
And I'm more afraid of her than the lava.
Maybe we're all in a dream again. I'm dreaming, I'm dreaming...
I don't think that's how that works.

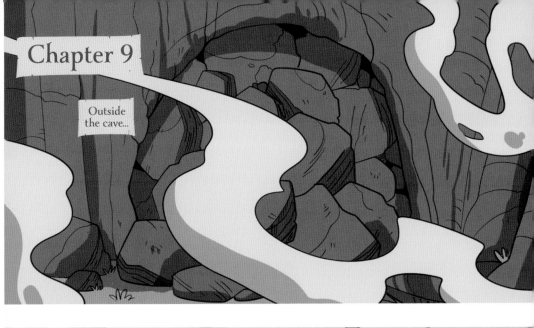

Chapter 9

Outside the cave...

...another fire was forming.

Come now.

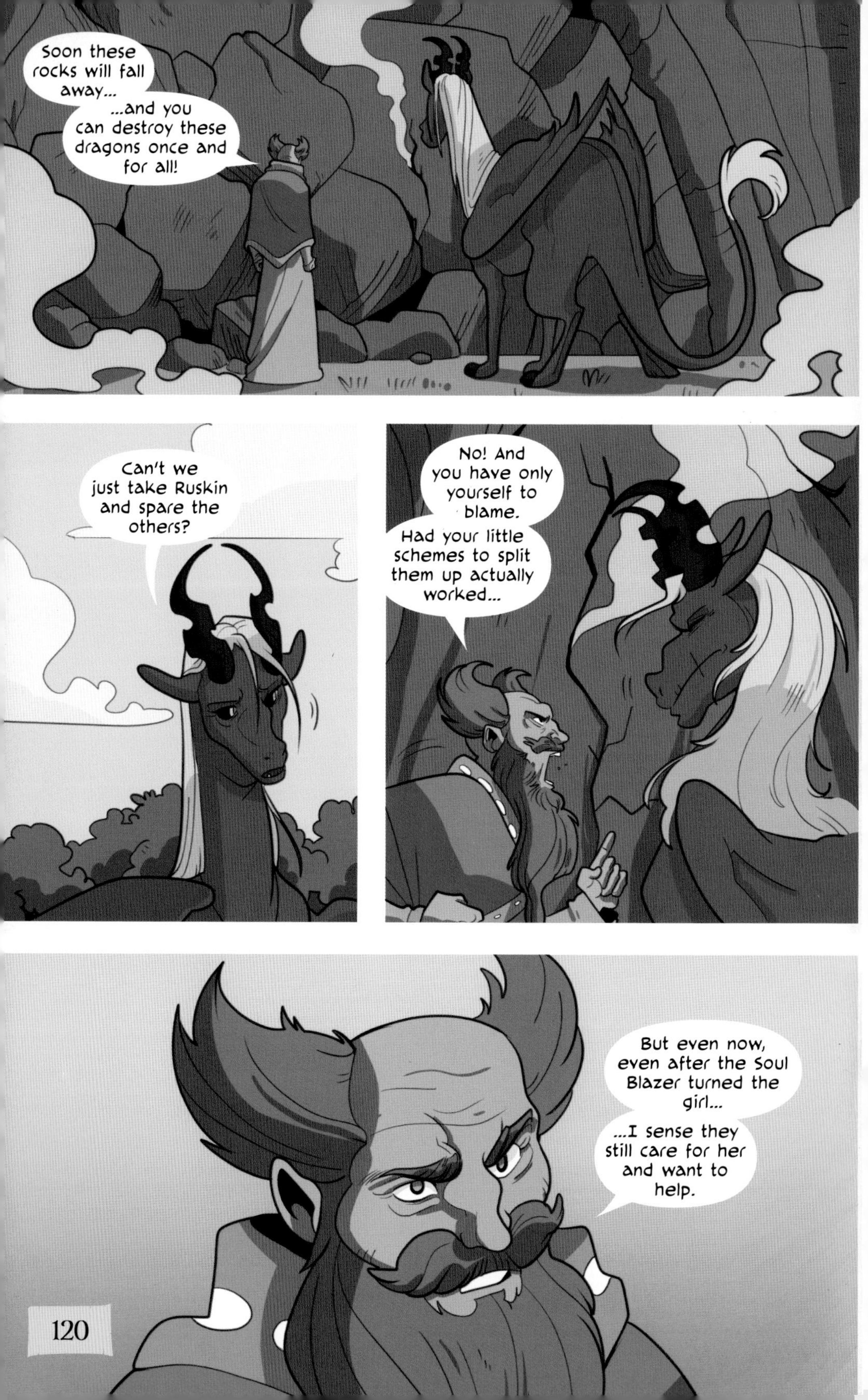
Soon these rocks will fall away...
...and you can destroy these dragons once and for all!
Can't we just take Ruskin and spare the others?
No! And you have only yourself to blame.
Had your little schemes to split them up actually worked...
But even now, even after the Soul Blazer turned the girl...
...I sense they still care for her and want to help.

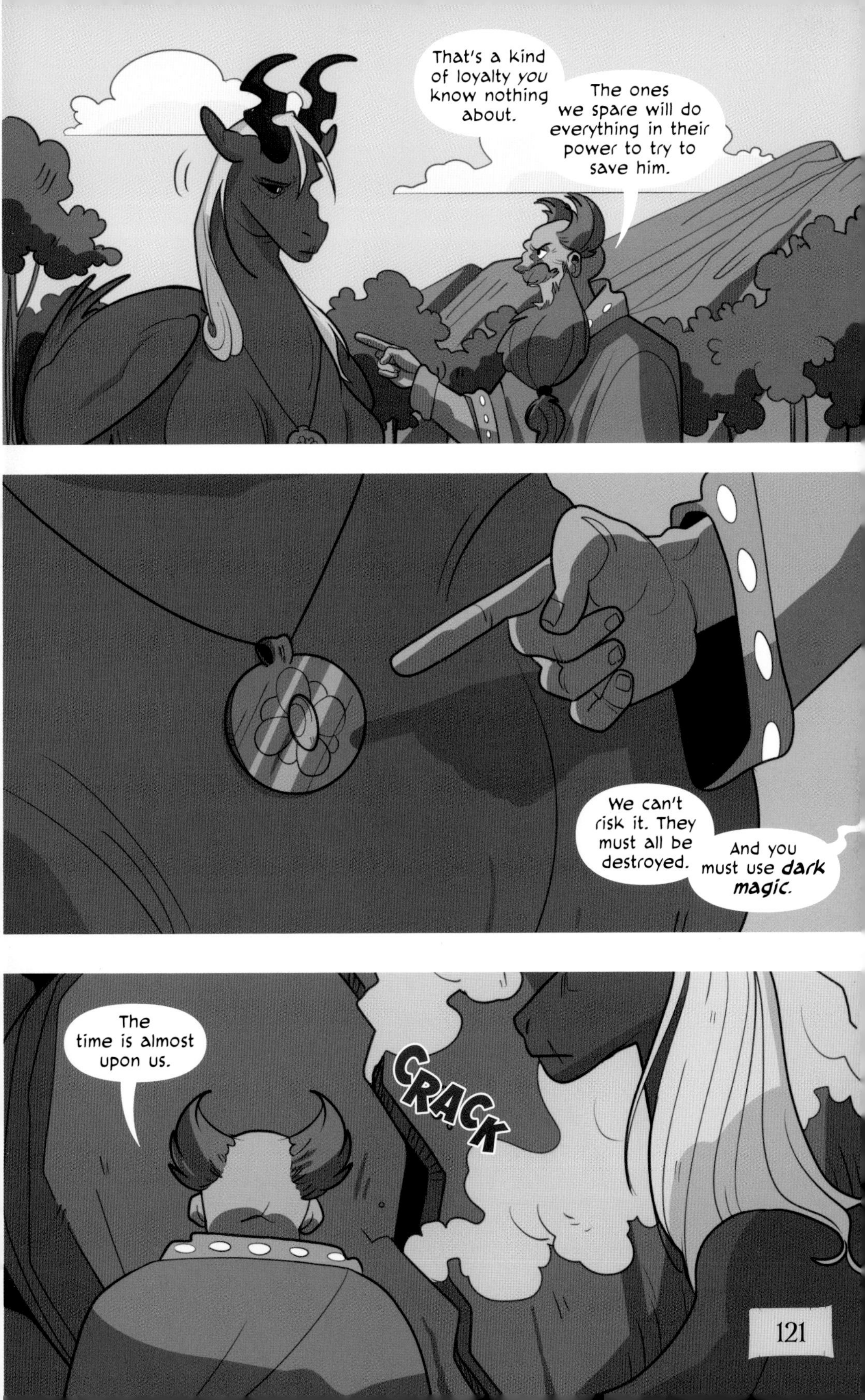
That's a kind of loyalty *you* know nothing about.
The ones we spare will do everything in their power to try to save him.
We can't risk it. They must all be destroyed.
And you must use **dark magic**.
The time is almost upon us.
CRACK

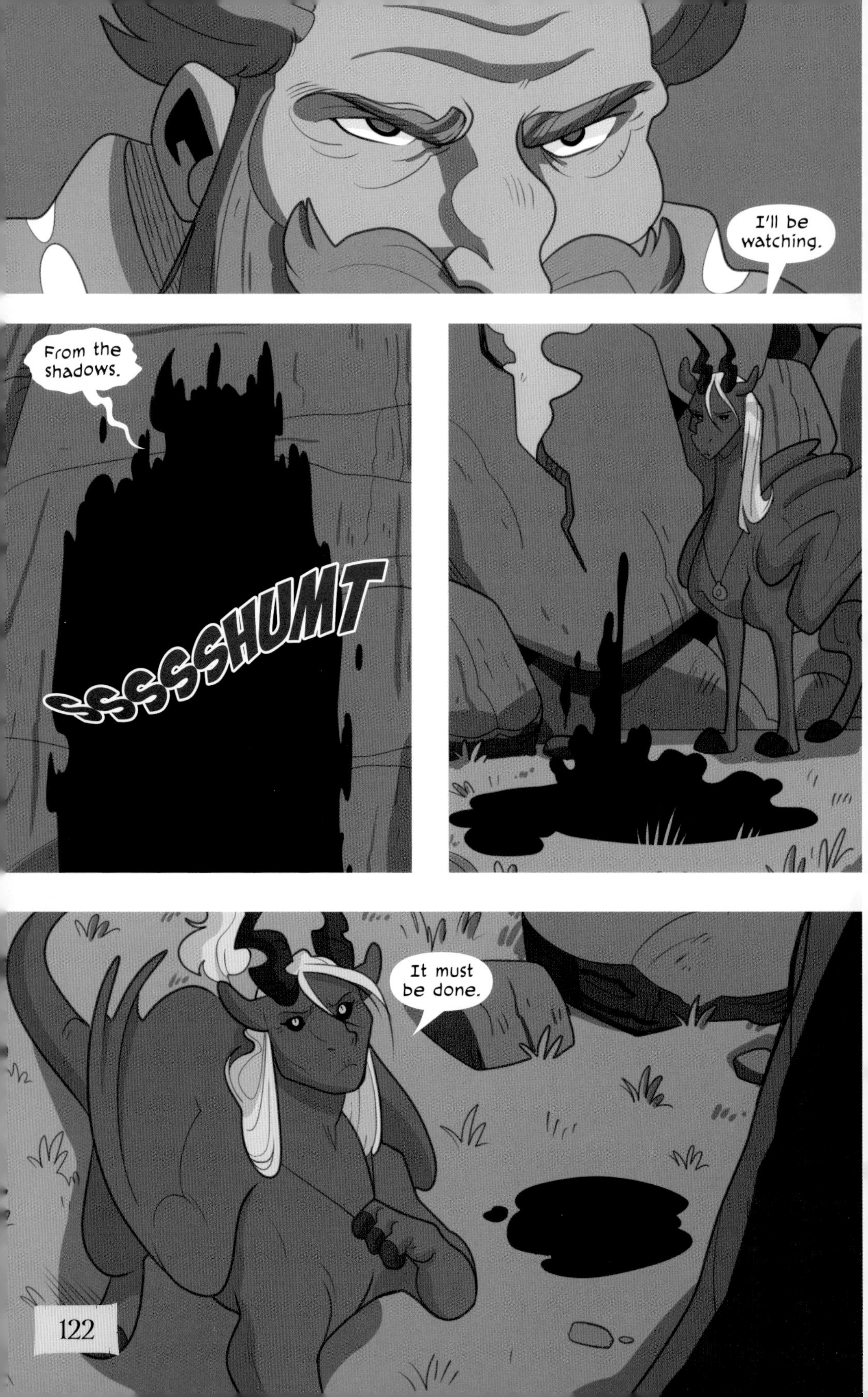
I'll be watching.
From the shadows.
SSSSSHUMT
It must be done.

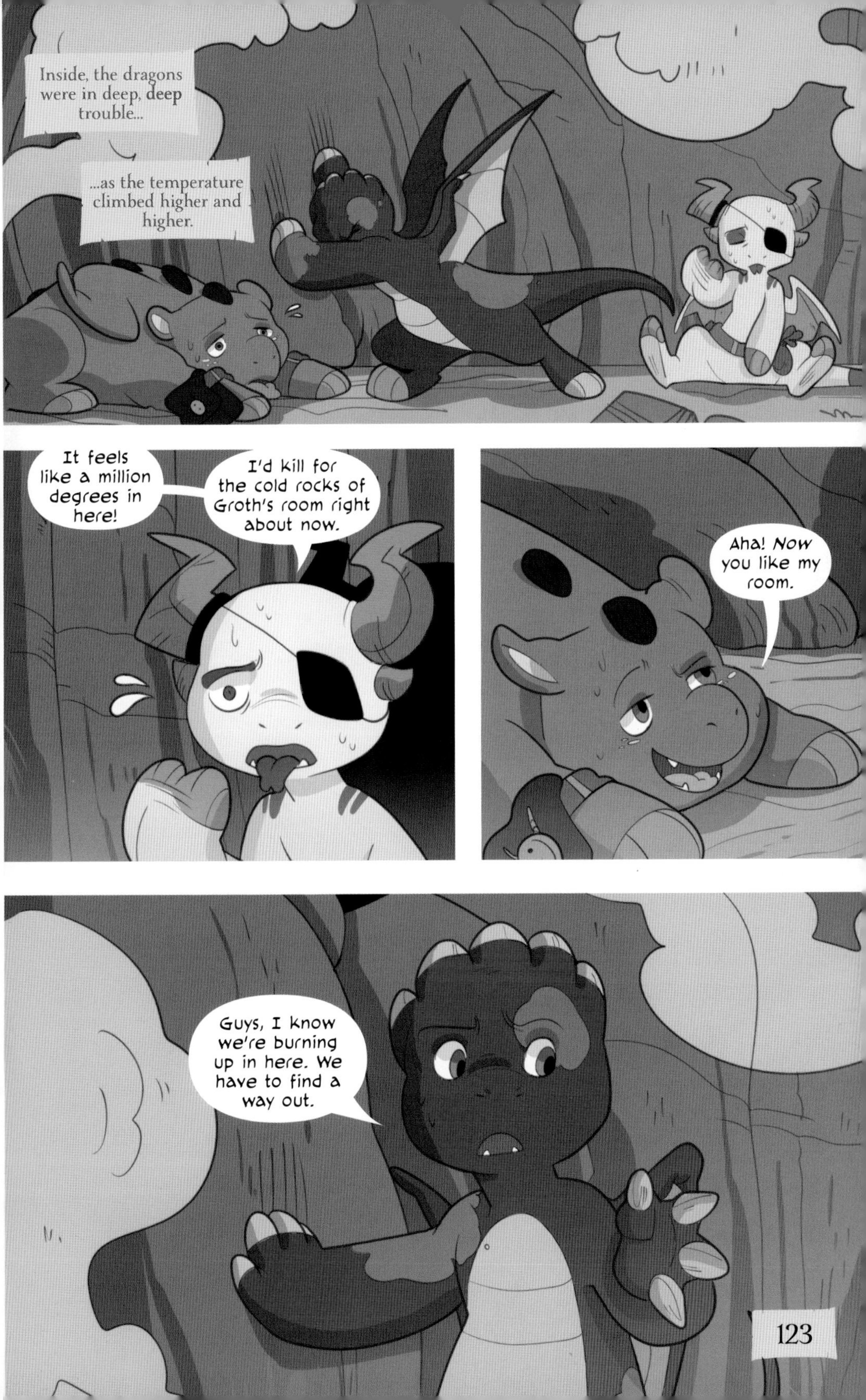
Inside, the dragons were in deep, **deep** trouble...
...as the temperature climbed higher and higher.
It feels like a million degrees in here!
I'd kill for the cold rocks of Groth's room right about now.
Aha! *Now* you like my room.
Guys, I know we're burning up in here. We have to find a way out.

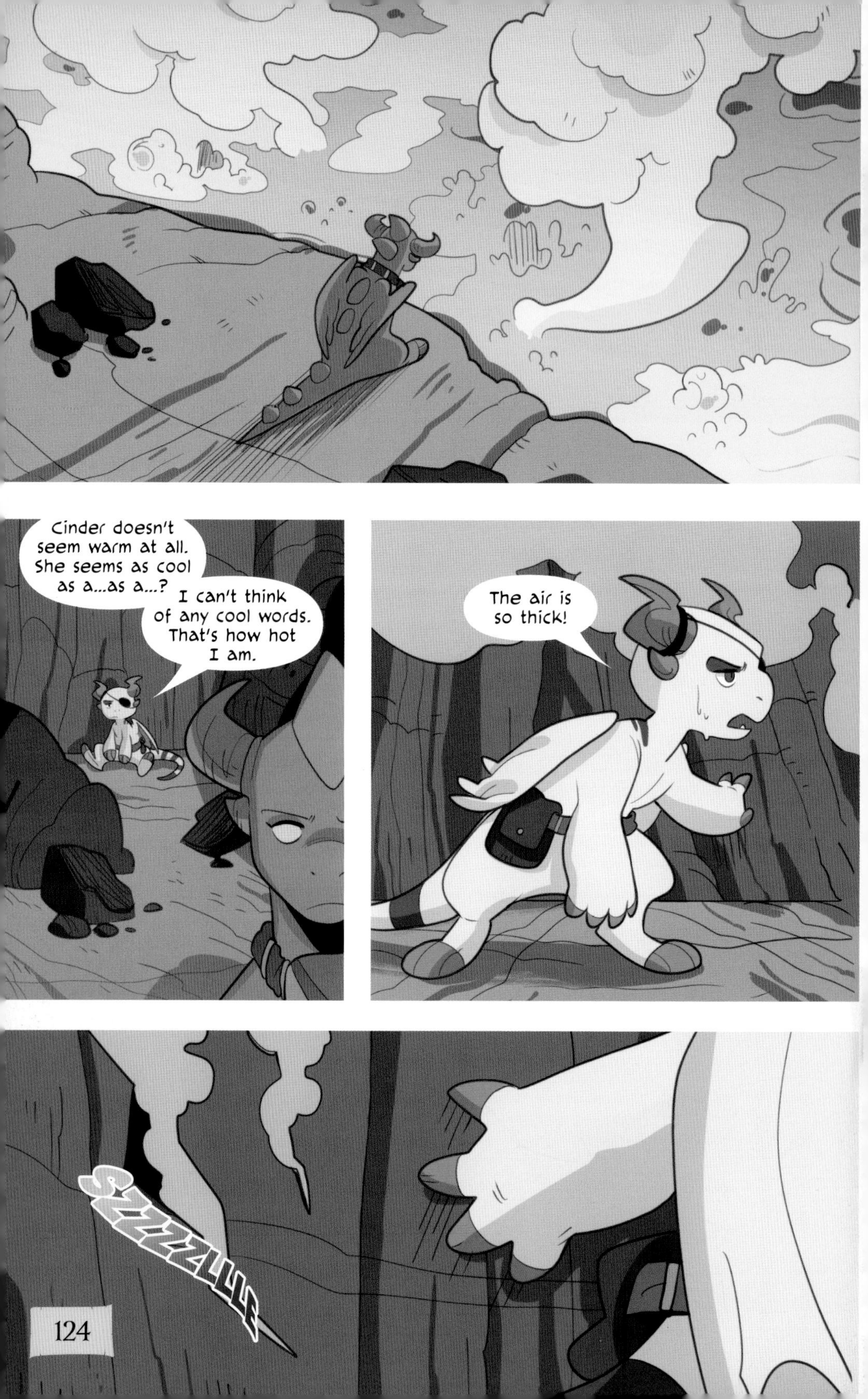

Cinder doesn't seem warm at all. She seems as cool as a...as a...?
I can't think of any cool words. That's how hot I am.
The air is so thick!
SZZZZLLE

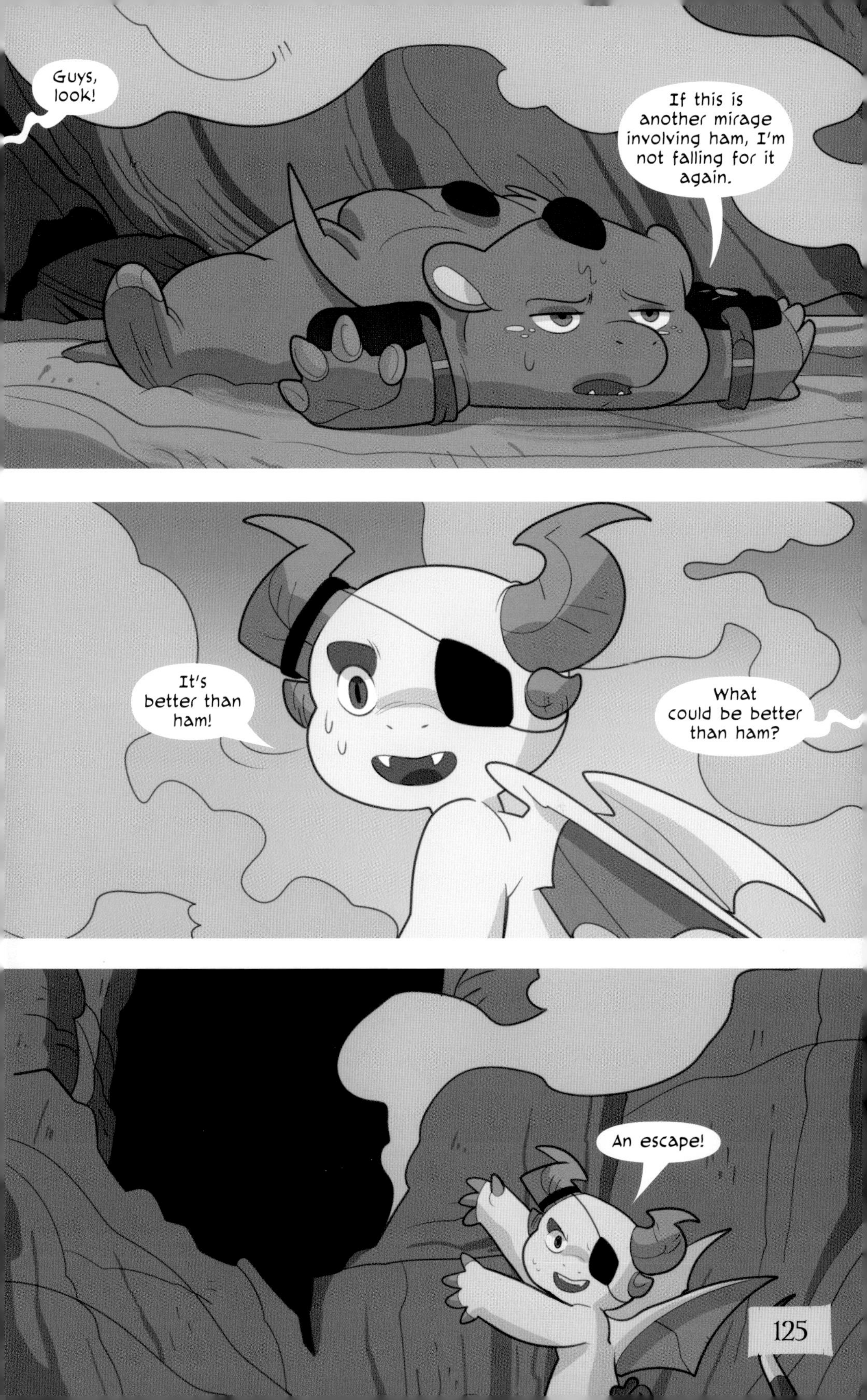
Guys, look!
If this is another mirage involving ham, I'm not falling for it again.
It's better than ham!
What could be better than ham?
An escape!

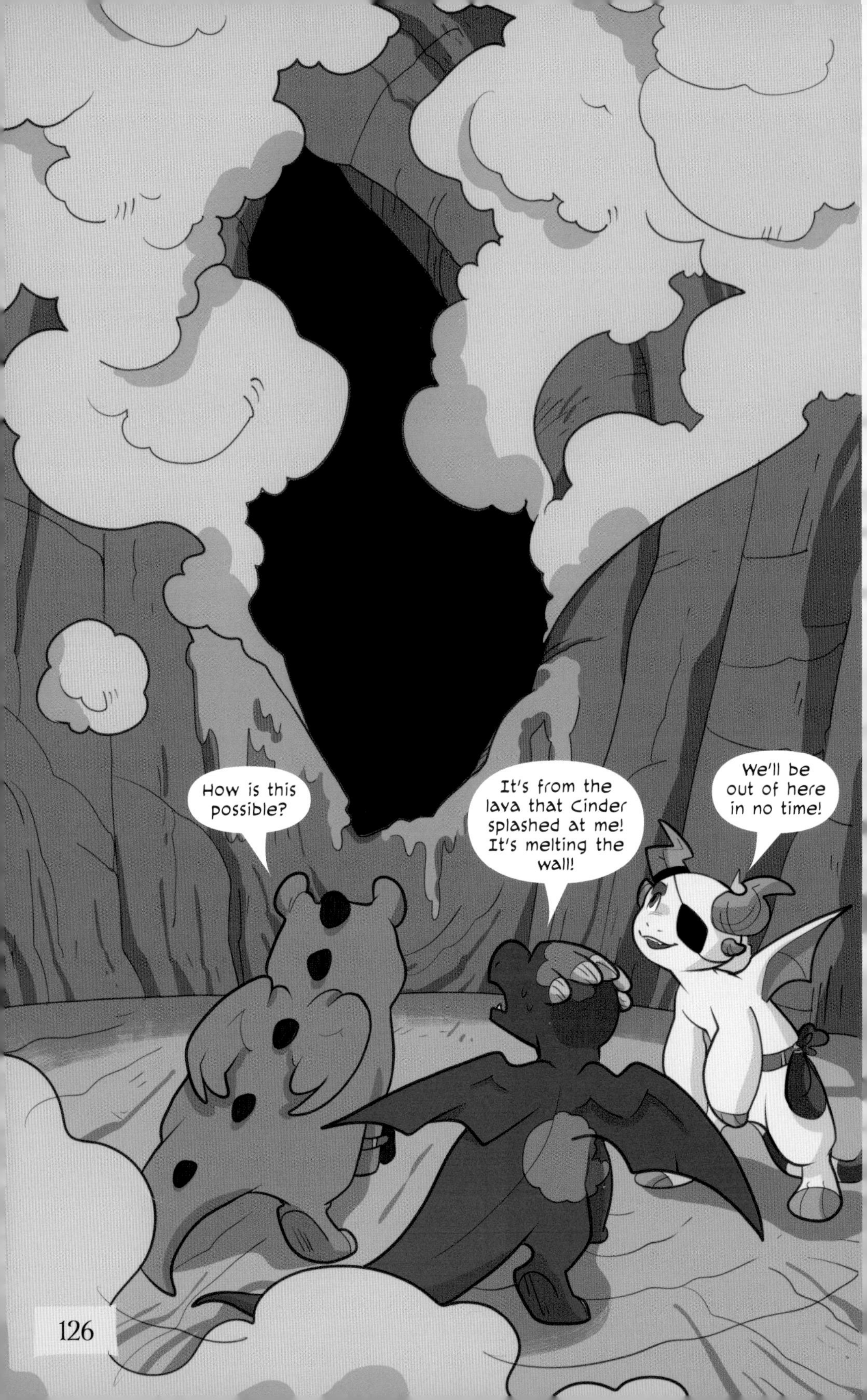
How is this possible?
It's from the lava that Cinder splashed at me! It's melting the wall!
We'll be out of here in no time!

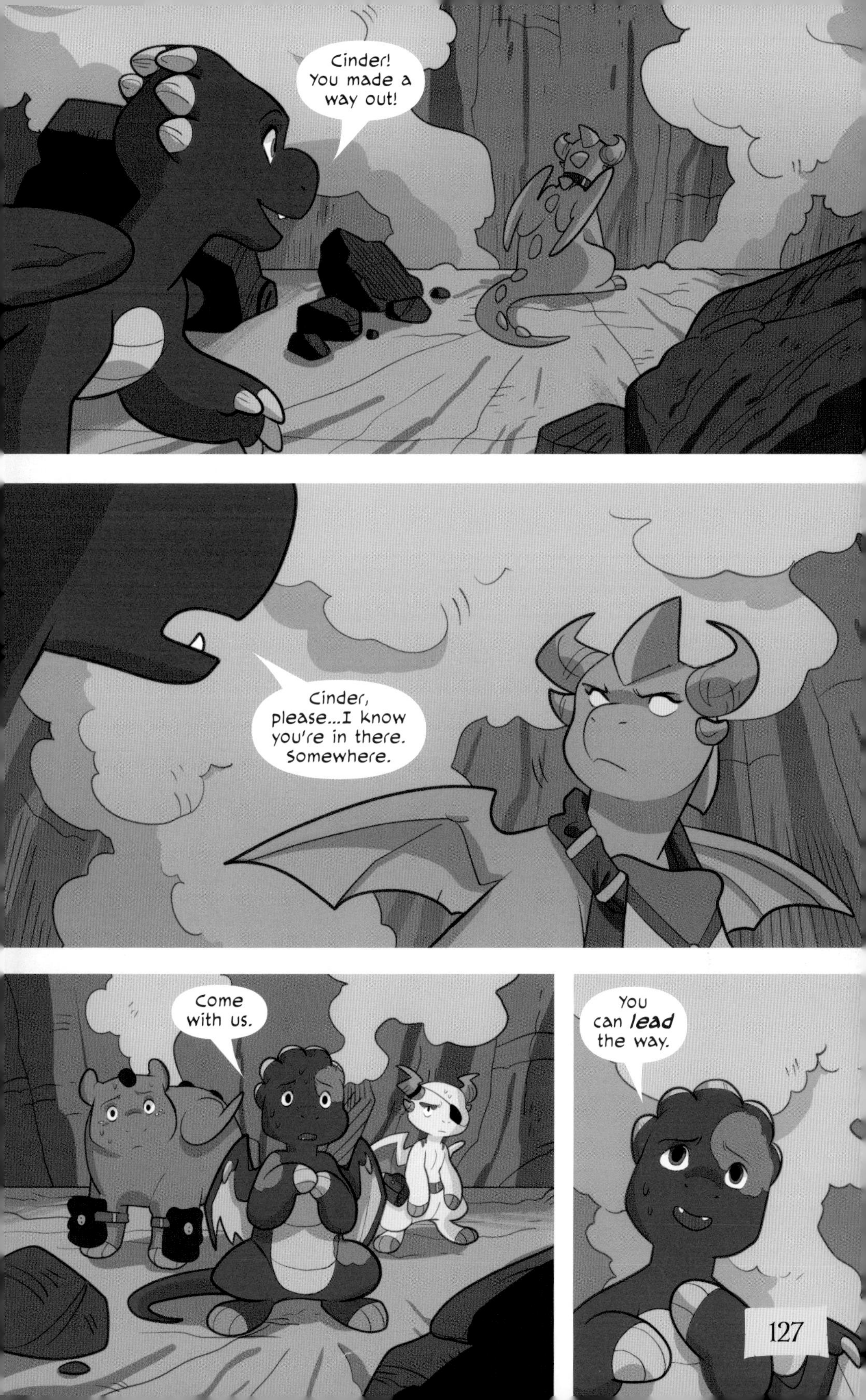
Cinder! You made a way out!
Cinder, please...I know you're in there. Somewhere.
Come with us.
You can *lead* the way.

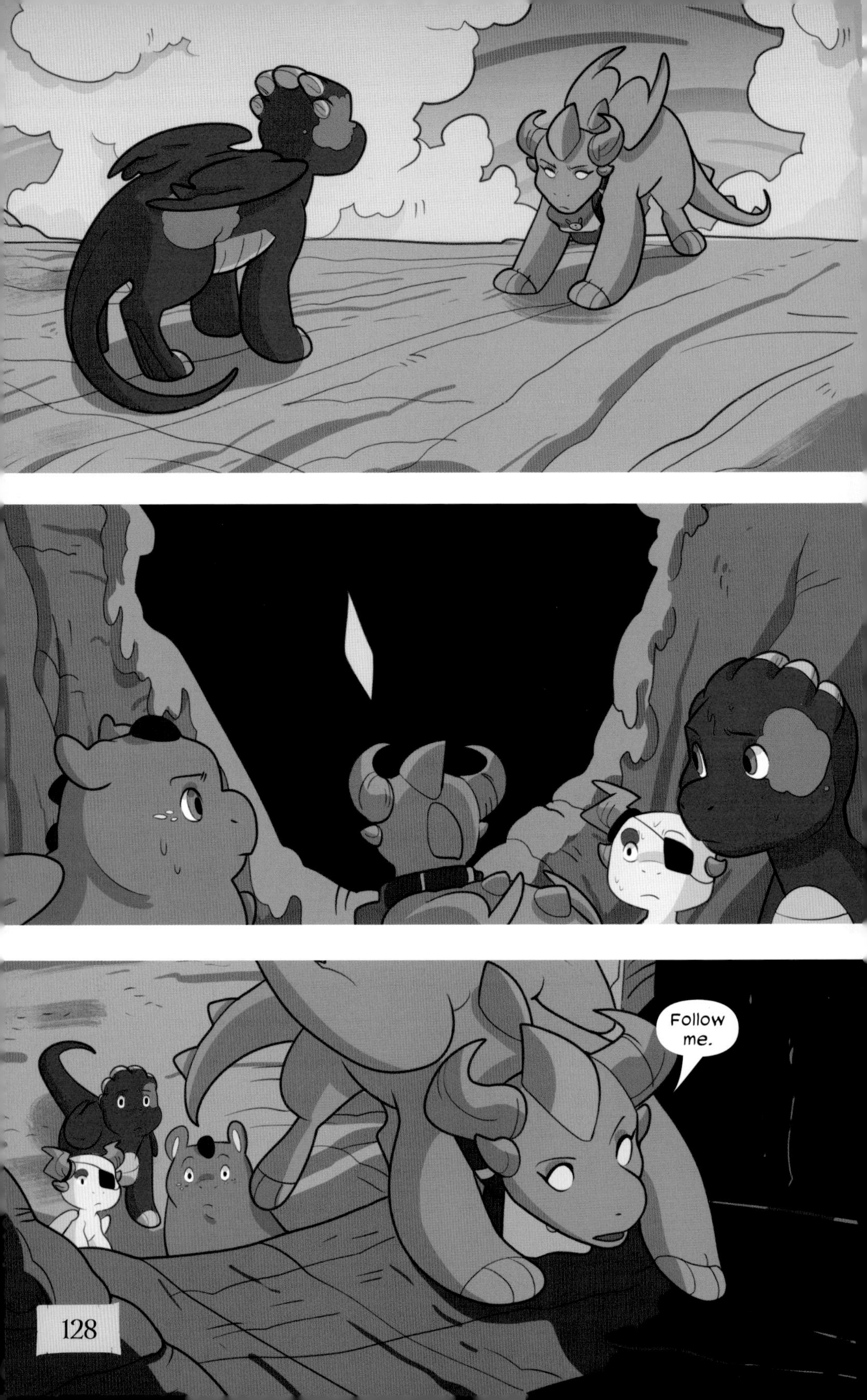
Follow me.

Chapter 10

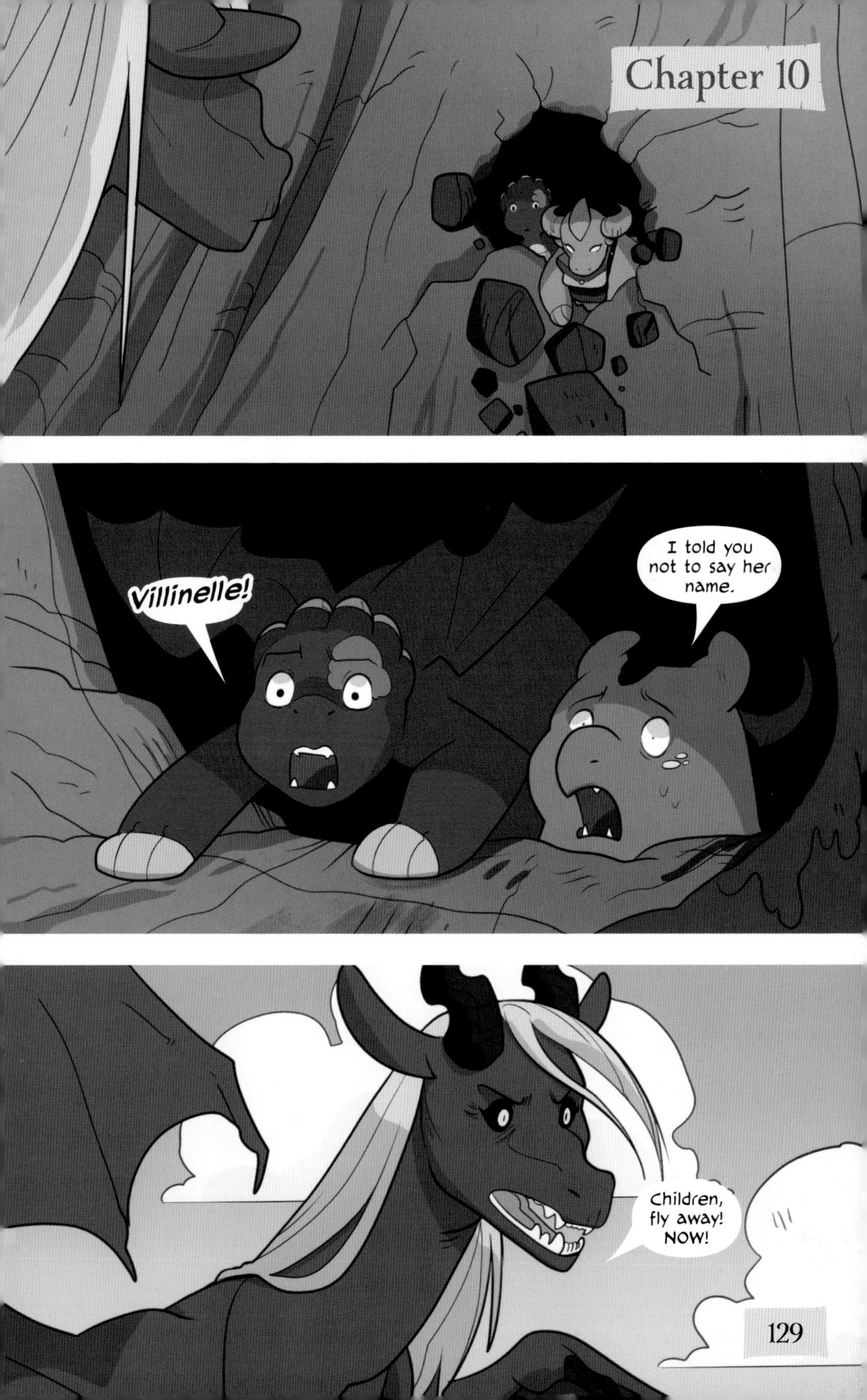
Villinelle!
I told you not to say her name.
Children, fly away! NOW!

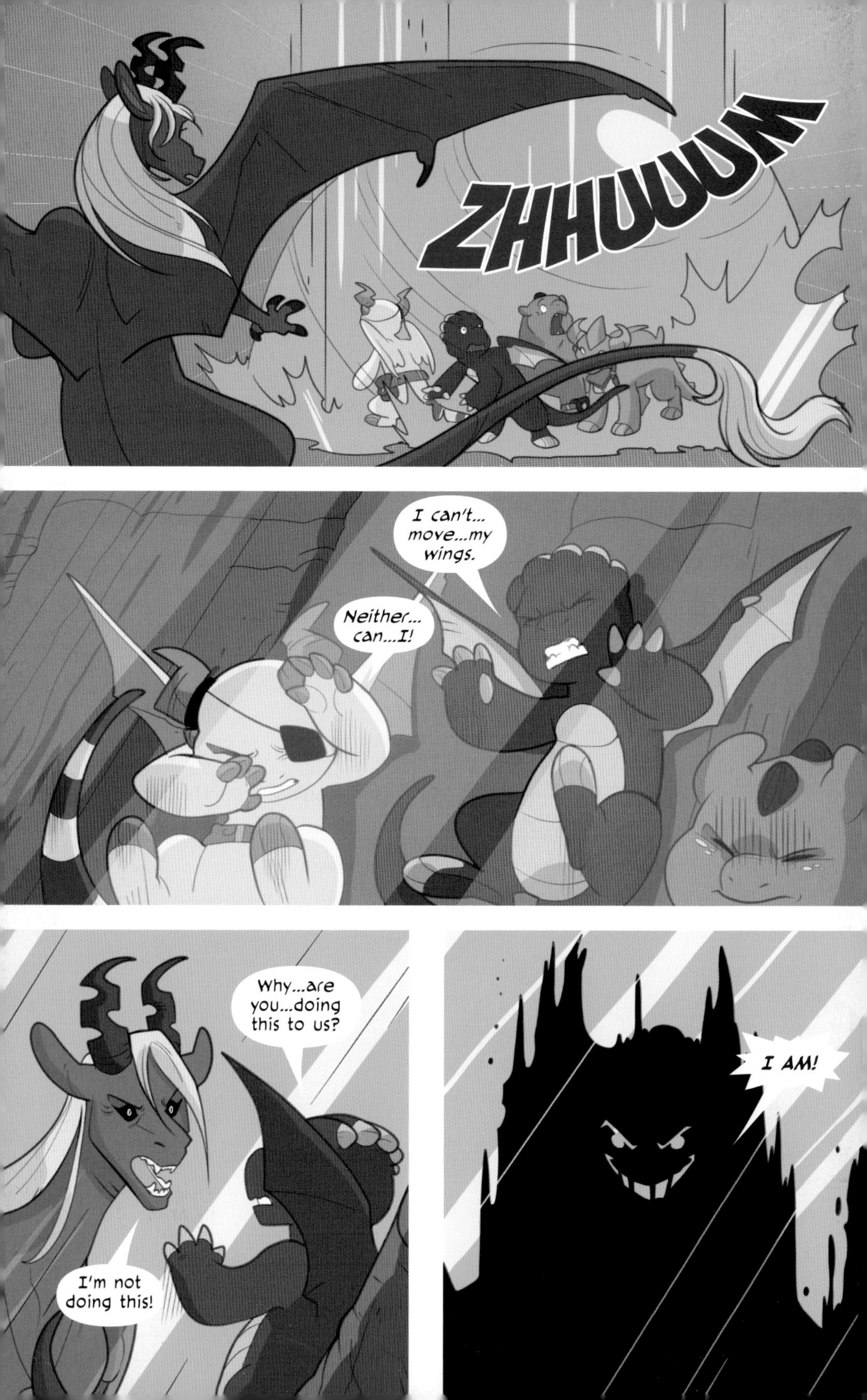
ZHHUUUM
I can't... move...my wings.
Neither... can...I!
Why...are you...doing this to us?
I'm not doing this!
I AM!

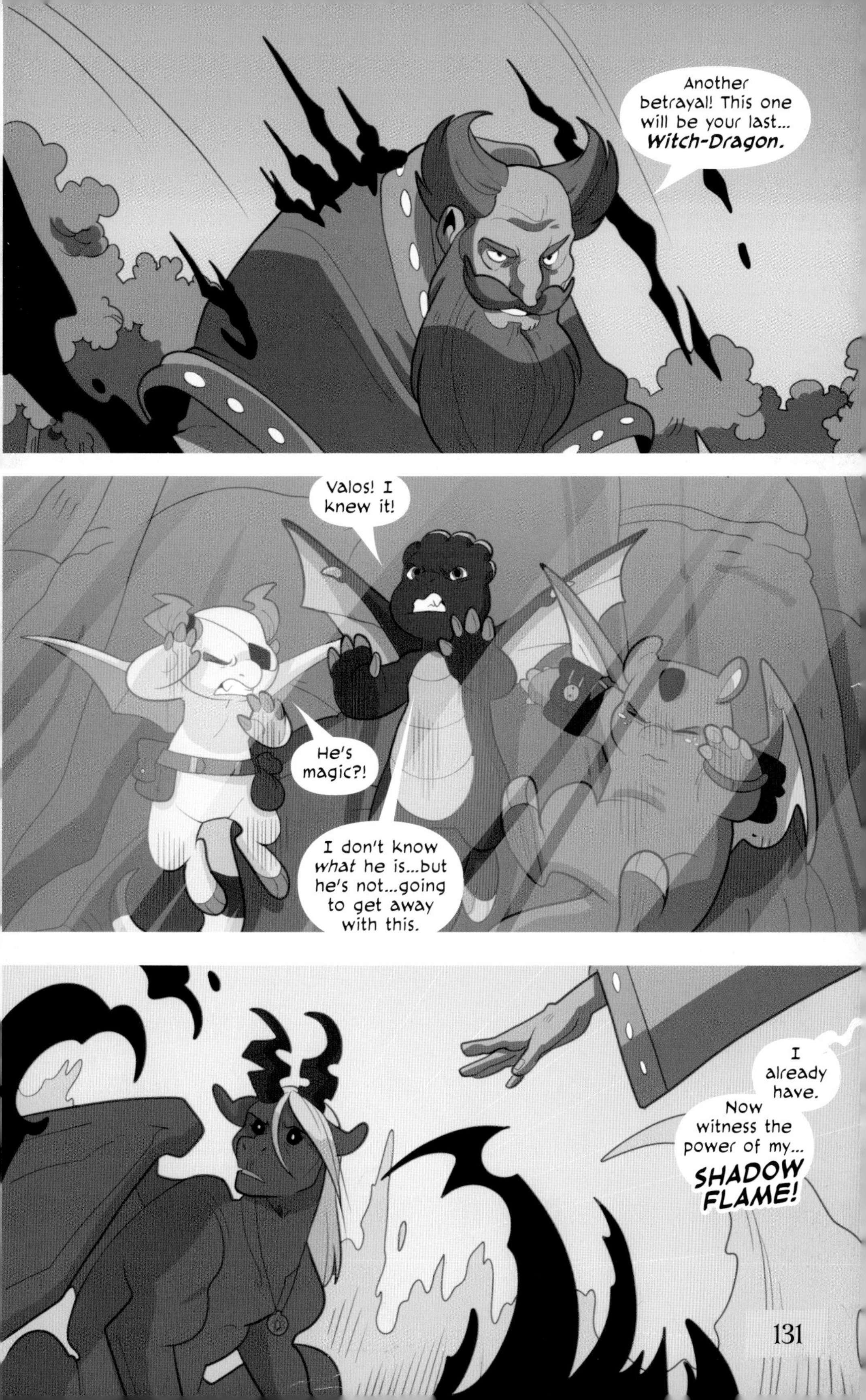
Another betrayal! This one will be your last... *Witch-Dragon.*
Valos! I knew it!
He's magic?!
I don't know *what* he is...but he's not...going to get away with this.
I already have.
Now witness the power of my... **SHADOW FLAME!**

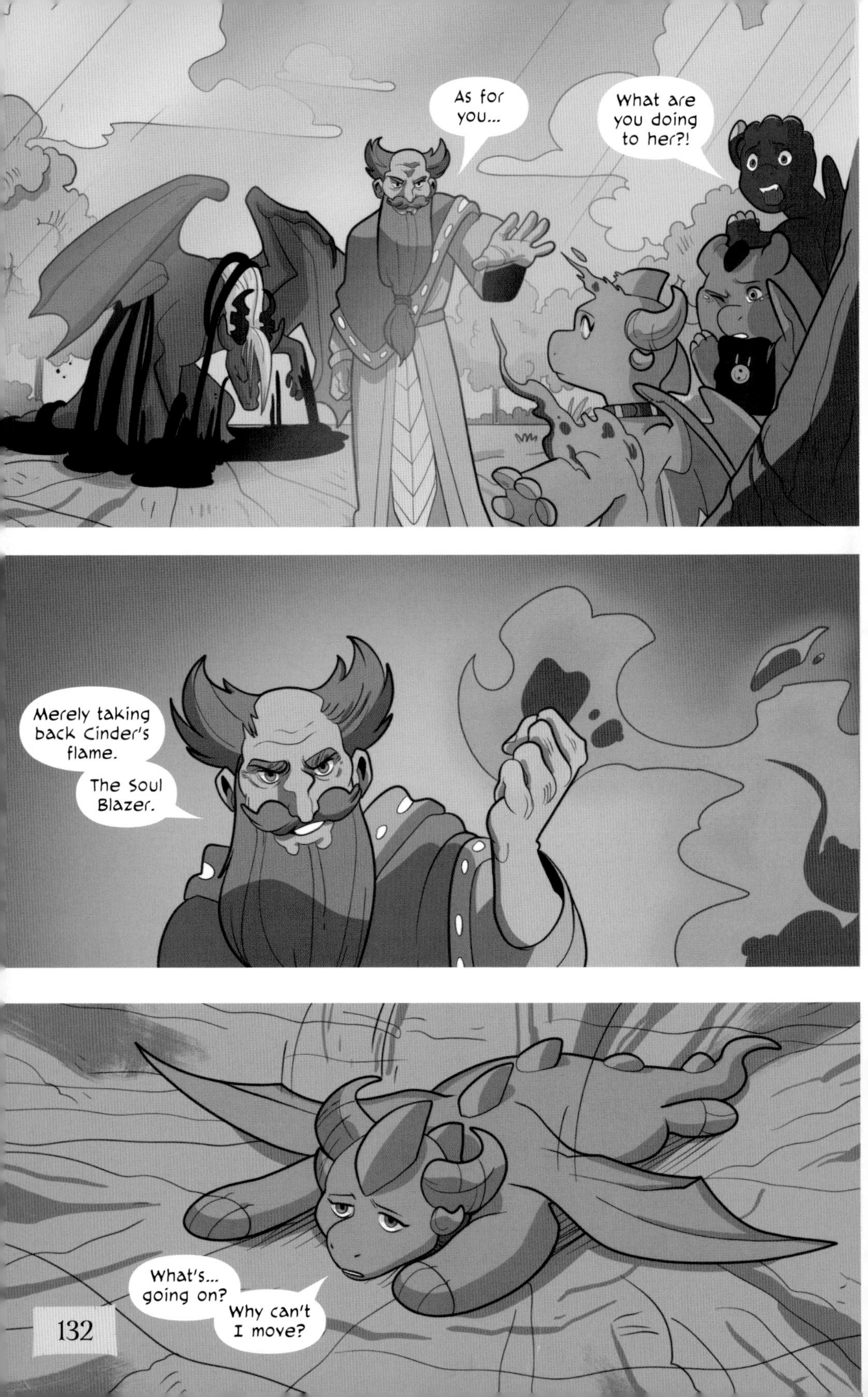
As for you...
What are you doing to her?!
Merely taking back Cinder's flame.
The Soul Blazer.
What's... going on?
Why can't I move?

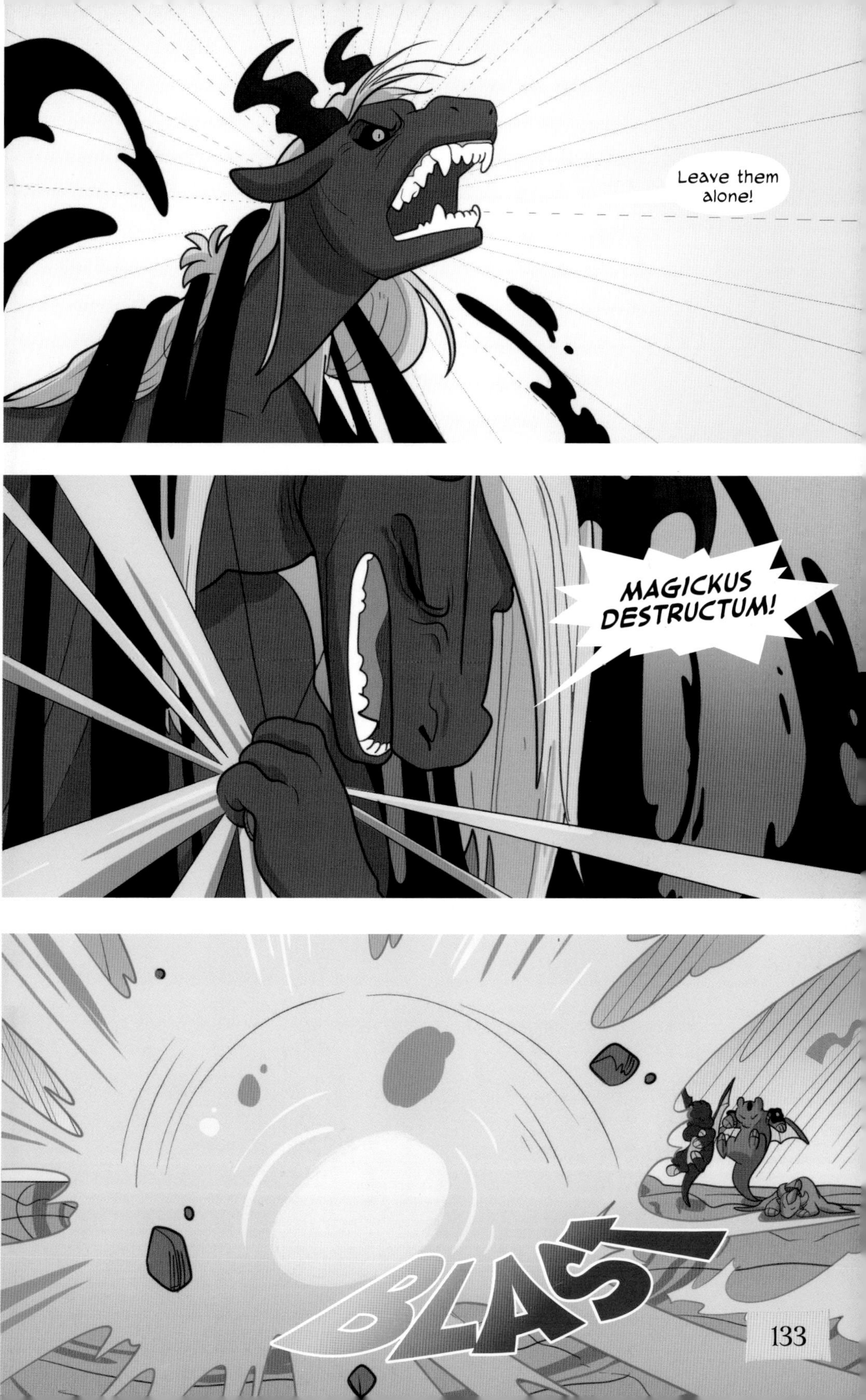
Leave them alone!
MAGICKUS DESTRUCTUM!
BLAST

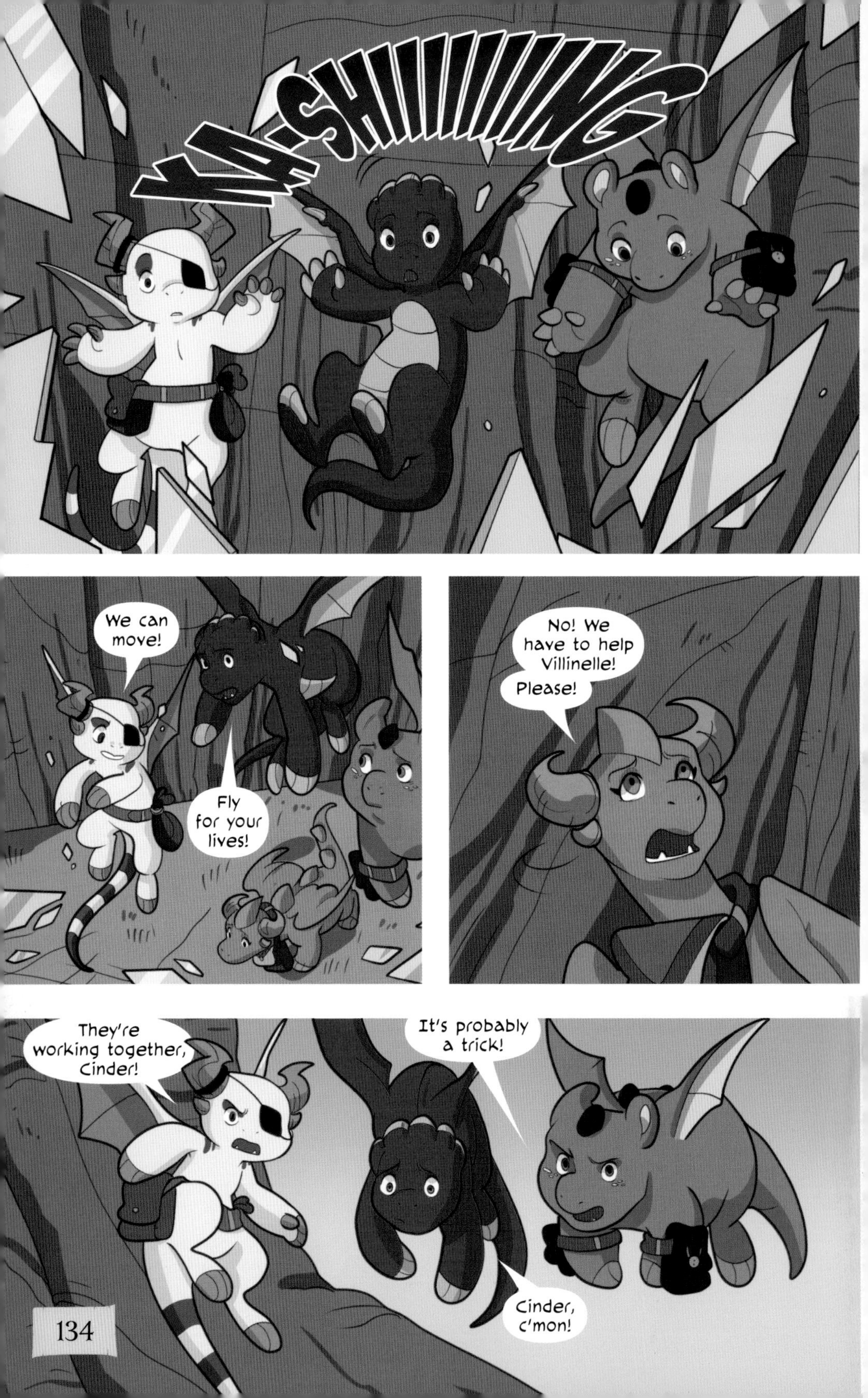
KA-SHIIIIIIING
We can move!
Fly for your lives!
No! We have to help Villinelle!
Please!
They're working together, Cinder!
It's probably a trick!
Cinder, c'mon!

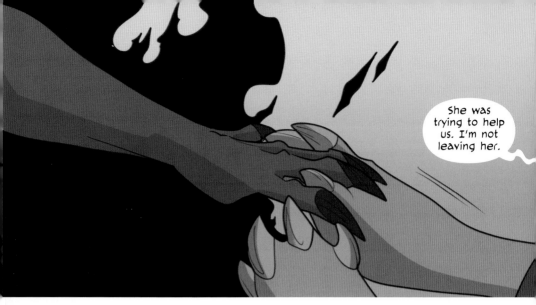

She was trying to help us. I'm not leaving her.

What do I do?

It's too late, child.

There has to be a way! Please!

I'm so sorry, Cinder. I'm sorry for everything I've put you through.

Everything I've put you all through.

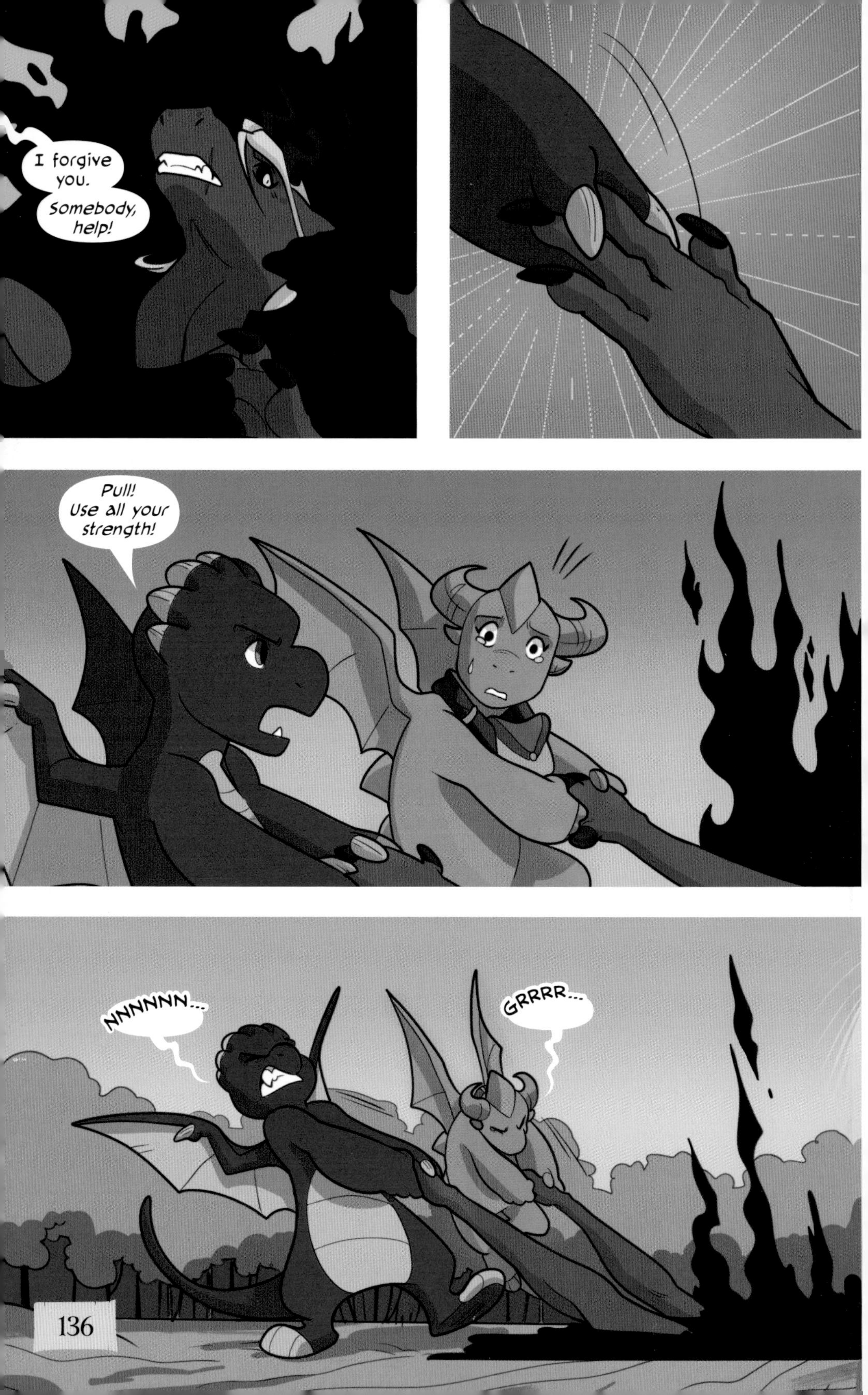
I forgive you.
Somebody, help!
Pull! Use all your strength!
NNNNNN...
GRRRR...

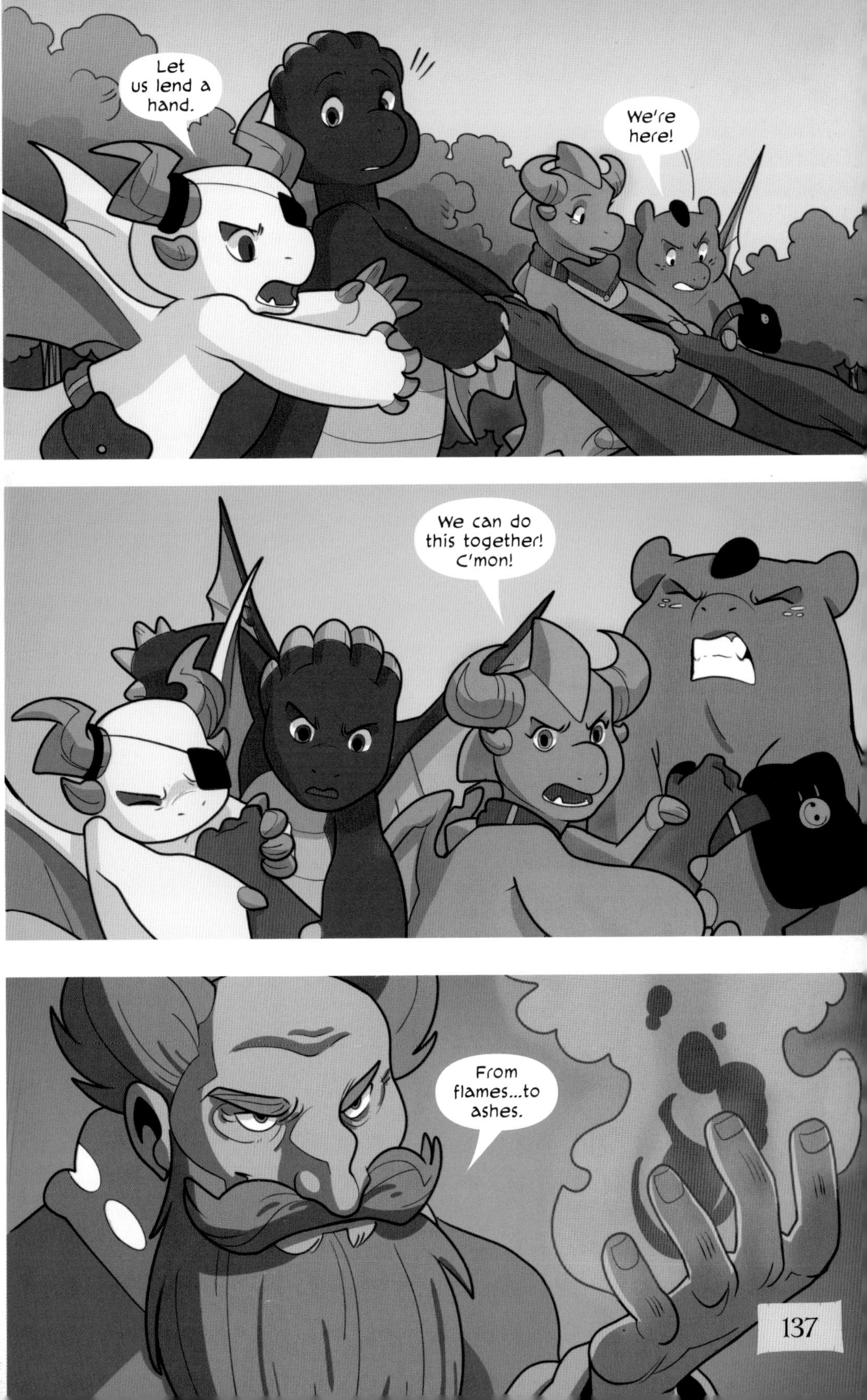
Let us lend a hand.
We're here!
We can do this together! C'mon!
From flames...to ashes.

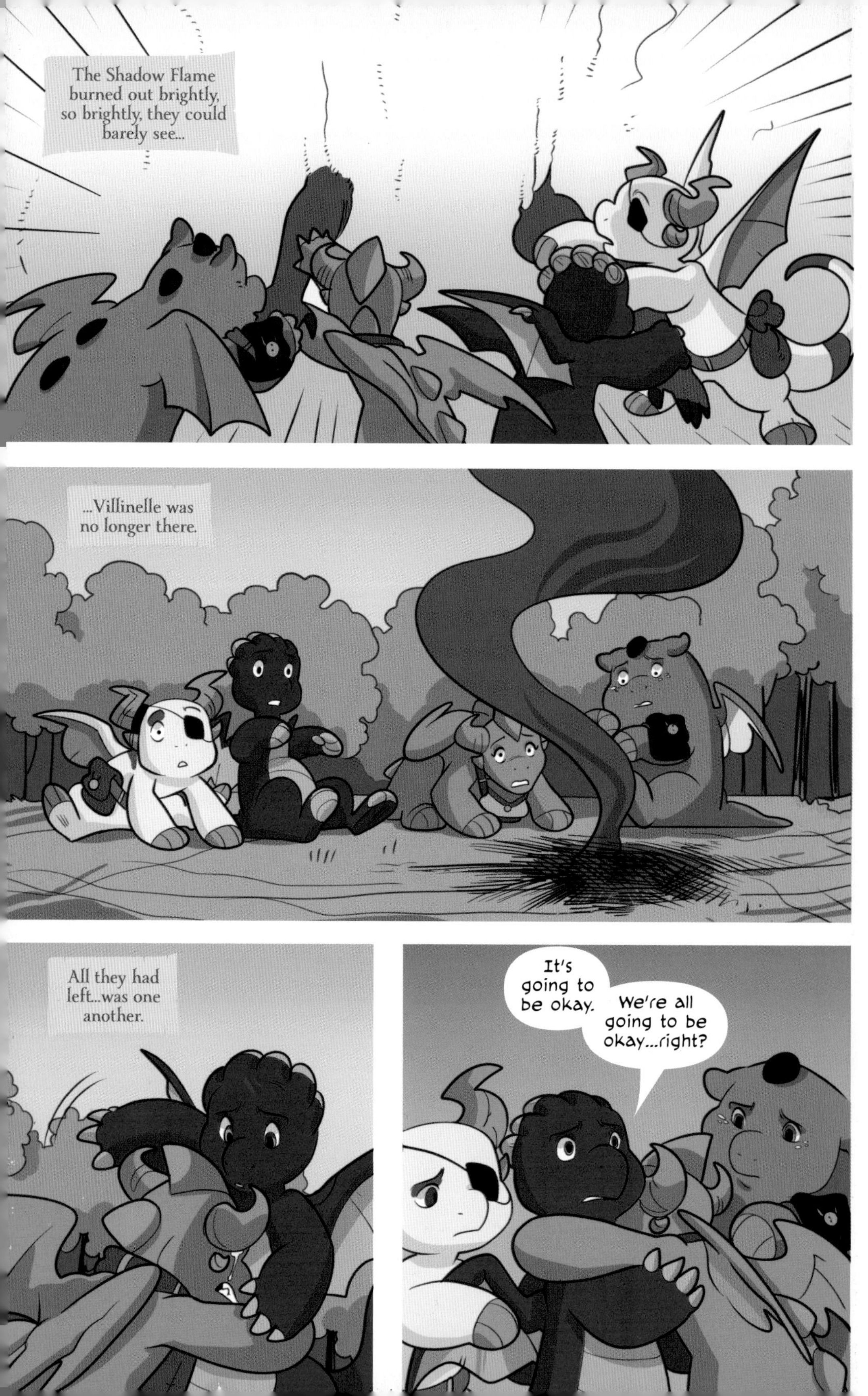
The Shadow Flame burned out brightly, so brightly, they could barely see...
...Villinelle was no longer there.
All they had left...was one another.
It's going to be okay.
We're all going to be okay...right?

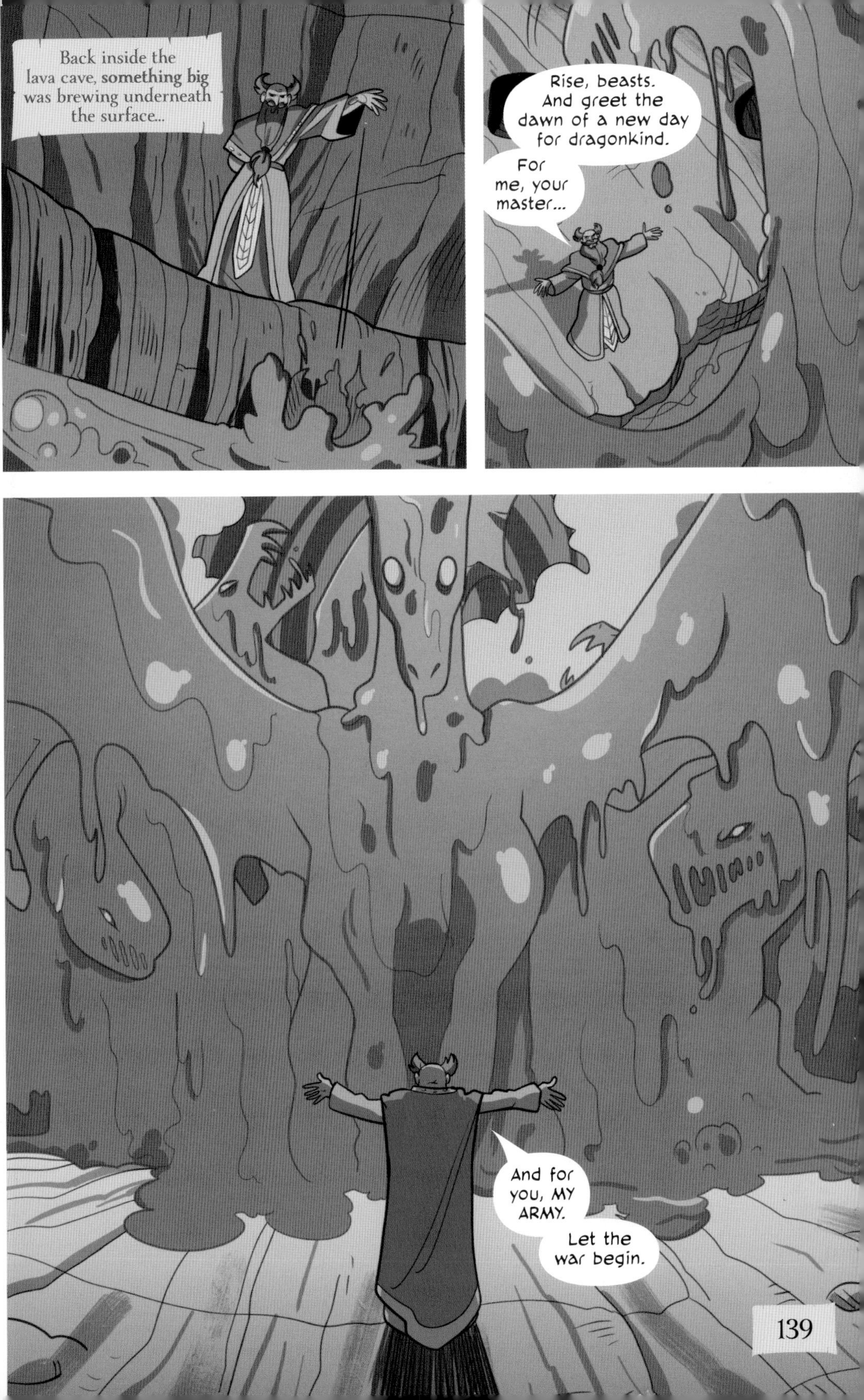
Back inside the lava cave, **something big** was brewing underneath the surface...
Rise, beasts. And greet the dawn of a new day for dragonkind.
For me, your master...
And for you, MY ARMY.
Let the war begin.

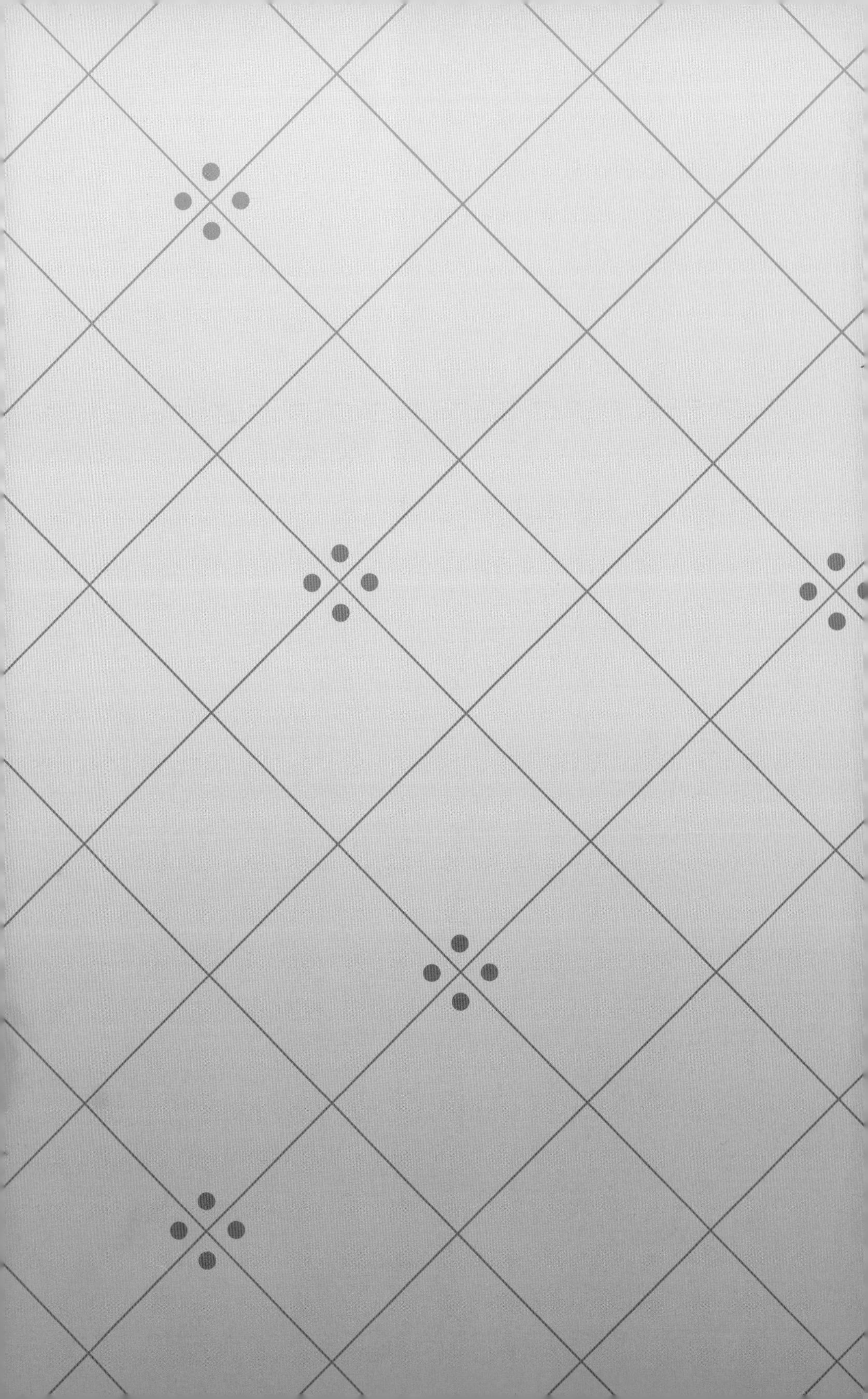

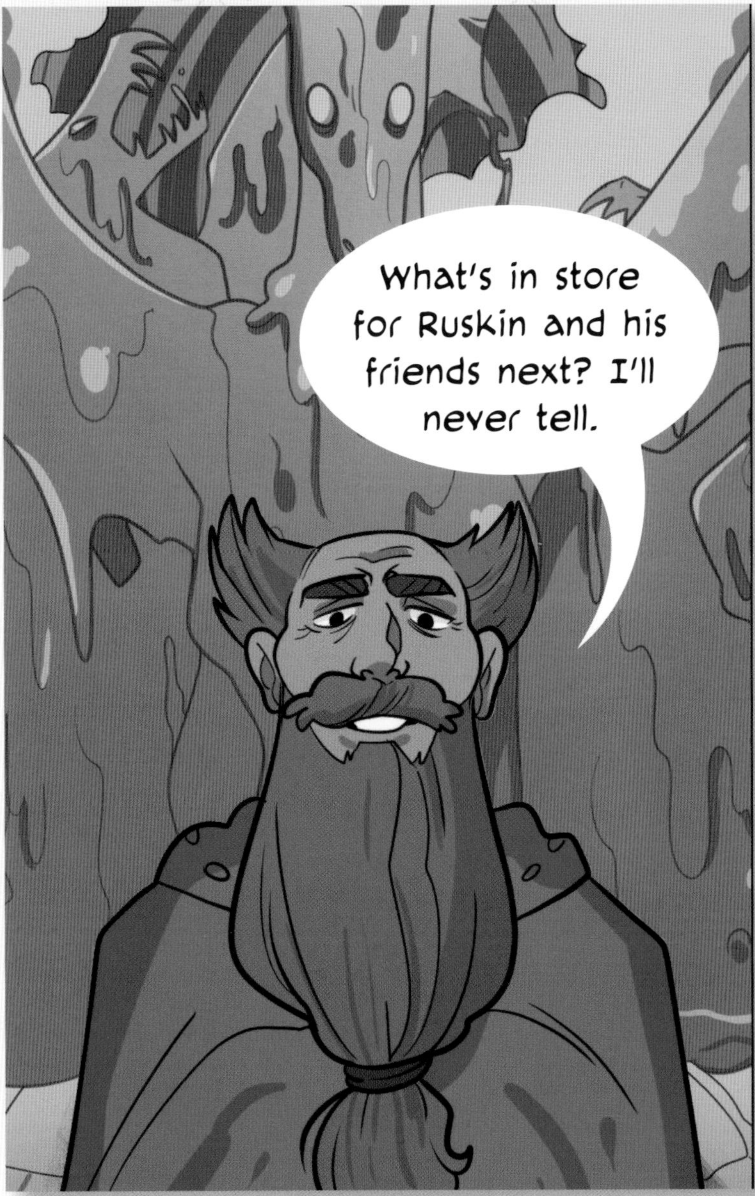
What's in store for Ruskin and his friends next? I'll never tell.

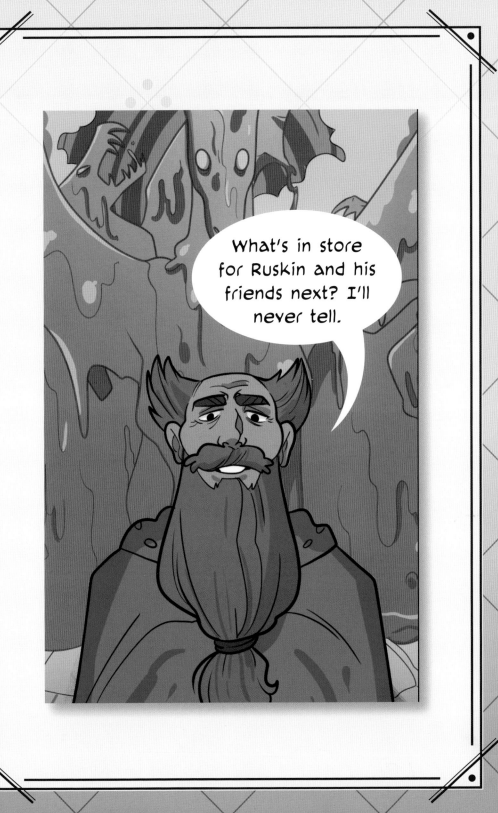

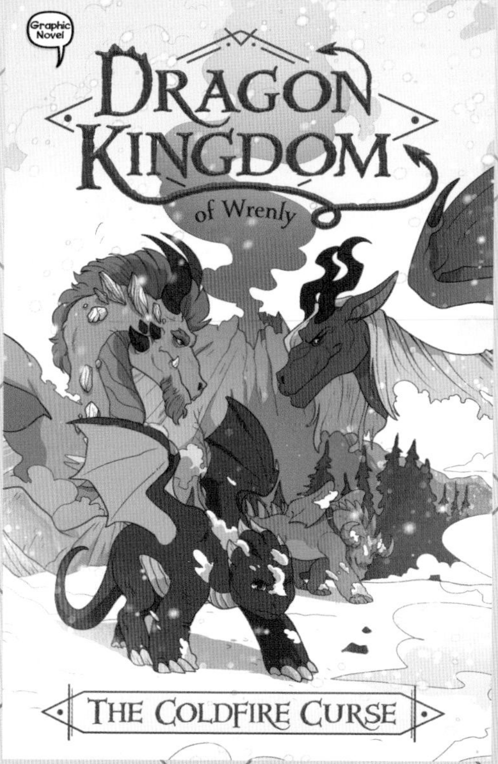
Graphic Novel
DRAGON KINGDOM
of Wrenly
THE COLDFIRE CURSE

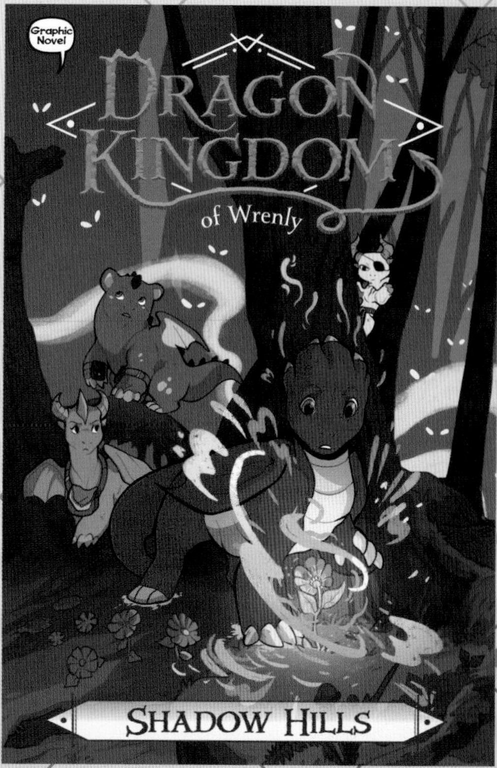
Graphic Novel
DRAGON KINGDOM
of Wrenly
SHADOW HILLS

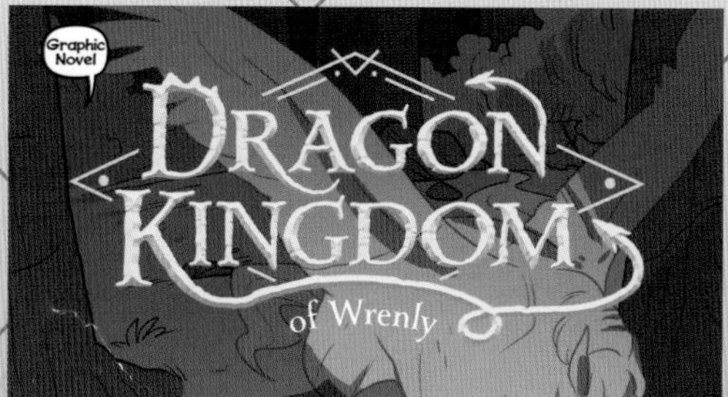
Graphic Novel
DRAGON KINGDOM
of Wrenly
GHOST ISLAND

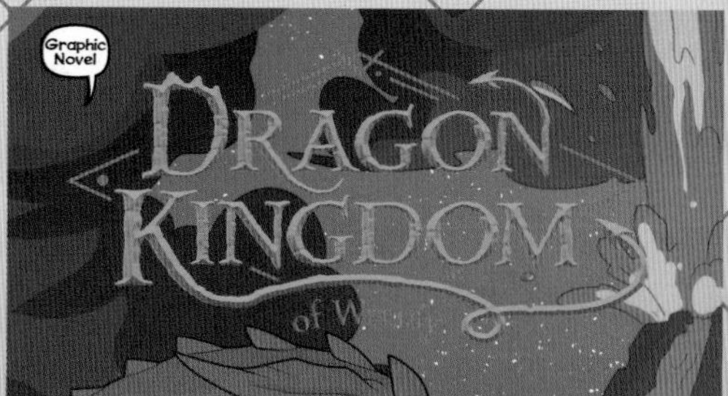
Graphic Novel
DRAGON KINGDOM
INFERNO NEW YEAR

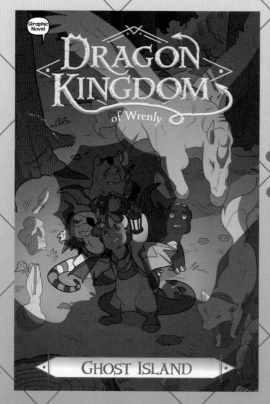

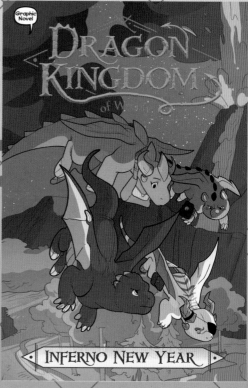

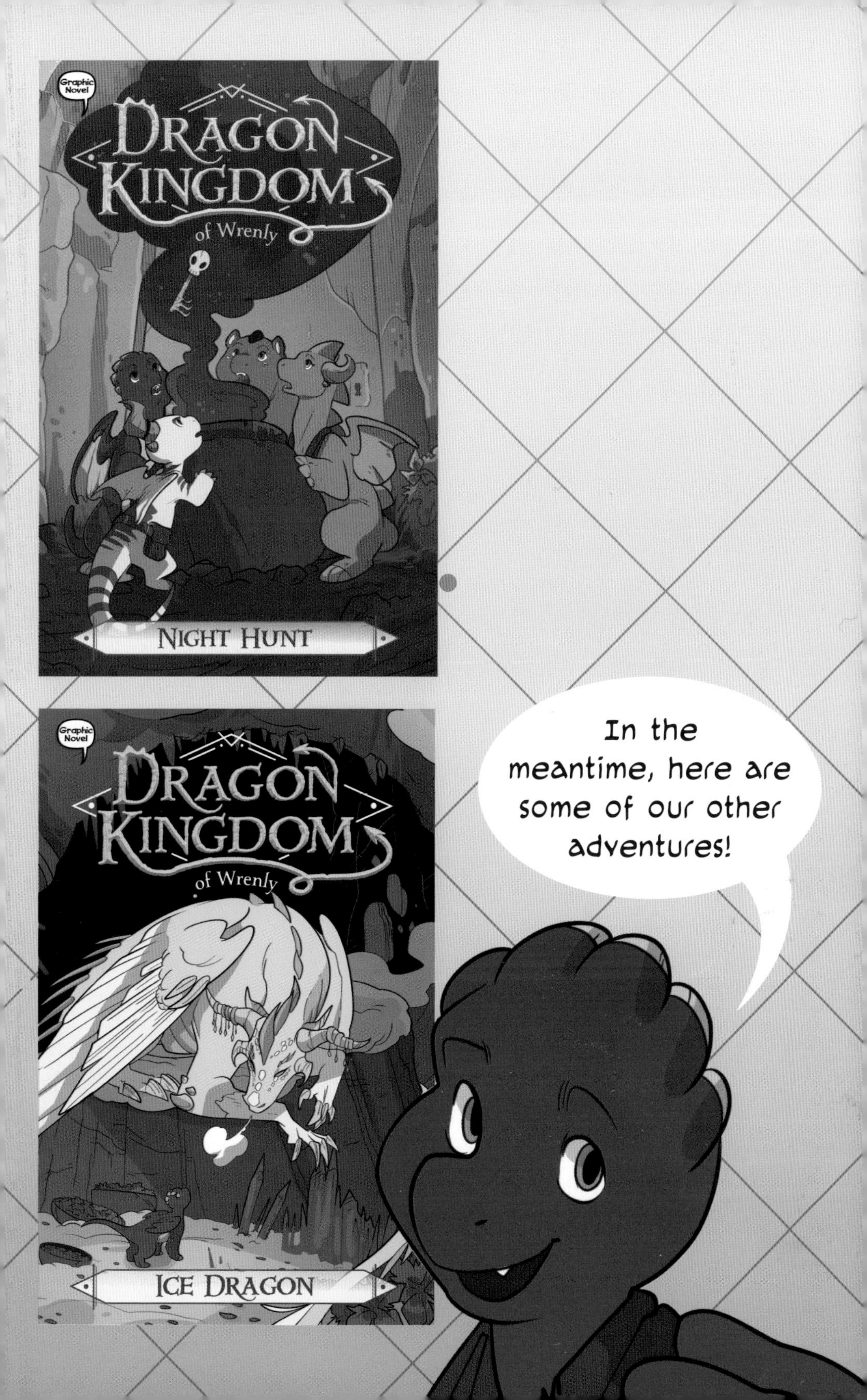
Graphic Novel
DRAGON KINGDOM of Wrenly
NIGHT HUNT
Graphic Novel
DRAGON KINGDOM of Wrenly
ICE DRAGON
In the meantime, here are some of our other adventures!

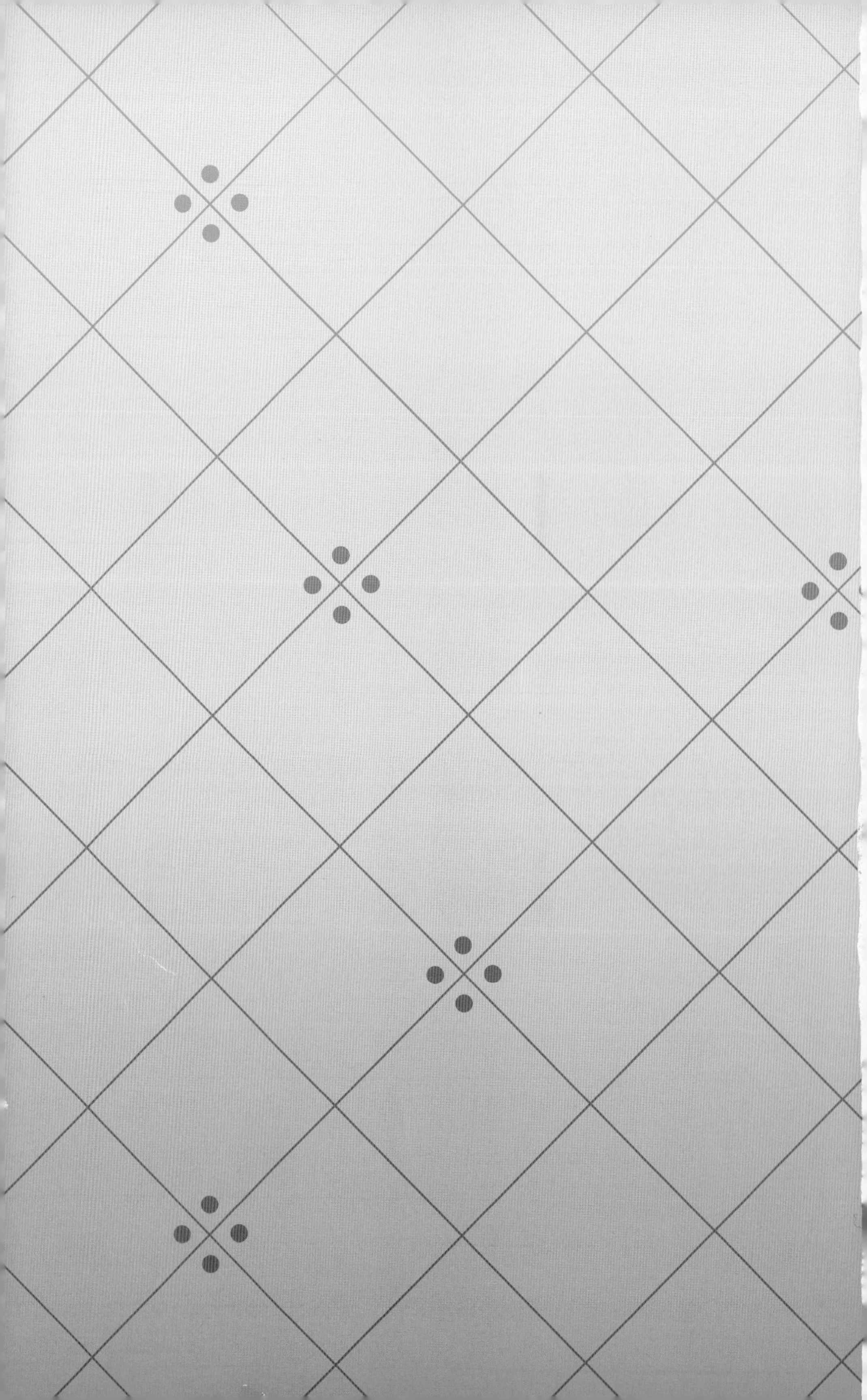